Also by Brad Leithauser

Seaward

Seaward

a novel by

BRAD LEITHAUSER

Alfred A. Knopf   New York   1993

THIS IS A BORZOI BOOK
PUBLISHED BY ALFRED A. KNOPF, INC.

Published in the United States by Alfred A. Knopf, Inc.,
New York, and simultaneously in
Canada by Random House of Canada Limited, Toronto.
Distributed by Random House, Inc., New York.

Library of Congress Cataloging-in-Publication Data
Leithauser, Brad.
Seaward: a novel / by Brad Leithauser.—1st ed.
p.   cm.
ISBN 0-394-58587-9
I. Title.
PS3562.E4623S44   1993
813' .54—dc20   92-31047
CIP

Manufactured in the United States of America
First Edition

FOR

KIM TOWNSEND—

Friend

for the long run

When she turns back toward the shower, in the eclipsing light, she detects a body in the mirror over the door, a body not so distant and yet all but lost in the room's distant fog. And this time it's as though it's she, come for a visit, it's Harriet, her own Harriet Dwiggins, to whom she adds, aloud in a voice that cracks upward to become almost a little girl's, "Or am I wrong? Oh, dear, I pray I'm wrong."

Hence

The bride hath paced into the hall,
Red as a rose is she;
Nodding their heads before her goes
The merry minstrelsy.

The Wedding-Guest he beat his breast,
Yet he cannot choose but hear;
And thus spake on that ancient man,
The bright-eyed Mariner.

Coleridge, *The Ancient Mariner*

Contents

Part One

A SINGLE MOMENT

Horizontal Chitchat

"Who ever would have thought it—and yet this is really shaping up into a very traditional, very old-fashioned affair, and who in the world would ever have conceived of such a thing?"

Me, for one, is what Glenn feels tempted to answer. Instead, after allowing the matter some deliberation, he replies, "Mmm."

"Well, I mean a very traditional and old-fashioned affair with you can bet a few totally unexpected zingers thrown in." Kaye laughs softly—but with unmistakable pride. "You know Diana."

He does, though just a bit. "Mmm," he says. He would rather talk about something else, which is what these close-mouthed assents of his are meant to convey, but Kaye isn't getting the point, quite. She carries on.

"When I asked was she going to wear white, she says to me, *Mah-ahm.* Just like that. I thought she meant, *White would be,* you know—I don't know, *too corny for words,* or something, but what she meant was, *Mom, don't you think your only child's entitled to white on her wedding day?* Isn't it just to die for—entitled? Well of course, of course the girl is . . . Whatever does she think?" In the darkness of this room Kaye has no trouble seeing in her mind the girl once more, puzzlement all over her young face— puzzlement on both their faces. "Do you suppose she's thinking her own mother's so, I don't know, so unhip or something as to suppose that in this day and age it's only a virgin's entitled to white? Or is she honestly thinking I'm actually thinking that even though she's been practically living with this, this well obviously very ro*bust* young man for months on end, I'm still cherishing the hope that she has nonetheless been saving herself for her wedding night? Or that I'm thinking Peter's too much the Southern gallant to—to deflower my precious baby before the nuptial rites? Is that how I come across? Like some sort of, I don't know, *prude* or something?"

Glenn waits for another laugh, which follows. A soliciting pause establishes itself. This time she's waiting on an answer. "No-o," he says, "Uh-uh. I don't think that's how you come across at all."

"And if I was a little slow in getting what she was getting at—well, does that make me dense or something? I ask you. Honestly now, who'd have thought it—that *Diana* would choose to go the old-fashioned and traditional route . . ."

It isn't clear to him (though he hasn't, admittedly, given the matter much thought) why this notion of Kaye's, this conception of her daughter as some sort of Bohemian-beatnik-hippie-rebel, is so regularly annoying. But you'd think to listen to Kaye that the girl was steadily pumping her veins with heroin, or panhandling on behalf of a Satanist cult. In fact the wildest thing about Diana—so far as he knows—is that a couple of months ago, home during summer vacation, she slipped out one day and had her ears pierced a second time, so now she can wear a total of four earrings at once. And this decision to get married at the comparatively tender age of twenty-two simply isn't, as Kaye would have it, another unpredictable, iconoclastic stroke: the smart money would probably have bet on it.

Not that there is anything the least bit annoying about Diana herself. The girl is a winner. And (more than there was any solid reason to figure) a real looker.

"And she told me she isn't even going to invite her father," Kaye continues. "I said, *Well that's purely your decision.* I said, *Baby, it's got zilcheroo to do with me.*" Kaye savors the sound of these words. They reverberate; she pauses to listen to them echo in her mind.

Glenn swallows another remark: *I'll bet that's what you said.* He knows the expression that has seized Kaye's features, although her back is to him and, even if it hadn't been, the room is too thick with shadows for any subtle deciphering of faces. Her large eyes have widened and her lower front teeth have emerged to clamp her upper lip. It's an expression common to her when, challenged, she sees herself as hanging tough in support of a principle.

Kaye goes on: "I said, *But I'll stand right by you.* And I added, *You don't owe that man a single solitary thing.*"

"That's true," Glenn concurs, glad to have found a point of ground on which he and Kaye can stand together.

But, almost as though she'd rather not have him at her side, Kaye says, "Well, it's something various of us might at times prefer to overlook, but he *is* Diana's father. There's no getting around that. And leaving him out's a pretty big step familywise, future-relationshipwise. Although," she adds, "if you want my own personal opinion, Ralph'd be more relieved than hurt to be left out. You've got to ask yourself, *Does that man honestly belong here?*"

There's another pause and Glenn shifts his hand, which had been curled upon her belly, to Kaye's upper arm. It's hot in here. This room—Kaye's guest room—has its advantages over the bedroom (it seems somehow less imposing than the bedroom, more spontaneous and relaxed in its atmosphere, and he'd thought spontaneity and relaxation would perhaps be an aid to him tonight), but the air-conditioner's broken. Things might have gone altogether differently just now had there been a working air-conditioner.

"She said she's going to have Terry give her away."

"That makes sense."

No, apparently Kaye won't stand for agreement just now. For she jumps on his remark: "*Sense?* Don't you think it's going to look pretty darn peculiar? Pretty damn irregular? To have the girl's uncle be giving her away when her father's still living?"

"You could have nobody give her away . . ."

"Didn't I tell you it was a very traditional, very conventional affair?"

Purely in hopes of flummoxing Kaye, Glenn says, "But didn't you say we've all got to expect a few zingers? After all, you know Di*ana*," he says, and ventures a little chuckling laugh of his own.

She merely exhales in reply—a slow, depleted sighing that seems to say, *Men . . .* or, perhaps, *You . . .*

And could it be that *she* is feeling just a little put out with *him*?

At the thought, all of his own hot disgruntlements melt away on the instant—for this woman must be placated. Though Kaye's a pretty good sport, taking all with all, her annoyance can mount with frightening speed to become a formidable thing. Glenn says, "Is he going to handle it all right?"

"Is who going to handle what all right?"

"Terry. Is this the sort of thing he can handle?"

"Handle? Glenny, what in the world's to handle? Handle? He isn't the one who's marrying the girl."

Does he know that? What Glenn actually says, though, is, "Sure, hon. Sure, sure."

"He's just giving her away is all. Not that even getting married's such a godawful Broadway production these days. Or doesn't at least necessarily need to be." She rolls over, toward him, and Glenn feels her sweaty breasts against his chest, and the larger, solider nudge of her belly against his belly, and she laughs, and he experiences a kind of abdominal unclenching, from navel to sternum, an easing of a sort that hadn't fully come—though it ought to have come—a few minutes ago. He *has* this woman. He isn't feeling annoyed, she isn't either, and if he'd encountered just now a touch of the old problem, was that such a grievous and debilitating thing? Life could be worse for a fifty-seven-year-old man than to be going off like a teenage kid—*too soon*—especially when we're talking about a fifty-seven-year-old man who bears on his chest a scar more than twelve inches long. Things could be a whole lot worse than to be knowing, just now, in this warm dark room, with a week of vacation still before you, that the cells of your body are briskly aswim in the ample belly of a woman—a woman thirteen years younger than you are and a woman who is (let's face it, let's have no who's-kidding-who here) pushing hard for marriage, even though you represent, objectively speaking, a very bad investment.

The phrase had come to him a couple of months ago, at a glimpse of himself in the mirror after a shower, and it came to stay. Catching sight of that pale plump soft-sloping body that has become his own body, with its even paler scar there where the bones over his heart had been opened up like a mail slot, he'd said aloud, *Mister, you know you represent a very bad investment,* and the phrase became, through a single utterance, his for life.

That scar isn't something he likes to expose to anyone's gaze but his own. It makes him nervous, to have other people eyeing it. He feels about it something like what—ages ago, just a kid— he used to feel about baring his genitals or his backside.

"If Terry could only hear you asking if he can *handle* it—I mean the old Terry, the before-the-accident Terry, you didn't know him then but I can assure you he'd be one furious dude."

Glenn feels how amusement has taken her; her body's gone sweet and roly-poly with mirth. Slip-slop, slip-slop. "Always so cheerful and competent," she continues, "my super-cheerful, super-confident baby brother. Not that he isn't still competent . . . It's just that he's gotten so, I don't know, broody or some-thing?"

"Well, he does seem very . . . distant?" Glenn suggests. "Not quite of this world?"

And as a sort of joke as he speaks the phrase *this world,* or as a way of highlighting for Kaye that he, Glenn, is still very much of this world and still has some change jingling in his pocket— that he is, for all the valleys of death his body has marched through, still a *player*—he takes in his hands her hot breasts, which are little for a woman of her size and weight, and squeezes firmly once, twice, three times.

"Terry, *Terry* not quite of this world . . . Yes," she sighs, ex-tending and relishing her mirth, agreeing with him fully at last. "That *is* new."

"Still," Glenn says, "if the girl wants to be given away, I don't see how it could be anybody *but* Terry. Anybody else would be an injustice plain and simple." Though he hardly knows him well, Glenn has had, it's true, his difficulties with Terry—specif-ically, with Terry's constant quick scrutinizing looks, those small sharp eyes that are so much more discerning than the baby-face they lodge within. Eyes that forever seem to say, *Are you worthy of my big sister?* A very possessive guy, Terry can be.

According to Kaye (and Glenn could well believe it) the before-the-accident Terry was a very different variety of Terry—before, that is, Terry's wife, Betsy, drowned off a beach in the Cayman Islands. It was only to be expected that something like that would permanently change a man. Not that Terry made a point of parading his grief. Quite the reverse, in many ways: the step was springy, the baby face unlined. But there was a vacancy to him, a way of disappearing right in the middle of a conversation—a tendency, it had to be said, that was perhaps something of a self-indulgence. What everyone seemed unable to recognize was that the accident had taken place what?—a year and a half ago? Two years? A long time, anyway, to be rendered a social paralytic—which is what, catch him on the wrong day, Terry could be. It was as though Terry failed to understand that life rolled on, that the meter kept on running—a lesson which Glenn himself, with two divorces squarely behind him, felt particularly qualified to offer. And yet, and yet . . . if Terry didn't do everything he might to put his sister's boyfriends at ease, still there was no disputing his generosity. When it came to his niece Diana, Terry had been a prince. Nothing short of princelike. Kaye didn't quite seem to perceive how extraordinarily generous her little brother had been. On that score, at least—the bottom line, the let's-not-forget-the-hard-cold-cash—Glenn saw it as his duty to stand up for Terry. Kaye didn't understand money— it was as simple as that. Just didn't.

"He'll loosen up all over the place this weekend," Kaye says. "You'll see—you'll see a brand-new Terry. He'll surprise you. Just getting out of town, getting him out of that office he lives in, and out in some real fresh air, a chance to hike around a bit, will be a total release for him. Believe it or not he's got a wild and woolly side—he always used to love to party. He can be a real scream." But in her mind as she talks of parties she envisions him somewhere else entirely. He is hiking toward her in a plaid shirt and a pair of bright tennis shoes, looking even younger and more little-brotherish than usual, and she feels cheered. "You guys are just getting started. I see the two of you becoming fast friends."

"He's so much younger. Nearly twenty years."

"Real pals."

"Yes . . ."

"Oh I'm looking *forward* to this. The drive—everything, Glenny."

"You don't think it's permanent with Terry?"

Kaye responds quickly: "Oh *no,*" she insists, and then, sensing that the question, which belongs in a category with *Do you still beat your wife?*, has asked her to concede far too much at the outset, she adds, "Whatever do you mean by *it?*"

A Single Moment

He needed a couple of moments, on waking, to understand where he was (an airplane), and a couple more to recall where he was coming from (Marquette, Michigan) and where he was headed (Dulles; the office; home). But these little mysteries having been disposed of, they opened up before him a mystery larger by far: up and down one side of his body he felt an odd indwelling pull, a kind of hunger in muscle and bone. It was there in his left arm, in his left knee, sunk into the bones on the left side of his face, there in the pumping half of his chest: a sense that something—but what?—was missing.

On his left . . . But over there, on the left, lay only an empty seat, and beside that a little oval window, rimmed with sun, and it occurred to him, lightheadedly, that the source of attraction might have something to do with the stacked clouds, or the river down below, or the good green land on the river's either side, whose patchwork cultivations at this height revealed themselves as exemplars of large-scale planning. The sun had turned the river into metal, a glittering impenetrable expanse on which a person might walk securely, head held high, and he heard a name, *Kelly,* and everything loose and indeterminate in the air cohered around a face—the girl's, the woman's, Kelly's, who had been sitting right here, before, on the leg of the flight from Marquette to Detroit, and who'd been such an appealing girl, with earrings that were a pair of emerald birds, bobbing and fluttering on either side of her plump, pretty face. She had taken him by surprise, the feeling she brought him.

Improbably enough, with the deepening of conversation he'd found himself drawn to a woman who was more girl than woman and who worked in a video store ("Of course it does mean I get to see everything when it first comes out—first comes out on video, that is"), and he'd hoped she, too, was destined for Washington. When it turned out she was bound for Pittsburgh, he'd urged her, a number of times, to come visit him, and gave her his business card. (She'd seemed genuinely keen on the idea of a Washington visit—oh, she would come some time with her girlfriend Marty, who lived in Pittsburgh, who had boldly packed up one day and moved there from Marquette.) He had even promised (though this was so uncharacteristic he could hardly credit it; surely it was a detail added subsequently, in his brief but disorienting sleep) that he would take the two of them out for a "night on the town." A *night on the town* . . . What in the world did the phrase even mean these days—or mean, anyway, to a girl like Kelly? Did it mean discotheques? (Probably they weren't even called that any more.) At the thought of *discotheques,* a door swung open in Terry's mind, revealing a dark cavern—deafening music, plunging heads, drugs passed hand to hand . . . was that what he'd promised her? You had to laugh, really—oh, this had been quite a conversation! He'd confided in her all sorts of things . . . About Betsy's death, and even about some of the problems Betsy'd had before her death. And about his vaulting, years ago, and indeed about the day (a big blazing immeasurably blue afternoon in May—May of 1970—with the sun shining from one open end of Iowa to the other) when he broke the Gawana High School pole vault record by seven inches. ("I shouldn't be boring you with something that happened, hell, twenty years ago," he told her, and she said, "You weren't in high school twenty years ago"—her tone conveying not flattery but an alert, able skepticism, as if letting him know she wasn't easily taken in.)

Well, people were always showing surprise on learning his age. The varied evidence of accumulating years observable in his contemporaries (the graying, the balding, the etching of the forehead, the thickening of the middle) so far had, seemingly less by some special dispensation than by simple inadvertency, failed to touch him. Actually, it made a sort of sense that this would be the case, for he was, in one way or another, accustomed to being overlooked—an experience that came naturally to somebody who in childhood had always been "small for his age," and who in adulthood, never having quite reached five feet eight, retained a sense, a "little guy's" ingrained sense, of his own unimposingness. In addition, as though further to ensure that he would never appear to be somebody you had to reckon with, Nature at birth had woven a large cowlick at the top and center of his forehead, which pretty much mandated, for life, that his hair be parted down the middle.

"Twenty years," he'd laughingly protested, "at *least* twenty years"—to which Kelly said, "Get off it," and "You know, I wasn't born yesterday." Ah, but Kelly, that's exactly what you were: born yesterday. He'd known this the moment he asked if she'd ever been to Washington and she said, as though this somehow marked her out, "No, but I've seen pictures, the monuments and stuff"—as if thereby distinguishing herself from those of her countrymen who'd never once laid eyes upon a single photograph of the nation's capital . . .

He'd told her about Coach Kramm, the chemistry teacher who was himself an odd bitter chemical compound of a man, one part technical advisor and one part lunatic guru. Coach Kramm standing out there by the vault pit in his half-zippered windbreaker, day after day intoning, "It's in the mind . . . It's in the mind . . . It's in the mind . . ." And he'd told her about Kaye, sweet old luckless Kaye, and about his having agreed to go away this weekend with her and her new man, Glenn, and maybe this was going to work out splendidly—the weekend— but all the same, he confessed to Kelly, he was dreading it. ("You'll have a better time in Pittsburgh," he said to her, and she said, "Me, we're going to have a *great* time, Marty's a riot, everybody *loves* her.") He told her about Diana ("She's sort of a niece slash daughter to me"), and though he didn't explain it outright, he hinted, pretty explicitly, about the arrangement he'd worked out concerning Diana's expenses at Dartmouth. And he told her about calling his mother Mob instead of Mom. ("Years ago, just a little kid, I was in bed with a bad cold, and every time I called her it came out Mob. The name stuck.")

And Kelly, she of the airy dancing hair in the early-morning stratospheric light, around whose head emerald birds were endlessly fluttering, she'd told him all sorts of things . . . About her husband, whom she had left and was divorcing ("He's not a un-bright guy but my God he has no ambition. We're at this party, and I can't find Jim anywhere, and I get a little concerned be-cause tell you the truth there were some pretty slutty types hanging around around there, and so I go outside looking for him and there he is, in the backyard, with this buddy of his, Chuck, and the two of them are having a pissing-for-distance contest. You know, seeing who can shoot it the farthest?—and I said to myself right then, *Kelly, your husband has no true ambition in life*") and about her brother and his wife, both of whom had drug problems. ("It narrows your mind—that's why I don't go for them, they narrow your mind.") Her talk was full of *new plans,* of *new ideas,* of *new ways of looking at things.* She was just a kid but he'd relished the sense she gave him of somebody who was trying, with more energy than precision perhaps, to put the past behind her and to extend her horizons. She had blond, or blondish hair, which must have been treated to some sort of fancy permanent, since it was all over the place and yet basically under control at the same time. Small brown eyes, and a cluster of freckles on her bridgeless pug nose. And on the tip of her nose was perched a freckle-sized white dot, which might have been a feather filament, as though she'd spent the night on a down pillow, and glancing at that all but weightless bit of fluff he'd found an odd daring image darting into mind: how quick and easy it would be to lunge his head forward and—snap!-remove it with one lizardlike flick of the tongue. The thought was discomposing enough that, he discovered, he'd missed an observation or two. "Beg pardon?" he said to her.

"I'm interested in the media," she said. "That's why I took the job in the video store."

"The media? Well in that case we're sort of in the same field, you and I. You see, I'm a communications lawyer."

"Really? Yever meet actors? Any television or movie actors?"

"No, and this is funny, you might almost call it bizarre: I've never actually laid eyes on somebody famous or extraordi-nary—not in person. It's funny because I live in Washington, I'm often in New York, I'm flying all the time, and pretty much everybody I know has laid eyes, at one point or another, on somebody who's really really famous, who's truly larger than life. Betsy, my wife, my ex-wife, my you know late wife, she once saw Jackie Kennedy in an art museum when she took some kids on a field trip—she taught elementary school. And Adam, this guy at my office, Adam Mikolajczak, he's sort of my best friend, he's seen so many famous people I sometimes accuse him of lying to me. But he isn't. He's on the level, he's a very straight, levelheaded guy. But the fact is he can hardly go out for a slice of pizza without running into Gorbachev or Arnold Schwarzenegger or Katharine Hepburn. Even Mob, my mom, who's hardly ever left Iowa, she once shook hands with Dan Quayle. This was before he became the Veep. Mob's very much the Iowa Republican. My dad shook his hand too. But me, I've never really had that experience, though I'd like to just once before I die: the experience of seeing somebody who was some-how *larger than life*."

"I know what you mean," she said.

"What I do mostly is TV and radio licensing, and a little bit of other stuff—cellular phone franchises, cable regulation. The field keeps changing. The technology keeps changing. You heard of high-definition television? That's the sort of thing I ex-pect to be dealing with in the future. It's always moving. Some-times people try to stop the technology. They've got vested interests maybe in stopping the technology, but technology keeps winning out in the end."

"Uh-huh," she said, and nodded, and that little white feather filament on the end of her nose swayed. "You must meet a lot of inventor-types."

"Me? Not really. Mostly what I do is just write. You could say I'm a writer, but that's a bit more glamorous than the truth. I write briefs, reports, appeals, motions. No, I'm afraid there aren't a lot of movie stars in my line of work. It's mostly admin-istrative law judges and other lawyers, neither of whom is ever all that glamorous," he told her, but this wasn't strictly accurate. In fact, there'd been quite a glamorous lawyer in, of all places, Marquette. Yesterday. Allison Collier and when he called her Allie she corrected him as though he were a child: *That's Allie spelled s-o-n.* She'd flown up from Chicago, and was ever so slightly cross-eyed, and in the inexactitude of the gaze with which she met the world, its elusive leaping wobble, he'd sensed an uncertainty or an incompletion which he might answer or complete; her rapid dark glancing had confused and excited him. From a business standpoint, she represented the other side, a Detroit bunch. Which made her the enemy. And which was hard to keep in mind at all times, partly because she'd been— Terry was pretty sure—wearing no bra.

At the thought of Allison Collier, he felt a little pleasurable jet of expectation. It wouldn't be long before he saw Adam (at lunch, if the flight got in on time), who would want the usual debriefing. And here was a story with two good-looking women in it—Adam's sort of trip and story.

It was possible, he saw now, as the last of his sleep dropped away from him and the plane began its computerized descent on Dulles, that he'd overreacted with Kelly (a night on the town!) in response to Allie with an s-o-n Collier, whose mixture of signals had pretty much undone him. Intermittently, meeting her crossed eyes, sneaking glances at her chest, where dangled a crucifix so fine it might have been made of toothpick pieces, he'd had trouble following her—which, at some level or other, was probably the strategy. In any event, he'd felt drawn to her, drawn to both women. And this pure, thoughtless sensation of being drawn (all embarrassments and frustrations lodged further and further behind him, as the flat fertile sweep of Virginia rose up to claim his attention, his time, his day) was in itself encouraging. That was the way to look at it.

He had no checked luggage. Whenever he could, he avoided the checking of bags; it was amazing how much, provided you knew what you were doing, could be fitted into a medium-sized briefcase and a soft overnight bag that even when full could still be stuffed underneath an airplane seat. Both the briefcase and the bag were of brown leather, and both had been gifts from Betsy. Worn but still a long way from worn out, the two were his constant companions, for he was as often as possible on the road—which meant, in his line of business, as often as possible in the air. He was usually out chasing after depositions—scrambling from big planes into small planes, small planes into smaller planes, as he journeyed out from Washington to God-knows-where. Whatever their size and design, whether little noisy props or humming jumbo jets, planes seemed a second home, and the rhythms of modern flight—the little beeps and muttered unintelligible announcements and flashing signs—were in his blood. It all made *sense,* profoundly so: the way, just now, the wheels shuddered for a moment on contact and a final protest went up from the body of the jet, a whistle approaching a death-shriek at being rendered earthbound once more, fol-lowed by the slow taxiing forth, docile as a blinkered horse, to the arrival gate, which obligingly swung out to meet them. An easing, a little popping sound of release, and then, with the rest of the passengers, most of them carrying briefcases as well, Terry crowded toward the front of the plane.

Freed, on his own in the terminal, he went first to a bank of telephones and called Adam. After one of those absurdly terse conversations that were an ongoing, ever-satisfying joke be-tween them ("Heya, I'm at Dulles, you hold lunch?" "It's dan-gerous, what you're asking. This kind of deprivation's dangerous." "I'll get there soon's I can." Click. Click.), Terry stared at the phone with a squirming, itchy feeling that he ought to make a couple more calls. Somebody else he needed to reach? Kaye? Tell her he was back in town, firm up any loose arrange-ments?

At the thought of his sister, Terry marveled once more at how she'd maneuvered him into spending the weekend with her and Glenn in what was, evidently, little better than a shack some-where out near Virginia's Dismal Swamp. What *had* he been thinking? In fact, he'd almost agreed to drive down there with the two of them, but at the last minute, sanity ascendant, he had informed her he would arrive on his own steam—fly to Norfolk and rent a car. This was a plan offering a twofold benefit, for besides providing him with the safety hatch of his own trans-portation, it carried an air of heedless extravagance which could not help but impress Kaye—something which, if the truth were told, he never did fully tire of. If she were led to think her little brother *much* too busy to make the four-hour drive by car—well, wasn't that a small and a harmless stroking of his vanity?

What was the possible benefit in calling her now? He had his directions to the place—as well as a spare key, in the unlikely event of his arriving before them. No, whatever her news might be, it could surely wait until he saw them tonight. Out in the Dismal Swamp.

The bright sky he'd recently descended from began to darken as his cab racketed down the highway. Needed a tune-up. Though he hadn't wound up being very handy around the house, he was enough his father's son—the son of Everett James Seward, Iowa's premier amateur handyman—that he passed through a world in which sagging drainpipes, squeaking desk chairs, warped floorboards, peeling tool sheds, crumbling window sashes were forever calling mournfully to him. Outside, a storm was brewing with such speed it seemed he might not reach the office before it broke. Mob was another person who needed calling. *She'd* be pleased, anyway, to contemplate his heading off to the Dismal Swamp—always urging him, as she was, to devote more time to Kaye. She seemed to feel that he could "help" Kaye; but Kaye was fine really. Or was—take your choice—thoroughly beyond help. Kaye was Kaye: a simple enough proposition but one that, just maybe, Mob had never quite absorbed. Not that she was to be blamed for that. Perhaps (he was willing to concede) this was what being a parent was all about: forever thinking your children deserved better than they got.

Approaching the Key Bridge, he caught sight in the distance of his adopted city's most prominent landmark—the Washington Monument, bone-pale against the darkening heavens—and marveled, as now and again he did, at how little its slender aspiring shape stirred him, how faintly for him it seemed to spell *home*. At the moment he was tired, true, but the fact was that after fourteen years in this town he still sometimes felt Washington wasn't yet his real home. But where if not Washington? Charlottesville, which he'd fled so eagerly after law school? Princeton, which even while he was in the thick of undergraduate life had always seemed a mere interlude, a sort of sunny stepping-stone? Or Gawana, where he hadn't really lived since he'd left it in his teens?

By the time the taxi pulled up in front of the office a few drops

of rain had dotted the dusty windshield, but not so many that
the driver had yet felt the need for wipers. Though the bill came
to over forty dollars, Terry didn't bother with a receipt. One of
the advantages of having made partner was how little fuss there
was about collecting on expenses—even though his own were,
this past year, the highest in the firm. Nobody was on the road
more than he was. In the old days, Betsy still around, with all
her complaints about his being an "absentee husband," he'd
tried to curtail travel; now, he welcomed it, and sometimes
made trips that could probably have been handled by fax and
phone. He liked to think it was the pole vaulter in him, this
instinctive trusting to the corrective qualities of flight. Simple
movement was, by and large, the way he'd dealt with things
since the accident—a method that beat lying on a shrink's
couch, surely. *That* had surprised a lot of people, his choosing
to stay away from therapy after the accident, and yet this decision, wise or not, wasn't one he'd had many second thoughts
about. He'd pulled through.

It was a long-standing but still gratifying joke of Terry's that
he was the only man left in America with a secretary named
Bertha. The name suggested, of course, an aging, broad-
shouldered, robust, bifocaled matron—an office fixture—but
Bertha was, and not merely in appearance, unlike anything anybody would expect. She was young, for one thing (late twenties) and looked younger, in part because of her frequent attacks
of acne. And she was sickly; she often seemed, in her stooped
way, to be protectively draping her shoulders around a cough or
a cold. Although she did wear glasses, as any Bertha should, she
was sharply, bonily thin. Hers was a narrow little face with a
long and slightly crooked nose. Adam had once announced to
Terry, over drinks in some airport bar (on their way to Topeka?
to Honolulu? to Battle Creek? After a while, destinations were
all one) that the consensus among the men at Hamill, Hillman
(and at that time the firm's attorneys had still been exclusively
male) was that Bertha was the homeliest woman on the prem-
ises. What Adam hadn't known, however, was that a counterpart office poll—of the secretaries—had concluded that, after
the founder, old man Hamill himself, Adam made the least de-

sirable boss. (These days, the firm had twenty-nine attorneys, but at that time there had been twenty—a number that had stuck in Terry's mind because it meant that Adam and old man Hamill fell, precisely, in the bottom ten percent.) This little revelation from the other side of the looking glass—from the alter-office of the secretarial staff—had come from Bertha herself. And with it had come the news that he, Terry, was considered the best of the bunch to work for. This last was information that, if Terry had chosen to repeat it to anyone (which, despite occasional temptations, he'd never done), inevitably would have suggested that Bertha was seeking to ingratiate herself—or had even been flirting with him. That wasn't the case, though. No, and he had never repeated the poll results in part because of the impossibility of conveying to anybody unacquainted with Bertha just how she could manage, in that remote, confident, congested voice of hers, to offer such pronouncements without the slightest inkling of their likely effect. She was equally capable of bringing Terry not reassurance but disquiet—of announcing, say, as he was heading off to a meeting with a major client, "You ask me, that tie doesn't go with that suit *at all* . . ." (Clothes were one of the aspects of his life he felt most vulnerable about; he missed Betsy's guidance, and had taken to buying practically all his "serious" clothes at St. Ferri's, on the theory that he couldn't wander too far astray at the place where old man Hamill himself bought his suits.) For all the mundanity of her appearance, Bertha in the last analysis was otherworldly—and one of the last people on earth whom Terry would choose to make a confidant. But he had grown used to her—she had meshed into his life, somehow. He probably liked her far better this way, with all her quirks, than he would have had she been, in any conventional sense, likable.

"Tell me the truth," he said to her now, "while I was away he called, didn't he? The Bush-man, the President? Something about a Supreme Court appointment?"

"Your calls are right there." Bertha pointed at a tray on the corner of her desk. Her fingers were knobbier than any young person's ought to be; she had the hands of an elderly arthritic. The first time he'd noticed them, after she'd been working for him a couple of weeks, the word *rickets* had leapt into Terry's mind—though he hadn't been at all sure, in fact, what rickets was or were. He sometimes fantasized that Bertha as a child had been the victim of some bizarre and stupendous abuse, the sort of horror one saw headlined in those tabloids that, as a matter of fact, she sometimes brought to the office. MOTHER KEEPS GIRL IN CELLAR 11 YEARS—*nothing to eat but two cartons of cigarettes . . .* That sort of thing. "Right where they're supposed to be," she added.

"Anything important? Anything *earth*-shaking?"

"Important?" The light caught a lens on Bertha's glasses, throwing off a little signaling wink—as of mischief, as of teasing in response to his teasing—although her spoken reply was gravity itself: "That's for you to decide."

"But you understand my definition of importance as well as I do. It's anything that has to be done before lunch." He tossed off this observation while sifting through the little stack of message papers. Sam Marcellino calling about what must be the Tulsa licensing; a call from Mob, no doubt intent on offering some qualification or advice concerning the Dismal Swamp; two calls from somebody at Rose, McCall, which was probably in reference to next week's FCC hearing; a call from a Miss Eileen Latimer, who worked at a place called Pathpower, Inc., and who was almost certainly a headhunter (he received a number of such calls, for communication law was booming and Hamill, Hillman was an acknowledged leader in the field); and a call from Jerry Danley in Chicago, a colleague of Allie spelled s-o-n Collier. Nothing that could not wait.

"These are all my calls? Bertha, you don't honestly mean these are all my calls . . ."

"And also a woman called, just a little while ago, but she left no name or message."

"A woman?" Terry said. "A lady? Of the female gender? I don't see any message about her."

"No name," Bertha said. "No message."

"Ah," Terry said. "But surely she requires a memo all the same. *From: Unidentified Woman. Message: None given.* That sort of thing."

A comedian in search of a straight man would never need to look any further afield than Bertha. For a brief interval after she'd first come to the office, four years ago now, she had acknowledged Terry's little stabs at humor by cracking her face minutely into a mirthless grin; but this had been replaced—irrevocably, it would seem—by a habit of watching him with a look of unwearying forbearance that said, *Are you done?*

As it happened, however, Terry was not yet done. Bertha's imperturbability at times was itself fuel, itself inspiration—bad jokes, good jokes, no matter, it was all one, since humor wasn't the point, really. A trace of giddiness, which was perhaps a lingering effect of all the flying, or of last night's troubled sleep in a noisy hotel in Marquette, had crept into his soul today, and he proclaimed, "Maybe the mystery woman's extremely important message is that there *is* no message. It's all part of an uncracked code, Bertha, a very delicate negotiation. We're spies, she and I, on different sides. Part of a shadowy underworld." He searched Bertha's desk for anything employable as a comic prop, and seized upon a pencil. He picked it up with his left hand and beat it, metronome fashion, against the palm of his right. When it came to comic props, Bertha provided slim pickings: hers was a notably austere desk, with no knickknacks, no little furry animals, no cartoons or humorous quotations taped up on the gray partition. As for photographs, there was only one, and it was a puzzle: a dour black and white portrait of her paternal grandfather (who, it transpired, she'd basically never known, for he'd died when she was four). "You weren't honestly thinking— were you?—that I'm truly a mere communications lawyer, that this is what I do, that Hamill, Hillman is my actual life, that I am what I seem, that what you see is what you get, and tell me about the mail, Bertha, do tell me about the mail."

"It's right there in the box. Where it's supposed to be."

It had taken Terry a long time to discover that Bertha was, for all her neatness and spareness and unflappable humorlessness, an inefficient secretary. Not helplessly, disastrously inefficient— merely repeatedly and unapologetically so. It was that unflappability of hers which had initially hoodwinked him. She would greet emendations or outright corrections with a nodding, un-

fazed air of thorough understanding, as if adjustments of just
the sort he was proposing were only to be expected, and hence
were, at bottom, more reassuring than worrisome. Whenever
he could do so without hurting her feelings Terry shunted work
elsewhere. One had to be careful with Bertha. Though she
would shake off direct criticism with aplomb, even indifference,
a minor setback could unravel her. Once, six or so months ago,
she'd knocked Betsy's photograph from Terry's desk and,
though it fell only a few feet and onto a carpeted floor, the glass
shattered—at which, Bertha not only broke into tears but remained so shaken she wound up leaving the office early. (Silly
or excessive though it might have been, her response had
touched Terry. He'd sympathized with her, for he, too, had
shivered at the pane's destruction.) Given her volatile blend of
toughness and vulnerability, Terry never knew quite when precautions were advisable. Better to be on the safe side, of
course—since he felt so confused, so sorry, so gesticulatingly
impotent in the face of her distress. He was therefore wary
about soliciting another secretary's help, and more often than
not found himself doing the work himself, late. Running Xe-
roxes, typing letters after midnight. He was often the last to
leave the office at night, or the last except Adam, for whom
being a lawyer, like being a sports fan, was something that could
only be approached with a headlong fanaticism.

Adam—yes, it was time for lunch. Terry walked into his own
office and closed the door behind him. He set his briefcase on
his desk, deposited his bag in the closet. With the coming storm,
the room was as dark as though the shades were drawn.

Terry looked around and although everything seemed in order (at work, as at home, he kept things neat), a little punch of
nervousness struck him in the chest as he stood there in the gray
light, a hand on the closet doorknob. This was one of the dis-
advantages of travel: the way in which, sometimes, your own
office came to feel foreign. It was as if something had been subtly altered—but what? The desk? The blue armchair? The beige
curtains? No, everything was where it ought to be. The picture
of his parents at one end of the bookcase. The picture of Mob
on the other (even stronger-jawed than in person). And over

there on the desk, facing away from him, Diana's high school graduation portrait, and another picture of Mob, and Terry's favorite snap of Betsy (a sandy-haired woman behind the wheel of a Mustang, staring out through the lowered window with a look of sweet round-faced sun-dazed contentment). And beside Betsy his favorite photograph of himself, taken in high school, his bare legs nearly as thin as the supple pole in his arms. Standing at the head of the runway, ready to pitch himself once again at the heavens.

Why did the whole room seem slightly out of joint? The doorknob was cold against his fingertips. And Terry's head was hurting. Simultaneous with this realization of pain came the knowledge that it had been hurting for some time now—minutes, hours, steadily emitting a signal that had not been fielded. (More and more his job led him to think of the body as a scattered collection of radio and television stations, all throwing out competing signals.) When he was under stress, as he had been lately, he was prone to neck-aches (so constricting that they'd driven him to a masseuse), but this frontal affliction—a headache bang in the middle of his forehead—was a rarity.

Adam—it was time for lunch. Terry opened his office door and there at her desk sat Bertha engrossed in a magazine. She was on lunch break herself. On the cover of her magazine the half-familiar face of a beautiful blonde woman—someone Terry could not place, though he'd almost certainly seen her on one screen or another—beamed out over a headline that read IT'S LIKE I'VE BEEN REBORN. Though she seldom went to the movies, Bertha was forever poring over articles about Hollywood. It was as though she liked the movies best when they weren't moving—or so ran one of Terry's jokes. Actually, it was probably a matter of frugality, or perhaps of simply having nobody to go with. It isn't all that easy (as Kaye, forever educating her little brother about the difficulties of being a single woman in a big city, had repeatedly pointed out) for an unaccompanied female to walk into a cinema.

"Bertha, that woman claims she's been reborn," Terry said. "Why *are* people in Hollywood reborn more than the rest of us? It's—" He felt himself within reach of a neat aphorism, searched for it, found it: "The thing about Hollywood is that it's a spiritually promiscuous place. Not just physically, but spiritually," he explained, when Bertha said nothing and did not even glance up from her magazine.

What she said, after a moment's silence, was, "Hmmm"—a sound that slid first into a sniffle and then into a muffled cough. He knew she relished this little snub—and knew, too, that *she* knew he enjoyed providing the opportunity for it. Though Bertha rarely left her desk at lunchtime, she was always keen to demonstrate that she had no professional duty to answer even the most cordial off-the-job remark when it was presented during this, her own time. Her tawdry magazine, her burrowed head, the childish peanut-butter-and-jelly sandwich on her desk, the Reese's Peanut Butter Cup, the can of Coke—all were an assertion of temporary autonomy. It wasn't (Terry felt certain) that she resented being interrupted; rather, she savored, as a minor but an unslakeable pleasure, the exercising of her right to a justified brusqueness. To work beside Bertha was to partake in a multifaceted ritual. Positioned like this—him standing, her sitting; him talking, her grunting—the two of them were having fun. As best they knew how.

"I'm going to lunch," Terry said. "If there are any calls."

"I've already switched you over. To central switchboard." Bertha still had not looked up. What the telephone did was no affair of *hers*, clearly.

"Right," Terry said. "Carry on."

Bertha waited until he was nearly down the corridor before calling after him. "The flight to Norfolk? The four-forty? It's full."

Terry turned around with the heavy-footed, theatrical slowness that the unwritten script the two of them were enacting seemingly indicated. "Full?"

"I had to find another airline. Not to worry, you leave from National at five-fifty."

"I thought the ticket was already booked . . ."

Hadn't Bertha told him that? And didn't this mean she'd forgotten to make the reservation? Or screwed it up somehow?

"Totally booked. But I got you one at five-fifty." Bertha shrugged and lowered her head once more into her magazine.

Five-fifty. Which meant arriving later than he'd planned. Which meant he immediately ought to notify Kaye, who might not yet have left. But he didn't want to. What he wanted was lunch. And to see Adam.

"It's spiritual promiscuity," he called to Bertha, by way of a farewell. He enjoyed the phrase's unplumbed, somewhat racy sound and also the thought of how alluringly the words might drop upon any ears in adjacent offices—though, as for that, things were pretty deserted at the moment.

Adam worked one flight up, in one of the offices created the year before, when the firm, finessing a little real estate coup, had managed to grab a piece of the fourteenth floor. Needless to say, Adam's decision to move "up there" had been the talk of the office—scrutinized and analyzed and argued over for weeks . . . What precisely was the line of thinking that had led him, as one of the two most powerful partners at Hamill, Hillman, to position himself on the periphery? What was he planning? What did he know that the rest of them didn't? And what did this mean for everybody else? In any event, he had at one stroke rendered the six upstairs offices desirable. Spaces that had been intended for new associates had instead been seized by higher-ups.

Terry felt in his chest a flicker of pleasure as he ascended the carpeted steps of the internal staircase and a larger pleasure still when he stepped through Adam's open doorway and saw his friend—his best friend—seated at his desk in his shirtsleeves. Dents of concentration were worked, as by a hammer, into Adam's massive brow.

"You look weak," Terry said. "Dangerously weak."

"Marquette, Michigan," Adam countered. "Know something?—the single place in the whole world I've always wanted to go to but have never gone to is Marquette, Michigan."

"What's lunch?" Terry said.

"Your choice." Adam rose from his desk and threw his big shoulders into his suitcoat.

"You mean my treat," Terry said.

"Exactly what I mean."

The business of going out to lunch was something that Adam took quite seriously—almost as seriously as the business of going out to dinner—and when, after years of working companionably but not closely together, the two of them had suddenly become the best of friends, Terry had felt compelled to adopt all sorts of rituals of Adam's devising. Lunch and dinner checks were never split between the two of them; they were picked up in alternation, with final say as to where they would eat belonging, at least in theory, to the person whose turn it was to treat. In practice, Adam generally made the decision, whether or not he was treating; and this seemed only fair, in a funny sort of way, since the whole business of eating out was obviously far more important to him than to Terry. It wasn't that Adam was a glutton, exactly (he was far too avid an athlete to let himself go absolutely), but he did love his food, and a bad meal could suddenly turn him bitterly sarcastic about the firm, about the practice of law generally, about Washington, about women, about politics, aging, crime—life in general. He could be, in truth, a pretty moody guy and his low standing in the secretaries' poll was hardly surprising. He had a short fuse (or liked to act as though he did), and this, too, forged another bond between them. An unvoiced understanding had been arrived at, by which it had become Terry's responsibility to explain away his friend's bluntnesses and incivilities ("Don't mind him, he's having a rough year," Terry would say, or "And they call him Mr. Congeniality," or "Would you believe it? He's the optimist in our firm").

"I was thinking we'd go visit the General," Terry said—which meant Chinese food at a place on K Street called Captain Wang's. There was no captain, needless to say, but his absence had in no way impeded Adam—expansive with satisfaction at the end of a spicy meal—from vociferating about the need to raise the military man's rank. Eventually Adam himself had promoted the man, all the way to General, and unfailingly spoke with respect and even affection for the commander in the kitchen. This was another of the things they shared, the two of them, Terry and Adam—a penchant for jokes couched in nicknames.

"Whatever you want. It's your say," Adam replied, which meant, probably, that he'd been thinking along the same lines. "Looks like hell's coming our way."

"Hm?"

"The weather . . ."

Outdoors, the storm felt no closer—felt equally imminent. The few raindrops on the sidewalk might have been the same ones Terry had noticed when stepping out of the taxi. Everything was suspended. Still there appeared no question that a storm was coming; it was only a matter of things locking into place overhead. Everybody felt it. A sort of squeeze had been placed on K Street: pedestrians scurrying along, cars racing and beeping their horns, bicyclists leaning hard into their gears.

"Some weather," Terry said. "I hope I get out okay. I've got a flight in a couple of hours."

"From Marquette, Michigan, to the Great Dismal Swamp, and all in one day. Some fellas have *all* the luck. Me, I never get to go anywhere."

"I told you before, you're welcome to come along . . ."

"Oh but I wouldn't want to intrude—you, Kaye, and the brand-new Glenn. Sounds perfectly cozy."

"He's not so new and it'll be okay. It'll be all right."

"A chance to talk real estate. Didn't you tell me he's in real estate?"

"I've got my fingers crossed about Glenn. He may be fine, you know. I can't believe your average real estate agent is a *whole* lot more boring than your average lawyer."

"I'm with you *there,* anyway."

"And it'll give me a chance to talk to Kaye, who I haven't seen much of lately."

"Oh well Kaye, she's a sweetie."

"I'd feel better about this guy if he hadn't been divorced twice."

"Practice makes perfect."

"*And* hadn't had a heart operation last year. Wouldn't you think Kaye could find somebody a little more promising?"

"You said it yourself, he can't be any more deadly than your average lawyer."

Unmistakably, the two of them were gliding around a subject. Terry had tried once, a year or so ago, to interest Adam in Kaye—even though she was, at forty-four, three years Adam's

senior. Terry had contrived his plan in secret, letting his imagination unfold all sorts of improbable and beguiling daydreams.
Back then, the three-year gap had not looked insuperable; nothing had. But if the discrepancy in their ages wasn't, in truth, *all*
that great, and if Adam was undeniably quite available (divorced
now for more than ten years, from a woman Terry had never
met who'd followed her second husband, a doctor, out to
Maui), nonetheless Terry now found it rather incredible that
he'd ever conceived of his sister and his friend as a suitable
match. It wasn't merely that Kaye was too plain for Adam
(though there was that, and this *that* was a large that); it was a
matter of their living in opposed worlds. Adam, for his part,
had extricated himself quite dexterously from Terry's schemings. Wisely, he'd begun by refusing to acknowledge them. And
he'd sensed, in addition, Terry's deep sensitivity or vulnerability
or protectiveness—whatever—regarding Kaye. Adam, who
could come down quite hard on women, particularly homely
women (as he could come down hard about most things—for
he was a man of settled views and a caustic tongue), never had
anything but kind words for Kaye. He almost invariably called
her a sweetie. Actually, kindness toward Kaye was one of the
few requirements that Terry, who in the main imposed only
minuscule demands upon his friend, asked unconditionally;
whenever Terry expressed a worry or a reservation about his
beloved and hapless older sister, it was Adam's implicit job to be
hopeful and supportive—to be upbeat. And Adam (who was
generally not perceived as the world's most sensitive guy—and,
indeed, wouldn't want to be) had also intuited that Kaye's
daughter, Diana, wasn't to be made the subject of typical male
evaluations or speculations—although in Diana's case Terry's
protectiveness took a radically divergent form. When Adam
first met Diana, home from Dartmouth after her sophomore
year, he'd joked, all winks and leers, about Terry's becoming his
uncle-in-law. Diana was the girl he'd been *waiting all these years
for.* But he'd soon come to see that such humor wasn't appreciated (not at all, not even the slightest bit), and had abandoned
it. He'd started calling the girl Delightful Diana—a nickname
which, after Adam had drained his voice of any drop of the ac

quisitive and concupiscent, Terry had learned at first grudgingly to accept and later actually to favor. In Adam's company, he sometimes called her Delightful Diana himself.

"Kids?"

"Hm?" Terry said.

"This Glenn got any kids?"

"One. A boy. You should have heard Kaye reassuring me how perfectly all right this was, since the boy won't have anything to do with his father. Funny, I wouldn't have thought that's such a great recommendation myself."

"What's the kid do?"

"Do? He does drugs. Out in California. Or so Kaye tells me. And cruelly torments his father, whenever he finds the time."

Doubly driven (imminent rain, pressing hunger), the two of them marched rapidly down the street—so rapidly that the glimpse Terry caught of them in a mirroring bronze doorway was a hurtling blur. He was struck, nonetheless, by the squatness of his friend's reflection. At five feet nine-and-a-half, Adam actually had nearly a couple of inches on Terry, but probably most people, on seeing them together, would take Terry for the taller of the two. Terry these days weighed in at one hundred and forty-eight—a couple of pounds lighter than at his peak, in college, when, embarrassed always to be hovering below a hundred and fifty, he'd temporarily managed, through a combination of weightlifting and coffee milk shakes, to nudge his weight over that then-reassuring mark. Adam probably weighed close to one-eighty. When seen in a business suit (which was how he was usually seen, since he spent most of his time at work), Adam with his wide shoulders and big-browed thick-nosed face looked blunt, paunchy—or just plain fat. It had been a surprise, the first time they'd traveled together on business, to see Adam poised tiptoe on the edge of a hotel pool: it was muscle, most of that bulk was muscle. Those few things Adam cared about he was likely to be wholeheartedly devoted to—work, the Baltimore Orioles, the Washington Redskins, meals, and, it turned out, exercise. When he was traveling, hotels were often chosen on the basis of whether they had a late-night pool—or, better still, a pool which, though technically closed, could be easily invaded. In the South, or out West, wherever the weather was warm, he liked sleepy motels with outdoor pools, where no one seemed to mind a maverick, off-hours swimmer. It was like Adam to arrive somewhere on a dawn flight, work all day, go out eating and drinking with clients half the night, and wind up, at two in the morning—admirably, eerily—churning out lap after lap of butterfly, breaststroke, crawl in an unlit pool.

Something was rumbling in the distance like thunder but the rain held off for them; they arrived dry-haired at the General's. "You see the advantages of having waited for me," Terry said. "No lines."

A waitress, a rather pretty young woman, though branded with a burn-like scar upon her forehead, came toward them. She smiled warmly. Month in, month out, they were good customers, Terry and Adam. "Two for lunch?" she said, which was what she invariably said. Adam a couple of times had attempted a little banter ("He's having lunch, I'm having breakfast, I just got up"), but a flustered confusion had been the result. Her English wasn't up to it. "Two for lunch," Terry said.

"Smoking or the not smoking?"

"The not smoking," Adam said.

She led them to a partially cleared table by the window. Dishes had been pushed to one end but not yet carted away. One of the previous diners had ordered sweet and sour shrimp, Terry noticed, and evidently had chewed them up for a while, tail and all, before depositing the result, gathered into neat globular amalgams of pink flesh, breading, and shell, on the edge of the plate. Terry felt a quick, thrashing kick of nausea go through him, followed by a thump at the front of his head. His headache—he who never got headaches still was carrying around a massive headache.

"Enjoy your meal," the waitress chanted, as she always did, to which Adam, with mock grimness, replied, as *he* always did, "We'll do the best we can . . ."

"Thank you," Terry called after her, thereby capping the ritual. This was by way of instructing Adam to be less cutting and peremptory with restaurant staff.

"So you didn't see the game last night?" Adam began.

"You don't have an aspirin?"

"Aspirin?"

"I got a headache. I never get headaches, or *this* kind of head-ache, anyway, but I got a bad headache."

"Have a drink."

"You going to have a drink?"

Like most things in Adam's life, drinking was a highly regu-lated affair. Alcohol was almost never consumed at lunch and almost always consumed at dinner—usually in the form of martinis. For watching baseball, at home or in the park, beer was the only permissible beverage.

Adam for a moment peered oddly, pressingly at Terry. It was nothing Terry had yet put his finger on, but Adam didn't seem quite himself today. "Sure," Adam said. "I'll have a drink."

"Good," Terry said. "May be just what I need."

A stooped old man whose drooping moustache covered both upper and lower lip came to clear away the dishes. "We're ready to order," Adam told him. Adam *couldn't* seem to remember that this was somebody who took no orders—whose sole job was bussing tables.

The little man made no answer except to clear away the dishes a little more hurriedly: as fast as he possibly could with his shaky hands. The hunch of his shoulders, the downturned swing of his face, the mouth-effacing moustache—all worked to express his absolute hopelessness in the language of his adopted homeland.

Another, younger man came forward, ebony hair agleam with oil, and with a grin of self-congratulation he pointed at Terry. "Shrimp with the lobster sauce . . ." he announced. Terry's usual order.

"Shrimp? No, no," Terry protested, those regurgitated shrimp balls still fresh in the mind. "Not today. Adam, whyntcha go ahead."

"Garlic chicken. Hot and sour soup. But first a martini, extra dry, with a twist."

"I'd like a martini too," Terry said. "And the hot and sour soup. And—and the string beans." Terry handed his menu back to the waiter, who accepted it with a spirited grin, as though acknowledging receipt of an especially thoughtful gift.

"String beans?" Adam said. "You know what I think of vegetarianism. It's immoral. Animals were put on this earth to be *eaten*. Why in the world do you think God created anything so pathetic as a chicken if not for the backyard barbecue?"

"I don't know. I wanted a change. My head hurts."

"You just need a little of the General's M.S.G. That'll set you to rights. So tell me about Marquette."

"It's a beautiful lake, Lake Superior. I just caught a few glimpses of it. Looked as big as a sea. And blue—God what a blue it was."

"I mean how did things go?"

"Oh, the usual dancing, why *are* we so tiresome? Lawyers I mean."

"It's genetic. Give 'em a hundred years, you watch and scientists'll isolate the gene, the one that simultaneously drives a person toward law school and tiresomeness."

"Actually, this was worse than usual, since they weren't really communications lawyers—they're Chicago-based—and we had to go through a song-and-dance so everybody could show how tough and competent they are. And all this over a C-2 station, mind you."

"You got to start somewhere."

"It's the silly aggressiveness I can't stand," Terry said. "The playing at soldiers. People ask me why I went to law school, I tell them I didn't *go*. I *enlisted*. It was our generation's equivalent of the military draft."

"We eat better, on the whole. Than the military, I mean."

"Figure it out. Marquette, a Class C-2, we're talking about a potential listening audience of what, five years from now, ten years from now? A hundred thousand max? That's if you go along with some absurd population projections, if you buy into this 'capital of the North' line they're singing, if you ignore the fact that half your signal's going straight out over the water, heading off toward the North Pole, and yet we're all expected to treat this thing as though we're divvying up exclusive rights to trade with—with China for the next hundred years."

The smiling Chinese waiter set their drinks before them. One of the great advantages of General Wang's establishment was that food, drinks, the check all came with exemplary speed.

"And the other side had this woman, up from Chicago, she's at Freeley, Polk, okay, okay, a very plush firm but not exactly the *first* name you think of when you think communications law. Her name's Allison Collier, quite huffy when I call her Allie. She would have driven you nuts."

As a signal to his headache that he wasn't kidding around, Terry took a substantial swallow of his martini. At the first sharp bite of the gin, his skull gave another crushing throb, as in remonstration—but this was followed, almost immediately, by a beaching wave of gratifying ease.

"Tell me more about Allie," Adam said. "She good-looking?"

"Yes. Oh yes. Actually I'm tempted to say unfortunately yes. She'da driven you nuts. Full of all sorts of tough-slash-corny expressions. You know she *actually* said, I'm not kidding you, 'We could run it up the flagpole and see who salutes.' And I'm there thinking, That was corny *fifteen years ago*. Big dark eyes. Kind of cross-eyes."

"Cross-eyes," Adam protested. Clearly, he wanted her flawless.

Terry tipped into the hurting vessel of his head another large swallow of drink. "Not badly crossed or anything. Just this faint little wobble, this—this—"

"Jiggle?" And Adam laughed raucously.

"Well it was fetching, actually. Here's this tough pretty woman, saying things like 'They just don't want you pissing into the soup,' and—"

And at this moment, comically enough, the hot and sour soup arrived, which prompted Adam to cry, "Let's hope the General followed her advice!" His galloping laughter could be a little too loud at times—particularly in public places.

"—and at the same time," Terry went on, in a pointedly quiet voice, "she's pretty obviously not wearing a bra."

"How's she built?"

"Good. You know the way it is sometimes. You're looking at her in the hope of finding something you really don't like. Something that will let you say, I wouldn't have wanted her anyway. Thick ankles, or something of the sort.

"And on the way home today," Terry went on, still quietly

but eagerly; with the retreating of his headache he felt speech leaping to his tongue—"although God it doesn't seem like it was today, it seems like it was a couple days ago. Anyway, on the flight home I'm seated beside this very attractive woman, she's from Marquette, she's only twenty-four—"

"She sounds exactly like my type."

"—and she works in a video store. Anyway, we get to talking, about all sorts of things, including her husband, from whom she recently separated—"

"A very wise move. Did you tell her I'm looking to marry her?"

"No, but you know what I do tell her? I tell her to come to Washington. A number of times I invite her. You know what I tell her? I tell her I'll take her out for a night on the town. Do people even *use* that expression any more? I mean other than old farts like me? I say it and I see my parents dancing to 'Some Enchanted Evening.'" And with these words, Terry for a moment actually did see his parents dancing.

Somewhat unexpectedly, perhaps, given her build, Mob loved to dance, and was always dragging Dad up onto some improbable floor. It was a little cruel, all things considered, for Dad was an atrocious dancer. Moreover, he seemed acutely aware (as she grandly was not) that on a dance floor the two of them—the little gray-haired slip of a man, the big orange-haired woman—made a faintly ludicrous spectacle. "I gave her my card. I wouldn't be surprised, I honestly wouldn't, if she took me up on it."

"So what's she like? You haven't told me what she looks like."

"Blonde. Quite nice-looking. Big thick lion-like mane of hair. Or is 'leonine' the word I'm looking for? And very much, I don't know, in search of a new life."

"Now that's funny—because you know what? That's *exactly what I'm looking for!* This morning, in fact, I wake up, I look at my prematurely gray head in the mirror, and I say, 'Damn it, 'Dam' "—Adam's nickname for himself—" 'what you need in life is a new life.' God this soup is good. How does the General do it?"

It was odd that Adam would mention hair just now, for Terry

had been remarking to himself, just moments before, that in the light of the General's restaurant Adam's tousled hair looked much grayer than usual. It was possible, for the first time in their friendship, truly to envision, at some future lunch, Adam across the table as a snowy-haired man.

"So what have *you* got planned for the weekend?" Terry said.

"Well of course you know the O's are in town. And I can't believe you're going to leave me when the O's are in town. Who am I supposed to go out to the ballpark with?"

"You could take a date . . ."

"Tell you something?—I sometimes honestly suspect that women find me boring. It's incredible—it's *incredible*. I say to them, Football—you like football? No? Okay, *base*ball, and I'll take you to a night game, or a day game, or, hell, I'll even take you to a twi-night double-header. Diversity, honey, I'm offering you di*ver*sity." Adam released another baying laugh. At such times, his jaw—like that of some loose-stringed marionette—could swing wide and snap shut with ferocious rapidity. "Now how can you beat an offer like that?"

"Go figure."

Adam, who though a slow was nonetheless a sloppy eater, had somehow managed to get a fleck of hot and sour soup on the thick bridge of his nose. His appearance generally—his crumpled, food-stained suits, wayward hair, muddy shoes, badly knotted ties—was the stuff of great, affectionate office legend. "Women," he said. "I suppose I'm the first man who ever said I don't understand them?"

In fact, the larger mystery—from Terry's point of view—was not women *per se* but Adam's relationship to them. There were all sorts of inconsistencies—things that, on the surface, anyway, didn't make much sense.

Although, for a number of reasons, this topic wasn't something Terry felt comfortable pursuing, still he was aware of things not quite adding up. On the one hand, Adam was subject to powerful crushes. There'd been a period, a couple of months ago, when Adam, who'd always gone to a barber around the corner from the office, had suddenly taken to driving nearly an hour to get his hair cut. It turned out the woman who'd been cutting his hair had moved shops, nearly to Baltimore—and he'd followed her. It was, given Adam's indifference to his appearance, all somewhat hilarious: Adam driving some eighty miles, round trip, to get his rarely combed hair attended to. No question about it, he'd been smitten. And yet for all his talk about marriage, his declarations about wanting to settle down with every other stewardess or waitress or shop clerk he met, he seemed fundamentally skittish about being drawn anywhere near the altar—about, in fact, being drawn into feminine intimacy of any sort. Some answers to this puzzle surely lay out in Maui, with Adam's ex-wife. Of whom he so rarely spoke.

When, once, Terry asked him outright what had triggered the breakup, Adam said only, "She found greener pastures"—an explanation whose bitter emphasis on *green* suggested that she'd landed somebody with a good deal more money than he himself could offer. This was hard to accept, though. Adam had always had the Midas touch. These days, he was rich—maybe stinking rich. He pulled down a very hefty salary (along with "young" Hamill, son of the firm's founder, he was one of the two highest-paid partners at Hamill, Hillman), but that was only the beginning. He'd also made a killing in the market (as had Terry, ever since he'd begun to follow Adam's advice). Better yet, Adam had twice won the lottery. Not the DC Lottery or the Maryland Lottery or anything crass and plebeian like that: no, he'd hit on a couple of cellular phone franchises and the payoff had been phenomenal. "I really don't feel any pressing need to talk about her," he'd added—unnecessarily, for this was manifest in the look of hardness, almost of spite, that had flared in his eyes. "I've put my marriage behind me." And while there had of course been references, now and then, to his ex-wife, whose name was Nancy, these surfaced far less often than—given the closeness of their friendship—you would have expected.

And when, on another occasion, Terry'd asked to see a photograph of Nancy, the reply was, *I haven't got one.* But this, it turned out, was a bald-faced lie. In Adam's living room one night, while Adam was out on a beer run, Terry'd come across, under a pile of old law school texts, an entire album of photographs of the mystery woman—including wedding portraits, in which Adam, his hair brown instead of gray and his big nose almost laughably prominent on his younger, leaner face, had positively beamed at the photographer. Nancy was a soft-faced bride, at once sweeter-looking and less sexy than Terry had supposed. He'd studied the photographs avidly, one after another, until he heard the sound of a key in the door. . . . Guiltily, a little panicky, he'd shoved the album back under the law books, and had never reached for it since.

A further piece to the puzzle was the way Adam tended to be both flirtatious (often captivatingly so) and, in the last analysis, retiring. A couple of times in the past year Terry had found himself, at Adam's prompting, part of an impromptu and quite lively foursome (Adam was the sort of man who could actually approach women in bars), and it had usually been Adam who dissolved the group. "Oh, we weren't going to get anywhere with *them*," he would later explain, ever so knowingly—but the situation's hopelessness hadn't been at all clear, still wasn't clear, in Terry's mind. Terry had come to see, on the one hand, that his friend's interest in the women around him was no mere macho show; it was heartfelt and unflagging. On the other hand, there was no doubting that something, time and again, pulled him back. And whatever that *something* was, at times Terry was just as glad for its existence. Adam's hesitancies made it easier for Terry himself to keep his distance from women— which was, in the main, what he wished to do.

"The soup's hotter than usual. Spicier," Terry said.

"Not that I noticed."

"No, a good deal hotter. It's got me sweating."

"Sweating? Sweating's normal. Welcome to the club."

Adam sweated freely. He could sit in an air-conditioned conference room, in which the other men had kept their jackets on and the women wore sweaters, and the hair at his temples would be licked with perspiration, the dents and creases in his big forehead would hold mica-like flecks of moisture. This was but one of the ways in which he was, from a bodily standpoint, a heavy *producer:* he was forever having to go to one specialist or another to have various things stripped or cleansed—his teeth of their tartar, his ears of plugs of wax, his feet of plantar warts. There'd been boils that needed lancing, jock rot and athlete's foot that called for fungicides. It even seemed that his eyes exuded more "sleep dust" than other people's. His lids often looked crusty.

"It's a lot spicier," Terry said.

"You're just feeling nervous. Cold feet about the Dismal Swamp?"

"Cold feet wouldn't make me sweat. No actually, I keep telling you, the weekend's going to be fine."

"Then why are you sweating when I'm not? You're not turning sensitive on me, are you? I don't think I could stand it if you turned sensitive. I choose my friends exclusively on the basis of their extreme insensitivity . . ."

"I just hope that it doesn't all feel a little *close*, claustrophobic? This weekend, I mean. Kaye can go *on*, you know how Kaye can go on."

"Kaye's a sweetie," Adam said again, and then as though in acknowledgment of the empty, reflexive sound of this, he added—"She's still in cahoots with that billionaire dentist? How's that going?"

"Dunphy, Or Dumph, as Kaye's always calling him. Fine. It's just fine."

"He still got a hundred good-looking women working for him?"

"Something like that."

"And still seeing a thousand patients a day?"

"So far as I know."

Adam's joking wasn't all that far from the truth. Last spring, after floundering around for years in the job market, Kaye had landed a position with a dentist, Brendan Dunphy, who, to all appearances, managed to see hundreds of patients a day, spending no more than a couple minutes with each. He had quite an arrangement going. His female staff not only seemed to do all the real work but were a remarkably good-looking bunch besides. Kaye had been hired to look after accounts and appointments—a curious choice on Dunphy's part, since (as Terry knew all too well) her own personal records were a permanent muddle. It was almost as though, in her early-middle-aged stolidity, she'd been hired to play mother hen to Dunphy's "chicks." Once, a couple of months ago, Adam had gone with Terry to pick up Kaye, which had led to all sorts of jokes about dentists' offices that fronted for brothels. Although Terry had never actually visited anything like a house of ill repute, and so had no basis for judgment, it *was* true that there was an unsteadying sexiness about the place—not only its good-looking uniformed young women but its ugly opulent furnishings (so unlike any dentist's office Terry had ever seen), the lush string music oozing from the loudspeakers, the padded, abstruse equipment, the muffled cries echoing from rooms within rooms. And Terry had for a time found the joke amusing—until his gathering realization that it made Kaye into some sort of madame had eventually forced him to cut such humor dead.

"I just hope Kaye doesn't bore me to tears about the wedding."

"The wedding?" A queer light—a greasy shine, like the film of soup still on his nose—came to Adam's eyes. "You don't mean this new guy, Glenn, is actually going—"

"No no no. Diana's. You know how Kaye can go on."

"Our Delightful Diana. I would call this whole thing cradle-robbing, but I gather the groom's fresh out of the cradle himself."

"Peter. I have every reason for thinking that he's going to work out just fine . . ."

"Gadzooks, I don't like the sound of that. 'I have every reason for thinking . . .' *Uh*-oh." Adam hooted.

This was one of Adam's great charms, actually—his homemade, hybrid way of talking. He really could manage to say things like *gadzooks* (even at an FCC hearing) and get away with it. Terry himself usually avoided any sort of outlandish expression—in large part because he was so keenly aware of how bumbling and fatuous Kaye managed to look in her attempts to sound hip or hep or whatever she might choose to call it.

"What asinine thing are you on about now?" Terry said.

"No wonder you've seen so little of him. Don't you see she's hiding him from you? You make a very tough daddy for a girl to bring a young man home to."

"And what's that supposed to mean?"

"Isn't that the role you've pretty much assumed in this case?"

"I guess so," Terry said. "Actually," he continued, picking up his napkin; the peppery spiciness of the soup made him aware of the heat coming to his face, "she's asked me to give her away. You know, walk her down the aisle."

"Go ahead—admit he's insufferable."

"Who?"

"Who? Diana's heartthrob. Didn't you tell me he's good-looking?"

"I suppose most people would say so."

"And rich?"

"His family is."

"And smart? Isn't he going to Columbia for grad school?"

"He hasn't gotten in yet. I don't know how smart it makes him that he hopes to get in . . ."

Terry had forgotten that he'd ordered string beans. When set before him they seemed, in their thoroughly pervaded greenness, their surprisingly ambitious length, a sort of exotic puzzle to solve: a wondrous Oriental knot.

Terry always used to eat Chinese food with chopsticks—somewhat slowly, but with the satisfaction of receiving a passing grade in the little test of dexterity they imposed—but he'd given them up at Adam's prompting. It was one of Adam's jokes, quite insistently advanced, that for Americans to employ chopsticks was not merely an affectation but a perilous abdication of cultural identity. Terry considered calling for chopsticks nonetheless; instead, he said to the waiter, "I'd like another martini."

"And you're the one not dreading the weekend," Adam said.

"My head," Terry said. "The ache. It's feeling better."

"I'll bet."

"What's happened to Susie?" Susie was somebody Adam went out with now and then. She worked for a congressman from Arizona, a Republican, whose name Terry could never remember—a lapse of memory never to be admitted to Susie herself, whose easy-flowing chatter always presupposed a deep conversancy with dealings on the Hill. Actually, neither Adam nor Terry was much interested in politics. Both had voted for Bush over Dukakis—as had most of the crew at Hamill, Hillman. Reagan's deregulation of the airwaves, which had sounded potentially disastrous to a firm that specialized in communications, had turned into an ongoing bonanza. For this "deregulation," among other things, opened up the spectrum for hundreds of new radio stations. Reagan had started a real feeding frenzy. Adam was a habitual if cynical Republican (he accused the Democrats of not understanding business) who was drawn to the party emotionally, uncynically on the issue of Russia; the Republicans could be counted on to be tougher with "those bastards who overran my homeland." (This was something of a joke, since Adam had never been to Poland and both his parents had left it more than fifty years before, but it wasn't completely a joke.) Terry saw himself as an Independent. To some extent this was a distinction without a difference, for when the time came to cast his vote he (like his father, who had also held out nominally as an Independent, despite Mob's longstanding involvement with the Iowa Republican Committee) could usually be counted on to vote a Republican ticket.

"Nothing's happened to Susie. It's quite reassuring in its way. In a world of dizzying, bewildering changes, nothing ever happens to Susie. In any event, there hasn't been another speech about her biological clock. People talk about the noise of the city, the horns, the sirens, trucks—but you know what that sound is that's roaring up from every corner of this overcrowded metropolis? The one that's deafening us? It's the sound of thousands upon thousands of female biological clocks. I'm waiting for scientists to discover why it is that biological clocks have become so much louder than they used to be. Let all the clocks run out, I say. Can you *imagine* anything worse than having a child on your hands?"

"Twins," Terry replied, hoping to make Adam smile—even though a number of things in this monologue had vexed Terry just a bit. The truth (which was standing a little ways off to the side during this conversation, looking on with bitter amusement) was that if everything had gone as Terry once had hoped, he and Betsy by now would have had a couple of kids. Three— she'd wanted three.

Adam was always seeking to make outrageous pronouncements (it was one of his great appeals that in a traditionally straitlaced firm he was forever rocking the boat), and the best policy was not to take him very seriously . . . Now in this matter of children—well, had things worked out differently for Adam, he might easily have become the contentedly over-busy *paterfamilias* of a demanding little brood. It was easy to visualize, somehow: the same tone of happy complaint from Adam, only a radically altered subject matter. Still, this business of biological clocks was for Terry an especially ticklish issue—for the fact was that, not so many years ago, Kaye had gone a bit off her head on the subject. She'd suddenly gotten it into her brain that she wanted another child. A boy. She'd rattled on about this "need" for months on end—half a year maybe. Her clock, her clock, her clock . . . To Terry this development had seemed (given Kaye's age, her lack of a husband, and her inability to put the one child she already had through college without a huge subsidy from her "little brother") pathetic and, in all sorts of ways, unseemly. But he'd felt sorry for Kaye. And that was the way things always turned out: however foolish or misguided or unreasonable Kaye's lamentations might be, in the end they touched you. Adam could joke about the perils of sensitivity, but surely few things could so sensitize a man's nerves as having a somewhat plain older sister who was forever holding herself up as a victim of the male sex.

Sometimes, admittedly, with good cause: Kaye's ex-husband, Ralph, had turned out to be a first-class shit. Whatever justification he'd had for abandoning Kaye, there was none for abandoning his daughter—which to all intents and purposes was what he'd done. He had refused to pay her college expenses, and this huge, inflation-outrunning burden had fallen, after many complicated psychological turnings, on the shoulders of Uncle Terry. Ralph evidently wasn't even going to be invited to the wedding; it was Terry, in any event, who would walk the girl down the aisle.

These beans were good! They had plenty of crunch. This process of maneuvering their awkwardly elongated shapes into his mouth, there to be ground down into a spicy and fibrous pulp, was in its primitive way far more satisfying than anybody would have supposed.

"I want to hear more about Allie Collier."

"No you don't," Terry said. "You want to hear about Kelly. I invited her to come out to Washington with her friend Marty."

"I'm very much hoping that this friend of hers Marty is female. Otherwise, you really are losing your mind, Babe."

And this was another of the little routines they'd evolved. Adam was always addressing him in the language of sports—calling him Babe and Kid and Tiger and even Rookie. It was a joke, of course, this business of converting Hamill, Hillman into some sort of minor-league baseball franchise, but it carried its note of gravity as well. For all of Adam's patent satisfaction in skillfully playing the role of a beer-drinking baseball-watching regular guy, at bottom he was in many ways a beer-drinking baseball-watching regular guy. The quite endearing truth was that the only time Terry had ever seen tears in his friend's eyes was when, after leading for eight innings, the Orioles had dropped a night game to the Yankees in the bottom of the ninth. Hence, to be addressed by Adam in the language of sports was to be granted admission to a world of honor, dexterity, glory.

"Oh, she's female all right. I've seen her in a bathing suit."

"You've seen her in a bathing suit?"

The look on Adam's face—exaggeratedly incredulous, but with a touch of roused, authentic curiosity in the eyes as well—was just the one Terry was seeking.

"Her picture. Kelly showed me a picture of the two of them in bathing suits."

"Kelly showed you a pic-ture of herself and her friend in bathing suits," Adam repeated with histrionic slowness. Oh, the look on his face! "What were you supposed to do—choose between them?"

"I was supposed to take a look at them. And that's exactly what I did."

"How's she look?"

"Who look?"

"Marty. The woman you're going to set me up with when the two of them come to town."

"Well," Terry said, in a tone of sober-minded understatement, "I don't think you'll have cause to complain . . ." He found himself reveling in a sense of his wheeler-dealer powers—just as though he were, in actuality, providing Adam with a woman. The drink, he realized, had gone to his head a bit. "Beans," he added. "Adam, you've got to examine the possibility of eating more green beans."

"*That's* what I'll do with my weekend. And here I thought I had nothing special to do . . ."

Another pause took shape, during which Terry, as a sobriety-seeking gesture, consciously expanded his gaze from the food before him, and from the face of his friend, to the restaurant itself, now almost deserted of its lunchtime crowd (what time *was* it?), and to the narrow stretch of sky visible over the street. And for just a moment it seemed incredible to him that in a few hours he would himself be seated in the hollow metal tube of an airplane, humming at hundreds of miles per hour through that selfsame sky. Simultaneously he recognized, in an altogether other sector of the mind, that he was experiencing one of those rare moments when the pure miracle of flight—the unlikelihood of a world in which you could purchase global destinations with the same ease as bread, sugar, milk, a leg of lamb—for an instant stood highlighted. Rare as they were, such occasions always held an inkling of connection, one with another, as though a man's life were best perceived as a string of instants in which, briefly, most of his life fell away. (And for Terry they were also allied, these instants, to an odd inarticulate disgruntled sensation—one burrowing all the way back into his childhood—that there was something, some not yet divulged *some*thing, for which, or to serve which, he had been placed upon this planet.)

"Hey you lucky pig, it's yours if you want it . . ."

"Mm?" Terry said.

"Yours . . ." Adam pushed his plate, which held a few shreds of chicken in garlic sauce and a small mound of rice, toward Terry. Adam generally left a bit of his lunch unfinished, as a means of controlling his weight. For all his bulk and energy, Adam honestly didn't eat that much. No, Terry ate far more.

"I tell you," Adam said, "I can't think of anything, *any*thing I'd rather receive from Santa than a splendidly inefficient metabolic system like yours."

This was a favorite refrain of Adam's, and one that had some solid grounding. The truth was that Terry, month after month, did eat just exactly what he wanted, including sweets by the handful and plateful—cinnamon rolls, jelly doughnuts, candy bars, cream-cheese brownies. He never fretted over calories and never gained an ounce. If he ever *wanted* to gain weight, it seemed he would have to resume the weight-lifting regimen he'd adopted briefly at Princeton, but he'd grown content to tip the scale at just under a hundred and fifty pounds. Adam used to enjoy warning Terry about the advent of a "great metabolic shift"—but evidently the pleasures of gloating over that distant day of reckoning had faded. Lately, Adam had turned, with re-awakened relish, to advocating the reverse: Mother Nature, forever doling out inequities, had created Terry solely for the purpose of stirring envy in virtuous dieters everywhere. *That* was Terry's mission on the planet.

"Are all the Seward men like that?" Adam went on. "Born pigs destined never to look like pigs?"

"Well it's true Dad doesn't carry an extra pound. But my genes are a mix. Kaye's always struggling with her weight and Mob—well you've seen her."

"It's comforting to know that *some*body in the family's fat."

"Oh, Mob's not so fat. I mean she is *fat* but that isn't really the impression she gives. Just big. Formidable." Terry laughed jubilantly; the resonances of *formidable* pleased him. That's what Mob always had been (or was until recently, when things had begun to take a worrisome turn): unignorably and reassuringly formidable.

Terry recalled another restaurant, Marianna's Soup and Sandwich, in Gawana, Iowa—specifically, the afternoon when, half his life ago, he'd wandered into the place alone, taken a seat at the counter, ordered french fries and a root beer, and, after a couple of minutes, discovered that the little gray man in the end booth, whom he'd perceived with his peripheral vision only, was his father. "Dad!" he'd called just as his father called "Terry!" The recognition seemed, on both sides, unaccountably embarrassing: shamefaced. Terry, his plate of fries in one hand, his root beer in the other, went and joined his father, who also was drinking a glass of root beer. "What are you doing here?" Terry said, and Dad, with that deft, knowing, winning little wink of his—the wry wink of a man seemingly born for expressions of wryness—replied, "I'm fleeing an angry Mob."

Dad had not only latched on to Terry's nickname for his mother but was constantly embroidering little jokes upon it. He spoke of Mob scenes and Mob justice and of taking your appeals to the Mob.

"What did you do?" Terry asked him.

"A very bad thing, Terry. Very bad. I broke her gravy boat. Trying to get something out of the cupboard."

"Not the one that was Grandma Chapman's . . ."

"The very one. That one and no other. Broke it into a million pieces. Ka-powee."

If there was unease to be found in Dad's eyes, there was also, deep down, a buoyant glinting merriment. It was *amusing*—this strategic decision to sit for a stretch in Marianna's Soup and Sandwich, secure in the knowledge that, before too long, the storm would die down utterly. "I left her a note about it. Said I had to run some errands. And came here."

No doubt about it: the Mob *would* be furious. And it was wisest to treat her fury as one would a tornado—lay low, run for cover, go underground. And yet father and son shared, in addition to their cautious, healthy respect for this whirling force at the center of their lives, a knowledge of its ultimate harmlessness . . . Whatever anger Mob was feeling would, in its time, howl away over the horizon. It would pass utterly. She was, for all her occasionally titanic displeasures, as unshakable by her own emotions as by anything else.

At this thought of his father in a booth at Marianna's Soup and Sandwich, Terry felt a physical climb of emotion; up from his chest it mounted, to his face, which was already warm with the soup's excessive spices, and for a moment it stung his eyes. And in its wake came a sense of forfeiture and mourning—which was perfectly absurd, since in this particular matter nothing had been lost or taken away. Dad was not only still in Gawana but was living there in remarkably good health for a man of seventy-three . . . and at this very moment might well be sitting in Marianna's, nursing a lukewarm cup of coffee. But still a sense of loss floated in the air, as well as an attendant feeling of gratitude—oh, what a great stroke of good fortune it had been, what a kind kiss from Lady Luck, to have been born Everett Seward's son . . .

"I'm going to have to cut you off at one."

"Pardon?" Terry said.

"One drink. Two seems to shut down your conversational powers."

"Sorry. I was thinking."

"You want to push off?"

"In a minute . . ."

There was here a thought remaining to be voiced, or at least pondered, and it was as though to depart from Captain Wang's would be to abandon something he was on the verge of divulging . . . Or maybe he just needed another moment to rest. Christ, he was tired—which was a bad way to start a weekend with Kaye and her newest new man.

"You know," Terry began, "I was wondering about Nancy."

"Nancy?"

"Your wife."

"Ex-wife. Hey when I was a kid there was a comic book, the X-men, who were this group of mutants? All sorts of special powers, you remember? Now these X-men were so very, very special that nobody could be told about them. Secret identities, and all that. But you grow up and you see that in fact the world is full of X-men: ex-husbands, ex-wives, ex-in-laws, ex-stepchildren."

Terry nodded solemnly before, abruptly, joining Adam's spirited laughter. It took him a moment to comprehend that Adam was closing off an unwanted subject.

"But you weren't finished," Adam said. "You haven't painted a proper picture for my mind's eye. Were these bikinis or one-piece suits?"

"Mm?"

"Don't look at me as though I've got a screw loose. You were the one who insisted a moment ago, altogether improbably I should add, that a good-looking woman you'd never laid eyes on before was actually pushing snapshots of herself in a bathing suit at you."

"Oh, Kelly." The sound of her name in Terry's throat was hugely cheering. He felt her eyes again on his face, saw the eager exploratory jumping motions of her hands as she called for *a new life,* while those green bird-earrings were fluttering beside her face like birds around a feeder . . . And he felt once more inside him the little abdominal sway and rotation that her proximity had aroused.

"Hey, what do you *mean* you don't get headaches? So what about all these trips to the masseuse, huh? So, can you explain Angelina to me, huh?"

"Those are neck-aches. They're quite another thing."

It would be easy to ridicule Adam's tenderness toward his lady-barber-from-Baltimore had Terry himself (as if driven to demonstrate the humbling principle that while nothing is more amusing than somebody else's misguided infatuation, nothing is less humorous than your own) not managed to wind up in a strikingly similar situation. It had begun two months ago, when *he'd* been at the barber's.

Maggie, the woman cutting his hair, had asked him to turn his head, and he'd replied that that wasn't so easy when your neck was killing you, and the next thing he knew he was being almost literally dragged off to meet a masseuse in the back room. For Maggie's was no mere barber shop, it was a "head wellness center," and Maggie had recently taken on a woman who specialized in Indian-Japanese massages, and by chance there was an hour opening up *just now,* she would *realign his life* . . . and so it had come to pass that he'd been introduced to this life-realigner, whose name was Angelina.

She'd had him leave his T-shirt on. That had been fine with Terry, who'd sensed in the air (as in Dunphy's dentist office) something illicit and potentially dangerous. And yet, at the touch of Angelina's hands upon his neck all such misgivings had vanished. Oh how much better she made him feel! Time and again (since that first visit, he'd been going once a week) she made him feel so much better! He would lie on a paper-wrapped bench, which was very much like what you'd find in a doctor's office except that there was a grooved extension at one end for your forehead, with an opening below it for your eyes, nose, and mouth. Looking down through the opening, he would study, for steady minutes at a time, Angelina's feet. She wore old-fashioned pointy canvas tennis shoes. On the outside edge of the right shoe her baby toe had scraped and ripped its way to open air. Though she ostensibly discouraged all speech ("empty your mind of words and thoughts") she kept up a steady chatter. She had a boyfriend named Howard, who was some sort of computer whiz. She'd been a psych major in college (U. of Maryland), until she dropped out. Her father had been an alcoholic. She had a brother in the navy. And another brother who was gay and who worked as an "outfitter" in Montana. Her mother lived solely on hamburger, practically.

Well, was Adam still driving out to Baltimore to get his hair cut? Terry didn't know. He didn't like to press Adam on the subject of women, and hoped thereby to discourage Adam's pressing him back. At the moment, anyway, Terry was sexually dysfunctional. It was a term whose coldness proved strangely reassuring—for the words had the virtue of removing his shortcomings from the tender, queasy bog of the psyche and placing them within the firmer, simpler realm of body pathology. This inability of his was like being incapable of digesting lactose or of manufacturing insulin or of focusing your eyes upon distant objects—he couldn't screw—but with the principal difference that in his case the condition was almost certainly temporary. It had originated after Betsy's death. Some months ago Terry'd read a long article in a men's magazine about various forms of male sexual dysfunction and had come away both generally comforted that these were far commoner than he'd supposed and squeamishly convinced—having edgily glanced at the section devoted to physical therapy and prosthetic aids—that in the sexual area, anyway, cures tended to be spectacularly more oppressive than maladies. For the meantime, he was content to let his life go on just as it was going on. He was hurting nobody. Whatever his lacks, no one else suffered from them. Actually, he had come a long way, in the last year or so, toward putting the accident behind him, and these days he was working well and sleeping well; his health was good and he was taking pleasure anew in all sorts of incidental things that, for a time, he'd been blind to. He had reached—as Adam, too, in regard to his own needs no doubt had reached—a state like equilibrium. There was something missing, of course, an unignorable hollowness—but around this hollowness Terry had constructed a sort of shelter for himself.

And it was possible that "sexually dysfunctional" was, under the circumstances, an overly severe choice of terms. Nineteen months now—nineteen months since Betsy's death, and in that time there'd been two women, though in neither case could he have been called the instigator. With the first, he'd been unable—flatly unable—to make even a start at a start. That had been a mistake—more than that, *it had been wrong,* for the woman, Donna Kaistalides, had been an acquaintance of Betsy's, a schoolteacher colleague of Betsy's, *one of Betsy's friends.* Things had gone, technically speaking, somewhat better with his second partner, whose name—astoundingly enough—when he'd woken in the middle of the night a couple of weeks ago he'd been unable to recall. In itself it was no easy name to forget—Joan Steptoe—and besides there was the almost daily reinforcement of having her surname blazoned around town on the front of one or another of her ex-husband's retail outlets (Steptoe Hardware—Home and Recreation). But it had been blotted out all the same. And the power of the mind to forget something so central, to repress, even for a couple of minutes, something so ubiquitous, had seemed extraordinary. When he'd woken up temporarily unable to recall either of her names—the names of the woman he'd been to bed with most recently!—he'd felt diminished and frightened, of course, as anybody in such circumstances would, but he'd also felt, even then, dispassionately impressed with himself. He was displaying a kind of power, was he not? To block her out so thoroughly required, in its way, vast expenditures of internal force . . . With Joan (who was something of a sad case, her husband having left her just a year or two before his business really took off) he'd managed, on a couple of occasions, to complete the act (though failing dismally on a couple of others), but even when he'd "succeeded" he found the whole business unsettling.

More unsettling, actually, than the outright failures had been those other occasions, when the physical motions were accompanied all the while by a sense of smothered turbulence—something ugly or mortifying or malign concurrently being enacted at the roots of the psyche. And, in all of this, something unrecognizable: *this* was orgasm? oneness? catharsis? What was taking place physically had in the end little to do with what was taking place psychologically. At one point, in the gray light he'd looked down at himself, swollen and upright, and an internal voice had said the strangest thing a man has ever said about himself: *That's not my dick . . .*

And the confusions afterwards . . . Of course it was possible to lend these a certain dignity—call the whole mess of emotions *post coitum tristesse,* as though there were something noble and learned and continental about it—but *is* there any experience more regularly debasing than that of the man who goes off for his post-coital pee and, in the sharp glare of the bathroom, confronts the slimed, angry-red swelling of his misspent self? It had all gone wrong, something had gone wrong since the death (though perhaps this was only to be expected, and was perfectly normal, in the face of such a loss). (And as for the death itself, very little to be said . . . He'd said what needed saying, done what needed doing, including, one raw fall day in Charlottesville, hurling himself headlong, eyes hotly blind with weeping, onto Betsy's grave. What was left was a silent awareness of a sort of mute fraternity out there, scattered around the planet, made up of those among the living-damned who at some point in their lives had seen, as he had seen, something so unthinkable it was never once more, even in dreams, to be fully approached: your wife unreally bleached and unreally bloated and lying closed-eyed on a tableclothed table, in a hot room whose windows were ever open, no glass, no screens, the boundaries down and man-sized leaves out there that had turned to metal in the tropical sun: nothing, ever, could bear to inch itself, step by step, close to that vision again. Never. Not again.)

Not getting involved with anybody else also carried the advantage of leaving unconfirmed the self-diagnosis of "sexual dysfunction." In his case surely there were, from a medical standpoint, too few examples to generalize from. It was comforting, this notion of insufficient data . . . And yet he'd felt, these past months, toward Angelina, and now this morning toward Kelly (toward a twenty-four-year old! who worked in a video store! and who'd left her husband because his idea of a challenging experience was a pissing-for-distance contest!), an intimation of ease, a sense of direct, eye-to-eye accommodation, of bracing plausibility to the notion that going to bed would be, on both sides, an occasion of joy. Joy and—more than that—thanksgiving.

"You really must wipe that soppy expression off your face. You honestly look as though you'd gone into some sort of poetic trance. Or, even worse, are about to take up oil painting."

"Oh you don't have to worry about me. I'm not artistic—and I'm not going to start." Terry laughed and the laughter felt surprisingly solid. "I'm a very regular guy."

Although this comment was, on the face of it, a repudiation of Art (or at least of everything Art seemed to stand for in those magazines and newspapers—the *Atlantic Monthly, Harper's, The New Republic,* the *Post,* the *Times*—that Terry regularly read), it held for him nonetheless something akin to artistic richness. Ironically, it was a boast to take pride in. As for Art—well, Terry rarely went to museums, almost never read fiction, never read poetry, and agreed wholeheartedly when Adam dismissed opera and ballet as "gay gaga." It was true he enjoyed the movies; he even liked photography, provided it didn't take itself too seriously. But what Art seemed chiefly to stir in him was a sense of having been shortchanged—a repeated recognition that it could not reach the sectors of his life it was grandly reputed to reach. It did not touch, for instance, that region in his soul wherein he felt (still felt, though he was on the very edge of forty and no longer could confess this to anyone, it all sounded so flighty and romantic and insubstantial) that he was born for some as yet undivined purpose.

How amusing, how *right* it was, that if Art failed you, your own pride in ordinariness—in being regular—did not. In a world in which grown men in suits and ties were constantly seduced into ever more novel and mortifying ways of publicly making asses of themselves by exposing their *sensitivity,* their *playfulness,* their *creativity* and *vulnerability,* it was a considerable satisfaction to enlist yourself among the ranks of the insensitive, industrious, uncreative, callous. In this conviction lay a powerfully affectionate bond between Terry and Adam: their common horror, best expressed by blasts of incredulous laughter, at the ways in which grown men these days were encouraged on television and radio to sniff and blubber and generally carry on about the problems of being male, or about (worse yet) *caring* and *growth,* or about (worse still) *creative needs*—a far more squeamishness-inducing term than sexual needs. As Adam was forever pointing out, the world had far, far more artists than it could possibly use; what it was acutely short of, at the moment, were people of sanity, evenness, clarity of temper—regularness, in short.

"You know you talk about creativity," Terry said, "now you know who really was creative? I don't mean painting soup cans, or writing novels about how Mom and Dad mistreated you—but really creative? Kevin Kopp, that's who. You know, my—"

"Your college roommate."

"God I wonder sometimes what Kevin's up to. Or do I want to know? I told you about Kevin and the beans?"

"Maybe. I think so."

Obviously Adam knew the tale backwards and forwards, but he was being good about it—good old Adam. He seemed to understand that Terry suddenly very much wanted to recount it once again.

"Okay, it's November, my freshman year at Princeton, and my roommate, Kevin Kopp, also known as Curly Kopp, also known as Squirrely Kopp—and God he did look like a squirrel! I mean he really did honestly and truly look exactly like a *squirrel!* Anyway, the notorious tightwad Curly Kopp goes out and makes a purchase. And it turns out that if you add up all the money Curly Kopp has spent from September to November on meals outside the dorm, on dates, on movies, on records or tapes, on furnishings for the room, on booze, on dope, on—on you just name it! Anyway, you add up all these expenses, and the sum total is *less* than the purchase Curly has just made. And what has our little Squirrely Curly bought? Little Squirrely Curly has bought jumping beans."

Adam laughed appreciatively. It *is* a good story.

"Good old Squirrely-the-tightwad-Curly has suddenly broken down and bought hundreds and hundreds of Mexican jumping beans. And what does Curly do? He puts up signs all over campus, he puts up signs saying, *Until you've felt their warm rapturous throbbing in the palm of your hand, you have not really lived.* We've gone into the jumping bean business, he and I. No, better still: we've gone into the jumping bean *escort* service, for that's how he bills them. And who on the Princeton campus is most keen on jumping bean escorts? Well, pie-eyed eating-club boys returning from parties at two in the morning, that's who. There'd be a knock at the door, late, way after I'd gone to bed, I'd go to the door in my underwear—Squirrely slept like a log—throw it open and there'd be a couple of these pie-faces, and one of them saying with the gravel-voiced solemnity of the truly shit-faced, 'You the guy with the jumping beans?' So I'd invite them in, drop some beans into the lid of a metal potato chip can, set the lid on the radiator, to get the beans warmed up, watch 'em wiggle for a while, sometimes make a sale and sometimes not, and go back to bed. Now you talk about creative," Terry concluded, "and that was Kevin Kopp in a nutshell. In a jumping bean.

"You talk about creative," Terry started up once more, as Adam glanced at his watch, "and that's what Dad is. I mean genuine creative, not artsy-fartsy creative. I've told you about all the stuff he's made. Beautiful stuff. Genuinely beautiful and imaginative stuff. I mean we're talking about a man who built a solar doghouse! A man who got his picture in papers all over the country by building a solar doghouse."

"That is amazing. We better go."

"We better go," Terry said. "We need a check."

"We've got a check."

"Money's what we need then. I've got money. It's my treat you know."

"That's right," Adam said.

Terry peered at the check, got out his wallet, and counted out the necessary bills—three tens, a five, two ones. "More expensive than usual," he said.

"We've been drinking."

"So we have," Terry said and realized when he mounted to his feet that the martinis had worked on him more than he'd realized. He felt fine.

The two of them stepped out into a street in which not a minute had passed. Same dark, hushed, suspended air. Same hot clammy clatter and hurry.

"We're talking about a man who, when I was a kid, not only sets up a model train arrangement in the basement that's an absolute marvel, an engineering *marvel,* but who constructs his own model train cars. Better, more original than you'd get in any store or catalogue. The E & T Railroad—that's what he called it. Everett and Terry. Our initials, you see."

"Looks like all hell's going to break loose."

"What do you mean?" When Adam didn't respond—perhaps he didn't hear over all the noises of the street—Terry answered his own question. "The storm." Terry perceived that he needed to bring himself down a bit. His head was flying. "I'm not quite myself today," he apologized. "Maybe it's the lack of sleep? I hardly slept at all last night. In Marquette."

Silently, but at a good clip, the two friends marched back to the office. In the elevator, just the two of them, Terry said, "I'll drop by before I take off."

"You all right?"

"Me? Fine," Terry said. "Except for my head—headache. Headache."

Terry got out on twelve, one floor below Adam's floor. "You watch yourself," Adam said. It was his familiar call of farewell, and was—bless him—about as openly solicitous as he allowed himself ever to be. And yet, undemonstrative as his care and concern remained, it had been Adam who, after Betsy's death, had done more than anybody else to ease Terry's way. Not Mob, not Dad, not Kaye, not Betsy's sister Heidi, each of whom had encouraged him to "talk about it," to reminisce, to pine, to sort things out, to weep. No, the greatest help had come from Adam, who'd cringed in undisguised mortification on the couple of occasions when Terry had shattered into tears. It was Adam, always discouraging reflection and reminiscence, and simply saying, "We've got work to do," who'd been the greatest support of all. "Sure, sure," Terry said. "See you."

He marched off the elevator and was at once hit by a panicky suspicion that he might look, under the warm lights of the lobby, visibly drunk. He dropped his head and scuttled toward his office. Bertha was typing away on something at an impressive speed. God how efficient she could sound and look! "Hold my calls for twenty minutes," he told her as he veered by. "I've got a headache."

"You had some calls."

"Tell me about them in twenty minutes. I'm going to lie down. I've got a headache. Was up most of the night and got up at the crack of dawn this morning."

"Including your niece."

"Diana?" An odd time of day for her to be calling. Usually she called after five o'clock, when the rates fell. Terry had told her more than once that she could call collect whenever she wanted to, but she paid for her own calls—a symbolic gesture that pleased him. Rather than take him up on this little extravagance, this young woman whose bills he was largely footing displayed an instinct for frugality.

"And someone named Angelina called. She wouldn't leave a last name. She assumed you knew her."

He felt the blood from the depths of his lower body rush to his face. "Who?"

Though he avoided Bertha's eye, the image he presented to her came to him brightly: a florid-faced drunk, slinking back from a long lunch only to discover that his masseuse had called him at the office.

"Angelina? She wouldn't leave a last name. She said something about your joining her yoga class."

"That's right," Terry said, and slapped his thigh, as though only now recollecting the obvious. "She *said* she'd be starting up a yoga class."

"She said you have her number."

"Do I?" Terry said. "I guess I do"—and turned into his office, clicking the door behind him.

He did not head directly toward either the couch, to lie down, or the phone, to call Diana or Angelina. It seemed there was something he ought first to do. He wandered uneasily over to the window, looked up at the sky, down at the street. A tall young black man with a blue scarf wound round his neck had set up an impromptu umbrella shop behind a cardboard box. Waiting, hoping for rain. Perhaps it was the man's scarf that brought to Terry's mind Delbert Douglas, someone he hadn't thought of in years, who'd gone to Browning High and wore a blue scarf around his head at the Tri-League Meet. A black vaulter? He was the first Terry had ever seen, and on his third and last attempt Delbert had cleared twelve-nine, bettering Terry by three inches.

Terry went over to the couch, unstrung his shoes, lay down and closed his eyes, and though it didn't seem he'd fallen absolutely to sleep his head jerked spasmodically when the phone rasped.

He walked across the carpet in his stocking feet and picked it up.

"You told me to wake you."

"Yeah, thanks. I wasn't sleeping."

"You want your other calls now?"

"In a minute."

Terry hung up the phone and padded back over to the couch where, slowly, he relaced his shoes. He checked his watch— nearly four o'clock. Bertha'd given him a break of nearly forty minutes, twice as long as he'd requested, and whether this was to be attributed to a kindly feeling that an ailing man needed ample rest, or to mere inefficiency, would be (as in so many of his dealings with Bertha) hard to say.

Nap or no nap, he felt a good deal better—ready to face a few legal documents, ready even to face a weekend with Kaye and Glenn. He opened his closet and stared quizzically at himself in the full-length mirror that lined the inner door. A little rumpled looking, but nothing too alarming. His head was hurting still, or again, but the pain had changed into a dull, metallic ache that could be ignored. He tightened his tie and straightened the part in the middle of his hair, recalling as he did so Adam's reference at lunch to going gray. How many years off into the future, Terry had wondered then, was the day when Adam might fairly be described as white-haired rather than gray-haired? And how much further off was the day when Terry himself, who had seemingly no more than ten gray hairs on his head, might be thought of as snowy-haired? No, it was Kaye, with her dyed hair, who'd picked up the Seward tendency for premature grayness. He felt a little guilty about that, for it was almost as though, in taking on the gene, she'd absorbed something that might otherwise have attached itself to him. And he felt even guiltier—much, much guiltier—about the way her hair had thinned a bit, on top, so that, at various times and angles, you became nervously aware of the scalp below. Who ever would have predicted, of the Seward children, it would be the girl whose hair would thin?

In his closet hung a couple of suits, slippery in their transparent dry cleaner bags, and in drawers to the side were to be found, neatly stacked, shoes in shoe bags, shirts, socks, underwear, ties. He'd freed himself from his home—where he spent very little time, really—by setting up a sort of bedroom closet here. His home was in the District, though just barely. It—the only house he'd ever owned—was out near the Friendship Heights Metro Station, at the very edge of the Maryland border. Betsy had found it. He'd thought recently again of moving—perhaps to an apartment like Adam's. The house, too, was in its way a source of guilt. On the one hand, he had no interest in maintaining a house—in painting it, repairing it, keeping up a garden. And yet it bothered him, burned his conscience as the son of Iowa's greatest amateur handyman, to hire others to do these things.

The phone buzzed—another call from Bertha—and he drifted over to answer it.

"Terry," she said, "there's a guy on the line named Stan Duggar, if I've got the name right, from somewhere called Venture Ventionality. He called before. He's sort of inferring that maybe he knew you, some time ago, but maybe that's not right."

Terry exhaled into the phone. "Put him on."

There was a click, another click, and Terry said, "Afternoon."

"That's Terry Seward, isn't it?"

This was nobody Terry knew. As strangers sometimes did, the man at the other end of the line elongated the *e* of the surname, creating *Seaward*. It was a common mistake, and one that often nudged Terry into a bit of family history, but at the moment he wasn't about to offer either a terse correction or a longer clarification. "Pretty much," he said. The fact was that, but for an obscure twist of events, Terry might have been a Seaward. When the original ancestors, Dad's ancestors, came over from England in the eighteenth century, the spelling evidently hadn't been fully fixed. Some branches of the family became Sewards and some Seawards.

Terry's paternal grandmother had held all these people—Sewards and Seawards—in her head. He hadn't known her well. For one thing, she'd died when he was ten. For another, she'd lived out-of-state—in Wisconsin, where she'd taught school. And yet, to be informed by Dad, five years or so after her death, that she'd done some research into the family tree, and to be shown the yellow papers in the dead schoolteacher's lucid hand—that had been strangely moving. And when, at Princeton, Terry'd become a history major, the decision had fulfilled, he liked to think, a sort of compact with her. Later, he'd fulfilled another by marrying a schoolteacher.

"This is Stanley Duggar of Venture Potentiality."

"I don't think I've heard of it."

"You'd be surprised how many people I talk to who say that . . ."

Terry was tempted to reply, *I don't see anything so surprising about it.* Instead he said, "Would I?" When the proper mood was upon him, which required just the right proportions of boredom, inquisitiveness, and leisure, this peculiar and usually quite obnoxious form of hustle—the telephone hustle—provided a welcome challenge. As contests went, it presented unique demands on each side: for the caller, it was a matter of bluffing and dissembling one's way through a faceless maze in order to reach the targeted person; for the target, the callee, the task was to extract as soon as possible the caller's concealed purpose. What was Stanley Duggar selling? Real estate?

"I suppose you could say that we are Tulsa-based, Tulsa, Oklahoma, I don't suppose that you, living in the nation's capital, have ever been to Tulsa, fine country, very fine—"

"I have, actually. Many times."

"But in a very real sense we are everywhere . . ."

Tin mines? Terry had once received a call from someone who honestly had hoped to induce him to sink ten thousand dollars into a South American tin mine . . .

"I'm not exactly sure what I can do for you, Mr. Duggar."

"Our organization is multiplying at a rate that would astound you. I'm quite sure of that—astound you. We touch everyone. We feel it's all just a matter of time."

"Mr. Duggar, what do you want from me?"

"I want nothing but a few minutes of your time. That's what I want. Literally a few minutes, which if you stop and think about it, if you come down to earth and view the matter long-term, isn't much at all to be asking. You may just discover that you need us. I want to talk about human transformations. I want to talk about downside risk . . ."

"Mr. Duggar, how in the world did you get my name?"

In a changed voice—a steady and insinuative voice that echoed with an almost insectivorous hum—Mr. Duggar said, "Oh we've had our eyes on *you* for quite some time, Seaward," and Terry, abruptly, his gaze on the street below, where rain had still not fallen, experienced a chill. Just like that. He went cold, his skin went *cold,* all of a sudden.

He felt it on his back, up and down his ribs, along the tops of his thighs. This was nothing to take seriously, surely, but these words of Duggar's (*We've had our eyes on you for quite some time, Seaward*) did seem laced with menace. It was for Terry as if dozens, hundreds of film moments (from movies and television, from last week and from twenty years ago) instantly flashed upon his soul, and all of them so densely packed as to provide nothing distinct, nothing discernible—just a sense of dark figures gliding across a screen. Blackmail, protection money, extortion . . . He had stepped into another world.

His voice was not quite his own, not his everyday voice, as he said, "I don't know what your particular hustle is, Mr. Duggar, but I can tell you with near-absolute certainty that I'm much too busy to be interested . . ."

"Lissssen—" the other voice hissed: "You seem to think we're after material things. What I'm concerned about—"

Terry hung up the phone and strode to the door.

And could a person's life offer any sight more reassuringly earthbound, if you were feeling faintly unnerved by nebulous threats and misgivings, than that of Bertha Kulick typing a letter? She had a pencil tucked behind her ear, Bertha did, like some sort of door-to-door salesman. Her pencils were a sight to behold. She chewed on them, often nipping the eraser right off (did she swallow it? or did she spit it out?), and left amid the flaking golden paint the indentations of her little crooked teeth.

"Bertha," Terry said, "I *don't* know anyone named Stanley Duggar, who by the way is some sort of absolute lunatic, some sort of fruitcake or nut-case, and you don't need to let him through next time."

"You remember that's what I told you. You don't know him."

"Right," Terry said, nodded, retreated once more into his office, shut the door. It occurred to him that Duggar was probably a religious fanatic—and hence almost certainly harmless. Wasn't that the direction in which the conversation had been flowing when Terry, so precipitously flustered, had hung up? ("You seem to think we're after *material* things . . .") Still, even if you took that business about having *an eye on you* as a bluff, or some sort of religious metaphor (didn't God always have His eye on you?), there remained the vexing question of where Duggar had got hold of his name . . . And that voice: there really had been something unsettling—creepy—about that voice. What was it Duggar was about to say? Maybe hanging up had been a mistake: maybe he should have heard the man out . . .

The story would surely amuse Adam, though, and Terry briefly considered going upstairs with it. Instead, he took a seat at his desk, telephoned Bertha in order to collect the lunchtime messages, concluded that none needed to be acted upon right away, and pulled out some of the documents pertaining to the Marquette licensing. These included a letter from Allison Collier, whose signature he examined closely. Her name inhabited that middle ground between printed and cursive writing, the pair of l's in each name standing apart, like the mathematical symbol for parallel lines . . .

He turned to another project, one that could only sound ab-

surd to anybody who wasn't a lawyer: the composing of an op-
position to a motion to compel the production of documents.
His clients, a Dallas-based group, were being challenged by another Dallas group who seemed to sense irregularities. It was a
question of, among other things, the authenticity of some sig-
natures. In addition, there were copies of complaints about
Terry's clients addressed to the FCC. These were ostensibly
grass-roots letters, composed by "concerned citizens"—voices
of the public at large—and like most such letters to the FCC,
they were almost certainly a put-up job, a hoax orchestrated
by the enemy. But such things were almost impossible to prove.

Somewhat surprisingly, the work went well. It seemed that
the last of the gin had drained from his mind, leaving his thinking almost unnaturally sharp. What headache persisted was, in
its clenching steadiness, weirdly stabilizing; he felt none of his
usual restless urge to pace, to joke with Bertha, to get a drink of
water. Paragraph succeeded paragraph. Even after all these
years, he was usually a slow writer. But today he was finding
that everything was right there, in his head—he needed merely
to transfer it to his computer screen.

At about five he dialed the one number that—twenty years
from now, a hundred years from now—he would still be able to
dial in his sleep.

"Hello?"

"Mob . . ."

"I thought you were going away . . ."

"I am, I am." Terry laughed merrily. "And how do you know
I'm not calling from away?"

"Aren't you at the office? You sound like you're at the office."

"What good ears you have. Isn't that what the wolf said to
Little Red Riding Hood? Or is it what Red Riding Hood said
to the Wolf?"

"Terry, what in heaven's name are you talking about?"

"So what's new? How's every little thing?"

A pause. "Well it's pretty much what you'd expect. It's just
what you'd expect here. Nothing too bustling or exciting. This
isn't Washington, DC, you know."

She informed him of this regularly—as though he stood at

fair risk of forgetting that Gawana, Iowa, was not in fact the nation's capital.

But she sounded fine. Terry was listening hard for something which, a year or two ago, he could never have believed he would be listening for in Mob's speech: the slippages and stiffly righted precisions that come with overindulgence in alcohol. For it appeared, unbelievably enough, that in recent months Mob (*Mob*—in whom resided all that was controlled and measured and autonomous in the world) had, on occasion, taken to drink. It was back in February that Terry had first detected odd hesitancies in her voice. Illness? Fatigue? Or a shift in her medicine, perhaps? (She'd been treated for years for high blood pressure.) And yet, the next time he called, finding her out of the house, he hadn't been able to extract a thing from Dad, who either hadn't understood him or hadn't yet perceived anything out of the ordinary. It had been Kaye, some weeks later, who'd turned all of his own explanations on their head: "Maybe she'd had a few."

"Had a few?"

"A few *drinks,* Terry. My God, you know there are people in this world who, instead of going back to the office after dinner, like to unwind a little at the end of the day."

Oh there were times when he wanted to throttle Kaye! (Vividly he could picture her face becoming even more bug-eyed than usual when, for one delirious moment, his thumbs pressed into her neck, and he shook her—shook her up and down. Long years ago, when they were both growing up, *she'd* always been able to throttle and punch and pound and bully *him*; by the time he'd advanced far enough into adolescence to know that he could "take" her, the age of physical tussling between them was long past. He'd never had a chance to get his own back . . .) He could put up with feckless Kaye (who whenever she made any major purchase usually managed to lose both receipt and warranty, and would then call him up seeking legal redress) or luckless Kaye (who for a time couldn't seem to hold a job) or whiny Kaye (who found Baltimore's summer heat so oppressive), but he simply could not, *could* not bear Gay Divorcee Kaye—the liberal, liberated, slangy, foul-mouthed middle-aged woman who was always urging him to loosen up, lighten up, put his feet up.

"On the other hand," Terry pointed out, "Washington isn't Gawana."

"I'm looking forward to your report."

"My report?"

"On the weekend."

"On Glenn?"

"Kaye says he works in real estate."

"That's right."

"What they say is absolutely true, you know. You can hardly go wrong owning land. You remember I tried to get your father to buy that lot next to the Westcotts? I should have pushed him. Do you know what it recently went for?"

"Actually, it can be kind of a headache. Owning land. Taxes and things—there's all sorts of hidden costs."

"You talk about land, now would you believe they're honestly talking about taking a wedge right out of Fielding Park? I've got an appointment with the Mayor tomorrow—incidentally, fifteen minutes was all he was prepared to give me. But that should be time enough to make clear to him they're taking a wedge out of Fielding Park *over my dead body*. I speak for the community, you know."

Terry laughed. "You sure do. You give him hell, Mob. Remember, he's a public servant."

"It's easy to laugh, Terry, but you know *that's exactly what he is*. There's no sitting back in *this* world, Terry. That will have to wait for the next . . ."

"Dad around?"

"Oh he's just where you'd suppose he would be. Off to the hardware."

"What's the latest project?"

"I'm sure *I* wouldn't have the slightest clue. I just hope it leaves the air breathable. We had sawdust everywhere you looked a while back. And what goes in the air, goes into your lungs. *That* ought to be clear enough for everybody to understand."

"I better go, Mob."

"Kaye says he's quite intelligent, incidentally. This beau of hers."

"Beau? You make it sound as if they're school-kids. He's got to be in his mid-fifties. Late fifties? And we'll see about the being intelligent. You know Kaye. She does say all sorts of things."

Terry had stepped onto tremulous ground. Provided that he show tact and moderation, he was permitted in Mob's presence to criticize his sister; in fact there were times when Mob seemed positively to relish having Kaye serve as a shared burden between them. But push this approach ever so slightly too far— as, apparently, Terry just now had done—and a rebuke was merited. "Now don't you go doomsaying, Terry," Mob said. "Not when you have scarcely met the man."

"Doomsaying? Who's doomsaying? I'm looking forward to the weekend. Listen, I got to go, Mob. Love to Dad."

"Remember what I said . . ." Mob entreated, although it wasn't at all apparent to which remark of hers this plea referred—or whether to the whole of her conversation, or even (as the outflung desperation in her tone suggested) to the whole sweeping panorama of her life.

"Bye-bye."

He set the phone down only long enough to, in effect, cancel this conversation and bring himself a new dial tone. He punched Diana's number and got a recording, a new recording: "Hi. This is Shawn. Diana isn't in at the moment. Now if you want to leave a message for her—"

Another recorded voice—Diana's voice—broke in. "Hi. This is Diana. Shawn isn't in at the moment. Now if you want to leave a message for her—"

Speaking in unison, and riding a wave of not quite suppressed hilarity, the two girls continued in a sort of chanted singsong: "then please, oh *please* leave a message right after the beep."

It was cute, deeply appealing really—these two giggly young feminine voices coming at you in a sort of stereophonic effect. He could imagine that for a young guy, somebody their own age, it might actually be intimidating to have these two good-looking girls (Terry had twice met Shawn—Diana's best friend and future maid of honor—and if she wasn't quite so pretty as Diana, she was still a very pretty girl) urging you to say something that would later be played back by one or both of them. He wished he himself had something witty-sounding to say and for one pressured instant, absurdly enough, he considered hanging up the phone. "Diana, it's Terry," he began. "Returning your call. I'm off in moments to—to where else? To Virginia's Dismal Swamp for the weekend. I'll call you Monday, or you call me. Hope everything can keep till then. Be good. Bye."

He set the phone in its cradle and was immediately jarred by a feeling of having somebody else he needed to call. All day long this same squeezing sensation of neglecting something—of leaving something crucial behind.

A knock at the door presented a welcome distraction. He knew this diminishing knock: a little tap followed by a littler tap.

"Bertha," he said. "Come in."

She hung in the doorway a moment, peering at him. Stray light wobbled on the lenses of her glasses. "Your ticket's on your desk there. I am leaving now."

Night after night, Bertha was capable of turning a simple departure from the office into an august ceremony. She might almost be resigning, after long years of service, from a topflight governmental post. With balancing solemnity he said, "All right, Bertha. You have a class tonight?"

It was one more of Bertha's peculiarities that she seemed, from a professional standpoint, resolutely unambitious (Terry a number of times had suggested, gently, the possibility of some sort of graduate school—and always met a stiff if unspecified resistance). And yet she was devoted to non-credit adult education classes. She was always plunging into something new—astronomy, the American political process, even woodworking.

"A class? It's Friday night."

"Right. Of course. Well you have a good weekend."

There had been a period (it had not lasted long) when Terry used to tease Bertha about her weekends. He'd implied that she spent her time wildly, dissolutely—in bars and discotheques, in pool halls and bowling alleys, crack joints, opium dens. But the jokes had been met blankly—as though Bertha simply could not grasp what was so farfetched about such envisionings—and her blankness, in combination with a gathering suspicion that there was something ever so slightly cruel about this brand of humor (Bertha lived—inevitably, it would seem—with a pair of widowed aunts, and the thought of her weekends truly wasn't, at bottom, all that amusing), had led to its abandonment. He had chosen in substitution a quiet, avuncular manner. "You get yourself some rest, Bertha," he told her now.

But Bertha replied with something outside the routine. "Terry," she said, "now I want you to be careful."

"Careful?" he said.

"Maybe you're having a rough day," she said.

"Me?" he said.

She nodded; he nodded; she nodded; he nodded a little more deeply, with hoped-for finality; she nodded; he nodded once more; she peered at him and then turned away.

Bertha's departure seemed a signal for his own. After locking his door from the inside, he changed out of his suit and into a pale blue corduroy shirt and a pair of khaki chinos. He emptied his papers and some dirty clothes from his suitcase, leaving within it only his bag of toiletries and a book, a biography of General Patton. (He enjoyed all sorts of American history, but the Second World War—Dad's war—was a special interest.) From the shelf of the closet he took down, all of it neatly folded from the cleaners, a sweater, a white dress shirt, a plaid sports shirt, a pair of jeans, two pairs of white cotton socks. He added a brown leather belt and a pair of running shoes. There was room in the bag for more, but did he need anything more?

He needed his ticket, of course. He gave his desk a final glance-over, his gaze momentarily alighting on Diana's face—her high school graduation portrait. She had changed in three-plus years, and not just in the obvious ways, but even in things like the shape of her mouth and eyebrows. She pretended these days to despise this picture and the last time she visited the office she'd pleaded with him to get rid of it. She would supply him with another, a more recent photo. And he'd pretended to cherish it even more than he did: nothing, *nothing on earth,* could induce him to part with it.

He turned off the light, shut his door, and carried his suitcase upstairs, in search of Adam—whose open door revealed an empty desk. Terry left his suitcase in the doorway—at once lightening his load and creating a signal—and went off in search of his friend, down the corridor, into the johns (upstairs and down), into the library. Nowhere. Terry checked his watch and abruptly realized he was running late . . . A talk with Adam would have to wait . . . In fact, the taxi would need to make good time if he was going to catch his flight, and there was a storm coming, if it hadn't already broken.

Am I trying to miss this plane? he had to ask himself as he stood on the corner of 19th and H, under a black sky, hoping to flag a cab. The question pleased him in its way, for it imparted a sense of unstinting mental rigor, of self-penetration. He usually allowed himself plenty of time for flights. *At some level of my mind I must be trying to miss this flight.*

And yet, whatever was operating on him subconsciously, it certainly felt like a pure relief to see a cab pull over, to slide into its black interior, and to recognize, within moments, that he had found a sharply aggressive driver. Everything moved much more quickly than could have been expected. The storm held off, the cab roared forward. It was as though forces everywhere were contriving to get him aboard the plane. When he climbed out of the cab, a safe twenty minutes before flight time, handed the driver a twenty-dollar bill and waited for change, he laughed with delight when a loud smacking crack of thunder broke overhead. "Looks like a real storm," he announced. He spoke slowly, lest the driver, who was evidently Vietnamese (his surname, according to his taxi ID, was Nguyen), flounder with his English.

But Mr. Nguyen's reply was fluent enough—fluent and it would seem consummately melancholy, as his slanted eyes took on a further, squinting slant: "All my life, I have never liked thunder."

"I know what you mean, bye, thanks," Terry called, as the sky rumbled a second time.

And a third: Terry heard another crackle and boom as he stepped through the makeshift, adjustable corridor that linked the terminal to the body of the plane. He found his seat. The round windows were raindrop speckled. His race through the airport had been so hurried that he now couldn't be sure, quite, that he'd glimpsed in one of its corridors what his memory told him he'd glimpsed: an extraordinarily fat man—a human colossus—who was eating a dripping brown ice-cream cone and wearing a black T-shirt with white letters on the back that read: TOO BIG TO FUCK WITH. Out there in the world at large, was there truly somebody who'd risen this morning and said to himself, "Looks like a fine day to wear my TOO BIG TO FUCK WITH T-shirt . . ."?

Surprisingly, the flight went off on time. Little zigzags of water—miniature models of zigzagging lightning—slid across the windows but it wasn't apparent, given the competing roar of the plane, whether these represented cloudburst or mere drizzle. In any event, the rain soon lay underneath them, below this little seated gathering of strangers who, from a historical standpoint, had one thing in common, anyway: an urge to travel, on a Friday afternoon in October, 1989, from Washington D.C. to Norfolk, Virginia. They had beaten the storm.

Terry opened up his biography of Patton and, adjusting his mind to the vibrations of the plane, read steadily for a while. Patton's nickname had been Old Blood-and-Guts. By all accounts he was a brave man, but then you could afford to be courageous, Terry supposed, if like the General you were a lifelong believer in reincarnation and in the notion that the battle never ended—that you had been "a Greek hoplite, a Roman Legionnaire, a cavalryman with Belisarius, a highlander with the House of Stuart, a trooper with Napoleon and Murat."

Another flight, another ascent into the heavens, and a bumpy touching down . . .

"I tell you, Mistuh Seawood," cried the woman behind the rental car desk, who was wearing a name tag that read SHARI ANNA, "ah was so con-cehned about your cah." You would think, from the loam-rich layerings of her accent, that Terry'd flown a couple of thousand miles south, rather than a couple of hundred. This was one of the things that always amazed him about entering Virginia from Washington—how quickly you felt you'd stumbled into a variant realm, how tenaciously these

people had held on to what was, if you took the historical perspective, a pretty embarrassing heritage. "On account of the
weather. But your cah is here safe and sound."

"The weather?"

"You know we've had the most *gigantic* storm. Rain *pounding*
on the roof."

"I seem to have missed it all."

Terry drove with the window lowered, through a puddled
parking lot and along a puddled road. The sun was down but a
little of its light still seemed to linger. Leaves and branches had
been torn from the trees and the air had that smell of release, of
pressure come and gone, which follows a heavy storm.

The turn-off onto Route 11 came up as expected. One thing
you had to say for Glenn: the guy sure knew how to give directions. These had been mailed to Terry's office. They were typed
out, on crisp stationery, and they came complete with estimated
mileage for each leg of the trip. Of course, if a real estate man
couldn't be depended on to tell somebody how to get somewhere, what possible good was he? Still, given Kaye's hopelessness in such matters, Glenn provided a useful service.

Terry thought of the man in the obscene black T-shirt, whose
letters had been stretched out of shape by the monumental bulk
of the body within, and he felt inside himself a historical pronouncement stirring. He revised it over and over in his head
until it seemed invested not merely with insight but with grace
as well: *I belong to that last generation of Americans which contains a
sizable subset of people who have never heard either of their parents
utter the word "fuck."* He was one of that subset. So far as he
knew, the term had never once issued from the lips of either
Mob or Dad.

Yoga? Yoga lessons? It was a thought . . . In the two months,
in the eight forty-five minute sessions he'd had with her, Angelina had inspired all sorts of improbable and beguiling notions,
his imagination in no way curbed by the utter lack of curiosity
she'd shown about every facet of his life except the condition of
his neck and shoulders. It might be fun, he'd often conjectured,
to go out with her. It might be fun to come home at night to
somebody who would rub your neck while the two of you

watched a video. The aspect of this fantasy that most appealed to him (and which could not be confessed even to Adam, since it sounded so crass and unimaginative) involved money. She seemed a little strapped for cash and he saw himself elevating Angelina-with-the-ripped-canvas-tennis-shoes onto another socioeconomic plane. The fact was, he needed something or somebody to spend his money on, if only to vindicate the hours and hours he devoted to its accumulation. Peculiar though it might sound, he didn't much enjoy lavishing it on himself. And since it disturbed him to spend money on fixing up the house (was Terry Seward, son of Iowa's greatest etc. amateur handyman, actually going to hire perfect strangers to put up wallpaper or lay linoleum?), he wasn't left with many outlets. His interest in clothes did not extend very far beyond a desire not to look outlandish or goofy. He traveled often enough on the job that the idea of traveling for pleasure—popping over to Paris for an extended weekend, say—seemed almost grotesque. And he ate out so often at the firm's expense that when it came time to open his own wallet for a meal what he craved, often as not, were things like hot dogs and sauerkraut at home. (The tidiness of hot dogs and sauerkraut—everything cooked together in the same pan—was keenly satisfying.) Whether he was to be praised for his uncluttered existence, or damned for his blindness toward life's glittering perquisites, he felt no impulse to buy a motorboat, a mezzotint, an elaborate DAT stereo system like Adam's, an antique desk, a summer cottage . . . Various people had told him, after Betsy died, that he needed to move—buy a smaller house, or a newer house, find something closer in or farther out. *Buy something just to buy something* seemed to be the gist of their message, and in the end he'd responded obliquely to their urgings. One day he went out, a couple of months later, and put down close to thirty thousand dollars for an Audi 100. And, surprisingly, he'd never suffered a serious qualm over that. He *loved* his bright red Audi. But since then, as if sated—as if having made his soul's one essential expenditure—he'd hardly wanted to buy a single thing. And when the impulse to purchase something did hit him, it was apt to be hazy and impractical, as when, watching a television commercial recently, he'd found himself yearning to buy jewelry. But it had touched him!—to watch a pretty brunette's face light with such brightness, more bright even than the glittering string of pearls she'd lifted adoringly from its little box . . .

Angelina's boyfriend was some sort of computer whiz, and when Terry, lying on his stomach, had grunted surprise on learning this, she'd become a little indignant. Wasn't there something a little incongruous (he had hesitantly, stumblingly inquired) in this matching up of a woman who talked about psychic energy distributions with a man who spent his days punching commands into a keyboard? No, there wasn't, she'd explained to him. *We're both channelers,* she said, and added, with a kind of smugness that Terry thought sure he could feel not just in her voice but in her fingertips, *Howard's a man of the spirit . . .* The words had hung troublingly over Terry's head. To describe someone as a *man of the spirit*—did the phrase really mean anything? And whether or not it did, was there any chance in the world that Angelina would describe himself, too, as *a man of the spirit?*

One of the many things he most missed about Betsy's being gone (and would never have expected so deeply to miss) was her ongoing reports about a community he'd never met: the little world of her classroom. Boys and girls who were only names to him—and yet who were spoken of so often that they'd come to seem as real as anyone. Even now, all these months later, sometimes in the middle of the night he'd wake to the sound of one of their names in his head: Bucky Walsh, Johnny Johnson, Alwyn Powell, and the "three Annies"—Annie Close, Annie Hilbert, Annie Parsons. The odd thing was to realize that these were lives as real now as they'd ever been. Their stories went forward. He'd simply lost the link to them—that was all. Ricky Nevin—what in the world had happened to Ricky Nevin, who, banished to the hall for incorrigible mischief, had somehow got his hands on a janitor's hammer and nails and had actually *begun pounding nails into the school floor.* It was almost as though nothing so shocking had ever happened to Betsy. For some reason she'd been unable—simply unable—to believe it: the boy was so depraved in his instincts, so unruly, so *bad* that he'd pounded nails *right into the school floor!*

When Terry turned off the highway onto Route 33, which was a two-lane blacktop, his destination came to him in a premonitory flash. Glenn had described the place, which was owned by a client of his, as "no great shakes," and in Terry's mind now suddenly rose a dilapidated wooden structure half-hidden in foliage. A slanted porch. Entangling, burying vines growing round the remaining pales of a white wooden fence. "Soon now," Terry said aloud and unexpectedly a phrase of that man Duggar, Stanley Duggar, returned to him: "downside risk." Hadn't Duggar spoken of *downside risk?* Not the words you'd expect to hear spouted by a religious fanatic . . .

Terry pulled off the blacktop and got out at a little roadside store, a gas station where you could buy cigarettes, bread, soda pop, snacks and candy. You could also rent videotapes, and Terry recalled a woman he'd met a few days ago, only it wasn't a few days ago it truly was this morning, Kelly. He felt a thud in the middle of his skull; his headache hadn't completely left him. He drew out one of the dozens and dozens of Coca-Cola cans from the freezer and carried it toward the homely young boy behind the counter, whose mouth was encircled by painful-looking acne.

"Do you sell hot sandwiches? I see you've got a microwave."

"Doritos."

"Beg pardon?"

"We do sell Doritos." The boy pointed to a sort of goldfish bowl, in which a gummy golden substance was stored. ELDORADO'S REAL MEXICAN CHEESE SAUCE was emblazoned on the front in red letters. The machine reminded Terry of a soft-ice-cream dispenser; a skillful operator might even make of the stuff a tolerable-looking cone, complete with decorative curlicue tip.

"I think I'll pass, thanks. I guess you had quite a storm. I just flew in," Terry explained. He felt a need to talk.

The boy muttered something that, given his accent, might have been *hail* and might have been *hell.* There were two open bags of potato chips by the cash register—Down and Dirty Cajun Flavor and Extra Sour Cream 'n' Onion.

"We're not so far from the Dismal Swamp, are we?"

"I dunno, there's swamp out back."

"Out back?"

"Back of the store."

"Is it dismal?"

Terry hoped to get from the kid some sort of rise—a smile, a joke, a glint of amusement in the eyes. There was an odd flatness, of gaze and voice both, about this boy.

"I don't know." It seemed this was all the reply Terry would be treated to, but as he was carrying his can of Coke toward the exit the boy added, "I buried my cat back there. A couple of weeks back. She threw up a mouse just before she died."

"Is that right?"

Funny—he remembered his rental car as blue, a blue T-Bird, but the one car in the lot, which was parked where he'd parked, was red, a red T-Bird. He got in tentatively, as though expecting the key not to fit the ignition; but the engine started with a spirited roar. He rented so many cars it was becoming hard to keep track. And how many drivers, he wondered, had this car had? Dozens? Hundreds? There were nearly sixteen thousand miles on the odometer. This was a new and curious phenomenon, if you took the historical perspective: whole fleets of transportation drifting inexorably toward the junk heap without anyone's ever forming any personal attachment to them. These were cars from which any sort of lived-in personality was scrubbed away between each use.

He had another twenty minutes or half hour of driving, he figured. Although night had fallen a while ago, the darkness seemed to have suddenly deepened—as though the world had rushed toward blackness during his few minutes inside the store. The air was dense with watery smells, floating on an understratum of decay, and for all his interesting reflections on the impersonality of rental car fleets it felt good to roll up the window and surround himself with the cool dry inorganic odors of a still newish automobile.

The road was surprisingly deserted for a Friday night. What about all the kids heading off to movies, parties, bars? His headlights turned up what looked like a dead dog on the road's gravel shoulder and Terry was relieved to discover, slowing as he passed, that it was actually a raccoon—a creature nobody was going to cry over. As a kid Terry'd had a dog—the great dynas-

tic Pretzel, forefather to a number of Seward family pets—
who'd been killed in a hit-and-run. It was for Pretzel's grandson
Biscuit that Dad built the solar doghouse that had landed his
photograph in newspapers all over the country.

He turned off Route 9 onto Route 116, also a two-lane blacktop, but here the shoulder narrowed, as though the swamp were
closing in.

At the corner of 116 and Route 22 stood another gas station.
Terry gave some thought to stopping. It might not be a bad idea
to pick up a few food essentials. But anything he were to buy
might only duplicate what Kaye and Glenn had brought with
them. The soundest course was first to check in with them, then
to come back out here, if necessary. According to Glenn's directions, which had been impeccable so far, there were only seven
miles to go.

Terry turned onto Route 11. This one was packed dirt, with a
scattering of gravel that could be heard ticking like rain—only
more cuttingly than rain—against the underside of the car. He
hit a bump that hadn't shown itself in the bleached wedge of the
headlights and a voice within said, *Thank God it's not your car.*
For all the dread he'd professed to be feeling about this weekend, he was pushing the accelerator. He was eager for company.

Just as the directions had promised, five miles after turning
onto 11 another turn-off materialized. This one said Private
Property. Separate signs, nailed to a common tree, heralded Absen, Butscher, and Coldwell. The last was the confirmation he
wanted—he would be staying the weekend at the Coldwell
place.

He turned the car and immediately a dip in the road lofted the
headlights to illuminate another, homemade sign. PRIVATE—
KEEP OUT. This road was a pair of ruts that enclosed a center strip
of tall, drooping weeds. These, too, ticked against the underside
of the car, making a sound that was indeed very much like rain.

God, the night was black! Full darkness had come down some
time ago, and yet everything seemed to grow still darker, still
darker. A road, or driveway, angled off to the right, beneath
another sign that read Absen. No lights burned in that direction.
No, there were no lights anywhere in the lush-leaved darkness,

except the white lights the car threw forward, the red lights it trailed behind. In the white lights the fan of weeds seemed to fall as to a scythe, and where they sprang up again, behind, they blazed red for a moment in Terry's rearview mirror, waving like the arms of someone signaling for help.

Another driveway, on the left this time, went snaking off into blackness. This one, too, was marked: Butscher. He was nearly there.

The road ended abruptly, in a tight little loop. It was blackness on all sides.

He stopped the car without turning off the headlights and got out. Creatures—insects, amphibians—were calling, calling, calling. Through the watery, smell-packed darkness dozens, hundreds, thousands of messages were crisscrossing. The world over, the air thronged with signals—radio, television, telephone, satellite transmissions, frogs, cicadas, bats. And there it was, in a clearing before him: a house, a decent-sized boxy house, its rooftop wanly aglow in the moonlight. But surely this couldn't be it. It looked nothing like the elaborate structure he'd envisioned, the one with the vines and the broken fence pales and the deep dark porch.

Where were the lights, where was Glenn's car, where was Kaye? This couldn't be it—and yet what else could it be? The evidence was indisputable, it left as little maneuvering room as a mathematical proof . . . Behind him was the Absen place, the Butscher place, and didn't Glenn's directions say that the Coldwell house was to be found where the road gave out? What else could this chill and forbidding moonlit structure be?

He left the headlights on, as some illumination for himself, and walked across a freshly mowed lawn toward the front door. Coarse, spiky, the grass gave beneath his weight with some resistance. Then it shifted, without warning, and his left foot plunged into a sinkhole; cold water lunged over the top of his shoe. "*God damn it,*" he cried with a fierceness that wasn't merited. But it had unnerved him, for just a second; the quick cold clasping of the water had scared him.

Proceeding more slowly, he made his way to the cabin. There was a screen door, which screeched when he gingerly tugged it open, and beyond that a wooden door whose varnish, even in this scrappy light, revealed blisters. Though he knew there could be no one inside, he went ahead and knocked—absurd though it was—waited a moment, knocked again, and, more absurd yet, called out, "Anybody there?"

Anybody there?

Anybody there? His voice echoes and bounces, it sounds strange, his knocking on the door echoes and bounces in conjunction with it, and he senses, all round him, the presence of those for whom he is an unwanted irruption, a big-bodied interloper. He has broken in upon them, the creatures, the lives in the leaves with their alien ear- and eye-mechanisms. They've had to take him in. He comes to them with lights, with grave heavy big-footed steps, with demands, he comes to bang on a wooden door in the moonlight. Terry shivers. It's colder here than in Washington.

Knowing that he might be viewed (by any outside observer in the woods, stationed out there with a pair of binoculars) as a criminal, a common thief, he draws out from his back pants pocket and holds up to the moonlight, for all to see, the legitimating key Glenn had sent him through the mail. At the time this had seemed an unnecessary precaution, since Glenn and Kaye were supposed to arrive well before him. And Terry is arriving now even later than scheduled. So where are they?

It seems he expects the key not to work, or at least for the lock to put up a struggle. The ease, even eagerness, with which the lock lets itself be tripped and the door springs open is all a little unnerving. Almost as though the door is being gently eased by someone on the other side.

He stands there—does not enter, only leans forward, to catch something of the air seeping out of the place. Darkness inside— what looks from here like absolute darkness. He has been riding for hours in a car that holds not a trace of any of its former inhabitants, not a single stray ash or odor, but here's an enclosure in which past lives come rushing up to brush against you the moment you contemplate its threshold. He smells something like an old sofa, or an old rug—a room out of childhood, a friend's house, maybe, the grandparents of a friend. For these

are the imposing territorial smells that old people used to give
off and used to live within. Informing you, from their very
doorway, of your distance from them . . . He takes a step inside
and halts.

As his hand, dartingly, flutteringly, pats the wall beside him
in search of a light switch, he is hit by a flurry of panicky questions—what if this *is* the wrong house? What if he finds here the
leavings of some grisly crime? And what's he going to do if the
electricity's off? For he has no matches or flashlight, doesn't
know *where* the fuse box might be . . . And just as it occurs to
him, reassuringly, that he can always drive back to that little
store and buy a flashlight (one of those big boxy four-battery
numbers that throw a beam like an automobile headlight's), his
fingers close on what must be a switch. He pulls upward. There.

This, too, is a sensation as old as childhood: the relief (tinged
perhaps with a dollop of disappointment) on discovering that,
with the flick of a switch, a blackness packed with rapid mobile
shapings instantly gives way to an utterly unremarkable tableau.
Here is a round table, chairs, a sagging couch, a table piled with
magazines, an old refrigerator, a stove, and a window in which,
obscurely, this ordinary, slightly run-down room is duplicated.

He steps inside. The ceiling is low and the room presses upon
him, not exactly uncomfortably. It is a small-scale house; he is a
large-scale presence inside it. "Hullo," he ventures, and thinks
he hears a sort of transformed echo: a little scurry, a four-legged
scramble toward the cover of greater darkness. A mouse—
nothing larger than a mouse.

There's a fireplace and on the mantel a pair of twin skulls.
These are smaller than a man's fist and yet with something com-
mandingly feral to them all the same. They're tough—tough
little predators with teeth made for ripping flesh. Foxes, maybe?
Weasels?

His clumping shoes are wet and muddy. He takes them off
and, after a moment's hesitation, peels off—one wet, one dry—
his socks as well. He proceeds barefoot into the house.

Aware of himself in the picture window as a loose draping
assemblage of lights, deliberately ignoring himself, he drifts
around the room. The top magazine on the pile cries out HOME-

TOWN SLAUGHTER in big red letters. It's an issue of *Time,* but what is it, exactly—what's the particular atrocity it's referring to? Coffee, or some other dark liquid, has been spilled upon it, obscuring and crinkling the photograph, so that in the room's insufficient light very little can be discerned except some horizontal bands and a dim sense of commotion and mayhem. He leans over and reads FERNDALE H. S. GRADUATION and the incident comes back in all its nauseating reality. Those horizontal bands are bleachers and those other lines, transecting the horizontals, those are corpses in the bleachers, but how quickly even such horrific things pass from the mind—are supplanted by other, fresher atrocities. The magazine is only a year old.

The walls are of varnished wood, the ceiling is of wood, the fireplace is of stone. The floor is covered with indoor-outdoor carpeting, except around the stove and sink, where linoleum has been laid. He tries the hot water tap and there's a splutter, a gasp, a distant unhappy whistling sound, and then water begins to flow. Lights on, water running. Despite the age of the magazine, the place does not feel long deserted—none of that dusty cobwebby feeling that accumulates with extended disuse. No, someone has been here recently.

He thinks about bringing his bag in from the car and recalls that he left the headlights on. But he doesn't feel ready to bring his stuff in yet. That needs to wait. First he has to feel he's grown a little used to the place. There are still rooms he hasn't entered—rooms that await him in unbroken darkness.

He crosses the living room, to a door that stands ajar, nudges it open, and his left hand (as if he has stood here before, and knows exactly where to look) reaches inside the frame and instantly locates the very low switch. The light comes on with a sturdy click. Although there's a bed in here, the room seems mainly devoted to storage—boxes, tools, fishing gear, a cane chair with a ruptured seat, an orange life jacket, a deck of cards warped away on either side from the blue rubber band that binds them in the middle.

The second bedroom, which is all but empty, contains a narrow bed with a bare mattress. Some blankets are folded at its foot. On the wall there's a picture of a buffalo planted on the flat bald crest of a hill, staring morosely off at an antiquated, smoke-puffing railroad, and another picture, perhaps a companion piece, of a lank-haired bare-chested Indian huddled at a solitary campfire. It is nightfall and the Indian is peering out at the rectilinear, illuminated skyline of a modern metropolis.

The third and final bedroom is larger. It has a double bed and, for all the room's tidiness, actually feels lived in. There's a bedside table and a reading lamp, a chest of drawers, a small print of Botticelli's *Birth of Venus,* and another print, Oriental, of a frog squatting on the end of a long leaf. It's a fat frog and a delicate-looking leaf, and the impression is that, any moment now, all must give way and the frog take a dunking. This room will be Kaye and Glenn's—but *where the hell are they?* Could they have gotten into some sort of trouble? Terry generally does not worry about such things. He's not a worrier the way, say, Mob's a worrier. But the simple truth is that the two of them ought to have arrived hours and hours ago—unless there's been a breakdown, maybe. Or a minor accident?

And what is he to do if they're not here in an hour? In two hours? Go to sleep? Out of the question until the two of them arrive . . . No, if they don't appear he will have to leave this place, go and call somebody—but who? Where in *hell* could they be?

He goes into the one room he hasn't yet entered and unzips his fly before the toilet bowl. In his shaky hand his penis feels little but tough—wiry, gristly. He clearly needs to pee and yet, as has happened on only a few occasions in his life, something inside him clenches itself tight as a shell—a closing up that he can't quite locate, and so has no control over. It's all a little unnerving and he wonders, dartingly, whether this might be some new twist, some new aspect of dysfunction? Penis in hand he waits, and waits, feels the urine burning in his belly—but evidently the clenched thing within him is prepared to out-wait him.

"I need a drink," he says aloud and, oddly, this phrase operates like a password: at once, with a warm and pleasant sting, he discharges a golden stream into the rusty old bowl.

At parties, at restaurants, at Adam's, at home, he has often declared to somebody, or even to himself, *I need a drink,* but rarely have the words carried any heartfelt impulsion. Booze of any sort always has been something he can take or leave. He drank when and what others were drinking, and in the old days, with Betsy, there'd been occasional parties during which she'd fretted, for the most part needlessly, that he would drink too much (while he'd fretted, just a little, that she would eat too much—those parties had been something of a strain). But he'd loved parties once—in an earlier era of his life, the bachelor era. At college, especially, he'd gone to so many parties.

Now, he does need a drink. In his bare feet he pads out into the main room and, still paying no heed to his reflection in the picture window, or to his sense of monitoring gazes fitted into the blackness out beyond it (it's another world out there, and beyond that another other world, one which includes Ricky Nevin, who once *hammered nails into the school floor*), he begins a ransacking of the cupboards over the stove. Salad oil, Bisquick, Campbell's pepper pot soup, Green Giant peas, Green Giant green beans, deviled ham, a tiny jar of Hellman's reduced calorie mayonnaise, coffee, tea bags, pineapple juice, French's mustard, Eternal Flame Barbecue Sauce, and—ho, ho, ho—Green Giant beets . . . But the closest thing to any sort of liquor is a bottle of cider vinegar.

One glass in the cupboard stands taller than the rest and Terry lifts it down and fills it nearly to brimming with tapwater. "Cheers," he announces and hoists it up, recalling once more, as the water sloshes down his throat, that he left the headlights on. He ought to put on his muddy shoes, go out and bring in his bag.

Instead, he settles into a seat at the kitchen table, turning the chair slightly to avoid looking at himself in the window. He feels as though he's being watched. A lunatic picture flashes in his mind: his watcher is the man in the T-shirt, the fat man, who is out there in the bushes, armed with binoculars and a sickle, still wearing his TOO BIG TO FUCK WITH T-shirt. The water has a rural taste. If you were handed a glass of it you would know, even if you'd been brought here blindfolded (as in some sort of fraternity hazing, or a kidnapping by terrorists), that you were a long ways out from a big city.

"A fraternity stunt," he says and laughs, for the phrase brings to mind another of Curly Kopp's little escapades. After the Mexican Jumping Bean Escort Service folded up shop (scores of the little worms inside the unsold beans eventually drilled their way free of their egglike shells and disappeared from out of the metal potato chip can lids, presumably making their way to the ancient dormitory rug, where perhaps to this day their descendants continue to find a home), Kopp had announced plans for a penny pitching tournament (an *international* penny pitching tournament), which, improbably enough, had drawn twenty-plus Princeton undergraduates, and which, more improbably still, he'd won.

Thoughts of Kevin Kopp inevitably bring on guilt and remorse—still there, and still potent, after two decades. At the end of freshman year Kopp had wanted to continue on as roommates, and Terry had found the whole business of refusing him immensely awkward. Having the class eccentric for a roommate had not been, in itself, such a bad thing. In fact in some ways it was a positive boon; it put you in demand, made people eager to talk to you. Everyone wanted to know: what was it *really* like to room with the Amazing Squirrel? But living with Kopp had been *hard*. Kopp made you nervous.

Looking back on it, that whole freshman year had been a nervous time. Terry liked sometimes, in unfolding a story, to play up the innocence of an Iowa boyhood, but in fact nothing in his upbringing had prepared him for someone like the Squirrel, who really was not to be believed. Kopp was an orphan, for one thing, though up until freshman year it had always seemed to Terry that this was a condition properly belonging to distant lands or to biographies set in earlier centuries. *An orphan?* Terry had never met an orphan of his own age before. But be that as may be, Kopp's parents had died when he was a boy, within a year of each other, and he'd been raised by an aunt and uncle. In addition, Kopp refused to go to parties, never went on dates, rarely drank, and wouldn't smoke pot. He often stayed up all night, sleeping through the next day's classes, and would still be in his bathrobe when dinner rolled around. In best Squirrel fashion, he was forever bringing back from the dining hall peanut butter sandwiches wrapped up in napkins, which he would eat through the night; he never spent a dime if he could avoid doing so. At times it seemed the only thing that could get him out of the room was a shrink appointment. He was always heading off to be shrunk, which in itself made Terry nervous, and to make matters worse Kopp wouldn't disclose what really went on there, even while belittling Terry's naïveté. And Kopp was constantly unearthing in everyone he knew a malignant motive—a covert aggression, an oblique play for self-aggrandizement. Worse still, he was always hinting at some dark secret inside himself—was always nudging you with it and then withdrawing behind that odd, cackled laugh of his.

"A toast to Squirrely Kopp," Terry announces, holding up his water glass, which has only a few drops left within it. "Wherever he is."

Actually, Terry has a fairly good idea where Kopp is. He's in Baltimore. A couple years ago, the two of them ran into each other—almost literally—on a street corner in Washington. Terry had been hurrying toward an FCC hearing. And Kopp's disbelieving or disapproving way of gaping at Terry's pinstripe suit (Kopp had been wearing a baggy pair of Bermuda shorts and a sweatshirt with a panda on it) had been a further incentive to cut matters short. Conversation lasted only long enough to establish that Terry was now in D.C. and Kopp in Baltimore, that each was listed in the phone directory, and that they would get together soon. "I'll call you," Terry cried over his shoulder but—one more brick for the wall of guilt inside him—he never had.

Not that in the course of an average month he thought many times about Kopp (tonight was unusual), but when he did there was always the suspicion that, in refusing to room with him, he had not merely hurt Kopp's feelings but also cut himself off from a disquieting and yet useful provider of insights. Behind that decision there'd lurked a kind of cowardice perhaps.

"I need a drink," Terry reasserts and rises from the table. A little nonsense phrase pops into mind, "Here boozie, boozie, boozie," which he calls out in much the same tone you'd use to lure a cat into the house before retiring for the night: *Here pussy, pussy, pussy.* He peers again into the cupboards, whose doors he has left open, and there it is, a little miracle of substantiation: right behind the bottle of salad oil stands (how *could* he have missed it before?), stands a pint bottle of Seagram's VO. It's nearly half full.

"My prayers have been answered," Terry concludes and with a whoop of laughter empties the contents of the bottle—five or six ounces, probably—into his water glass. He takes a good-sized but not altogether greedy sip. Where *is* Kaye? The headlights are still burning and he will have to step into those squishy wet shoes and go out, in just a moment, to turn them off and bring in his bag. But he doesn't want to go out there yet. For twenty minutes now, or an hour, or however long he's been here, he has felt pushing in upon him Virginia's dark forests (the same forests the first permanent European settlers to this country met, nearly four hundred years ago), and he has just this moment discovered the one force—it is swaying languidly in the glass within his hands—that will even the pressure. He takes another hefty swallow.

Instead of heading to the car he returns to the bathroom and this time there is no nonsense. The urine surges forth from the moment he lowers his underpants. "Thataboy," he says and takes another swallow. They'd called this *equalizing* at Princeton—drinking one drink while you pissed away a previous one. And all sorts of jokes about keeping up your osmotic levels. Such sophomoric jokes.

Later in college, after the two roommates had gone their separate ways, Kopp had organized a raft race on the Delaware River. There were to be all sorts of prizes for categories like Biggest Eyesore and Least Likely to Float, as well as a grand prize for whatever improbable craft first crossed the finish line. Kopp, it turned out, had somehow got hold of a mile or so of very strong rope—spelunker's rope—as well as some rock-climber's pitons, and with the help of a few co-conspirators he'd hooked up an underwater network. He and his raft were to be towed by a cluster of friends located in a clump of bushes hundreds of yards from the starting line. The pitons, secured underwater, would keep the rope from rising out of the water into visibility.

The result was the funniest sight Terry in his entire life had ever seen.

At the starter's pistol, Kevin Kopp, seated atop a plain inner tube, took one stately, leisurely stroke with, not a paddle, no, but an old metal tennis racket—and pulled away from the pack! He smiled benignly, waved at the cheering but uncomprehending crowd, and then, fixing on his face a look of dignified resolution, took another stroke—and pulled away at an astounding rate. . . .

Would Princeton offer its undergraduates such entertainments today? Terry has to doubt it—for hadn't things changed, life changed, in some fundamentally un-fun way? Diana, say, at Dartmouth, is she building memories as rich as the best of these? He can't help thinking that she isn't, that times have changed, that he was extraordinarily fortunate to have gone to college just when he did—in that time of giddy released energies when the Vietnam War was closing down and Tricky Dick Nixon, showing himself to be far less scary and pernicious than everyone had supposed, had obligingly shot himself in the foot. The heyday of the hippie had receded by then and no one Terry knew at Princeton had talked much about living without money—but neither, as students, had they aspired to be investment bankers.

"Thataboy," Terry repeats and heads back into the living room and stands by the sink. Where is Kaye? What the hell has happened?

Seawood is what the woman at the car rental desk had called him. That was twice today he'd been called Sea-something and neither time had he offered a correction. Given that Seaward was what the family name had evidently been, in its original, its historical form, really it was unfortunate that the old spelling hadn't been retained. In a way, Seward was a corruption. It was a pity, in any event, that Terry, for whom the issue roused such strong associations, should happen to find himself born into one of the branches of the family that had long ago adopted the shorter form. What a small difference it was—but what a huge difference it was! In dropping the *a*, you were only a step away from the *sewer*. Reinstate it, creating *Seaward,* and you had vista and grandeur: you had a thing of poetry.

Or so it had seemed once—in college, that era in a young

man's life when you longed with such raw-nerved longing for that trifling but miraculous modification of circumstances (the shifting of your surname by a single letter, or the gift of even one more inch to your height, or the overnight vanishing of that cowlick which forced you to part your hair, nerd-style, in the middle) whereby all those things that you yearned for (women, mostly—and yearned for them in the faintly disbelieving way that only a freshman in college who was also a virgin could), and that had always been so tantalizingly withheld, now might companionably come your way.

Terry turns toward the sink to pour more water into his whiskey. Enough of the bottle remains to make this little dilution seem a task worth bothering about.

(And later on, in the next few months—indeed, in the radically new life that awaits him—when he tries to sort out what precisely it was that happened during these next few compressed moments, this will come to appear a condition of unshakable significance: *I was nowhere near drunk. You see, there was still enough whiskey in the glass for it to seem worthwhile to dilute it rather than to swallow it outright.*)

Terry feels himself on the verge of meaningful action. He plans, in just a moment, the last of his drink downed, to put on his shoes and go out to the car, turn off the lights, carry in his bag, and begin to make some claim upon this place. He will unpack some of his things, as a sign that he is here to stay . . .

He turns to the sink, flips on the cold water tap with his right hand, and is bringing his whiskey glass to it with his left hand, when behind him—where no one is located, where no one can possibly be standing—a voice outside himself, speaking to his back, speaks. The voice chants, softly but unmistakably, the voice says, *Terry, Terry, no one's fault,* and he knows, in this single instant, the only one from whom these words, this voice could possibly issue. He *knows*—yes, *already he knows*—and turns toward her, just as she would have him do. The voice passes as if through a miniature door, and in his turning toward it a compact is established with her, and his body swings right through that door. It is as simple as that, really. (And yet, how cold he has become!)

There is no one else, there has never been anybody else, who'd stroked his name quite like that, *Ter-ry,* and he swings round, the glass in his hand, to face up to a miracle—and the air is so dense with light it must of course thicken, he is moving through something thicker and brighter than water, his face is sliding through a kind of grease that has congealed and that cracks intricately with his turning. It could only be *Betsy* (who would have thought otherwise?), and for all the dim light she stands right there at the door, Betsy herself, on the threshold of the dark, and from underneath itself her very skin communicates a glow.

Betsy stands at the door and she is dressed more simply than anyone would have imagined, in a T-shirt, one of those she would borrow from him to sleep in or clean in, and a white towel around her waist, and he swings through mounting, ridging sheets of grease for her, while the lights go humming-humming and his hand goes loose, and there's a shattering (and to hear the whiskey glass shattering is profoundly reassuring: the sound confirms that *everything is here, every object is still at hand, as real and solid as ever, just as it always was*) and the humming of her light is summoning him forward, to where his bare foot goes down (and he hears the cry, the loud illuminated squelched cry as the bite takes place, deep in the tissued arch of his foot, his much-magnified giant-sized foot). He stumbles, drives the glass deeper through the living laminae of skin and muscle, nerve and tendon, lifts the cry higher, glass, the shattering you can't leave behind, the scattering scurrying mouselike pieces, glass, shattering the way the light shatters at the fierce pressure of the darkness, the eyes out there, hurting, he's hurting, and he goes down.

Part Two

A SINGLE SEA

Horizontal Chitchat

When the phone rings, at this odd hour, he considers answering it. It's closer to his side of the bed. But she gives a grunt, to mark it as her own; rises, and comes round the bed, moving with that surprising lifelong quickness of hers. "Hello," she says, in a firm voice. Staking out another sort of claim.

There's a pause, then she says, "Kaye?" then she says "No" and "No" and "No" and "What do you mean?" She says this— "What do you mean?"—a number of times.

Uh-oh. Problems of some sort, but judging from her voice nothing too troublesome. Nothing he'll have to get right out of bed over. He hasn't shaken his tiredness off, though there are mountains of things needing doing today; all kinds of good projects calling him. Odd, though, Kaye's calling at this hour, on this day—not yet eight o'clock on a Saturday morning.

"What do you *mean?* I don't understand what you're *saying . . .*"

Of course it's one hour later over in Kaye's part of the world. He can hear her voice, a little thread of sound coming out of the receiver; and fast, faster than usual, she seems to be talking a mile a minute. On, on it flows, the two of them pushing at each other a little in the struggle to hold the floor—always, between them, this gentle womanly pushing. Whatever has happened, Mob needs to have it explained a number of times before she's prepared to allow Kaye off the phone: "Now you listen," Mob says to her. "I'll be right here. You call me when you hear anything more.

"I'll be right here, Kaye," Mob repeats, and heavily sets down the phone. She says nothing for a moment; then makes her way, much more slowly this time around, over to her side of the bed.

He feels the mattress give generously, with an old patient sigh, beneath Mob's weight. She grunts. "That was Kaye," she tells him.

He thinks a moment. "Oh?"

"She was wondering whether we might have heard from Terry."

"From Terry? Why, you talked to him yesterday."

"*Yesterday?* She wanted to know if I'd talked to him this morning."

"This morning?"

"This morning. Yesterday wouldn't be much good, under the circumstances."

Circumstances? Clearly, she wasn't about to rattle off the whole story right away. That wasn't her style. And so there's very little point in trying to hurry her along. The funny thing was, she couldn't bear it when other people held up information—she had too much hunger to know. But let the tables be turned, give *her* the story first, and nothing on earth could nudge the Mob along. Oh, she was going to take her own sweet time.

"I suppose so," he tells her.

"Last night, Kaye and the man I told you about, this Glenn of hers, they arrive at that cabin place. I told you, you remember I told you they were all heading to Virginia?"

"Sure. I remember . . ."

"And the two of them are late because of a terrible storm and also because Glenn needed to look at some property. You remember he's in real estate?"

"I remember." It's odd the way she's always asking this of him, if he recollects this or that. His memory has always been better than her own.

"And they got lost for a while, but anyway eventually they do pull up at this place and there's a car with its headlights on, only they've gone all dim, you see, and the car door's wide open . . . And they go inside and call and no one answers but there's blood all over the floor . . ."

He can't help himself, the word leaps from his throat: "Blood!"

She brushes him off—dismisses him: "Oh it's nothing like *that,*" she says. As though he'd leapt to some sort of wild conclusion.

He waits. "No one's seriously *in*jured," she goes on. "But somebody's blood is all over the floor, and broken glass, and the car outside—all these signs of Terry, you see, but no Terry. Where is Terry? Now can you imagine? Can you? Can you imagine how poor Kaye must have felt? Terry had cut his foot open on some broken glass, you see, but how in the world was Kaye to know that? Can you imagine how Kaye reacted?"

Oh, he could imagine, all right: Kaye wasn't the sort of person who took a shock like that in stride. Never had been, even as a girl—always so sensitive, so quick to shriek, to jump, to flood over with tears.

"So the two of them, Kaye and Glenn, they go outside, looking for Terry, and where do you think they find him?"

But at this point in the story Mob hears her voice thin away. She stares up at the ceiling. Her eyes have gone dry and when she blinks she feels the sliding of her lids. The other aspects of this story are merely colorful; they go into making this a tale worth the telling. But here's the one detail that pulls like a drawstring at her throat, nearly closing off her voice entirely: "They find him standing in the creek. There's a creek right by the cabin, and Terry's just standing in the middle of it."

How is she to explain it—this feeling, lately more and more, of not comprehending her own children? It is as if they have pulled back from her and when she comes at them directly they kid her, they tease her, they humor her. It is as if they are dancing around her, and she cannot turn quickly enough to keep up with them, her little ones, she has become this big heavy lumbering creature in the center, around which the little ones go yapping and dancing, like dogs, like snapping dogs.

"Washing out the wound. He was washing out the wound."

"Yes," she says, and instantly feels much better. "That's got to be it, doesn't it? But—but wouldn't it make more sense to wash it out inside? And if he's just *standing* there—well, wouldn't that make it bleed all the more?"

"He was trying to keep the blood out of the house."

Everett, too, ponders the ceiling. For a long time, for years, the side of the bed he is now lying on had been hers, but then one day Mob announced she needed the better air circulation on the other side. And that may well have been the reason. Or maybe she'd noticed that, under her weight, her own side had begun to sag more than his. If it was merely the sagging, well it was the simplest thing in the world to flip the mattress and springs around. There was no need to switch sides. But no matter. He doesn't mind sleeping on the softer side.

What he does now and then miss, however, is being close to the window. For it had been something of a heart's comfort, when his insomnia got at him, to peer straight up and out at the outflung night-swayed branches of the honey locust he'd planted just when Terry was born. That tree was his own handiwork, and he had cultivated well; or been lucky. He has always been a lucky man. The size of its branches, so thick and forthcoming, was reassuring. In the darkness branches of that sort could make a man feel better.

Still, the switch hadn't been something worth making a fuss over, when all was said and done.

"Anyway, when they got him inside the house the thing was still bleeding, evidently, and he was so pale, with loss of blood, and acting so funny, saying such peculiar *things,* according to Kaye, as if he was in shock, so at first they thought they ought to take him to the hospital. But Kaye bandaged him up, and Terry calmed down, and everything seemed all right, and Glenn got Terry to drink some wine—to calm him down?"

"Yes . . ."

"And finally they all went to bed."

There is still something troubling about this story; something that nags and gnaws; but he tells her, "So everything's all right, then."

"All right? Is that what you're saying? When Kaye gets up this morning and what do you think she finds? All *right?*"

"I don't know . . ."

She has him at this point, and he feels it coming: another blow. But it will indeed be all right. Whatever the boy's done, whatever's happened, Terry can handle it all. That was something he proved once and for all at Betsy's death: the strength inside him. No faking a strength like that—but where *did* the boy get it, that sort of fortitude? Not from Mob, who might seem so strong, solid as a house, but wasn't quite what she seemed to other people. No, not so strong; just a girl; in some ways, just a girl. And not here, not from his father, who was maybe a little tougher and a lot more resourceful than people might suppose, but who all the same could never have handled something like that. *Neither one of us, we don't have that kind of strength,* Everett thinks, and there's a sort of accountant's riddle to this: how could two people, coming together as parents, give a child something that neither one had?

"Terry's gone. And his car's gone. And *their* car, Kaye and Glenn's car, has been moved. Now you go and explain *that*. It wasn't moved far, and it wasn't moved to get it out of the way of anything. Just moved a little bit. And how do you explain *that*?"

Everett pinches his nostrils together for a couple of seconds— a gesture that often seems to help him think. Much more is called for here than an explanation of Terry's behavior, though that in itself is going to be no small feat. Mob wants something in addition. She is challenging him at the middle of things, right there in the central role he plays for her: she's questioning his deductive powers. She is challenging him to demonstrate for her just what those methodical processes that he represents in their marriage can make of facts like these. This was his line of work, after all; this was how he'd put bread on the table for all the years of their married life. Here is one of the key things that people simply never understand about the insurance business. People see it as *dull* but in its various applications it calls for nothing less than the reasoning powers of a Sherlock Holmes. What is insurance, after all, but an ongoing attempt to foresee the future, to reconstruct the past?

Well, he *does* have an answer for her, and for a moment it quiets her utterly. "The headlights," he tells her. "Now stop and think. In all the excitement wouldn't it make sense that no one remembered to turn off the headlights? And so Terry gets up early the next morning—you know what an early riser he always has been," Everett notes parenthetically, and feels with these words a familiar pride in the boy, his hard-working big-money-making son. "And what does he discover? That the car's totally dead. And so what does he do next? He goes back inside quietly, finds Glenn's keys, pulls some jumper cables out of Glenn's trunk, moves the car close enough to do a jump start, returns the keys to where he found them, and drives off."

Everett rolls over on his side, away from her, and allows himself a sleepy-sounding sigh.

Mob goes on staring at the ceiling. She listens to her breathing, which slows. Yes, it is all right.

There had been people in this town, she knows, who'd wondered what she could possibly see in Everett Seward. (One of them, Dora Glover, actually spelled it out: "You're not really going to marry little Everett Seward, are you?" and that was *that,* though the two of them had been friends for years, that was the end of their friendship.) (Dora's comeuppance came later, and just as you'd figure, when the story broke about how Hugh Glover had been running after every little high school tart in town.) But what people couldn't see was the fineness of his mind, how *deft* almost like an acrobat the little man was. It had been no surprise to *her* when, for one thing or another (a model railroad, a stage design, a doghouse), he'd ended up in the newspapers. And if he'd only been able to put himself forward (if she'd only been able to push him more into pushing himself forward) there really would have been no limit to what the little man might have done with his life.

Still, he did have a habit of sometimes ignoring a problem when he couldn't quite account for all of it; he required careful watching in that way. And when the doubts hit her now—questions he had failed to answer—they come thick and fast. She says, "Yes, but why did Terry go off without leaving a note?" She says, "Why not wait until Glenn and Kaye got up?" She says, "And where did he go in such a hurry?" She says, "And where in heaven is he now?"

A Single Sea

"But let's suppose, let's just for a moment suppose—"

"Let's suppose I don't want any of your supposing."

"Purely for argument's sake—"

"I don't want any argument."

"—Just let's suppose it was no illusion . . ."

"I will do no such thing."

"I'm not saying it wasn't, Adam. In fact, I'm saying it probably was. But I'm only saying, purely for the purposes of argument, Let us suppose, for just a minute, that what I saw, what I saw *and* heard, wasn't an illusion."

"And I'm only saying, Let's not. I'm only saying, You and I, representing as we do ten trillion years of evolution or whatever it is, and representing as well the firm of Hamill, Hillman, leaders in the field of communications law for half a century, have a responsibility to suppose no such thing."

"Adam . . ."

"No, I mean it, Babe."

"I'm just asking you to entertain a possibility."

"Entertain? You know what I did in honor of your visit tonight? I went out and bought two six-packs of beer—which, I feel compelled to add, you have churlishly refused to touch. And I made popcorn with my very own bare hands. Now from where I sit it seems to me I've done all the enter*tain*ing tonight that I'm obliged to do."

"Adam . . ."

"No, I mean it."

He did. For all his joking, and the obvious pleasure he was taking in his pseudo-solemn lawyerly grandiloquence, he did mean it: he didn't want to talk about this.

He was feeling a little surly, naturally, at the way the Redskins had managed to bungle the game; and it was possible that all the beer inside him (he'd downed five or six cans) wasn't sitting well; but his obduracy in the end could not be laid to anything so fleeting. Clearly, everything in his temperament instructed him that the line Terry was pursuing wasn't to be pursued.

Decor in Adam's apartment was inspired solely by considerations of comfort. Although Adam was very well-heeled (he was sitting, by Terry's estimation, on a fortune easily surpassing a million dollars), he lived in a place not far removed from a dump. The old tan velour couch was bald in some patches and stained in others, but it was endlessly hospitable; Terry had slept many nights upon it. There were two big easy chairs and an Oriental rug of sufficiently bold and busy coloring that you didn't have to worry much about spilling anything on it. The place had achieved, in its way, a kind of grubby perfection. Only the two standing lamps struck a discordant note. They threw forth a sickly glare in which, with Adam on the couch and Terry in one of the easy chairs, faces stuck out harshly. Adam's eyes disappeared under his brow ridges, while his thick sweat-filmed nose gleamed in the light.

One of the room's few touches of grandeur, the panoramic view from the living room window (which looked out across Calvert and Connecticut Avenue, to a wide green swath of Rock Creek Parkway, with a hazy intimation of Virginia in the distance), had vanished with the fall of night. Another grand touch, an enormous TV that had knocked Adam back nearly two thousand dollars, flashed silently. As dumps went, this place was extremely well-appointed. Adam was a sucker for gadgetry. He had a talking microwave, a fancy juicer, a talking chess set, a DAT stereo, computers that spoke with other computers, an espresso machine. Actually, the expensive "toys" fit in with the Salvation Army couch and chairs and rug—everything in the place was a comfort-enhancer. "You've got to let this go," Adam was saying. "Now this event, or visi*ta*tion, or however you want to label it, is no longer a recent event. We're talking a couple of weeks now. And I'm tired of hearing about it, frankly. You've got to put things behind you, Babe. Honestly, don't you see that? Don't you see that?"

"That's exactly what I'm trying to do. Put things behind me."

"Okay, you've been under lots of pressure. Generally speaking, you work what most people would call long hours. You're flying all over the place. Half the time you're sleeping badly. You're going to meetings and writing briefs. In short, you're suffering from overwork, right? And you know what, under these circumstances, is the only cure for you? *Going back to work,* that's what it is, keeping at it, with occasional evenings like this one where you watch a game and drink some beer and piss a lot and bitch about a lawyer's lot in life. Trust me."

"I do trust you, Adam. What I'm saying is, Trust me."

"You want to go crazy? Let's go crazy. Let's order up a couple of large pizzas and eat till we puke. Let's pop the bottle of champagne I've got in the fridge. Let's play gin rummy until dawn. But if you're going to go crazy, let's not go crazy in a crazy way, huh?"

"I see what you're saying, Adam. What I don't see is what possible harm there is in supposing, if only for a moment—"

"Terry, you've got to deal with the reality of the situation."

"Okay. Fine. But what's that?" In his excitement, Terry felt his voice turn a little shrill. "What is reality?"

"Oh God, this *isn't* happening to me, is it? Tell me I didn't invite somebody to my house, offer him beer and genuine, homemade popcorn, and what does he wind up doing? He winds up saying to me, What is reality?—that's what he winds up doing. Terry, get the hell out of my house. You know as well as I do that I choose my friends exclusively on their willingness to avoid hitting me with questions like *What is reality?*

"Reality," Adam went on, "is the knowledge that when you put butter into a hot popcorn pan, it's going to melt. Terry, you want to go for a run? Let's go for a run. Burn off all this crap . . ." With a sweep of his hand Adam indicated the strew of empty beer cans, the crumpled, buttery napkins, the popcorn bowl empty of all but its unpopped kernels.

"Adam, it's the middle of the night. We couldn't *see,* for one thing."

"We'll hop the fence at the high school. That's what you ought to do. Get on the track. It's good fun."

"Adam, I'm beat. I'm going to go home in a minute."

"That's what you ought to do. Go home, get some sleep."

"That hasn't been so easy lately. Sleeping."

"Now you listen to me." Adam was sternness itself. "I'll get you through this. Haven't I always got you through everything?"

"You're a real lifesaver," Terry replied, and to his embarrassment his voice splintered over *lifesaver.* The word called forth—instantly, unexpectedly—more feelings than he felt ready to deal with. The truth was that there was no one, *no one,* who'd done more for Terry after the accident than Adam had. Outrageous Adam, crazy but proudly sane Adam . . .

But caught up in his own designs, Adam evidently missed the rip in Terry's throat. He went on, "Didn't I cover for you just this week? That was a real sweetheart—what you did with the Tulsa request."

"Not my finest. Conceded. Not Terry Seward's golden hour. Adam, my mind wasn't on it."

"Your mind wasn't on it. You want reality? You screwed up. Struck out, fumbled the ball, missed the rim. That's reality."

"That, too, is reality."

"Of *course* you can't sleep. You've suddenly become a teetotaler on me. Terry, get the hell up and go get yourself a beer."

"Okay, I'll have a beer, I'll have a beer."

Terry rose from the easy chair and went into the kitchen on knees that had gone a little soft and indecisive. This was an odd phenomenon but one he'd noticed many times before: how, being around somebody who was drinking, you soon began to feel you'd had a few.

It was slim pickings in Adam's cavernous refrigerator. There were some hot dogs, a white cardboard carton half full of what looked like beef and pea pods, some low-fat yogurt, some quarts of low-fat milk, a couple of old, loose-skinned peaches, a jar of olives, a block of unidentified yellow cheese, a bottle of champagne. And three six-packs of beer. Terry wrested two cans free of their plastic rings and returned to the living room.

He handed one to Adam, dropped back into the easy chair, and popped the tab on the other. Instead of drinking from it, though, he sniffed at its open oblong wedge. He hadn't had a drink in a couple of weeks. Not since the night in the cabin.

It smelled okay. With an infusion of sudden purpose, a liberating inkling that he was, commendably, preparing himself for sleep, he tipped back his head and threw down a long swallow—discovering, the moment it splashed frothing into his mouth, that this wasn't at all what he wanted.

With Adam's eyes upon him, he took a second swallow—but this one was not so much a swallow as a French kiss, a laying of his loose lips upon the open metal mouth—and deposited the can on the coffee table. "So where do we go from here, Adam?"

"Go?"

Terry exhaled loudly through his nose. "I don't know." He started again. "I talked to Diana today."

"Our Delightful Diana. How's she?"

"I don't know how *she* is. She seemed to want to know how *I* am. It was pretty clear Kaye had been talking at her. Lord knows what *she* said . . ."

"And how's Kaye?"

"I dunno. Haven't talked to her, haven't seen her. Not since I went out to Baltimore, *at* your suggestion, to show her that I haven't become—yet, anyway—a raving lunatic. Which was, let me see, the same day I went to the eye doctor, also *at* your suggestion, and was told I have the eyes of a teenager. The point here, Adam, is that it's not as though I've suddenly started ignoring your counsel."

"I should have been a shrink. Listen all day to women talk about their sexual fantasies . . ."

"Should I go see a shrink? I've been thinking about going to see a shrink."

"Go to a tea-leaf reader first."

"Anyway, you want to know the truth, I'm kind of pissed at Kaye. She can be pretty hard to take when she's Florence Nightingalish. I thought we'd got past most of that big sister little brother stuff, especially now that, you know, now that it's little brother who's doing the lion's share of putting big sister's kid through Dartmouth. But she's wearing the nurse's cap these days all right. Goes from playing mother hen to all the little chicks at the office to playing mother hen to me."

"*I* should have been a dentist. And hire me a dozen girls in white frock coats . . ."

"In fact, they're *all* calling me. Mob. Even Dad. Oh, Jesus, Dad's the worst, you've got to feel so sorry for the guy, here's the old insurance man trying in his polite decorous probing way to determine just what *sort* of a phenomenon we're talking about here, under *which* category it falls, it's enough to break your heart. It's enough to break your heart. Wouldn't you think that life would have had the ordinary common decency to spare old Everett Seward any suspicion that he might have fathered a lunatic? And then to*day*. Diana calls today. I mean what the *hell* is Kaye going into any of this with Diana for, which she clearly has, though I *ordered* her not to. She did say she didn't. Am I being paranoid? I mean am I being crazy in thinking the word's gotten out about my craziness when suddenly I'm getting fifty-two calls a day? Jesus, Kaye." He brought his hands up over his tired face, his fingertips tight against his closed eyelids, and began a little massage. As he did so, Kaye's face popped into mind, and he said to her, aloud, "What the hell are you doing, mm?"

"I'm thinking about having another beer. What are you doing?"

Terry dropped his hands into his lap, opened his eyes. "I'm thinking about going home. Correction, I *am* going home. G'night, Adam." He stood up.

"'Night, pal. Get some sleep."

"That's where I'm going, right to bed," Terry told his friend, but when, fifteen minutes later, he stepped through his own front door he moved—with an unswerving deliberateness belying the notion that this was any spontaneous impulse—to his telephone. He called directory assistance and once he'd obtained the number he wanted he allowed himself no time for second thoughts. He dialed again and to the man's voice that answered—possibly familiar, possibly not—he said, "Hi, is that Kevin Kopp?"

"Who's it wanting to know?" Oh, it was Curly all right.

"Hey there, geez, it's Terry, Terry Seward. How are ya, Curly, how are things?"

"Terry?"

"Sorry to be calling so late. I know it's after eleven."

"I go by Kevin these days and it's after twelve, actually."

"Well then I'm even sorrier. So how are ya?"

"Terry? What do you want?"

Never one for the social graces, old Curly Kopp. Terry was tempted to comment upon this, to complain about the lack of civility. But he held himself back. He had to watch himself, his impulses; suddenly, lately, he'd grown so impulsive. What he did say to Kopp was, "Well I was wondering how an old college pal of mine was doing and so I thought I'd give him a call, what the hell. I said I would, remember. What the hell. It was the last time I saw you. Here in Washington. A couple years ago."

"That was more than a *couple* years ago."

"Was it?" Why in the world had he thought there might be any point in telephoning Curly Kopp? He had forgotten the barriers Kopp put up: the arch corrections and the needless, whiny haggling, the suspiciousness, the absolute lack of anything resembling everyday courtesy. He'd thought perhaps that Kopp had changed over the years, but already it was manifest, after a minute's conversation, that Kopp was still Kopp. The thing to do now was to sever this reawakened, doomed connection. But how? Seemingly this was to be accomplished only by moving forward, not backward. "I was thinking maybe we could have dinner sometime. You know I'm often in Baltimore. My sister lives there."

"So when are you going to be here?"

"Well, that depends on you. I travel a fair amount, but I'm going to be around all next week. Is any day all right with you?"

"You mean you'd be making a special trip?"

Terry denied this readily, instinctively: "No, not really. I mean I've got all sorts of things to do in Baltimore." Too late he realized he should have taken the opposite tack; should have said, *Yes, Kevin, I thought I would make a special trip, drive nearly a whole entire sixty-minute hour expressly to see you.* Was that such an outrageous thing? "I'll take you out to dinner."

"No," Kopp replied, and in one way, evidently, he wasn't the same old Kopp—no longer the skinflint who never spent a dime on anything, unless it was jumping beans, or a wooden box containing five thousand steel ball bearings, or a fingerprinting kit: "I'll take *you* out. That way, if you hate the place, I don't have to feel guilty." And this was followed by that high sharp snort of a laugh, which Terry had almost forgotten. A little self-congratulatory announcement of his own cleverness is what it was. An audible smirk. "I'm vegetarian, by the way."

"Me, I eat lots of vegetables," Terry said, which came out sounding pretty silly. "How's next Monday night? A week from tonight?"

"Monday?"

You would think, to hear how taken aback Kopp managed to sound, that Monday was some outlandishly implausible day; Terry might just as well have proposed they get together for breakfast on Christmas morning. But in response to Kopp's show of surprise Terry felt a time-tested, intricately interlocking pattern of behavior cohering inside him. Though it was long ago now, he did have a great deal of experience—months and months of side-by-side living—in the handling of Curly Kopp. At this juncture, the thing to do was not to back down. "Yeah, Monday. Dinner Monday night. You free?"

"Monday?"

"Monday."

"For dinner?"

"Exactly."

Pause. "We'll go to a place called Belinda's. It's South American food—that okay?"

"Fine."

"It's not so far from the Inner Harbor. How well you know Baltimore? You need directions?"

"Just give me the street name."

"The street name? Don't know the street name."

"You have a phone book there? Maybe it's in it."

"A phone book?"

"A phone directory." Why, why in the world had he ever concluded that the best way to wind up this evening would be to resurrect Curly Kopp?

Another pause. "It's at 850 Throckmorton. Near the old Bromo Seltzer tower."

"I'll find it. Say eight o'clock?"

"You eat late."

"Say seven-thirty?"

"Okay, if you insist, I'll say it: 'seven-thirty.' But why *don't* we make it eight o'clock?"

Again a pause. "You working these days, Kevin?"

"I own a couple of pet stores."

"Pet stores." Terry did not quite succeed, perhaps, in removing every last quiver of mirth from his voice—but how could he be expected to? Life really *was* too perfect when it came to people like the former proprietor of the Mexican Jumping Bean Escort Service. Of *course* Kopp ran a couple of pet stores . . . Hurriedly, seeking to put all hilarity behind him, Terry said, "Me, I'm a communications lawyer. Handling applications for radio and television stations, cable franchises, and some cellular phone work—that sort of thing."

"Mostly Greek to me. I don't own a TV."

"You don't own a TV?" Another pause opened and Terry was tempted to add a joke—something along the lines of *The pet store business is really that depressed, huh?* But Kopp would probably take him seriously.

"Nope," Kopp said.

"Never have?"

"Oh, I *had* one. But I gave it away. Television rots the mind, Terry."

"There is that . . ." And still another pause. "Well. Yes. Anyway. Sorry about the hour."

"Nothing to be sorry about. No one can change the hour. Of course behavior can be modified."

"Right . . ." Oh, the same old Kopp—always literal-mindedly pouncing upon some exaggeration or imprecision or simple colloquialism, as though he'd truly been misdirected by it. And, given his queer take on things, half the time you didn't know whether there'd been a genuine misunderstanding or not. Freshman year, ignoring his academic advisor's pleas on behalf of diversity, Kopp had plunged headlong into the study of philosophy—with an emphasis not (so far as Terry had been able to make out) on the meaning of life but on little meaningless puzzles, paradoxes, conundrums. What does one make of the billboard that says *This billboard is a lie*? And does the barber who shaves every man in the village who does not shave himself shave himself? That sort of thing. "Well. Sorry about calling so late. I thought it would be okay. In college, you often stayed up until dawn."

"College was a long time ago . . ."

"That means we have all the more catching up to do, doesn't it? See you Monday, eight o'clock, Belinda's, 850 Throckmorton." And added, though he didn't mean, or for the most part didn't mean, to revive the repudiated nickname: "'Night, Curly."

Unlike Kopp, Terry had actually been to South America (he and Betsy, five years ago, had combined a trip to Barbados with a few days in Caracas), and knew for a certainty that the fare offered at Belinda's bore little connection to what was actually eaten down there. What was found on Belinda's menu were things like fried plantains and black beans in pepper-garlic sauce and pork with star fruit and curried coconut chicken. What people actually eat in South America is, needless to say, what people eat anywhere: potato chips, fried chicken, hamburgers, hot dogs, Snickers bars, Doritos, Chinese food. Not that there was any point in being a stickler. What Polynesian has ever tasted Polynesian food?—but Terry found the whole ersatz cuisine, with its rum and coconut drinks, its pineapple-on-plastic-toothpicks and paper parasols and maraschino cherries, quite appealing. What he would quarrel with at Belinda's was the cooking itself.

Not about to let Kopp corner the market on adventurousness, Terry had ordered green banana fritters and beef in guava sauce. The fritters had come encased in a breading evidently devised not for its flavor but for its capacity to absorb grease, and the beef, which was fatty, had such a peculiar taste that the first bite had actually caused him to halt, dumbstruck, in mid-chew.

The last time the two of them had met, with a flutter of words on the streets of Washington, Kopp had looked almost unchanged since college days. Since that brief encounter, though, serious alterations had overtaken him. His curly hair had receded from his forehead and thinned on top, leaving the hair on the sides, which was as thick as ever, to form two clownlike balls over his ears. Another clownlike ball, this one composed of the flesh at the end of his nose, had seemingly been inflated. Meanwhile, his eyebrows had thickened considerably, if that were possible, and—which probably wasn't—he'd shrunk an inch or two and the gap between his always narrow eyes had dwindled. And he'd put on ten pounds—at least ten.

"Does vegetarianism go along with running a pet shop?"

"You're not the first person to suggest a connection."

"It hadn't occurred to me that I might be. I was just interested . . ."

"Well, I suppose it does. The two are part of something else—an entire integrated way of life," Kopp declared, but his voice was too adenoidal to lend a phrase like this the grandeur he clearly aspired to.

"And you're strict about it? You don't even eat fish?"

"That's right."

"Me, I do like fish," Terry said.

"So do I, Terry. That's why I don't eat 'em."

Terry greeted this remark with a little laugh. But the lifting of one of Kopp's eyebrows, and the hard sharp self-satisfied glint in his eyes, announced that it wasn't easy laughter he was striving for. Oh, no: he still wanted—as much as ever—to be challenging. To make those pointed, pithy little observations that might be called thought-provoking. Terry suddenly felt sorry for Curly—and recognized, in the warm familiar wash of this feeling, just how large a measure pity had played in the composition of their original friendship.

"So what do you do for fun, Kevin?"

"Actually, the business takes up a lot of time. It's a lot harder than people think, running a couple of pet stores."

"I can imagine. But you must have some spare time. What do you do in your spare time?"

"I do lots of things. I read, I do all sorts of things. How about you?"

"Well, I don't go to too many parties, anyway. Don't you remember? What you wrote about me freshman year? In your journal?"

"You had no business reading my journal, Terry . . ."

"As if you wouldn't have read mine, if I'd kept one! We were *fresh*men, Kevvie, for Chrissake. Anyway, I've got it word for word. You wrote: 'Terry Seward was put on this planet in order to stand around at parties with a drink in his hand.' Remember? It was actually quite perceptive, if you want to know the truth. In college, and law school, too, I went to a hell of a lot of parties. But Betsy didn't like them that much—she wasn't all that sociable, to be honest with you. Except with her family, her sisters. They were very close. Especially her sister Heidi, who recently moved from Charlottesville to Germany. They were *very* close. And her kids—her students. She loved her kids."

It had been an enormous relief to discover, earlier in the evening, that Kopp had already somehow been apprised of Betsy's death. It wasn't a subject that, tonight, Terry could bear to lay out in detail—and there had seemed a substantial possibility that Kopp would seize on it, in his dogged and analytical way, and not let it go. But when Terry had said, "You heard about Betsy, my wife—" Kopp's eyes had swayed and dropped away; there had been no need to add, though Terry had gone ahead and added, "that she died . . ."

Terry went on: "But lately it's like I outgrew parties. The last year or so, I can hardly bear them. Not that I get invited to all that many any more. The last year or so, things have changed a lot for me, my whole life's different. I have basically no social life, for one thing. Truly. It's the oddest thing. The few people Betsy and I saw socially I never see, not that I can blame them. Of course I can't blame them if *they've* quit inviting me over now that *I* never invite them over," Terry said, experiencing with this announcement a lively compounding of resentment toward them (toward virtually every young couple who had once been friends with that other, vanished young couple, Terry and Betsy Seward) and of satisfaction in his own dispassionate and generous objectivity. "What else could I possibly expect?"

This juncture of the conversation was, Terry perceived, an opportunity to introduce the one topic for which he had arranged this meeting: the vision, or visitation, or whatever it was that he'd witnessed in the cabin. And yet he didn't feel ready to do so—indeed, wasn't sure this was a topic which, under any circumstances, he would let crazy Curly Kopp get his squirrel's big teeth into.

"Of course I didn't tell you I'd read your journal, Kevin. Not at first. But I made sure to leave out on my desk a letter to my folks, in which I said, *Poor Kevin still hasn't made any friends.*"

"You did?"

"Oh come *on,* don't give me that. Don't *give* me that. You read it, you know you did."

Though Kopp shook his head in denial, the squirming merriment in his gaze seemed not merely to confess to the crime but to joy in having been, tardily, apprehended.

"How's your aunt and uncle?" Terry asked.

"My aunt and uncle?"

"The religious ones. The ones you lived with before college."

"Them? I suppose the two of them are just the same as ever. *I* wouldn't know. We've had no contact whatsoever in over ten years."

"Ten years? Good heavens, and why's that?"

"That's just the way things have worked out . . ."

"You had a fight?"

"Not exactly."

"You didn't exactly share their religious views."

"Oh we shared more than I wanted to . . ."

"You live alone?" Terry asked, all but certain what the answer would be. After all, this was somebody who, having lost both parents in childhood, had subsequently succeeded in cutting himself off from the very folks who had raised him.

"Yep."

"You always lived alone? I mean since graduation?"

"No, I lived with somebody for thirteen months."

The way Kopp's chin proudly uplifted with this remark, as well as the specificity of the number, strongly hinted at some romantic attachment. But the thought of Squirrely Kopp in any sort of physical relationship was now, just as it had been in college, utterly ungraspable.

"What happened?"

"We broke up."

Terry paused and then inquired, "What was this person's

name?" The phrasing was warily selected, in acknowledgment of a suspicion—one which, now and then, had fluttered uneasily through Terry's mind in college days—that ever-dateless Kopp might be gay.

"Pat," was the reply, which of course was neither one thing nor the other. "Pat Dewitt. Nobody you know."

"And where did the two of you meet?"

"At the zoo, actually."

Where else? *Where in the world else?* The absolute beauty of this revelation at once shoved aside all social precautions. If his assumptions were misplaced, Kopp could simply set him straight. "What does she do?" Terry asked him.

"What she does now, I don't have the faintest idea. What she did *then* was work with reptiles mostly. She worked at the zoo. I met her when I went in with some questions. It's a complicated thing, running a pet store."

"I can imagine."

Actually, it was a little deflating to discover something logical—practical, businesslike—in the genesis of Kopp's one great romance. Better, far better if the two of them had met by chance in the monkey house, if a baboon had brought the two of them together . . . "Are you still seeing a shrink?" Terry asked, and added, "Forgive me if I'm getting too personal."

"It's nothing to be embarrassed about. I wasn't embarrassed even then. Back in freshman year."

"No," Terry conceded. "You weren't. Not even way back then."

And these words, *back then,* carried an unexpected verve: they resurrected for Terry a feeling, or set of feelings—an atmosphere—and it was just as though the two of them might once more be sitting in some Princeton eatery, freshmen again. Terry swung his gaze around this place—wan lights, walls covered in burlap, blue candles mounted in coconut shells, and a big shaggy sickly plant listing tiredly into a corner—and felt his head drift limply, as though pulled sideways by the simple traction of his gaze. It was a movement he attributed to the drink he'd had, then recalled he'd had nothing to drink tonight except ginger ale. This was dizzying—inebriating—nonetheless: to be sitting, once more, across from Kevin T. Kopp of Houston, Texas. (Before freshman year even started, the name and place of origin had arrived in an envelope from the housing office. Terry had imagined a big, drawling Texas longhorn of a roommate—and in had scampered a squirrel instead.) And though so much had happened since, it seemed that all of it had intricately connived to place the two of them in the situation that had defined them at the outset: two unattached males attempting, through moments of exasperation and lurching boredom, to entertain each other.

"You want some dessert? Desserts are real good here."

This, too, was something new, and it was quite winsome— the emergence in Curly Kopp of a proprietary solicitude. He wanted Belinda's to please.

"Sure, I'll have some dessert," Terry said, although he wanted nothing more to eat. He wanted only to be home. To be in his bedroom, with the door closed, the reading light on, a book of history propped in his lap. This evening had offered nostalgic satisfactions and moments of authentic amusement, as well as a befuddled sensation, both sweet and uneasy, of the yawning cavernous distances of his life, but concerning the matter that had inspired this encounter in the first place—the hope that Kopp, with all his bizarre experiences and his investigations into unusual states of mind, might actually be useful—the evening seemed fundamentally misguided. Was he really going to ask Curly Kopp for advice? "Didn't I see fruit salad? I'll have fruit salad."

"The coconut pie's awful good. So's the flan."

"Fruit salad sounds perfect."

"And coffee? The coffee's from Brazil."

"Sure, I'd love coffee."

The skin of the woman who came to take away their dishes was so black that the collar of her electric blue blouse seemed to be reflected in the flesh beneath her chin. Skin that actually glowed.

"How's the family?"

"The what?" Terry said.

"The folks."

"They're fine. They still ask about you. Really."

And this was true. Especially Dad, who was still captivated by tales of Kopp's ingenious idiosyncrasies. The raft race, particularly. Dad had loved the story of the raft race. "Dad's retired now. But he still goes around quoting statistics at whoever'll listen. Still calling himself a 'numbers man.' And Mob—Mob's Mob. You were telling me about your shrink."

"No I wasn't. You were asking about my shrink."

"Okay, so tell me about your shrink."

"Well, I didn't go for a long time. I started up again not too long ago. Her name's Amanda." And the chin rose again—as though with pride. "She calls herself a directionist. Does that mean anything to you?"

"Not a blessed thing I'm afraid."

"Well I don't know if it means anything much to me either. But you don't necessarily lie on a couch, although you can. It's all much more like talking to you here. We challenge each other. The session is supposed to be integrated into your life. We've even had sessions a coupla times in public places—restaurants, a park. Course you've got to be sure you're not bothering anybody. You never been to a shrink?"

"No. Does that seem strange?"

"How do you mean strange?"

"Strange to have gone through Betsy's death without going to a shrink?"

"Well you got through it, and that's the main thing, isn't it?"

"I'm not sure when, if ever, you get *through* anything like that. I've been a mess incidentally," Terry added, and was tempted further to supply, not so much for clarification as for exculpation, an account of the occasion when, on a wet raw autumn afternoon in Charlottesville's Blue Pine Memorial Park, he'd thrown himself flat out onto Betsy's grave.

Conversation had halted once more at a spot where the mysterious event of a few weeks ago might naturally be broached. In fact this was—in its intersection of the topics of Betsy and of psychological recuperation—a moment that simply could not be more opportune. But one glance at Curly Kopp (his newly emergent skull, his beady, unnaturally close-set eyes) proved powerfully dissuasive. Closing off the topic for good—at least, tonight—Terry said, "Now tell me, what sort of animals are your biggest sellers?"

Still, on departure, in the parking lot at Belinda's, it was Terry—seized by heaven knows what new impulse—who urged another meeting. "Kevin," he said, "Sorry I've got to go now, believe it or not I've got some dreary lawyer-type business that needs doing tonight, but I've really enjoyed this, honestly, and I wonder if we might get together soon. This week in fact would be good for me. You free any other night this week?"

"This week?"

"Yeah, I'm happy to come back into Baltimore."

"Well I don't know. I don't have my calendar with me."

"You see, there are some things I wanted to talk to you about. That I didn't bring up tonight."

They were negotiating, as so often in the past, and looking down at Curly Kopp—who'd always claimed to be five feet six, but surely he was shorter than that—Terry relished an old manipulative mastery. For all its simplicity, this approach—that of directness, of clumsy candor—was one that Kopp, in all his obliquities and evasions, had never been able to counter effectively. How many times, how many times in the past Terry had wheedled or cajoled something out of his roommate by making, as now, an open-handed plea! Terry went on, "Well I've had some odd things happen to me lately, and I've started wondering about all sorts of questions, and I thought you might be interested. I thought you might be able to help me . . ."

Kopp's gaze bobbed, bounded away. He rubbed at the ball of his nose, scooting it back and forth. "You want to see one of my pet stores, maybe? Thursday night?"

"I'd like that. I'd like that a lot."

"Come by a little before nine. I'll close it up at nine. It's in the Bighunt Mall, you know where the Bighunt is? Cavendish Road, coupla miles past Whigley? My place is called Just Off the Ark."

"That's swell—really swell. The name, I mean—I like the name. You come up with it?"

Kopp's eyes glittered. The question seemed to amuse him—

or, perhaps, to wound his pride slightly. "All by myself," he said.

"And I'll be there," Terry said. "I'll be there a little before nine. It's been great to see you, Kevin."

"Yeah. Okay. Night."

It was just after eleven when Terry slid the Audi into his driveway. He took off his sports jacket as he marched upstairs. The message light was blinking on his answering machine.

"Hi, Terry, it's Kaye. Just called to say hi and to see how you're doin'. Everything's fine here. I just talked to Mom and Dad and they seem fine. Also, Terry, I wanted to talk to you a little bit about Diana's wedding. I know it seems a long ways off to you but there are all *kinds* of preparations, and of course expenses, you probably don't know anything about."

Expenses?

"I'm going to be up late tonight," Kaye's voice rattled on. "So if you get home before eleven-thirty, why don't you give me a holler?"

Terry reconsulted his watch. It was 11:17. Still time to call—but he was totally bushed, he was going to go straight to bed, he would wait until tomorrow.

The second call was from Diana. "Geez, I was hoping you could help me escape from under a rockslide. I've got a geology quiz tomorrow. Just called to chat. Bye-ee."

Terry dialed Diana's number. Sometimes he had a little trouble telling Diana's voice from Shawn's, but this singing "Hello-o"—playfully elongating the second syllable—was his niece positively.

"Are you breaking stones with a sledgehammer? Is that what you do for a geology quiz?"

"It's you."

"Did you find any diamonds in the rough?"

"Just a couple. But they were teeny-weeny, so I threw 'em back."

"Am I interrupting anything?"

"No, no. Peter's off with some friends, male friends, he's out being macho."

Terry dropped into the chair beside the phone. "And Shawn?"

"At the movies. She's seeing this *horrible* new guy who's always taking her to see blood 'n' guts pictures."

"He's at Dartmouth?"

"Yeah, but he's a graduate student. In English. He's twenty-five."

"Twenty-five? What is this with the older men?"

"He's twenty-five and he smokes a pipe and he's always holding forth about authentic American archetypes—what in hell are authentic American archetypes, Terry?"

"Beats me."

"How do they differ from inauthentic American archetypes?"

"You have me there."

He liked this about Diana—the gift she had, rare in somebody so young, for quickly smelling out pomposity and pretension.

"She's got a new name for guys, incidentally, or *we* do. I've taken to it like a duck to water."

"And what's that?"

"We call them newts."

"Newts? You call guys newts?"

"It's from this guy Newton on a soap opera who Shawn's been hyperventilating over. So we started calling guys, especially good-looking guys, newts."

There was a momentary pause, which Diana broke by asking, "You don't think it's funny?"

"Sure I do . . ." Ah, but it was much, much more, it was much, much better than funny. Terry *loved* to be let in on little confidences of just this variety. By way of Diana, and especially by way of her stories about rooming with Shawn, Terry had gained admittance into a kind of miraculous club. From an early age—ten? twelve?—there'd been for him a constant gnawing worried wondering about just what it was, exactly, that pretty girls talked about among themselves, when no male eyes and ears were present. He'd always known their conversation must be enchanting, but what would it consist of, exactly? What in the name of heaven did they talk about? Well, now he was beginning to find out. They talked about newts . . . "What soap opera is that?" he asked her.

"As if you'd know . . . I mean honestly, Terry, you ever seen a soap opera? All the way through?"

He answered truthfully—nonetheless his own answer, when spoken aloud, somehow surprised him a little. "No, I guess not," he confessed. Why had he never once watched a soap opera? "Which one should I start with?"

"Newton's this big lumberjacky guy with this bright red *beard*. He's so dumb I guess you do have to love him. Shawn does. She says she's going to marry him and"—pause—"cultivate his mind." Diana giggled. "You were away when I called."

"I was seeing an old college roommate. Curly Kopp. I've told you about Curly?"

"You mean the jumping beans guy, the if-you-haven't-felt-their - warm - rapturous - throbbing - in - the - palm - of - your - hand-you-haven't-really-lived guy?" Diana giggled again.

"The very man."

"How was dinner? Did you eat Mexican food, Mexican jumping beans?" And giggled again.

This, too, he liked—how she had retained, side by side with her precocious gift for spotting a fake, a teenager's quick, unforced hilarity. It rolled right up out of her. Shawn was that way, too—put them together, and the two of them were soon in stitches.

"You're close. South American. Dinner was fine, it was fun, it was all right. I mean dinner it*self* was godawful. But it was good to see him again, I guess, after all these years. Funny thing, you get to be my age—"

"Terry, come off it."

He liked this as well about Diana—she constantly made him feel as though there really weren't so many years between them. "No, I just mean there's something strangely reassuring about it. You have a lunatic for a roommate and twenty years later you discover the guy's still a lunatic. It really is reassuring."

"I've got a sweetheart for a roommate. Does that mean Shawnee in twenty years will still be a sweetheart?"

"You and Shawn in twenty years . . . Surely *you* two will never be forty. Add your ages together and you hardly have forty."

"Put me and Shawn together and you have forty-four. Put me and Shawn together and you get Mom."

It was an odd thought. It was hard to believe, at times, that Diana was truly Kaye's daughter. "She called tonight. Your mom."

"Wha'd she want? Don't tell me she wanted to rag about me."

"I don't know. I didn't call her back," Terry said, and added—an impulsive and wholly unnecessary untruth—"I'm returning your calls in order."

"How's your foot?"

"My what?"

"Your foot. Your poor old wounded cut foot."

"Fine fine. I'd forgotten all about it. So where's Peter?"

"Oh it's all very macho and tight-lipped. 'I may be back later, I may just crash at my place.' I say to him, 'You know there won't be a *my place* before too long.' "

"You're going to scare him off."

There was a flutter at the windows. Wind?—or had it begun to rain?

"He's going to scare *me* off you mean."

The bedside clock said eleven-forty-seven when the last bits of news were relayed, the last bits of kidding and well-wishing exchanged. Terry padded into the bathroom, looked at himself in the mirror, combed his hair, washed his face, brushed his teeth. The trouble he'd had lately in falling asleep made it all the more imperative to proceed as though everything were in order—as though he would be dead to the world in ten minutes. A stiff drink might help put him over, but he didn't want a drink. No . . .

He closed the bedroom door behind him. He removed his pants and shirt. He would sleep, as he generally did, in his T-shirt, underwear, and socks—items which, in the morning, he would place in the dirty clothes hamper on his way to the shower.

He never used to sleep with the bedroom door closed. This was something new—and something that no one need be told. His own secret. But in the event that Betsy revisited him, appeared again in a remote bath of light, he wanted an indication or warning—some few seconds to prepare himself, as the door-

knob turned. Provided, of course, that she would need to open
a door before entering any room.

"Compared to cats or dogs, say, saltwater fish are a high-
casualty item. You wake up one morning, you say, *Hey guys, get
up,* and they already *are* up, they're belly up. Of course *I* know
how to handle them, but that doesn't mean the customer does. I
don't much like handling saltwater fish. Or the very cheap freshwater stuff either. You pretty much have to in this business, I
guess, but I don't much like it. It's one of the reasons I don't sell
so much of the cheap stuff."

"Cheap stuff?"

"You know—fifty-nine cent guppies, ninety-nine cent goldfish . . . *That* kind of business I'd just as soon leave to the dime
store. Or the less scrupulous of my colleagues. You know what
a betta is?"

"Only as a sort of cosmic ray. Something like a gamma ray?"

"It's a fish, a really fine-looking freshwater fish from South-
east Asia that can live in brackish water. No pump, no filtration
system required, right? So what do my colleagues do? They sell
these betta bowls—put your betta in a bowl the size of your fist.
Literally—your fist. The thing can hardly turn around. Save a
buck, right? I mean for another buck you could actually get
yourself a decent-sized bowl. Now it may well be that bettas
really *are* so stupid and godforsaken that they don't know the
difference, but you know I can't quite shake this feeling that if
you treat something like it's dumb and miserable, it's going
to stay dumb and miserable. You think I could be evolving a better class of bettas? Just give me a couple of millennia, willya?
My thought is, You make somebody pay something for something, they're going to take care of it. They're going to learn
something about filtration systems, ammonia levels. They're
not going to come in here, the way I had somebody come in a
couple of winters ago, saying, The fish I bought was acciden-
tally left in my car overnight and the little bugger froze solid so
could you give me another huh?"

"Your policy sounds quite admirable."

"Does it? Shouldn't. Should sound commonsensical. But given some of the bastards you get in this business, maybe that's what I am. Admirable."

The characteristic edge to Kopp's voice—that whine which was always thinning toward a squeak—was blunted in this place, where the air hummed and gurgled with the ongoing purification of multiple stacked aquariums. This was another world. Here were the emphatic, spirited circus colors of the tropics, flaming reds and yellows, darting iridescent blues, outrageous oranges and purples—creatures got up as clowns and tarts. Some of the fish moved decisively, in sharp-angled veerings, others drifted as if through drugged dreamlike mazes. Electric pumps spewed wavering strings of pearl-like bubbles.

"Actually, some people think I'm despicable. I like to think I'm a real animal rights booster, but some of the righters think all pet stores ought to be firebombed. Me, I think getting people, especially kids, to take care of a pet is one of the few ways we have of getting them to value animals. All animals. Pets are good for people. Or a necessary evil, anyway."

"And they're pretty," Terry said. "These fish are pretty."

"Pretty? Course they're pretty."

"Maybe that's what I need. An aquarium."

"Probably you don't. Most people think they need aquariums don't."

"You're not much of a salesman."

"Well I don't know about that. Hey, I've got two stores. We're paying the bills and still making a little money. You might say I'm not doing so bad, Terry."

"Maybe you're right, and I don't need an aquarium, but they just seem so pretty."

"Pretty? Well, I grant you these guys are pretty, but they're not my favorites. You want to see my favorites?"

Kopp's face, too, was benefitted by these surroundings. In the bathing, darting light of the fish tanks, his features had taken on a blazed expression of enthrallment. He had looked so queer, so ill at ease, at Belinda's. Here, manifestly, he belonged.

Reveling in his role, he swaggered down the aisle, Terry behind him, and pointed—by means of a casual outward swing of his elbow—at one of the aquariums. Terry obediently leaned over and peered into it. For a moment his glance turned up nothing remarkable. Then he spotted, half-hidden behind foliage, a creature of contours as graceful as those of a question mark: an ivory sea horse, its elegantly elongated nose tucked into its mailed chest, its tail spun into a circle. Kopp reached forward and scratched at the glass, as one would at a simple itch, and the sea horse dipped its body and tilted its head, apparently staring full at their two faces. "Thataboy," Kopp said, in just the tone you'd use in addressing a real horse.

"That's no boy. Look at the belly. She's pregnant."

"It's a boy all right, although you *could* call him pregnant. He's got eggs in his brood pouch. A pregnant female put them there. With an ovipositor."

"You got to be kidding."

"Not kidding. Welcome to the world of Nature, Terry."

"Listen to you."

"I overcharge like crazy on sea horses, if you want to know the truth, I'm a real price-gouger. Pick 'em up for a couple bucks and sell 'em for twenty-five or thirty apiece. They're so fine and delicate, you see, that I hate to sell 'em at all. Each one goes out the store, I feel I've given him a death sentence. The female's in there too, but she's playing hide-and-seek. I like to give 'em a choice—they don't have to come out on exhibit unless they feel like it."

Terry's gaze nudged here and there through the glinting water in search of the female. The middle of the tank held a rust-red stone the size of a head of cabbage, and riddled like a cabbage with involutions and recesses, and down one of these, a crevice no larger than a keyhole, Terry caught a rusty sparkle—a fluent swaying quick as a blink—which, with a blink of his eyes, was gone.

"Come on," Kopp said. "I'll show you some birds."

The two of them were alone in the store. Kopp had locked the front door and said farewell to the teenage boy—a gangly bespectacled kid whose pants and shirtsleeves were both too short—who'd worked the cash register tonight. It had been odd for Terry to confront the notion that (for somebody in this world, anyway) Squirrely Kopp was "the boss." But it had come to seem less odd during the last ten minutes or so. In his speech, his movements, the set of his gaze—everything—Kopp was obviously meant to be the place's proprietor. This was Kopp's domain, Kopp's animal kingdom.

There were a dozen or so parakeets, and two comical birds with tufted roosterlike ruffs that turned out to be toucans, and one spectacularly polychromatic parrot, whose periodic gargantuan cries ripped the room in half.

"Look at those, those are amazing," Terry said, pointing at the parrot's stony-gray feet, which were fissured with innumerable wrinkles.

"Aren't they? Aren't they *ugly?*" Kopp exulted.

"Where's he come from—Africa?"

"The States, he's bred here in the States. Me, I'd never deal with imported birds—too many of them die along the way. And it depletes the jungle."

"Is that right?" Terry said, and at once a broad, undifferentiating envy brushed over him. He had expected that Just Off the Ark would interest him, entertain him, possibly even enlighten him about the Kopper—but never in a million years would he have expected it to instill envy. And yet, surrounded by the unexampled ingenuities of Nature herself, he couldn't help feeling that a store of this sort was a positive, tangible, visible social good—and that it wore its usefulness more openly than Hamill, Hillman ever could. It was theoretically possible, Terry knew, for a communications lawyer to enjoy a sense of forthright social utility; there was the comfort, if always somewhat tenuous and abstruse, of knowing that you were helping a complicated legal process to function. But such feelings were chancy and fugitive. Far more readily graspable, whether deserved or not, was a sense that, since the firm (like pretty much every firm) worked in effect for the highest bidder, what was daily being transacted was at bottom a kind of prostitution. That was Adam's view—who had to be credited, anyway, with a desire to strip away all conscience-salving constructions and face the truth head on. *We do snuggle up to them that pays,* is the way he would put it.

Kopp gave Terry a tour of the mammals: Siamese kittens, Persian kittens, two golden retriever pups, a cocker spaniel, a toy poodle, rabbits, and some hamsters, including one that—throwing himself hopelessly into a cliché—ran round and round inside a wheel. "I won't keep monkeys. Used to, but they attract the wrong sort of people. Real weirdos and crazies. I've got all sorts of theories about people want to keep monkeys. I used to try to steer people away from them—I even wrote up a little booklet about them, and I'd ask people who were interested to take it home and read it before they made any purchase—but in the end I just gave 'em up.

"I confess there are times," Kopp went on, "when I do think it's wrong to sell a pet to *any*body—at least to anybody hasn't been certified sane by a reputable shrink. I'm not kidding, there are all sorts of sickos out there. I could tell you stories would make you vomit."

"Try me . . ."

Terry was given an assessive look, which was followed by a little toothy bray of laughter, and then, immediately, by a treatise on animal ailments. There was a good deal of technical detail. Kopp sounded ready to be licensed as a veterinarian. It all came forth in a tumble of mostly unfamiliar terms: hypospadia in golden retrievers, distemper and eye infections in bulldogs, herbal flea collars (citronella, pennyroyal, eucalyptus, cedarwood, rue), FUS (feline urinary syndrome), colloid coating to protect fish from abrasions, sterilizers, bioreactors, chillers, heaters, calcium leaching, ammonia poisoning, the calcium/phosphorus balance in reptiles. He interrupted a disquisition on ringworm to say, "You hungry? Want something to eat?"

"Sure."

"I thought we might go to my place. That sound all right?"

"That sounds fine," Terry said. "Fine and dandy."

It turned out that the most striking thing about Kopp's apartment was that it smelled like Kopp. Terry had forgotten the smell—had forgotten, even, that there was such a thing as an individuating Kopp-odor. Not a strong smell, and not such a bad one either—almost comfy in its way. But, like one's fingerprints, a characteristic of personal fidelity over the decades: this was just the way Kopp's room had smelled from the first, from freshman year.

The furnishings were, from the standpoint of anyone collecting Kopp anecdotes, disappointingly ordinary. The place was dark, but not obsessively so. Dominating the room, incandescently illuminated, were three aquariums—a huge one devoted to a wide array of freshwater tropicals, a saltwater tank for sea horses and anemones, and another saltwater tank given over entirely to clownfish and one hefty lemon-yellow tang fish. There was a desk and a deskchair, a black imitation-leather couch, and a glass coffee table seemingly identical to one that Terry had picked up at Sears, long years ago, when he'd gone down to Charlottesville for law school. This was piled with magazines (*Natural History, Smithsonian, Scientific American, Time,* and, somewhat surprisingly, *People*) and books (what looked like a college biology textbook, an Agatha Christie novel, a science fiction novel called *Solaris,* Joseph Campbell's *The Hero with a Thousand Faces,* and—another unexpected choice—something called *The Art of Micronesia*). Nothing in all the decor that deserved to be filed away as a Curly Classic.

Kopp greeted his fish—said "Hey guys"—peered into each of the tanks for a moment, and, evidently satisfied, took a seat in the deskchair. "Sit down," he said.

"Thanks." Terry took a seat on the couch.

"You want a drink? I don't drink—not alcohol drinks—but there's a bottle of sherry or whiskey or something."

"I don't either. I quit. Or've temporarily given it up, anyway."

"There's pot you prefer pot. I'll sometimes light me up a joint after work."

"No, nothing like that, thanks. So," Terry said, "you like Baltimore?"

"You know I think I *do.* I think I like living in a place that's always needing to be apologetic. Course, Baltimore's always apologizing for not being Washington. That was one of the few things I liked about Princeton, actually—the way everybody felt a need to explain why they weren't at Harvard or Yale. You like Washington?"

"I guess I must. Though I wish I had some ready reason for liking it, the way you do. Obviously, after all these years it's *home,*" Terry said, but this really wasn't so. The strangest thing about living in Washington, really, was how little even now it felt like home to him. "I've considered moving. It's a little hard to move, actually, given my specialty. I mean most communications lawyers are headquartered in Washington. It's just—well it's not as if I'm *trapped* or anything."

"I'll get us something to munch on," Kopp said, and bounced out of his chair, reminding Terry how an earlier Kopp, in the old days when he must have been fifteen pounds lighter, was forever bouncing out of seats.

As Terry had already begun to suspect at Belinda's, Kopp's vegetarianism went unaccompanied by any nutritional concerns. He returned from the kitchen with a big bag of something called Doodle-O's ("crisper than any chip" the package promised) and a bag of Cajun Cookin' Corn Crunchies and a plastic container of Velvet Green Onion Dip. He certainly hadn't given up meat for his health.

"So what led you into pet shops?" Terry asked him. "Back in college days I don't remember you as—as any sort of Nature Boy."

Kopp threw down a pair of Corn Crunchies, heavily weighted with onion dip, and said, talking while he chewed, "I'm still not. I mean I don't much go in for hiking. Or camping with the bloodsuckers."

"Mm?"

"Mosquitoes, deerflies, vampire bats . . ."

"Vampire bats?"

"I do most of my traveling in this chair, courtesy of *Natural History* magazine."

"Of course even then, way back then, you were selling Mexican jumping beans."

For just a moment Curly halted his chewing and a flicker of emotion passed over his face, but so fleetingly it wasn't clear whether of embarrassment or pride. "Actually, I sort of half-walked, half-fell into pet stores. You remember I studied engineering for a while at M.I.T."

"That's right."

"That's what I was doing the time I came to see you, in Virginia, when you were in law school."

"That's right. You did come. I'd nearly forgotten that."

Terry *had* forgotten—but, in his defense, the visit had been forgettably brief. Kopp had been heading down to Texas, to visit the aunt and uncle who had raised him (and whom, evidently, he'd now not laid eyes on in ten years), and, proceeding under some obscure Kopp-motivation, he'd decided to drive rather than fly the however-many thousands of miles from Massachusetts to Texas. He'd arrived in a rusty orange VW bug, had spent one night with Terry, and departed early the next morning.

"Betsy's parents still live in Charlottesville," Terry said. "She was from there. That's where we met. She was always going down there. Sometimes almost every weekend. Her father was sick. He's better now I guess."

"That was the last time I saw you," Kopp went on. "Until that day on a DC street corner."

"Is that right? That's right, isn't it?" Terry said, and added, for Curly's surer command of their friendship's dissipation seemed a tacit rebuke: "You didn't show up at any of the reunions."

Kopp laughed—that high little strangled snort of a laugh. "Can you see me showing up at a class reunion?"

"Not very easily, no."

"Anyway, I quit M.I.T., went to work for Blare, Keating, they do aerodynamic design, quit them about ten minutes before they were going to fire me, went to work for an outfit called Advec, engineering consultants I guess you'd call them, worked there five years, did okay I guess, but it got clearer and clearer I was never meant to work for anybody."

"Oh? And why's that?"

"Come on, Terry, come off it." Kopp picked up a couple of Doodle-O's and a couple of Corn Crunchies and threw the combination into his mouth. "Hey, you know it as well as I do. That I don't exactly fit into organizational things. Let's face it, I'm a weird guy, at least in most people's eyes." And in Kopp's own eyes—despite the exaggeratedly pinched, close-set narrowness of his gaze—Terry beheld a spaciousness he'd never found there before. No, this sort of ability—Kopp's being able to perceive himself lucidly from the outside—was altogether new. After a fashion, anyway, Kopp clearly had been busy over the years. He had made progress, had (as the radio and TV talk shows would have it) *grown.*

"So I decided I'll start my own business. And I look around, try to figure out where I might make a go of things. Figured I'd do better at a business didn't require lots of connections, lots of chumming around. And figured I'd do better where you had to learn lots of things. I've always liked learning things, provided I could choose what they are, and I'm good at it, learning things, and having to learn things might also keep me from getting bored. So somebody was selling a pet store, and I didn't buy it but I almost did. I was interested. Did a lot of research, went to some conventions. The next time I found one up for sale, I bought in."

Curly bounced out of his chair and over to the glass coffee table. He opened a Band-Aid tin and upended its contents into his palm: a thin little joint and a pack of matches. He lit the cigarette, puffed upon it a couple of times, and returned to his chair, carrying the Band-Aid tin, which had become his ashtray.

In college Kopp had been opposed to pot—for obscure reasons that at first seemed uncharacteristically moralistic and later looked like simple fear—and on those rare occasions when Terry, who'd harbored his own inhibitions, had been cajoled into sharing a joint with somebody, he'd always sought to conceal his state from Curly. And now it turned out that, for Terry, the complicated feelings of guilt which used to drift up from the end of a joint still lingered in the air—so that he expected Curly to display some counterpart trace of self-consciousness or sheepishness. But Curly seemed utterly insouciant as he puffed, puffed, puffed upon his withered cigarette.

Terry rose from the couch and strode over to the desk in the corner. There was a photograph on the wall. It was a girl from a magazine. "What did you cut her out for?"

This little symbolic action—placing the photo of an unknown girl over your desk—seemed just the sort of young, collegiate gesture that Kopp would never have made in college. The girl was dark and unplaceably ethnic—Eurasian, perhaps. Gazing out over a bare, bony shoulder, she offered you an enigmatic, sidelong glance. From between her glossy lips the tip of her tongue had poked out shyly, or daringly, or dauntedly, or even determinedly—it *was* a wonderfully ambiguous expression.

"Cause I liked her?"

"What magazine's she from?"

"I don't remember. It was an ad."

"An ad for what?"

Getting no response, Terry turned toward Kopp, whose clouded look suggested that the inquiry was a not-altogether-minor invasion of privacy. Finally, Kopp said, "I think it was Congam, the computer people. Speaking of photographs above a desk, whatever happened to your scoutmaster?"

"My scoutmaster? I was never in Scouts."

"The guy whose photograph you had over your desk . . . The guy in the windbreaker."

"Photograph? Over my desk?"

"Freshman year."

"Oh . . . You mean Coach Kramm! God what a memory you've got! I forgot completely about putting his picture over my desk."

"So whatever happened to him?"

"To him? Beats me. He moved from Gawana ages ago, crazy old Coach Kramm. He was sort of a religious fanatic, actually. Maybe like your aunt and uncle?"

"Let's hope not . . ."

"He took me to his church one time. They met in a garage—literally—and some of them went nuts, I'd never seen anything like it. Jumping all over the place. *Full* of the Holy Spirit. And on the drive home he explains how there's nothing unscientific, from his point of view, and he's a chemistry teacher remember, about how long they lived in the Bible, Methuselah and the gang, because the world was so *fresh* back then. Back then you see the world was so *fresh*." Terry laughed—and yet to speak these words was to invoke, even now, an atmosphere of murky betrayal, one in which it wasn't clear whether Kramm had betrayed *him,* by revealing a strain of lunacy within, or whether Terry, in sharing this belittling anecdote, was betraying an old mentor. "But he was also a real hero for me, standing out there by the vault pit in all his endless patience, saying over and over and over again, 'It's all in the mind, it's all in the mind, it's all in the mind.'"

"Back when you were battling on behalf of the Gawana Iguanas."

Terry laughed. "We were the Gawana *Eagles* actually."

"You wanted to talk about something."

"Mm?"

"You had something in mind you wanted to talk about. In the parking lot the other night, that's what you said."

"Oh a lot of things, lots of things I'd like to talk about. You want to hear about my job?"

Kopp exhaled a blue, enervated cloud of smoke. "Lawyers generally bore me . . ."

"Fair enough . . . Perfectly fair enough. You want to hear about my family?"

"How's your sister?"

"She's all excited about Diana. You remember she had a daughter named Diana?"

"Course I do. They came up to see us. Your sister, her husband, and the kid."

"Oh God that's *right,* isn't it."

"Cute kid."

"Still is. Only she's not such a kid. In fact she's actually planning—"

"And the oil got on her dress."

"Oil? On Diana's dress?"

"No. Your sister's. Don't you remember? It was sort of my fault. I'd found that really weird hunk of machinery in the dump behind the engineering lab, and I brought it in for a closer look, and that's how the oil got on her dress."

"That's right, poor Kaye, I remember now." Here it was again, Kopp's tenacious memory acting as an implicit reproach, though there was some comfort in supposing that Kopp could recollect everything with such tenacity only because so little of note had befallen him in the meantime. "She and Ralph, her husband, are divorced, incidentally. She's seeing a new guy, Glenn, who's in real estate. I told you she lives here in Baltimore. She's all excited because Diana's getting married."

"Married! How old's she, twelve?"

"Twenty-two. That was twenty years ago they came to visit us."

"Fair enough. Your parents are the same?"

"Pretty much exactly. Dad's retired now, but he still speaks in reverent tones about life insurance. I suppose I do too. It's a great invention, historically speaking. Insurance is one of the world's great inventions. And he still builds things. Amazing squirrel-proof bird feeders, that kind of thing. He's also become a stage-designer, in a manner of speaking. He helped do the sets for the high school play. And Mob, you remember I called my mom Mob, she's just the same." Which wasn't quite true, of course—and perhaps this was the place to take an initial, downward step, this the moment for the furtherance of confessions; Terry had a long way to venture, after all, if he was ever to open the topic he most wanted to discuss. "One thing, though—she seems to have started drinking sometimes. That's new. And it's very worrisome."

"Rots the brain," Kopp replied cheerfully.

"Yes . . ." But there was worse to it than that . . . How was Terry to convey just how profoundly upsetting—cataclysmic— was the vision of a lurching, drunken Mob? "You never met my wife," he said. "Betsy."

"No."

"She taught school. Fourth grade. She used to tell me all about her students, until I felt as though I knew them almost. She didn't always get along with Mob. I mean it wasn't that they *couldn't* get along. Maybe Betsy was a little bit too forceful, like Mob, and that was the problem. She was big, too, not quite so big as Mob, maybe, but boy"—Terry shook his head, marveling anew, with pleasure, at the remarkable woman who had once been his wife—"she sure could be headstrong."

Back then, there'd been a perception at the firm (he had gradually come around to understanding) that he was henpecked. Nobody was blatant about it—just little references, now and then, to what Betsy would "allow" or "put up with." To what she would "let him do." But all of that had been all right. He hadn't minded—had hardly minded at all. And there could be a kind of sweet, unwitting humor to it, like the time when, in a

phone conversation with his father-in-law, he referred to her as
the boss ("Hold on, I'll put the boss on") and she ordered him
(*commanded* him?) never to call her that again.

"She had a miscarriage, a couple of years before the accident,
and you know in retrospect I don't think she ever really fully
recovered. You read sometimes about postpartum depression
and I think that's kind of what she had." No, it hadn't been
Betsy's stubbornness or forcefulness that had been hard to live
with; what was painful, *really* painful, was the listlessness of the
last years. He'd expected, for instance, that she would go ape—
pitch a fit, hit the roof—on the day when he came home and
announced that he'd guaranteed to underwrite Diana's college
education. But Betsy'd done nothing of the sort. She'd stared
out the window. She'd stared for a long while out the kitchen
window and then what she'd actually said—mutedly, and as
though over a long, chilly expanse—was, "It won't do us any
good. Not as far as Kaye's concerned. It won't shut her up. She
still won't leave us alone." (And the odd thing was that Betsy
had always *liked* Kaye; they'd always gotten on so well together.)

"I should make us something to eat," Kopp said. "Come in
the kitchen. We can talk in there."

The kitchen, too, was dark, and seemed older than the rest of
the apartment. The gas stove, black with rust and grease, looked
like a museum piece. Terry leaned against the refrigerator and
went on talking—about the delight Betsy had taken in the car
he'd bought her (a red Mustang), her love of tennis, her almost
nightly long distance calls to her sister Heidi (in those days before Heidi and her husband moved to Frankfurt), and how
(later, when things began to turn a little weird or wrong) she'd
finally gone to some doctors, including a shrink, and she'd been
put on some pills, and then other pills, and then others. That
had been the worst of it—not that the pills had made her
strange, exactly, but they'd introduced a variable, an x in the
equation: it was the not knowing, whenever she seemed uncharacteristically vague or languid or lazy, what was to be attributed
to her and what to the medicine. When she began in a serious
way to put on weight, for instance—who or what was to be
blamed for that? Was he supposed to sympathize, or chastise

her? Not that he minded the weight *per se* (he'd somehow never succumbed to what he liked to call the adoration of the anorexic) but there was always the worry that in its ascent her weight might find no natural resting place—that she would just go on, go up, go higher and higher. And the thought that the difference in their respective weights might eventually reach the point of comedy—as Mob and Dad, particularly on a dance floor, sometimes looked comical—was disturbing. Oh, yes: the threat, Betsy's deadly implicit threat, that she was going to turn the two of them into something ridiculous—that *had* been unnerving. Meanwhile, on waking, on retiring, he heard the snake-rattle of the pills, and it had reached the point for Terry that the mere sound of them, their little bump and jiggle in a plastic cannister, had made him sick. He forgets this now sometimes, but it really had made his intestines slither—that's how godawful it had been. So that, when she started heading down to Charlottesville nearly every weekend on her own, because her dad was supposed to be so gravely ill, there'd been some relief in that. Though he'd missed her—he'd always missed her.

As Terry talked, Kopp went busily about his business: he brought out a pan, adjusted a burner beneath it, filled it with a shallow pool of grease, and poured some sort of batter into it.

"I think," Terry went on, "that's the main reason why, after the accident, I never went to a shrink myself. I'd found the whole thing so unnerving, the never being certain what was her and what was merely pharmaceutical. I think I was frightened of getting lost inside it."

Kopp's response was: "I defy you to tell me what it is I'm cooking." Was he listening to a single word? These were not easy things to confess to.

"Smells vaguely familiar . . ."

"I de*fy* you to tell me. Now have a seat. Have a seat."

The little kitchen table had been recessed into a corner, flush against the walls, so the two of them sat on the open edges, at a right angle to each other. Kopp brought forth from the fridge a container of potato salad and a container of cole slaw and a jar of sweet pickles and a carton of milk. No serving dishes, or anything of the sort. Terry helped himself to potato salad and cole slaw, using the same spoon for both; he decided to skip the pickles.

"Here we go," Kopp said, sliding from the frying pan onto Terry's plate what looked like a gray, thick, frayed pancake. "Now you tell me what that is."

Dubiously, Terry took a small bite. It was greasy—a bit like fried dough—but with a spicy, peppery under-flavor. "I haven't a clue . . ."

"Does it help if I say you introduced me to it?"

"That *I* did?"

"When I came to see you in Charlottesville. On my drive to Texas."

Terry took another, larger bite. There was a vaguely char-coaled flavor as well—but this was probably the result of Kopp's having burnt it slightly. "There's some mistake, Kopper. You've got to be mistaken."

"Don't you remember? What you served me? You'd cut the recipe out of a newspaper."

"This time *your* memory's got to be letting you down . . ."

"And I copied it out after dinner. Don't you remember? You served Salmon Diablo."

"Salmon?" There was no salmon here . . .

"Well I never *did* like salmon, even when I used to eat fish, but I liked the breading. I eat this stuff all the time."

Terry washed down the greasy spiced cake with a swallow of milk. "Let me see if I've got this right," he began. "What you're telling me is, you're telling me that what you eat all the time is Salmon Diablo without the salmon?"

"Actually, how I prefer to think of it," Kopp said, sliding a gray pancake onto his own plate, "what I would prefer you to call it when you dine Chez Kevin, is Salmon Diablo *sans* Salmon. Sounds classier."

This revelation was, in its way, vigorously liberating. Out of a desire not to seem slightly crazy Terry had been holding back his confidences—holding them back, that is, from somebody who regularly dined on Salmon Diablo *sans* Salmon. This was Kopp, after all. This was Kopp and Terry had gone to the trouble of renewing their friendship largely because Kopp was in no position to call anybody—anybody!—crazy. "Have you ever had a hallucination?" Terry began.

"A hallucination?"

"Yes. Okay. Because you see I did. Just a couple weeks ago, in fact. And nothing like that had ever happened to me before. I live in a rational world. That isn't a boast, it's just a statement of fact. But a very important statement of fact. That's the way my life is . . ."

"Go on."

"And then, just a couple weeks ago, I saw someone, just as clearly as I'm seeing you now, only this someone wasn't there. This was someone who in fact couldn't be there. You've got to understand, I don't live in a world where I'm the sort of person who sees hallucinations . . ."

"That's true almost by definition, isn't it?"

"How do you mean?" Terry said.

"As soon as you call it a hallucination, you're saying the whole thing was unreal—and most of us, by definition, don't live with what we consider is unreal."

"What are you saying?"

"That you're proceeding tautologically? Or maybe I'm saying, Suppose it wasn't . . ."

"What wasn't? Wasn't what?" In this dark kitchen Kopp's *Suppose* had a burnish to it. It carried glints of light. These were slips of light cast off from some faraway, vast, unreckoned body of light.

"Wasn't a hallucination, hm? In the first place, just from the standpoint of science, isn't that bad science, Terry? When something inexplicable happens, to rule out various things at the outset? That's just one of the hypotheses we eventually must test, isn't it? By the way, it was Betsy you saw, wasn't it?" Oh, Kopp's eyes held the glow of fierce industry! Of tough deduction. He'd been listening all along. He hadn't missed a thing.

"Okay. That's right."

"We need to test all sorts of hypotheses, don't we? Only one of which is Coach Kramm's."

"Coach Kramm's?" Things were moving fast—just a little too fast for Terry.

"It's all in the mind, it's all in the mind, it's all in the mind," Kopp chanted. Oh, those eyes of his—blazing away under the now-bald brow, blazing away between those clownish balls of hair above his ears!

And this was another reason why Terry had felt the need to call Kopp when Betsy, wearing a simple T-shirt and towel, had shown up before him: the little guy was *quick,* wasn't he? Oh yes. There was that, too. Such a clever, such a clever little squirrel.

"Gad, you're a pig."

"You're not doing so badly yourself." While it was true that Terry had already worked through four massive squares of their deep-dish pizza, the Kopper wasn't far behind. He'd finished three. One slice remained.

"Hey at least I pay the price. I'm ten to fifteen pounds heavier than college days. Have you gained a single pound?"

"I think I've lost a couple." Terry laughed buoyantly. "Adam's always going on about that. About my 'enviably inefficient metabolism.' It really drives him crazy—he's always dieting. Speaking of which, you want that last piece?"

"You go ahead. I'm saving room for the cheesecake. It's good here. Incidentally, I brought something along to help us."

"And what's that?" Terry reached toward the remaining slice.

"A notebook."

Terry's hand halted. "You're planning to take notes? What sort of notes? What about?"

"About you. More specifically, about the night when you had yourself an uninvited visitor." With scurrying little strokes Kopp scratched first at the ball of his nose, then at the bottom of one of his ears. His narrow eyes were bright as fresh-struck matches.

"Maybe I'm not sure I *want* you taking notes."

"Suit yourself. But it's like I told you the other night at dinner."

"What other night?"

"At that place—at Paco's Cellar. That's the first thing you got to decide—whether it makes you too nervous or whether you really do want to investigate this thing seriously."

"Suit yourself," Terry said, of the notebook propped against the table, and to illustrate to Kopp just how little such issues concerned him, he nonchalantly lifted up the last slice of pizza and took a substantial bite.

Kopp opened the notebook and held a pen at the ready. "Okay, so let's run through it again. The last twenty-four hours before the—the what? We need an unbiased term."

"Incident?"

"Good. The last twenty-four hours. You were in Marquette, Michigan."

"I was in Marquette, Michigan," Terry repeated. "Our clients are supposed to be based up there, but they're really based in Detroit. They're interested in putting up what we call a class C-2 television station. That's pretty small stuff. Class two's are restricted to a five-hundred-foot tower. Regular class C's can run all the way up to two thousand feet. We're talking an initial capital outlay of say a half million dollars. Meanwhile, there's a Chicago-based group that's filed a competing application. So we're talking to their lawyers. One of them was this woman, Allison Collier—she made quite a thing about being called Allison—and as I told you she was quite good-looking. Now why is it"—Terry interrupted himself—"that when I tell you about radio licenses you don't write anything down, but when I tell you about a good-looking woman your pen starts wagging?"

"Cut it out, Terry."

"Just kidding, just kidding."

"The woman, then. Tell me about the woman."

"Well there isn't that much more to say. We were talking business most of the time. She wasn't wearing a bra. She had kind of cross-eyes. She was fair-skinned, dark-haired. As I say, there isn't that much to say."

"We'll get back to her. Tell me what else you did in Marquette."

"Nothing really."

"Sight-seeing?"

"Not really. I did go out and look at the lake."

"The lake?"

"That's right. Superior."

"And what did you think when you looked at the lake?"

"What did I think?"

"That's think as in 'think.' What was on your mind?"

There was something just faintly annoying in the gravity of Kopp's expression, the poised-pen readiness. "I thought, Hey, wow, what a big lake."

Kopp busily scribbled something and Terry said, "Okay, I can see what you're getting at but isn't it all rather *too* obvious? I expected more subtlety out of you, Kevin. Lake equals ocean equals drowning equals Betsy, isn't that it?" The words came out boldly. Forcefully.

"And what if I tell you that that wasn't what I was thinking at all?"

Their glances locked. It was Kopp who broke the silence. "So you were attracted to this Allison?"

"Yeah—okay. Sure, I was attracted to her."

"And what did you do after you left her?"

"Went back to my room and went to bed."

"And?"

"What do you mean, 'And?' "

"And anything more to be said in relation to your being attracted to her?"

"Oh yes. Forgive me, how *could* I have forgotten. The middle of the night she calls me up and says, Come quick, lover boy, I want your body."

"You know something—you're a natural shrinkee."

"Shrinkee?" Terry repeated the term in a mincing voice, to register just how inane he found it.

"That's the one being shrunk. You're a natural—all your defenses are in fine working order. You were telling me about what you did back in your room . . ."

"I *did* have trouble sleeping—but it wasn't her. Anyway, I'm up at the crack of dawn, get on a flight, and happen to be seated beside another attractive woman. This one, her name's Kelly, she's blonde, early twenties, works in a video store, and you can put down in your dirty little book that I was attracted to her, too."

"Dirty?"

"Just kidding. Clean thoughts in a clean mind, right?"

"What did she remind you of?"

"Remind me of? Nobody."

"Who does she remind you of now?"

"I don't know. Maybe a girl I went out with in high school, Claudia Dowling, who was my girlfriend for a while? That was quite intense, actually, although we didn't sleep together. Or to be clinically precise, we slept together but never had penetration. But did you know, and I never would have admitted it then, that when I arrived at Princeton I was a virgin? That isn't something that's supposed to happen any more, I know, not even among us corny backwoods Iowans, but it happened to me. Do you suppose I was the only virgin at Princeton?"

"Beats me." Kopp had never been very forthcoming in such matters. But back then, for various reasons, Terry wouldn't have wanted him to be.

"I've sort of gone back to being a virgin, if you want to know the truth. I mean, I might as well be. That's pretty much my lifestyle these days."

Terry wasn't sure that he would be willing—ever—to disclose anything to the Kopper about being sexually dysfunctional. Certainly wasn't going to go into the details—the sense of turbulence, of panic, of estrangement, culminating in that lunatic moment when an inner voice had proclaimed, *That's not my dick.* But to go *this* far, to admit to living a life of chaste removal, was somehow quite satisfying. There was nothing pathetic about it at all, at least when the words were delivered in Terry's tone of matter-of-fact forthrightness. Indeed, it was almost an expression of mastery—revealing, as it did, an ability to accept ungrudgingly a very lousy situation.

"So I get into Washington, it looks like it's going to storm, it's a typical day at the office, I get and make a few calls, I have a long lunch with Adam . . ." Terry debated for a fraction of a second mentioning the two martinis, but decided not to. No point in making things too easy for Curly.

"Who called? Who did you call?"

"Well I got a call from a religious fanatic, for one." Terry brought up this particular call, which clearly had nothing to do with anything, in a spirit of perversity—as an illustration for Curly of just how futile were these grabbings after the least relevant minutiae of the day.

But Kopp appeared interested. "Oh?" he said. "And what sort of religious fanatic?"

"God only knows. Maybe he wasn't a religious fanatic. It occurred to me afterwards—I hung up on him, by the way—that he might merely be an economic doomsayer. He said something about 'coverage' and 'downside risk.' But I *think* he was a religious fanatic—he made all sorts of vague threats about the state of my soul."

"Oh I like that about 'downside risk'—that's good."

"What are you talking about?"

"I'm talking about your incident?"

"And pray do tell me what possible relevance does any crank call have to that? I'm afraid I don't see it, Kevin."

"Don't you?"

"No sir, sorry, uh-uh, nix. No doubt it's thickheaded of me but I'm afraid I don't."

"And don't you see at all how inconsistent you're being, Terry? On the one hand, wanting to uphold the notion—while the whole time denying that that's what you're doing—that maybe you've been visited by an actual spirit. Something genuinely supernatural. On the other hand, insisting that everything else in the world is just as it always was. Your so-described soi-disant rational world."

"Listen to you . . ."

"That's not a bad idea, incidentally. Listening to me." Curly shrugged. "Put it this way: if spirits are walking the earth, who's to say *who* it was who telephoned you?"

"Okay, shoot. Hit me, doctor. Who are you suggesting?"

"Voices from the *under*world? Hm? How's that for 'coverage'? For 'downside risk'?"

"Is that what you think, Curly?"

"Actually, it *isn't* what I think, Terry, as a matter of fact—but that's not the point."

"The point is that I may be getting phone calls from ol' Cloven-foot himself, is that it? Or, more likely, given what a busy guy he must be, from one of his henchmen. Is that it?"

"You want to know what the point is? The point is that you're saying, Let's pursue a possibility, and then you're saying, But let's not *really* pursue it. The point is, if what you saw is somehow real, then what the hell does that say about reality?"

"Are you asking me, What is reality?"

"I would be if I thought you had any sort of answer for me . . ."

Oh, Terry had been here before! This was the way conversations had so often proceeded—and *this* was the true reason why he'd refused to live with Kopp after freshman year. He hadn't liked this sensation of being outmaneuvered, outwitted, outflanked . . . The suspicion that Kopp, when it came down to the unsavory roots of life, had a rigor, an unflinchingness, against which Terry was no match.

Terry tried a new tack: "I'm just trying to keep things from getting out of hand."

"*Out of hand?* Terry, your deceased wife shows up wearing one of your very own T-shirts and you're talking about keeping things in hand?"

"There are—there are aberrations," Terry replied, feeling with this word that he still had available to him, could he but clarify his thinking sufficiently, a considerable body of fixed, mathematical evidence in his favor. Help lay in the realm of the actuaries: the statistician's understanding that, given an earth of sufficiently colossal numbers, even the miraculous was fully probable. Help lay in Dad's world—the world of the insurance man. "Just because something strange happens doesn't mean the laws of probability have collapsed. Quite the reverse, in fact. Quite the reverse."

"You're trying to fit it in, but it won't fit. Don't you see how inconsistent you're being?"

"Look, you put four billion people, or whatever the figure is, on one planet, and strange things are going to result. That's a mathematical certainty."

"It won't fit. It just won't *fit*."

"You sound like a tailor—try the other jacket, that one's a little tight."

"I like that actually. You could call this place the Fitting Room."

"I prefer to call it Antonio's Pizzeria."

"You said it yourself, not ten minutes ago—yours is not the sort of world where this sort of thing can occur. Don't you see how inconsistent you're being?"

Inconsistent? Yes, all right—and Terry experienced an abrupt collapse within. Kopp was right and there was no arguing with him: it wouldn't *fit*. And yet, in this moment before publicly conceding defeat Terry sensed, amid all sorts of misgivings, that he was agreeing to far more than the question posed: he was putting himself in Curly's hands. "I guess so," he admitted, and then could not help adding, in a voice suddenly turned respectful and importunate: "Kevin, what do you think? What do *you* think it was that happened to me?"

But if Kopp could stand up stoutly to Terry's petulance and sarcasm and evasiveness, he was again no match for this urgent, open-eyed, heartfelt candor; his Squirrel's eyes darted away, he scratched at the base of his ear: "I dunno. I'm just getting started, Terry. Tell me some more. Tell me what you saw in that other fitting room. Tell me what you saw in the cabin."

"I think I'd rather tell you about finding the cabin first."

So Terry chronicled the whole journey once more. The cab to National. The takeoff just as the storm was breaking. Renting the car at Norfolk. The drive through the gathering darkness . . . Only, in *this* retelling all sorts of details came back with lightninglike vividness: the car rental woman with her humorously thick accent, the dense sea of Mexican cheese sauce, the way the T-Bird changed colors while he was inside buying a Coke, even the names on the homemade signs as he drove that final mile, Absen, Butscher, Coldwell. There was, needless to say, a tinge of absurdity to all this: the dutiful trotting out of all these inconsequentialities, while Curly Kopp, head lowered, more squirrely than ever in his industrious determination to hoard away these nutlike kernels of information, busied himself with their transcription. (Kopp even seemed to make a note of the fact that the boy at the little grocery store had a mouth ringed with pimples!) And yet, ludicrous or even lunatic as this whole business was, when Terry found that he'd tracked his own footsteps to that moment in which, operating by the sideways glow of the T-Bird's headlights, he'd fitted the key in the lock (and how easily the key had turned! The door had, as it were, sprung open), he felt an avalanching coldness slide over him. It frightened him. Going back there, even now, truly *frightened* him.

"Good God," Terry said. "I haven't told you about Bertha! Now, you see, central to *any* understanding of my life is Bertha, dear Bertha, my cross to bear through all the years to come."

"Bertha?"

"My secretary. These days the preferred term's assistant, I know, but Bertha, for her own inexplicable reasons, dislikes it. Actually, that phrase *for her own inexplicable reasons* is something one uses a lot when talking about Bertha. Good Lord, she's weird—even *you* would think she's weird. She has this emaciated body and her hands are all sort of—" But just as he was embarking on a gruesomely hyperbolic portrait, a wild thought came over Terry. What if (just supposing)—what if Bertha and Curly were to hit it off? What if—what if a courtship were to be succeeded by a wedding, and then by Bertha's leaving her widowed aunts to bring her solemn inefficiency to Kopp's dark apartment and the pet-shop business? Wasn't it just possible that their coming together would represent a sort of mathematical one-in-a-billion? The chance encounter of two surpassingly bizarre souls who would discover themselves to be miraculously complementary, with each one's weirdness harmoniously *fitting* the other's weirdness?

"What about her hands? What's so odd about her?"

Absurd as this sudden, compressed daydream might be, Terry hesitated to jinx the works by running down Bertha. No, she wasn't somebody whose life could take much more jinxing. "Oh I don't know. She's actually a fairly bright woman, but she sits there on her lunch hour reading things like *The National Enquirer.*"

"Doesn't sound that peculiar to me."

"No, but you see at some level she really *believes* it. That's the thing about Bertha. At some level she believes that all these preposterous things are true and the scientists are conspiring to keep the truth from us."

"Maybe one of the truths they're concealing concerns visits from the dead . . ."

Quick—the guy was quick.

"Just wait until you meet her," Terry said.

So, for the moment, Bertha, too, had become a topic to be sidestepped. Terry switched the conversation over to Diana and told Curly about the time, years ago, when she fell out of a tree and he'd taken her to the hospital. (It made him shiver even now to think of the strange—the unnatural, the inhuman—way her broken arm had hung.) Terry produced a photograph of her, which Curly studied with frowning intensity in the restaurant's dim light, finally lifting his gaze to peer at Terry with matching incisiveness.

The pizza tray was taken away and two coffees and two cheesecakes were ordered. Feeling that he'd given too much of himself away tonight, perhaps, Terry tried to get Kopp to open up about life since college, but Kevin seemed either wary or perhaps just plain uninterested. Conversation fizzled. Kopp was no better at making small talk now than he'd ever been. He had none of that gift (which Adam possessed in brimming abundance) of taking the everyday objects around you—the menus, storefronts, clothes, passersby—and spinning from them elaborate jokey speculations.

Nor was he any better now at handling the little ceremony of departure. When they stood at last outside the pizzeria, under the streetlights, here was the same greased sliding of the eyes, and a jerky stammer of a handshake, and a voice trailing off just when a firming fellowship was called for.

"Why don't you come to Washington? Adam's dying to meet you."

"Yeah, I dunno, things get busy this time of year."

"He's like nobody you ever met."

"At our age, nobody's like nobody you ever met."

"Come again?" And was this little paradox one to file away with the barber who shaves everyone in the village who does not shave himself?

"It's got nothing to do with *him*," Kopp went on. "If you see what I mean. It's just that you get to be our age, you don't really

meet new people. At this point, everybody's just a reshuffling of
people you've met before."

"You don't really think so," Terry said. "Do you think so? I
meet new people all the time."

"How remarkable."

"Well let's say I come back up to Baltimore. Say Tuesday
night? How's Tuesday night?"

"Actually, you do something even more remarkable, Terry.
You meet people who are no longer among the living . . ."

And was this going too far, was this stepping over the edge?
Ought Terry to feel insulted? In any event, Kopp went on
quickly, in a conciliatory tone: "Well maybe that'd be all right.
You mean just you coming up?" Curly seemed in no hurry to
meet Adam.

"Just me. Tuesday. You working? I could meet you at the
shop."

"Maybe. Why don't you call me?"

"I'll call you." And Terry added, with a hearty amiability that
was meant to disconcert, "Well, it was *great* to see you."

"Yeah. Okay."

When Terry reached home, he headed upstairs first. He liked
this bathroom better. He peed, washed his hands, glanced at
himself in the mirror. He went into the bedroom, glanced over
at his answering machine. (The message light was dormant. It
was a little alarming, maybe, how few people called him.) He
took off his shoes. He padded downstairs to sort the mail, then
came back upstairs to wash his face and brush his teeth. Returning to the bedroom, he stripped down to socks and underwear,
and took a seat on the side of the bed. Something flashed at the
rim of his vision. It was the message light, but how could it be
blinking?

It hadn't been blinking before . . . Or could his eyes have
played a trick on him? Could he himself have blinked in perfect
tandem with the machine? Or perhaps he was just tired. He hit
the replay button.

A click, and then a silence, and then, in place of speech, a
rushed intake of air.

Then a moment in suspension, a holding interlude, followed

by a hard-pressed, grunted exhalation. And then another rushed indrawn breath.

And this time a further, longer holding, while the oxygen burned itself up (who *was* this? *what* was this?), and an abrupt urgent whistling release of air, and a sharp inhalation, almost a gasp. And then a click—the breather was gone.

Terry ran a hand through his hair, stood up, sat down, and played the message, such as it was, through once more: a breath, a pause, an exhalation; a breath, a longer pause, a sharp expulsion of air; and finally that hard desperate drowning gasp, and the click of departure.

The bedroom window was open and somewhere down the street a creature released an odd sound of its own, a low-throated clearing rumble. It was a bird, in all likelihood, though it sounded more like a frog. A car went by, its headlights lapping for a moment against the window screen. Terry played the message through again and halted the machine. He settled the thumb and forefinger of one hand into the sockets of his eyes, shutting out the light, and dropped the other hand into his crotch, crossing his left leg over his fingers and squeezing down upon them. There was comfort in the pressure. He removed the hand from his eyes, uncrossed his legs, and played the tape through once more, this time letting it run on.

After the breathing came another click, and a familiar voice: "Hi, Terry. Just called to see how you're doin'. I need to talk to you about something. Could you give me a call if it's not too late? Bye-ee."

Terry went into the bathroom, opened his fly, discovered that in fact he did not need to pee, returned to the bedroom and immediately dialed Kaye's number before he'd had a chance to talk himself out of it.

"Hello."

"Evening."

"Terry? How ya doin'?"

"Fine, how ya doin'?" He liked the way this came out; it seemed to match with commendable exactitude the dip and rise of her folksy cheerfulness. Really, she was beginning to sound *remarkably* like a nurse. The nurses—we all need protection from the nurses.

"Me?" Kaye said. "Well I'm okay. Of course there's oodles to do . . ."

"To do?"

"Oh *you*," Kaye said. "You *men*," Kaye said and she might almost be flirting with him. "Always so blissfully unaware. So beautifully uninformed. I mean about this wedding. You know we've got to figure out where it will be held."

"It probably's a good idea to find a place to hold it."

"But the really good news, the great great *fabulous* news, is that I think we're going to get him."

"Him?"

"Reverend *Foreman*, Terry."

"Who?"

"I've only told you about him a hundred times. He's only definitely the most famous Episcopalian minister—minister of any kind, probably—in Baltimore. He is a *legend*, Terry. I mean if you could *hear* him! Honestly this voice of his is to-die-and-go-to-heaven-for! This voice is not to be believed. Anyway, it isn't definite, but I think we're going to get him."

"Well that's great."

"And there are all sorts of decisions that can't be made until we make *other* decisions. I mean how big a wedding are we talking about? How fancy a wedding are we talking about?"

It became more and more clear, as Kaye went on, where this conversation was heading. Terry neither assisted nor resisted—merely observed its ineluctable march. "The problem, Terry, quite apart from all the planning and running around involved, which I am more than happy to do on my own, without troubling you in the slightest degree, I wouldn't have things any other way, is that frankly the whole thing's going to require a wad of the green stuff and I don't see where it's all going to come from. Of course, I do have my IRAs."

Out they had come, once again: Kaye's IRAs. It was something of a ritual for her, in moments of pressure or high drama—her magnanimous offer to sell them every one, to strip herself naked of all financial security, to sail forth protectionless toward a noble and necessitous old age. "You better hold on to those," Terry advised her.

"Of course I could go to Mom and Dad. Just for a loan,

nobody's looking for a handout. But you know, with Dad retired and everything, I think they're always worried about the
budget."

Terry said, "No, absolutely not, Kaye, you *don't* want to ask
them." It would just stir up trouble—get Mob all hot and bothered, leave Dad feeling uneasy and inadequate . . .

"Of course, like I told you before, Glenn's offered Diana a
wedding gift of five hundred of the finest. Which is a huge help.
I mean he's not even related to the girl. And he's got a child of
his own to worry about."

Tactically, it was unwise of Kaye to bring up Glenn's offer. In
theory, this was a generous gift, and ought to be accepted as
such. But the self-glorifying way it had been advanced, as
though Glenn had unburdened everybody at one stroke, irked
Terry. The truth was that, in view of the summed expenses of
the affair, the gift didn't actually add up to much. "And how *is*
Glenn's son doing?"

"Tyler? Oh he's the same as ever. Totally hopeless. A job? Did
anyone around here say *job*? The kid doesn't do diddly squat."

Troubling as Kaye's use of slang generally was, it was especially so in cases when, as now, she employed a term he wasn't
altogether sure he understood. Was there actually any sort of
meaning—beyond mild vituperation—attached to the term
"diddly squat"? Such questions recalled to Terry a time—a faraway but still in his memory deeply vexing time—when he'd
come upon, in a friend's dad's men's magazine, an ad for a book
that promised to enumerate one hundred and two sexual positions. He'd been no more than thirteen at the time probably, and
the magnitude of that number had positively haunted him. He'd
gone home and, good son of an insurance man that he was, had
methodically illustrated, with stick-figure diagrams, every position he could conceive of, including a number of real gravity-
defiers. Even so, he'd only come up with a couple of dozen.
That mountainously awesome number (one hundred and two!)
had confounded, troubled, *haunted* him—as had, to a lesser extent, the language of the ad as well ("Have you ever tried Crossing the Stallion? Or Turning the Spigot? If your answer is no,
then you *haven't really lived!*"), and for weeks, months, maybe
years afterward he'd been left to wonder whether everybody

else was a party to activities he'd never conceived of, whether he was locked out of things not only physically but mentally. Was it possible that there were whole other realms of "congress" (itself a disturbingly amorphous term) beyond his feverish surmisings? These days it made him laugh, to recall what he'd felt then, fresh into his teens. And yet, as much as anything now could, Kaye's use of slang occasionally roused in him a twinge of this old uneasiness.

"I honestly don't know how Glenn puts up with it," Kaye went on.

"I thought he didn't. Or at least didn't have to. I thought you said they weren't on speaking terms."

Kaye dismissed Tyler—or perhaps, Terry's questions about Tyler—with a weary, snuffling sigh. She went on, "You know, Diana's starting to think she wants a fancy humungous do, and I can see her point. She doesn't want to go into that Drill family looking like a pauper. On what is the very last occasion of her single life, she wants to go in feeling that she kept her end up."

Now this, on the other hand, was an argument of great potency. Evidently, they were deliriously rich, Peter's family, the Drills of Lexington, Kentucky—and Terry harbored, as Kaye perhaps had intuited, a resentment of the whole yet-unmet clan, sitting out there in horse country on their styrofoam riches. The family made thermoses, lunchboxes, disposable cups, and it had been weirdly discomposing for Terry when, a few weeks ago, his eye chanced upon the name DRILL on the bottom of his red and white thermos. This discovery had launched Terry on a sort of internal—a house—investigation, in which, right here where he'd lived for years, he quickly turned up a DRILL on the side of his red thermal picnic basket and a DRILL emblazoned on the bottom of each of the throwaway styrofoam cups in his cupboard. Now, if these Drill people were even briefly to suppose that Diana was lucky to get Peter, that she had in any way "caught" him—well, that would be intolerable. Nothing but intolerable. And just as though they'd already declared as much, had labeled Diana a vulgar fortune hunter, Terry's heart kindled with indignation and he felt a grand proclamation stirring. He had a moment—but just one—in which to ask himself whether he was being overly impulsive. Impulsiveness was a characteris-

tic fault, he well knew, particularly in regard to financial matters; and lately, more than ever and in many more ways than
ever, it had been a problem. There were good reasons, then, for
trying to shut himself up. And yet when the words did emerge
from his throat, they sounded eminently reasonable. They felt
consummately *right*.

"Well I tell you, Kaye," he began, "since this really is a sort of
departure for Diana, the start of a new life, I'd like to help out.
What the hell. What the hell, I tell you what I'm going to do. I'll
write out a check for five thousand dollars." (Ten times what
Glenn had offered!) "That can be my wedding gift to Diana—
my main gift. If Diana needs all that for the wedding—fine.
And if she's got some left over, she can use it to buy a sofa bed
or something."

What this grand moment seemed naturally to demand of
Kaye was some moving counter-display of gratitude, which
Terry was prepared nobly to shake off. But what she actually
said was, "Obviously once she's really in the Drill family, we
won't have to fuss about such things, will we?"

Fuss?

"If she wants to go to grad school," Kaye went on, "and you
know she is talking about law school, Terry, well we won't have
all this bother."

Whatever Kaye's design, the implication was that Diana was
being handed over to people more generously liberal than
Terry—though he himself hadn't been aware, frankly, of having
subjected anyone, while paying most of Diana's college bills
these last few years, to much *bother*. Worse still, wasn't there in
Kaye's tone just a hint of self-congratulation—as though she,
rather than Diana, had arranged this marriage to the styrofoam
heir?

Nonetheless, this was hardly the right moment for confronting Kaye. (It rarely *was* the right moment for confronting Kaye.)
Terry manifested his dissatisfaction by tuning her out, as she
rattled on about one thing or another—the effect of a softening
real estate market on Glenn, and some recent murder in Baltimore (the strangulation of an elderly woman), which she
seemed to think Terry knew everything about. The truth was

that Washington had its own barbarities, own rapes and mayhem, bludgeonings and strangulations, and local news teams had no need to import such stories from Baltimore.

"So which? What do you prefer?" Kaye was saying. The topic had clearly shifted.

"I'm sorry, what?"

"Terry, is anything the matter?"

He took her question to mean was he irritated about anything, and so he let her linger in suspense a moment: "N-no."

But apparently what she meant was *Is anything the matter with you?* For she went on, abruptly switching into her nurse mode, "If you're not doin' anything special, why dontcha pop over tomorrow night? We could just lounge around, maybe rent a video, make some popcorn." Oh, what her question had meant was, *Is my little brother going off his rocker?*

"I'm *fine,*" Terry said and, giving her ample cause to suppose him thick in the throes of further degeneration, he added, "Kaye, suddenly I've got a brutal headache. I'll call you in a couple days. Love to Diana"—and hung up the phone.

With the click in the cradle, anger dissolved on the instant into a sensation of unbounded fatigue. With thickening fingers he removed the little cassette tape—the gasping voiceless caller—from the answering machine and placed it in the top drawer of his chest of drawers, atop a bed of foreign coins he and Betsy had amassed in their various travels. Surely he'd be able to sleep well tonight. So drained was he, in fact, that he almost neglected, in preparation for bed, to close the door before everything went dark. He fell asleep without reflection, to the companionable echoings of his own breathing.

"Kid, this simply will not do."

All right, agreed, this simply would not do—but it wasn't clear whether Adam was referring to this place (a "hitech work and recreation station" called Mackey's Matrix Fitness) or to life in general, or, most likely perhaps, to Terry's behavior in recent weeks. The two of them were jogging. It was a good-sized indoor track, eight laps to the mile, and they'd covered nearly two miles already. Reggae music was being pumped out of what must be dozens of hidden speakers; it followed them round and round the track. Mackey (or whatever consortium of business interests Mackey stood for) had sunk a fortune into this place. Adam and Terry were here for purposes of inspection, to "get the feel of the place." They had both taken out one-week trial memberships.

In its eighth of a mile, the oval of the track made quite a diversified journey. It ran past a little bar, where you could buy "Victory Veggie Cocktails" and barley tea—and also beer. It ran past rows and rows of cryptically torturous machines, and stationary bicycles on which you could ride and watch TV, and rowing machines that combined exercise with some sort of video game. One section of the track was dark, and here you passed through a druggy tunnel in which ribs of pale pink and deep purple neon pulsated as you ran toward them, fell away at your approach. It was as though down the gullet of a whale you were pursuing these lights, a peculiar sensation that recalled to Terry his very dim and partial experiences with the "psychedelic"—that befuddling phenomenon which, when he was in high school, had suddenly broken out at either end of the country, leaving him with a queer feeling of being, geographically, at once central and completely out of it; for the first time in his young life he'd felt a piercing suspicion that there might just be something intrinsically a little comical about being from Iowa. One of the reasons, perhaps, why he'd gone to so many parties freshman year at Princeton (inspiring Kopp so viciously to write in his journal, "Terry was put on the planet in order to stand around with a drink in his hand") was to assuage his jittery misgivings about having missed out on things from the outset. How was it possible that one could grow up in the nation's heartland—a word whose suitability he'd never doubted—and yet be on the fringes of real life?

"I suppose not," Terry replied, which seemed an adequate counter to any of the branching possibilities toward which Adam's *This will not do* might point. The two of them entered once more the dark portion of the track; they were chasing, together, pale retreating arcs of light—pursuing a sort of nightrainbow.

"My advice hasn't been so bad over the years. Would you agree with that assessment?"

Terry kept his answer short: "Sure." For one thing, his wind was giving out. (Although *he* was the one who looked like the long-distance runner, stocky Adam could chew him up and spit him out on any sort of track.) For another, he wasn't *quite* sure where this was headed—though he had a pretty good idea—and therefore hesitated to commit himself too broadly before ascertaining what sort of assault Adam was contemplating.

"All kinds of advice . . ."

"All kinds, everything—psychological, professional, financial."

"And you know what my advice is now? You know what I'm going to say, don't you?"

"What's your advice now, Adam?"

"That you have to put certain sorts of things behind you."

"You mean, you mean maybe like the death of one's wife? That the sort of thing you have in mind?"

The words were meant to sound, if not quite contemptuous, at least breezy and snappish. Adam needed to be stood up to, now and then. Adam needed to understand the absurdity, the insurmountable unreality, of such appeals to positive thinking! Adam now and then needed to be stood up to, and even with the reggae music, the flashing lights, the pounding of their feet, Terry felt sure it came across: the sting in the words. For Adam answered bitterly himself:

"Yes, just exactly that sort of thing."

Neither said anything for a few seconds. There was, underneath the music, and the pounding of their feet on the track, a pristine silence. And then, in that quieter tone of measured finality which Terry knew so well—the one Adam used professionally whenever he was certain of having the right (that is, the devastating) rejoinder—Adam added: "Or at least the dead wife's subsequent reappearance. *That* sort of thing."

The truth was that there were indeed moments, and this was one, when the indefensibility of his present circumstances left Terry dumbstruck. Surely, *surely* it wasn't the case that he (Terence Seward—Terry—that man whose face he scrutinized morning and night in the mirror, whose hair naturally and with-

out the least instinct of cool parted neatly down the middle) had
come to regard himself as the sort of fellow who received messages from the dead . . . No wonder Adam was impatient!
No wonder, at various times, Kaye, Mob, Dad, Diana were
telephoning with such roundabout concern in their voices—
on all sides, day and night, these tentative, gingerly, probing
voices . . . If they couldn't believe what he told them had happened—well, neither could he! And that's what he would have
them understand: that he, too, saw that this wasn't to be believed! *Wasn't to be believed!*

And in such moments he would feel a sweet, a radiant impulse
to flee. It came to him even now, while in the middle of a run, a
yearning after greater speed, after truly headlong velocities—
outflung, outreaching sprintings that would put things far
behind him. Sometimes, lately, he felt it in his car, too—an impulse to test just how far to the right he could plunge the needle
of the Audi's speedometer. You had to put your foot down (the
same foot the broken whiskey glass had bitten into), you had to
step *hard* on the accelerator. You had to learn, just once, what
your fancy new car would *do*. Yes, Adam was right: the only
reasonable goal was to move so far, so fast, that you could truly
and solidly put things behind you! He felt contrite and yearned
for Adam's forgiveness, for everyone's forgiveness—he was
sorry to have put everyone through anything so absurd, so utterly, laughably unlike him.

"I'm looking forward to meeting old Squirrely Kopp, after all
these tales and all these years."

Clearly, Adam's words were a calculated easing off—a pal's
attempt to soften pressures, to lighten any residual traces of rebuke. But they had quite another effect. Adam inadvertently
had chosen a subject that nudged Terry away from the conciliatory thoughts he'd just now been entertaining. For Kopp—
bless him—represented another sort of perspective entirely. In
his eyes, what had happened in the cabin was nothing to be se-
creted, nothing to be held behind your back in foot-shuffling
embarrassment; no, it was something to investigate. Terry was
apologetic with Adam, and more than apologetic—mortified,
thoroughly abject—with Kaye and Glenn. (How could he have
permitted *any*one to discover all that blood on the floor? And to

have done such a thing to a delicate bag of nerves like *Kaye*—
to have ushered her into what was almost the set of a slasher
film . . .) He was apologetic toward Mob and Dad, and also
toward Diana (who, despite Kaye's assurances of secrecy, had
evidently been let in on the juiciest details) . . . Embarrassment,
in short, toward virtually everybody he was closest to—but
not toward Curly Kopp. No, on that score, anyway, Terry felt
pleased with things—heartened to have reestablished contact,
and excited to feel himself challenged once more by Kopp's
oddball mixture of eccentricity, scorn, clumsiness, aggression,
insight.

With bald-faced dishonesty Terry replied: "He's looking forward to meeting you, too."

In truth, Kevin had been putting off, for weeks now, with one
evasion or another, a meeting of the three of them. Having finally agreed to get together tonight, he had set up all sorts of
self-protective stipulations. They were meeting in Baltimore,
on Kevin's turf; and not for a dinner, as had been proposed, but
for drinks; and not until eleven o'clock, which—given that it
was a weeknight—seemingly ensured that talk would not run
long.

"He prefers to go by Kevin, actually," Terry added. One of
the reasons he felt a little anxious about tonight's meeting was
that—as he'd come to realize recently—he'd been unfair to
Kevin over the years. In his telling and retelling of the choicest
Kopp anecdotes he had turned his old roommate into a weirdo-
madman from the funny pages. Well, Kopp *was* weird, and at
times could appear even a little mad, but never without an ob-
durate logic and penetration that made a mockery of the cartoon
misfit Terry had erected in his place.

"Who wouldn't?" Adam answered, and laughed with the easy
high spirits of somebody who was far from winded.

Terry dropped out at the four-mile mark, puffing hard, and
stumbled over to the bicycle machines. These could be pro-
grammed to follow different "courses"—to simulate, by means
of shifting degrees of tension, the rolling gradients of a cross-
country ride. He set the timer for eighteen minutes and then,
consulting his watch, reduced this to twelve. It was already ten
o'clock: the two of them should be thinking about leaving.

But tonight there was no hurrying Adam along. Terry tried, Terry kept trying. Was Adam merely enjoying himself, having a good time in this initial exploration of Mackey's facilities? Or was he seeking, at some level, to be annoying? In any event, after a six-mile run Adam insisted on trying out the bicycles, the whirlpool bath, the sauna. It was nearly eleven before—their bodies pumping out heat into what had become a crisp fall night—they strolled across the parking lot and climbed into Terry's red Audi.

"So what do you think?" Adam said.

"Mm? About what?"

"Mackey. Mackey and his Matrix. Too glitzy, huh? Definitely too glitzy."

"You seemed to be enjoying yourself. It was hard enough getting you out of there . . ."

And it was after eleven-thirty when the two of them found their way into the Hatchback, a cavernous pizzeria around the corner from Kopp's apartment. Terry's preliminary nervous sweeping glance around the candlelit interior turned up no Kopp (of course, of course—no doubt Curly had stuck around for ten or fifteen minutes and departed), but a second go-round disclosed a diminutive, plump, balding figure seated at a rear table. Not quite having turned his back on anyone standing at the door, Kopp had nonetheless shifted his chair around so as to reveal himself in profile. He was reading something by candle-light. He was wearing glasses. It was the first time, ever, Terry had seen him in glasses.

"Kevvie," Terry cried, when they had almost reached his table but—though Kopp must have heard the greeting—there was no response. Terry came forward a couple more steps and called, "Heya, Kevin."

The seated, bespectacled figure swung around. On Curly's face was a look—visible even through the unfamiliar lenses—which Terry knew intimately, though he'd not glimpsed it in twenty years. It was a flinching unease that went well beyond mere social awkwardness. This was the look of somebody being caught out or exposed. And with this look Terry recalled something else he had forgotten or repressed: just how embarrassing and cumbersome it had been—particularly the first months of freshman year, when he himself had felt so upended by everything at Princeton—to be compelled to acknowledge that this squirmy squirrely little fellow was your roommate. Wasn't there something significant in their being paired up? So it had seemed, anyway, at the time. Terry'd been unable fully to quell a suspicion that Princeton was trying to tell him something. Everything was part of some grand East Coast, Ivy League design, surely, and what did it signify that the Powers That Be had considered Squirrely Kopp, of the seven hundred plus males in the entering class of 1974, the most suitable roommate for Terence Seward? Admittedly, things had gotten better after a couple of months, particularly after Curly started up his jumping bean escort service and his eccentricities became a source of campus-wide amusement. And by year's end there'd been a sort of social cachet, actually, in being linked to this little guy, for whom, more than once, a reporter from the *Daily Princetonian* had come knocking in search of some witty or sharp-angled observation.

Terry completed introductions with what he hoped was a graceful mock-solemnity: "Kevin Kopp, my old friend and freshman roommate; Adam Mikolajczak, my less old friend and colleague at Hamill, Hillman."

The two men shook hands. "I see you're working," Adam said, nodding at the papers on the table. "You're shaming us. We've been playing."

"A six-mile run is Adam here's idea of playing," Terry explained.

"I've never run six miles," Kevin said. The glasses were going to take some getting used to. At the moment they looked like a stage prop. "How far is it?"

"Oh—about six miles," Adam explained, and laughed much too loudly. Kopp winced.

Adam and Terry seated themselves on the same side of the table. This arrangement was all but inevitable, since Kopp had placed a briefcase on the chair beside him.

"What sort of work is it you do?" Adam asked, although this was information with which Terry had supplied him.

"I run a couple of pet stores."

"Pet stores? Pet stores? Well then our jobs have a great deal in common," Adam boomed, with the rapidity of somebody who has a line prepared. "We both work with monkeys."

But instead of laughing Kopp earnestly replied, "I don't carry monkeys any more, actually. Refuse to do so."

"Refuse to do so? And why's that?"

"It's just I don't like the way people treat them." A darkly thoughtful expression had come to Kopp's face. He made a fist, which he edged closer and closer to the candle flame. "They bring out the worst in people, monkeys do."

"I know they bring out the worst in *me*," Adam answered, and again laughed too heartily.

Kopp drew his hand away from the candle and did Terry only imagine it or was there afloat in the air the faint acrid smell of singed hair? Fortunately, the waitress came up just then: "What can I get you guys?"

She was a short woman, large-eyed and once pretty perhaps, with a pack of cigarettes in the pocket of her blouse, or shirt—for she seemed to be wearing a man's shirt. She looked tired.

"A change of heart?" Adam suggested. "We all need a change of heart." He grinned at her and after a moment she, somewhat improbably, broke into an authentic-looking smile. He did have a gift, Adam truly did, for getting the women his life brought him casually into contact with (the waitresses, stewardesses, shop attendants, even parking meter maids) to brighten. Anybody who did not know Adam well, and was unaware of that inner distancing mechanism which so often yanked him back from the lip of intimacy, would probably suppose him quite a ladies' man. "If you can't give me a change of heart, hell, I'd like a vodka and grapefruit juice."

"*That* we got," the waitress said and looked down at Kopp. "And what'll you have?"

"Gimme a Coke. Lots of ice."

"And you?"

The question placed Terry in a position of minor but hardly negligible conflict. For these were moments of symbolic decision-making, of tacit allegiances, and in the choice of drinks Adam was steering the evening in one direction, Kopp another. "I'll have a Miller Lite," Terry said.

"Something to eat?"

"We'll feed on broken dreams," Adam said.

"Them and also a grilled cheese sandwich," Kopp added. "And onion rings."

"Onion rings instead of the fries? Fries come with."

"Addition to," Kopp said. "Addition to."

The waitress shook her head at him, in apparent censure, and wandered off. Terry, to fill the silence that immediately opened, began for Kevin's benefit a detailing of the facilities available at Mackey's Matrix. He was just on the point of describing the dark, dreamlike portion of the track—where you felt as though you were pursuing something down the gullet of a whale—when the waitress returned with their drinks. "A toast," Adam interrupted. "To the man responsible for bringing us together tonight, to everyone's mutual friend, to the inimitable Terry Seward."

Terry could feel Curly stiffening at these words—which epitomized just the sort of corny, collegiate gestures he'd always abominated. Something in his nature instinctively recoiled from any whiff, however faint, of the ceremonial chumminess of the frat house or eating club. Still, his glass came up slowly—and it did click with the others.

"Well, thank you, gentlemen," Terry said.

"You always lived in Baltimore, Kevin?" Adam asked.

"No. Lived lots of places."

Not giving much away tonight.

"Where'd you grow up?"

"Houston."

"You an Astros fan?"

"What?"

"The Astros? The baseball team?"

"I've never in my life attended a baseball game."

"You have never in your life attended a baseball game?"

There was something exultant in Adam's weighty repetition—as though he had cleverly contrived to bring to light some priceless eccentricity. But Kopp was fully aware of the impression he was making. And he was proud of it. This remark was but one more boasting about his distance from the social mainstream. It was at one with his announcing that he didn't own a television set. "Well, we'll have to do something about that," Adam went on. "You'll have to come some time with Terry and me. Us, we go all the time."

"Kevin may want to keep his perfect record intact. After all, he's got a shutout going." Terry intended this to sound witty, but it came out sounding almost inhospitable. "Of course you're welcome to come if you'd like . . ."

"I think I'll keep my record intact."

Terry nodded. Kopp's expression was harder to read than usual, given the glasses, but Terry thought he could detect within it the flickerings of an old disdain. Oh, this was a scorn as old as their acquaintance.

Returning in high spirits from a party once, some twenty years ago, Terry had come back to the room to find Curly seated in his underwear in the shattered armchair he practically lived in (one he'd got for nothing by salvaging it, in Squirrel fashion, from somebody's trash), and Curly had looked up from a book to inquire dispassionately, indeed almost absentmindedly, "Terry, why *are* you so determinedly vapid?" (*That* time, Terry really had grown angry, and Kopp in the end had apologized, after a fashion: the next day, ripping the cobwebs from his wallet, he brought home a couple of fancy cheese danishes.) The words still rankled . . .

"So tell me about running a pet store," Adam said.

"There's not much to tell you. I'm a small businessman."

"Oh but there *is*," Terry prompted. "I mean all the stuff you were telling me. You know. The diseases and everything. When you gave me a tour of the place." Terry turned toward Adam and heard himself enthusiastically point out, "You've really got to be a sort of vet to run a pet store. Kevin really is a sort of vet."

Simultaneously, contrarily nodding, Adam said, "Oh, is that right . . ." and Kopp said, "No way . . ."

Really, the situation here at the Hatchback was far more clumsy than one might ever have supposed. But seeing Kopp in the company of another person was bringing it all back to Terry: how any sort of encounter with outsiders (with anyone, that is, outside the Seward-Kopp roommate club) had always veered toward awkwardness. It wasn't that Curly was possessive, exactly, although he'd shown a friendless freshman's share of that. Rather, it was his way of wordlessly accusing Terry in his social dealings of being what Kopp, the night of that party, had explicitly called him: vapid. In his peculiar style, which mixed psychological acuteness with an adolescent's tough, inflexible distaste for the phoniness and dishonesty of adult life, Kopp had been forever letting you know that pretty much every social encounter in your daily college life was a sham, a dissembling hypocrisy, a demeaning betrayal of your better self. Nothing in Terry's earlier, pre-Princeton life had quite prepared him for the biting severity of this view, and nothing subsequently had reaffirmed it: for after having decided to leave Curly, Terry in his remaining three years at Princeton had basked in a relatively uncomplicated—even vapid—sense of well-being. He'd *loved* college. Never been quite so happy, perhaps, before or since.

"So tell me 'bout running a pet store," Adam repeated. "What's your bread and butter?"

"Bread and butter?"

"How does business break down? Take dogs—what percentage of your gross is dogs?"

"My business is going to the dogs, right?" Kevin emitted a hard little bray of laughter—a metallic, almost robotic chuckle, and at *this* sound Adam seemed to wince. Terry had never before noticed this, or at least had never seen both the contrast and the similarity so lucidly: his two friends shared a too-loud and somewhat off-putting laugh. Adam's was deep and chummy, a poolroom guffaw, and Kevin's was high and harsh and whiny— the triumphant bray of the undersized schoolroom nerd—and the irony was that each found the other's so grating. And neither could see that their laughs were, in their abrasiveness, complements of each other.

Finding his mirth unshared, Kevin quickly went on: "Not that much. Ten percent, fifteen? Too much competition. There's your neighborhood poodle-breeder down the street, to say nothing of the Animal Rescue League . . ."

"How about cats?"

"Cats?"

Kopp was evidently supposing that in remaining so reticent he would discourage Adam—but Terry could have told him otherwise. When Adam wanted information, of any sort, he went after it hard.

"Meow, meow? Little nine-lived quadrupeds? Garfield, Felix, or the one that's got your tongue?"

Kopp paused to peer at Adam, in evident reappraisal, seemingly having glimpsed for the first time that here was somebody who—for all his limp jokes and loud social bluster—could be formidable. It wasn't for nothing that Adam, in a highly competitive business himself, had risen to the top. "I don't know, ten percent?" Kopp said. "Same problems."

"What about fish—tell me about fish."

"Did you know there are more than thirty thousand species of fish in the world today?"

"I didn't but it was the fish in the store I meant. What part of the business do they represent?"

"I dunno—maybe a third? They're a big part of the business."

In Kopp's view, Adam was having him on—feigning curiosity purely with the aim of getting him to talk. But what Kopp, who could see so much, simply could not see was that Adam's inquisitiveness was sincere. It was in fact one of the most impressive things about Adam: he was interested in how a thing— how almost anything—*worked*. If his job were to be taken away from him tomorrow, if he were somehow disbarred from the practice of law, he would find a new profession in a minute. Give him a few months and he'd be a crackerjack banker, restauranteur, travel agency owner. With Kopp, on the other hand, once you got used to seeing him in a pet store, you couldn't imagine him doing anything else.

For ten, fifteen minutes talk rambled on, as Adam inquired and Curly, resistantly, replied. The waitress reappeared. She addressed Adam: "You still looking for that change of heart? Or maybe you like another round?"

"Why do you give me all the hard questions?"

Curly said, "Maybe he's had a change of mind about that change of heart."

As bar-quips went, it was fairly witty—certainly in no way deserving of the dismissive, even derisive glance the waitress lowered on him. But when it came to women, this was the way things always had gone, probably always would go, for Curly Kopp. He was given no leeway, no benefit of the doubt. Other guys would draw a laugh with the limpest of witticisms. Curly would garner contempt even for a neat flash of wit. Something about his voice, his face, his size seemed to ordain that in all attempts at humor he would be regarded as nothing but a smart-ass. Decades had gone by, but this unmerciful decree hadn't softened. And here in truth was one of the most interesting things about Kevin—that his interestingness took the form of his being almost indistinguishable from an out-and-out jerk.

Adam ordered a new round of drinks and began a new round of talk. He had taken charge of the evening. And in doing so he'd grown happily damp at the temples, licked by that easy sweat which emerged whenever he was cheerfully engaged in just about anything.

"I want to hear stories about Terry. Tell me about our boy back in his freshman days."

In his bantering style, Adam seemed merely a step away from referring to Terry as "Babe"—which could be all but guaranteed to send Kopp up the wall.

But for the moment, anyway, Kopp didn't seem to know quite how to handle Adam's question. He scratched once more at the base of his ear and said, "What can you say about a college freshman?"

"But there must have been something distinctive, even then, about our Terry . . ."

"He wore round-necked sweaters to parties."

"Round-necked? You mean crew-necked?"

"I suppose so. He had four or five of these round-necked sweaters, and whatever else he might wear during the week, come time for a party he'd put on a round-necked sweater. It was his uniform."

"Surely I didn't do it *always*," Terry protested, in a show of flustered embarrassment more feigned than felt. If playing the buffoon would smooth things along—well, he was willing.

"Always . . . Without fail. Inevitably."

Terry said, "I told you, Adam, the unforgivably cruel thing

Kevin wrote about me in his journal? I quote: 'Terry Seward was put on this earth in order to stand around at parties with a drink in his hand.' "

"Did he seem," Adam went on, "a young man of special destiny?"

Kopp's reply came snapping back: "Did you say a young man of special density?"

The lawyer in Adam had to pause in admiration of this little play on words. The short, plump, balding, red-nosed fellow across the table was quick, nimble. Adam chose to treat the question as a simple misunderstanding: "Did you realize even then that our boy was fated for great things?"

"Well, *he* thought so. Used to go around talking about how he would—and now if it's all right *I'll* do a little quoting—how he wanted to accomplish at least one extraordinary thing in his life. I heard a lot about that *one extraordinary thing . . .*"

Having faked embarrassment a moment before, Terry said now, with sincere unease, "Once, maybe, I may have said something like that *once*. It's not as though I went on and on about it." The phrase *an extraordinary thing* did have, in fact, a remote but reverberative impact. It echoed through his head and he felt, momentarily, drunker than he possibly could be after one-and-a-half bottles of light beer.

Illusory as it may have been, this feeling of drunkenness immediately yielded to an illuminated certitude that was very much like one of a drunk's abrupt revelations: he saw that it had been thoroughgoing foolishness ever, *ever* to have supposed that Adam and Kevin could recognize the virtues in each other. But beyond this, and beyond the unprepossessing male trio seated at the back table of a run-down bar in a run-down section of Baltimore, was the realization that if in his life he, Terry Seward, had not managed and perhaps never would manage to accomplish any truly extraordinary thing, nonetheless an extraordinary thing had happened to him. One evening, alone in a stranger's cabin, he had witnessed something unaccountable—something that did not "fit." But that was weeks ago now, and it was drifting away into the bar's candle smoke, into the fall breezes and the expanding autumnal darks, into streams and streams of talk that, however well-intentioned, never could do it justice. It—she—was leaving him.

"Let's assume we're talking about a normal pair of eyes and a normal object under surveillance. Me looking at you right now, for instance. Now each eye has something like one hundred million photocells within the retina—"

"Research," Kevin announced, and looked up from what he was doing to bestow on Terry an almost blissful smile. "You've been doing some research."

"That's right," Terry echoed with satisfaction. "I've been doing some research. Anyway, in a moment of vision like right now's, in which my eyes are doing a decent job of taking in their surroundings, in which I note for instance that you are rolling a joint with E-Z Wider cigarette papers on top of a Tchaikovsky's Greatest Hits record cover, these one hundred million photocells are all hard at work, and what they do is being filtered through tens of millions of horizontal and bipolar cells, and what *they* do is being filtered to something like a million ganglion cells, each supplying one fiber to the optic nerve. And of course we have the backup of two eyes instead of one. Which is to say, if I am fooled on the primary visual level, that of the eye, if I am going to be successfully taken in by some sort of hallucination, this is going to be accomplished by simultaneously misleading— what? Half a billion cells? In other words, it's quite an elaborate trick."

"Want some?" Kopp held out a burning joint.

"That stuff makes me uneasy."

"You yourself make yourself uneasy. The stuff is beyond reproach. I grow it myself."

"You go ahead . . . Needless to say, it isn't necessary for my hundred million photocells actually to be misled in order for hallucinations to take place. The cells can be bypassed, you can see your hallucinations with your eyes closed, when no visual stimuli are coming in, as—"

"Dreams . . ." Kopp deposited the word atop a pillow of smoke. That old aroma—pot—tickled Terry's nostrils.

"Dreams," Terry repeated, but crisply, with a brisk corroborative shake of his head, by way of countering Kopp's airy utterance. There was a danger here, clearly, of the discussion's subsiding into the absurd. "My point is that the hallucination may take place higher up, not on the level of retinal cells and optic nerves at all. Hallucinations are of course more common among those who have been subjected to extreme physical want or hardship—the old mirage in the desert, hm? Or among those who are on drugs."

"You *said* you'd been drinking . . ."

"I was nowhere near drunk that night. Honestly, Kopper, you've got a totally unrealistic view of alcohol. You seem to think some genie in the bottle leaps out and takes you over—"

"And you seem to be describing your attitude toward pot. When you say, *That stuff makes me uneasy . . .*"

This was so clinching a rejoinder that Terry was seemingly left with no alternative. "All right," he said. "All right, hand it over."

In view of the weightiness of this snap decision—Terry's keen awareness of multiple menaces in the smoldering cigarette's transfer—the little stick of paper felt inappropriately light. Terry drew upon the joint and it turned out there was an expandable niche in his lungs still reserved, despite the years since he'd last called upon it, for this particular species of smoke. He drew again, deeply, and handed the joint back to Kevin.

Kopp began, "You said yourself you were feeling peculiar that day. The headache—and you never get headaches . . ."

"Everybody gets headaches . . . The point here, the point is that if what I saw was a hallucination, and that's the way I'd prefer to think of it, incidentally, then it wasn't any quote simple hallucination unquote. There's no such thing. Not on this scale, anyway. We're talking about a huge combined effort on the cellular level. You remember that French bicentennial bash? You thought *that* was elaborate? That was nothing. *Nothing* compared to the show my mind put on."

"You should have sold tickets. Sounds even better than a penny-pitching tournament."

"By the way," Terry said, "I was dishonest with you about something."

"Oh?" Kopp said and it was like flicking a switch: all of his features were lit with joy. Was there a sentence in the world that could so delight the Kopper as *I was dishonest with you . . .* ? To begin with, it held for him the never depleted pleasure of seeing some stroke of dissembling or dishonesty overturned. In addition, there was the enchanting promise that, through just this sort of endlessly investigative talk, they were actually moving closer toward some excavation of the truth.

"About Washington. About my living there."

"Washington?"

"You know the real reason why I'm still there? I think it's because I'm scared to move."

"Scared?" Kopp said.

"I've essentially lived in four places, right? And you know there's a pretty good case to be made that I've been less involved, less *engaged,* with each one in succession. You could pretty much chart it out, the down-slope I mean. I mean, I live my first eighteen years in Gawana and you could almost say I still live there. Half my dreams are set there. Hell, it's the first place I check out on the *USA Today* weather map. I'll be in San Diego or Boise or some crazy place, buy the newspaper basically to see what the weather is, and where do I look first? Iowa.

"So I move to Princeton and I know this confirms everything you always said about my great vapidity, but I *adored* it there. It's where in all sorts of ways I came alive. Suddenly, everything in the world is wide open to me.

"And while I couldn't say I loved Charlottesville, you can at least say I was fully *engaged* with it. There's where I met Betsy. There's where her family lived. There's where she wanted to go every goddamned weekend after we moved to Washington. And also, that's where she's buried.

"But Washington, somehow it's hardly like I live in Washington, and if I move somewhere else, isn't it possible I'd live there even less?"

"Smoke. We're all turning into smoke," Kopp said, and exhaled a dense but fast-dispersing cloud.

"I was dishonest about a second thing," Terry went on. "I left something out, in my accounts of that day, and while what I left out hardly seemed important to me, I thought it might seem important to you. When I got back from lunch with Adam that day, Bertha told me I'd had a call from a woman named Angelina. She wanted to sign me up for yoga classes. She's a masseuse—I'd gone to her for my neck-aches, it's a long story. Anyway, it occurred to me recently that since the incident in the cabin I haven't gone to her once. No, I've really avoided calling her. And when I realized this, I realized I might have connected her to it, psychologically, in some way. Why have I avoided her? I'd better tell you right away that I had sort of a crush on her."

"What was it like, going to the masseuse?"

"For me, it was like going to a brothel, though I don't know anything about such things. It was all in my mind. I guess I'm the only guy you know who goes to a brothel where you don't get laid, huh?" Terry giggled.

"Yungry?"

"What?"

"Yungry for something? Chips maybe?"

Kopp tonight seemed even more squirmy and skitterish—squirrelier—than usual. For hours now, Terry had been trying to channel the conversation along serious pathways, but with very little success.

"Not really . . ." Terry took the joint Kopp was offering and drew on it again, and again.

"No wonder. God, you were disgusting."

"They were delicate and delicious," Terry said, of the soft-shell crabs he'd had for dinner. "All six of them. And I'm not the one who finished things off with a banana bonanza." Three scoops of ice cream laid between a halved banana, topped with a mucilaginous banana sauce, whipped cream, and fudge sprinkles—Kopp's dessert.

"Mocha mocha raft," Kopp chanted. Two scoops of coffee ice cream on a mocha brownie—Terry's dessert.

"It was nowhere near the size of a banana bonanza."

"Mocha mocha raft . . . Mocha mocha raft . . ." Kopp was being witty: exposing this conversation as an exchange of childish taunts: *banana bonanza, mocha mocha raft . . .*

"I don't know how anybody could eat a crab," Kopp went on. "Not just a crab but a crab's shell."

"They're *soft*-shell crabs. It's like eating chicken skin."

"Something I don't recommend."

"Okay, the rind of an apple."

"Not even in my ugliest carnivore days would it've occurred to me to eat a creepy crawly creepy crawly crab . . ."

"But they *taste* so good. And why do you think anything would taste so good if it wasn't meant to be eaten, hm? Isn't that the whole *purpose* of a crab? Why in the world would it have evolved in just this particular exact way if it wasn't *meant* to be eaten? I'm the one who gives that creepy crawly crab's life some meaning," Terry concluded, and abruptly wished that Adam were here. He would have loved this line of argument . . .

Or was the argument actually Adam's? Terry had a free-flowing sense, come to think of it, of Adam's having said something very much like this. A number of times.

"The theology of the gourmet, is it? A this-sirloin-steak's-so-good-God-must-be-in-His-heaven argument? And think of the applications to the dung beetle."

"Curly, do you believe in God?" And good heavens, when was the last time Terry could have asked anyone so monumental a question in so abrupt and uncushioned a fashion? Ages, it must be ages, and yet why does it feel so familiar? Surely, the last time words of this sort could have come tripping off Terry's tongue in just this way—succeeded by a respectful hush, as though in preparation for some revelatory flash—would have been fresh-man year, when Terry Seward of Gawana, Iowa, had come thumping up against a roommate of heretofore unmatched weirdness, cynicism, and philosophical sophistication.

"Hold on. Let me get some chips or something first."

Kopp bounced out of his chair. His speed was something of a marvel to Terry, who had considered going over to look at the fish tanks but had finally judged the effort too considerable. Whether or not there was a God in Heaven, there were without question little zinging scintillae aswim in the air, even here in the unventilated half-dark of Kopp's apartment. They were swimming there all the time, dawn to dusk. The room itself was in the end revealed as a sort of aquarium, one that extended from room to room and down the stairs into the apartment lobby and out into the street, making of the entire city a single sea . . . A hum of well-being sang from his knees.

"God," Kopp began, in the weary tone of someone offering an oath rather than opening a topic. He had returned with some smoky Cheese O's—or, more accurately (Terry took a closer look at the cellophane bag, marveling at the particularity of his vision) Smo-Key Cheez-O's. "God, God, God. Now that's a funny subject, because college, you remember, I was such an atheist, nothing but scorn for all believers. Remember the night we were visited by those Jesus freaks? Me pounding my fist and saying *You trying to tell me you think this man actually rose from the dead? Come on!* And I still do feel that way . . . Only now, I feel the same way about atheists. *You trying to tell me you take a mat of algae, soak it in the sun for a billion years or so, and it stands up and starts building Chartres Cathedral? Come on!* You came to the right man, Terry, after you concluded you'd seen a ghost."

"I didn't see a ghost."

"Okay, okay, one of the walking dead."

"Cut it out."

"The point is, I don't treat you with any more scorn than I give to anybody else . . ." Kopp shoveled a handful of Cheez-O's into his mouth. "These days I save my vitriol for other sorts of people. You want to hear a story, a really ghastly horrible story?"

"Sure."

"A couple of years ago this dolled-up lady comes into my store. She's actually quite a good-looking woman, though she seems pretty flaky. She wants to buy a snake. She doesn't care what sort, just so it looks *vile*. That's her word—vile. I try to explain to her there's no such thing as a vile-looking snake, vileness being pretty much restricted to humans and mosquitoes, and then I try to talk her out of buying a snake at all, because as I say she seems flaky and she's not listening to a word I have to say about care and feeding and all the rest. No, she sees the snake she wants, she's got the money, big stack of twenties, she's doing this what-the-hell-is-this-I-know-my-rights number on me, and now she tells me she doesn't need all this information because it's a *gift* for a friend of hers, somebody who knows all about snakes, and the long and short of it is she goes out of my store with a two-hundred-dollar anaconda in a box."

Kopp paused for another handful of Cheez-O's. And another. One might almost suppose, seeing him happily settled on the sofa, that his story had come to a close. "And?" Terry said.

"And a couple days later a cop walks into the store, carrying another sort of box, and says to me, 'I was just curious if you could tell me what this is.' Well, it's my two-hundred-dollar anaconda, chopped up into four segments. It turned up in a trash container on Charles Street. And you know what I think? I think maybe she did the chopping. Before she gave it to this so-called friend of hers who knew all about snakes. Or maybe *he* chopped it up and sent it back? I've given this all a great deal of thought and you know what I think? I think that if he chopped it up, that that's just the sort of response she hoped to get with her so-called vile gift, that maybe this man had dumped her or something. And you know what else I think? I think when I die and go to hell maybe if I'm very, very good I'll get my wish and you know what my wish is? My wish is that the devil will give me the whip to take to the two of them. I'll whip 'em good, Terry. I'll flay those bastards." Here in this dark room an unprecedented, indeed an almost miraculous, thing had occurred: Kopp's eyes had welled with tears. This was something Terry had never seen before—water from a stone—and what a welcome, endearing sight they were: these hot, heart-sore tears of Kevin Kopp.

"Jesus," Terry said.

"Lucifer," Kopp replied, and reached forward for another handful of Cheez-O's.

"Hey, can I ask a favor of you?" Terry said. "A really super big favor?"

"Mm?" The question pulled Kopp erect on the couch. He blinked and his eyes were his own again; those tears might have been a trick of the light. His gaze caught Terry's and for a moment held it—always afraid, seemingly, you were going to touch him for a loan . . . His cheeks were puffed with cheese rings, though these might just as well have been acorns.

"Well," Terry said. "Okay. Okay, it's just something I've been wanting to ask you for some time . . . Okay, can I call you Squirrely? Or at least Curly? I've tried to get used to Kevin but"—he shrugged his shoulders—"I just can't."

They held each other's gaze another moment. Then Kopp sat back, resumed chewing, swallowed, scratched at his nose, at his ear, and finally, staring off at his fish tanks, he said, "What the hell. Whatever you want."

"You know I really do appreciate this."

"Whatever you want."

Terry reached toward the coffee table and took a couple of cheese rings. The little squeak they released under your teeth, like the sound a styrofoam cup (no doubt a DRILL styrofoam cup) emits when you chew on it, made him giggle. They weren't bad, actually.

And Curly was racing through them at a great pace, Terry noticed. His own share would be utterly consumed, if he didn't advance quickly. He scooted his chair forward and grabbed another handful. The two of them chewed in silence for a while.

He was feeling grateful to the Kopper and so he said, "You want to hear maybe the most embarrassing thing ever happened to me? Okay, I'll tell it to you, though I've never told anybody this before. Nobody . . . Okay, when I was fourteen or so, I briefly found religion, and I went on a couple of these Methodist Youth retreats, and one night I'm lying there in the dark in a cabin full of fourteen-year-old boys and the conversation turns to speculation about parental sexual habits, mostly how often we thought they might do it. We sort of go around the room and when it's my turn I begin, 'Well, my parents . . .' and you know what happens? You know what happens? Somebody giggles. And then the whole cabin, the whole goddamn cabin, explodes with hilarity, it goes on and on and *on,* because you see that to these fourteen-year-old boys there's evidently no funnier vision in the whole goddamn world than that of little Everett Seward climbing into bed with the big Mob. It sounds like such a stupid *stupid* thing now, I know, I know, but I remember lying there in the dark and being so mortified I wanted to die . . ."

Oh, but he'd felt something more powerful than mortification—indeed, feels it in the palms of his hands even now. For he'd been overtaken by a furious itching desire (one far removed from Methodist Youth teachings) to murder each and every one of those bastard gigglers in their beds. He, too, had wanted to whip and flay . . . "So tell me," he went on, "what's the worst thing ever happened to you?"

"The time my uncle chopped me up in four segments and stuffed me in a box?"

"What are you talking about?"

"You were talking about hallucinations."

"That's true. I was."

"What you need to do, Terry, is to make yourself a list. Break down everything according to our two hypotheses."

"That's just exactly what I was thinking," Terry said.

"First of all we've got our—you don't want to call it ghost hypothesis, do you? Didn't we settle on guest instead—Guest Hypothesis?"

"It'll do . . ."

"And then we've got the it's-all-in-the-mind, he's-gone-round-the-bend Loonie Hypothesis. Will you accept Loonie Hypothesis?"

"Sure. But I'm not loonie. How about the Coach Kramm Hypothesis. He's the it's-in-the-mind man. Did I ever tell you he'd been married once? And that day he drove me to that crazy church of his, the one that met literally in a garage, I asked him about it and do you know what he said? He got this rigid look on his face, squeezing the wheel as if he meant to shatter it in his hands, and he said, *She was unclean* . . . Now what do you think he meant by that? Plain old infidelity—was that it? Or did he really mean venereal disease? I mean you do have to take a sexual interpretation, don't you think? Or do you? Is it unreasonable to impose a sexual interpretation?"

"Now take that headache of yours. According to our Guest Hypothesis, that just might be a presentiment . . ."

"Or it just might be a headache."

"Terry, you're missing the point. You keep missing the *same* point. If you're going to assume that these so-called guests really do walk the earth, then merely for purposes of consistency you ought to assume all the ramifications that naturally go along with it. If you want to stick with rationality, let's move to Hypothesis Two, the round-the-bend theory, in which case the headache might be seen as a kind of alarm. It was warning you of temporary mental aberrations—the brewing of a sort of cerebral storm. But we've got to keep sight of which one we're looking at, Terry."

The marvel in all this was how Squirrely managed to keep so focussed on things. There were so many distractions aquiver in the air . . .

Kopp said, "I want to go back a couple of years. To right after the accident. I want to hear about the first time you saw the body of your dead wife."

A swirl, a dark swaying, a bee-like cloud, hands clamped to your face and a venom-laden stinging . . .

"I don't want to talk about it," Terry said. "Uh-uh. No."

He went on, "It's sometimes hard for me to talk about her," and halted.

He had brushed aside Kopp's request, had refused to enter the room Kopp would have him enter, and yet something in the air now mandated, by way of recompense, that some confidence, some privacy, undergo a divulging. This wasn't (Terry understood) a duty owed to Kopp but to Betsy herself. She couldn't be here, but she was a larger presence than the two old roommates who were. She was larger than life, and he was being summoned, strangely enough, to breach the intimacies that had once enclosed their marriage. "I told you how she lost a baby," Terry said.

"But I didn't tell you," he went on, "that the doctor told *her* that the baby'd actually been dead for a week or two. She'd been carrying around inside her this dead baby, you see. And what I didn't tell you, what I've never told anybody actually"—and Terry's voice dropped to a near-whisper, his voice was walking barefoot on stones—"is that this image kind of you might say haunted me. It *scared* me I guess, but that isn't quite the word I want. Anyway, it made me sort of reluctant to—well there was this odd strange nervous feeling—" Was he making a mistake? Even with all these delicate, evasive circumlocutions was he commiting a personal offense against the dead? "—about putting yourself, I mean sexually now, about in a sense entering the same general area where this as it turned out child had, in a sense, for a time been buried . . ."

"Well sure," Kopp cut in. "That's only natural," he went on. "It'd give anybody the willies to stick his dick into the lair of a dead creature."

Oh God, oh good sweet dear God, count on Curly Kopp!— who of course would cheerily manage, short minutes after looking more tender-hearted than ever before, to convert what was probably the most jittery and ghastly disclosure you'd ever uttered into something still more jittery and ghastly. For with this word *lair,* and still more with *creature* and the phrase *dead creature,* it was almost as though inside her pale broad belly Betsy had been carrying around a dead mongoose, a dead weasel, a whiskery dead muskrat.

"All right, okay," Kopp continued. "Let's jump ahead then. I want to hear about the very last person you laid eyes on before the guest in the cabin."

"I don't know."

"But you do."

"I don't remember . . ." What he remembered, oddly, was the man in the obscene black T-shirt, eating a dripping ice-cream cone.

"But it was the kid in the little grocery store, wasn't it? The one who said he'd buried his cat in the swamp out back? The cat that had thrown up a mouse?"

Of course Kopp remembered. He held on to such things and wouldn't let you get away with *anything.* Terry had put himself, once more, in Kopp's hands, had brought it all, the whole freshman experience, back. But why, why in the world had he done such a thing?

"That's right."

"What did he look like?"

"I don't know . . ."

"Well you said he had pimples, didn't you? Around his mouth?"

"That's right."

"What did they remind you of?"

"The pimples?"

"That's right."

"They reminded me of pimples. What the hell else?"

"Did he seem unclean?"

"What do you mean?"

"Don't you see, Terry—that if you want to follow the second theory, the Round-the-Bend Theory, then all these things have a significance? They must add up, the way things do in a dream."

"Well I don't think there's all that much *in* dreams, frankly. Nowhere near as much as people say." And Terry added, not affectionately this time but aggressively (and who could blame him? This was that old game—Kopp trying to dig his way into your mind), "Squirrely."

"Don't you see that the thing's going to have its own logic? Just the way a dream does, Terry."

"Some things just don't make any sense . . ."

From a lawyer's standpoint Terry knew what he himself was doing: adhockery. He was throwing out objections piecemeal, without any overarching counter-scheme. But he needed time. In all sorts of ways he was feeling pressed at the moment . . .

Escape, he sensed, just might lie in the direct approach, the challenge that answered a challenge, and therefore he said: "So what are you getting at? What does it all add up to—the storm, the Chinese food, the boy with the pimples, hm?"

"And let's not forget Bertha, and her newspaper full of miracles."

"Miracles?"

"What else do you think those papers are selling, Terry? Woman gives birth to tattooed baby, Elvis is alive but Paul McCartney is dead, drowned woman returns to speak with husband in cabin on the edge of the Dismal Swamp."

For just a moment, Terry had no words. In the distance, across the room, nearby, Squirrely Kopp, that odd old man, that twisted little boy, that accident in the Princeton admissions process, had come fully into his own. And it was toward this emergence that every floating word of the evening had been drifting.

"Terry, don't you see, at the very least, that it may be no co-incidence she comes back the very day you've been inviting a good-looking young woman to visit you in Washington? And the very day your masseuse starts calling you at the office?"

"But don't you see these things *were* a coincidence?" Terry had found his voice but it was scratchier—more sophomoric—than before. "I mean it happened to happen that the flights fell on the same day. And somebody called me up—an unsolicited call. *I* didn't arrange that."

"No, but you *processed* it, Terry. What am I getting at? Well, for one thing I'm getting at the idea that you've got very special reasons, which we've only begun to touch on, for wanting your wife to come back and offer you reassurances."

"Anybody would. Surely anybody would."

"But most widowers don't have wives that actually *do*. Now when the two of them found you, your sister and that guy of hers, you were standing in a creek. Isn't that right?"

"Look, I was out of my head. I'm not trying to conceal that. I'd just seen a—an apparition, or whatever. And I'd cut the hell out of my foot."

"Sounds to me like a good way to ensure loss of blood . . ."

"Look, I wasn't thinking straight. I'm the *first* to admit that."

"It was a kind of return to the scene of the crime. Isn't that right?"

"The crime?"

"The accident. The great accident of your life. The one that changed everything. The one that you sometimes fear *wasn't to-tally an accident*."

What Terry just at that moment recalled was a funny thing. It was the way Betsy—now and then, and always playfully—had called him Little Terror and Holy Terror. As a rule she wasn't one for nicknames (she'd not gone along with calling Mob "Mob"—after the marriage, she'd addressed her as Mom Seward), but this little turn on Terry's name had really tickled her—especially in bed, or after bed. He could recall the exact pitch and cadence of her voice as she would say it, lifting a plump arm to run a hand through his hair—*Little Terror, my Holy Terror.* And he had forgotten that . . . Until just now, this very moment, he had forgotten that. When was the last time he'd brought it up to mind? Where had it gone and what was happening to him?

What was happening? In the day-to-day, she was so close, Betsy always was, never was there any need to call her up deliberately. She was an accompanying force, a second observer, a sharer of experiences—real as the very air. What was unnerving, a little, was in fact just how very much with him she remained, how stubbornly undiminished she could be. Although it might sound arrogant, the truth was that nobody who hadn't suffered a loss on such a scale could ever understand the way this was— this closeness more intimate than mere memory.

And yet there would now and then be times, like this, in which some stray, intimate detail would surface up through him and he'd be left to entertain the notion that the woman who inhabited his mind, whoever it was, wasn't Betsy; no—no, *Betsy* had been somebody else, she'd been the woman who, lifting a plump naked arm to run a hand through his hair, had said to the spent, sated man at her side, *Now aren't you a holy terror?* And with this thought would come the thought that life had been doing something strange to him for months and months and months now: something stranger, crazier than any loss, death, explosion of tears . . . Stranger than remorse, mourning, waking to the weights on your face . . . He was holding on to something that was intact but wasn't, maybe, real or right. And meanwhile life was busily transposing things, so cleverly you'd scarcely know it—so cleverly you'd scarcely notice how blue had shifted into red, or black into white. He had read somewhere that if you place a frog in a pan of water and raise the temperature gradually enough, it won't bother to leap out—will make not a single attempt to escape as it's slowly boiled solid.

And with this thought came another thought which, trivial as it was, was utterly unignorable: he wasn't feeling well. For the last hour or so, he hadn't been feeling well. This had taken some time to surface, but it had been there awhile. Doubtless he would be feeling fine now, everything would be crisply in order if only Curly hadn't made that snide little quip about *creepy crawlies.* But the words had done their work and right behind the thin wall of his stomach lining he could feel his dinner coming swampily back to life, sidling and slinking, prowling, darkly prodding his insides with their multiple soft-armored arms. "Curly," he said, "you know I'm not feeling well."

"No wonder."

"No, I'm not," he said, rising to his feet, which caused the room to sway.

He made his way to the bathroom on shaky feet that were too small for him, for he was like an inverted pyramid, so large his thoughts had grown. Even as he swung the bathroom door open he wasn't yet certain what his business was going to be, knew only that it was urgent. But when he flicked on the light he met a shove low in the center of his chest, a rude elbowing upward, a spiteful explosion of a cough. He threw his head over the wide toilet bowl and the seething slop within him lunged up so powerfully that it shut down his vision. There was another clenching jerk, and then an easing open-eyed upflow, as the whole acidified collection, the cheese rings, the Coca-Cola, the taste of smoke, the cole slaw, the french fries, the mocha mocha raft, the protuberant gesticulating soft-shell crabs rained down into the turbulent water.

There was a voice, and this was Curly's voice—standing outside the bathroom door: "You all right? Terry, you all right?"

By way of answer, Terry pulled off a little magician's feat. For though he had, just a moment ago, voided his stomach of all contents, now was the moment for releasing a second hot generous ghastly gassy upsurge. Another splash, the fumes were revolting, and isn't it peculiar how the contents of your own body, released at either end, repulse you the way they do? The contents of your own stomach make your own stomach sick.

"Oh God . . ."

"You all right?"

Terry rose from his knees. "Yeah. I'm going to be all right."

But it turned out that in the blinding moments of delivery he hadn't quite managed to deposit all the vomit into the bowl. Some on the toilet seat, some on the floor, some on his right hand . . . He snapped a long segment of toilet paper, began to swab the vomit from his right hand, and saw that his left hand, too, was spattered.

"You all right in there?" Curly was scared—you could tell it without seeing his face—and this fear somehow was strengthening. Curly was on the run . . .

"I'm going to be all right but I better take a shower."

"I'll put on some water for coffee. I'll put on some water for coffee."

"You do that . . ."

Terry dropped his shirt, his pants, his underwear and socks on a clean patch of floor and turned on the shower. The water's touch bloomed forth memories of a party, years ago, him and Betsy at some neighbors, the Boggses, who'd later moved to Minneapolis; and fat-faced Bradford Boggs, who would always drink too much and then want to play stupid drunken party games, on this night asking everybody to write on a piece of paper a single word to describe yourself. And head a bit fuzzy with drink perhaps, but his principles all the more collected for that, Terry had written, in rebellion at being coerced into this silly touchy-feely game, SOLID. As if to say, Let's see you make something out of *that* . . . He lathered his chest and had just begun with his underarms when he realized he was going to be sick again. Oh, he realized the truth: he was going to die in here. He stumbled out of the shower and, dripping everywhere at once, dropped to his knees once more before the bowl, which he had forgotten to flush. Obediently he opened his mouth— and discovered he wasn't going to be sick this time. Not in this way, anyway. He was done. He lifted his hand fumblingly—not daring to take his eyes off the bobbing contents of the toilet, where living crabs were swimming, seeking on all sides to climb out of the bowl—and found the little latch of the flush mechanism. He pulled and there was a roar before his face, a fluid-wrinkling suction that would pull him in strand by strand if it only could, and the blessing of purified water descending in jeweled strings down the sides of the bowl. He stood. He struggled back into his underpants, hearing meanwhile little sounds—sickly kissing sounds—from under his arms. The pits were still full of soap.

He stepped from the bathroom in nothing but his underpants, looked around, called sharply, "Curly—Curly."

"Here I am, here I am." It was a scared little Kopper—white-faced, skittery—who popped out of the kitchen.

"I'm sorry, I need to go lie down."

"Go on, go on, go lie down on the bed."

"I'd rather lie down on the couch. I need a blanket. I'm cold."

He *did* feel cold, although it soon became clear, once he'd settled on the couch, with a scratchy blanket wrapped around him, that he was sweating profusely. The Smo-Key Cheez-O's on the coffee table were to be endured only by closing your eyes. The unquenchable smell of smoke was to be endured only by breathing shallowly, through your mouth.

"You're really sweating . . ."

"Betsy and I went to a party once at these neighbors, the Boggses," Terry said. "Bradford Boggs was always wanting to play these party *games,* you know? And this time he asked us, don't ask me why, to describe ourselves in one word, and you know what Betsy wrote? Do you know what Betsy wrote? Guess for a hundred years and still you wouldn't guess . . . She wrote ARTISTIC. I couldn't believe it, I couldn't believe it," Terry said, despairingly sensing, with this repetition, just how little of what was astonishing Kopp might reasonably be expected to *get.* In order to convey the jaw-dropping surprise of that moment Terry would first have to give Curly, through hours and hours of careful portraiture, a true, rich, ornate likeness of Betsy—and the enormousness of this task overwhelmed him.

"Don't get me wrong. Betsy was many many terrific things"—oh but my own dear love, dear girl, dear Heart, what in the world were you *thinking* when, in that huddled, private moment of composition, you wrote ARTISTIC? And what was the force that drew a flush to your face, that colored your features with a look that spoke of bared, vulnerable mischief (it was a look of modesty subverted by daring, and in that moment you might almost have been a nightclub stripper on her first engagement) but that also spoke of self-wondering pride (as though that novice stripper in the midst of her motions were suddenly to discover, *But yes I am—I am truly beautiful!*), when after a moment's hesitation, you bared your card, your ARTISTIC, to the world?

"You've got to understand, there wasn't a single artistic activity, you know like photography or music or even sewing, that really interested her . . ." But with these words he saw that he was not doing justice to her, or to the moment, or to his own wounded astonishment. "For Christ's sake she was no more artistic than I am, which is to say an artistic cipher," he said, and decided to give it up. He pointed at one of the tanks. "Look at that clownfish," he said. "All dressed up and nowhere to go." Terry laughed.

"You're really sweating," Kopp said again.

It was apparent to Terry, even in this condition, that at the moment Kopp was the more worried, Kopp the more exposed of the two. For Terry had the reassuring knowledge that he would be fine, just fine, the moment he had sweated his way to completion: the moment, that is, when every inch of the blanket was saturated with sweat. That was all he need do. It was merely a matter of time, of covering the inches, of turning this blanket into a sort of rag—one which a jolly giant with a giant's hand might wring dry in a single clenching, ho ho ho, the water rivuletting down his huge hairy green forearm, his giant's teeth flashing in a gigantic booming grin of triumph. Fine—he was going to be fine.

"Kevin, will you read to me?"

"Read?"

"Whatever. Whatever at all. Doesn't matter, could be *TV Guide*. Just read out loud to me. I'm going to be fine."

"Read, sure, okay, let me see, let me see . . . How's this? It's the first thing at hand, my little pamphlet on sea horses, maybe I can set you straight on what you hardly believed the first time I told you, the first time you came to the store. Here it is— gestation. 'Gestation is five to six weeks, the first two weeks in the body of the female, the next four in the brood pouch of the male, after the eggs have been transferred by means—' We can do better than this, can't we?"

"Anything. Words, words. It's all the same." Terry was on the couch with his eyes closed. Filling the blanket with water, just as he ought to.

"*A Handbook of Mythological Beasts?* This is quite interesting, actually, it's by Douglas Crodian. The anthropologist? What do you want—I've got land creatures, sea creatures, air creatures, subterranean creatures."

"Anything . . ."

"Should we stick to marine life?"

"Sure. Swell. I had this sense, this sort of vision a while ago, you might even call it a poetic vision, of this whole room as one big aquarium. Of the whole city as a single—"

"Sea serpents? Sea cows? How do you feel about mermaids?"

"Fine."

" 'The mermaid,' " Curly read, " 'is found in cultures on all continents. Generally she represents a force of temptation wrapped in danger. Although mermen are occasionally sighted, and have on occasion been prominent, as in Matthew Arnold's poem "The Forsaken Merman," one might say it is the nature of this beast to be feminine in form and sororal by temperament. The desire to walk on terra firma . . . ' "

The text was flowing, word by word; the blanket was filling, inch by square inch. It was all just a matter of time, Terry understood. He was going to be fine.

"Of course you're doing this purely to irritate me."

" 'This'?"

"The facial appendage. The beard, Babe."

"I'm not doing it to irritate you. Furthermore, there's no reason why it *ought* to irritate you."

"I'd've thought simple embarrassment would've protected you, even if my advice didn't. Don't you see what a cliché you're becoming?"

"I'm sorry if I'm becoming a cliché."

"Isn't this just what every college-sophomore-turned-dropout feels it necessary to do? Grow a beard as a first step to turning mystical? Is that the point you're making?"

"I'm not making any point, Adam. I'm simply growing a beard."

"Don't you understand that you're falling in with a long tradition of fakes and lunatics?"

"There's a very honorable tradition of lunatics, too—but that's beside the point. I'm not joining anyone or anything."

"But you're dropping out, aren't you? Just like some college sophomore? It's as if you're going back to college so you can drop out of college."

"I'm not dropping out of anything. I'm just pursuing other things . . ."

"Okay, here's your chance, kiddo, give it to me from the horse's mouth. Tell me exactly how it was you decided to grow a beard. You looked at yourself in the mirror one morning, said to yourself, 'Terry old boy, you're not bad-looking, you're still youthful, not going gray like my old pal poor old 'Dam, still trim, not fighting a paunch like good old 'Dam, but grow a *beard,* Terry boy, and the girls'll come at you so thick and fast you'll need a stick to keep them off.' Is that it?"

Adam made a few swashbuckling sweeps with an imaginary stick, then dropped abruptly into the blue armchair, propped his elbows upon his knees and set his chin upon his cupped hands, in a look of exaggeratedly respectful attention. He was in fine form this morning, protesting Terry's beard with a mournful hyperbolic grandiosity that wasn't easy to parry.

"How I decided to grow a beard . . ." Terry began, and turned away from Adam. It was a shame that the firm's offices offered so little in the way of vistas. Even the windows of the biggest office, what used to be old Sam Hamill's and now was young Sam Hamill's, offered no sweep, no sumptuosity. For new associates, for young partners, there was little to aspire to in this department . . . Once, some years ago, Terry'd gone out to Colorado for a radio licensing and had wound up in the offices of a dinky little firm whose name was—what? He'd forgotten. Strictly local, these guys had been in way over their heads when it came to FCC matters, but the windows in the office where Terry had carried out negotiations commanded snow-fissured mountains which, on that day and in that light, bathed upon the horizon in a pink glow of almost surreal lucidity. One had a sense of the individual flakes, miles away. The view had filled him with envy. The view had told him there was something missing in his life, an imbalance that might actually be rectified: for wouldn't the practice of law, the sixty, even seventy hours a week he was devoting to it, take on an unassailable profundity if only enacted against such a backdrop?

"You're treating this as though everything's deliberate," Terry said, keeping his eyes on the far side of the street, "as though I willed all of it. But I didn't will any of it. I'm just trying to respond to what happens. Adam, I'm not a malcontent. I never set out to rock the boat. When I was married, I was happy to be married. You know I never cheated on Betsy, and I could have. I don't mean there were weekly opportunities, but I had my chances. I'm not saying I was a perfect husband, and you know as well as anybody we had our problems—my always working weekends, her depression, her weight, her heading out to Charlottesville every chance she got. I'm only saying I was perfectly content to let things go on that way forever . . .

"And then comes the accident, and you know better than anybody what that did to me. For one thing I became a sort of amnesiac—I looked up one day and it turns out six months of my life have gone by. Chopped right out of my head. Where did they go, huh? What was I doing? And who was it exactly who'd been living my life in my place? Or ask me right this minute to give you fifty words describing what it's like to fly home in a plane that's also carrying the body of your dead wife and I break into tears, right here before your eyes, that's what I do. But in time I found a new way to live—more travel, even longer hours, fewer parties, more ball games and exercise . . . You know what my life's been like. And okay, I could live with this arrangement, too. I'm not a malcontent, Adam—you know that. I have my daydreams, we all do, but I've got to be one of the few lawyers in Washington who isn't talking about opening a restaurant or writing a novel. But then something else happened to me, something that wouldn't fit into the world I'd made for myself. I didn't choose any of this. You'd recoil at the word fate, I know, but the truth is that all of this is less like choosing than like being chosen."

The satisfying eloquence of this closing epigram was undermined by a nagging suspicion that he had lost sight of his point. Oh yes: "So one day instinct tells me to start growing a beard and I say, 'A beard, Jesus, you got to be kidding . . .' And I say exactly what you said a minute ago: 'But under the circumstances isn't a beard a cliché?' But instinct says, 'You heard me, a beard,' so I finally say, 'All right, a beard it is.' Because what else have I got to go on these days except instinct?"

"Now about this sabbatical of yours . . ."

"Yes?"

Terry turned to face his friend. He knew he stood on much shakier ground here. This issue was serious, and sensitive, and delicate. This was his life. "The first thing is: You're not calling it a sabbatical."

"No?"

Adam meant every word now—a gravity he registered by adopting a much less grave demeanor. Gone was that look of concentration so fierce it had pitched him forward, elbows on knees and chin on hands. From the glass coffee table he had picked up a magazine whose back cover (a cigarette ad, in which a laughing man in a paint smock was slathering thickly with clay a laughing paint-smocked woman) he appeared to study intently. He spoke with mildness, offhandedly. "This isn't an academic institution, you know? This ain't no liberal arts college, Babe. You're not taking a semester off, if you see what I mean."

"I don't think it matters much what we call my time away . . ."

"Well if it doesn't matter much to you, then why don't we indulge old 'Dam on this point, huh? Now we're talking how long a period?"

"That's the thing. We're only talking three months."

"Who's talking three?" Adam looked up from the magazine. "Two. Let's say two's the max. Now, to do what? No, don't tell me. I don't think I want to know."

"To do research. Into hallucinations, visitations. I mean real research, incidentally. I've already begun sending out letters, I should tell you. To researchers in the field. And in Manhattan there's the Psi Center for Research into the Paranormal, where they've been—"

"No, no I was right. Rightrightrightrightright. I don't want to know."

"And maybe also I'd go somewhere else."

"Somewhere else?"

"I feel this need to make a—" He managed to cut off the word that leapt first to mind: *pilgrimage.* "—a trip. Maybe get in the Audi and go somewhere. I'm not sure where."

"I'd've thought that's the one thing you got enough of around here."

"Adam, I'm talking serious study. I'm talking things like physiology."

"And I'm talking things like office politics. So the first thing is, You're taking a two-month vacation. Not a sabbatical, not a leave, not time off. That's very long but it's not unprecedented. And you're not doing psychic research as far as the powers that be are concerned. We'll tell them you're kicking a coke habit before we'll tell them that. Or being treated for pedophilia. Terry, lately there's been some talk about you around here . . ."

Terry felt an impulse to snarl *So what?*, an impulse to retort, *Fine and dandy!*—and he felt, as well, a cringing impulse to inquire, *What kind of talk?* After all, "talk" could be dangerous. "Talk" could be deadly. For *this was his life*—that was the message Adam meant to convey to him. And to convey, as well, that when other things had passed away, the folks at Hamill, Hillman would still be here, as would his position here with them. That was how it had been in the aftermath of the accident, and that's how it would be once again. At some level Terry did understand this completely: knew that the presence of "talk" was the most important thing in the world. For this was his life.

"Christ, I haven't killed anybody. I'm just growing a beard for Christ's sake."

"You know as well as I do it ain't no beard I'm talking about."

A silence opened—opened and purposefully widened. Terry again stared out the window. Up H Street, a silent bus exhaled a dark breath of poison. Somewhere, far away, tons of snow were hanging suspended from a chain of mountaintops. But around him here, fully closing him in, were halls and offices and elevators where talk—poisonous talk—was circulating.

"Now you know as well as I do that whatever you do—go join the circus, or move into an ashram—you've still got 'Dam for an ally. And let's face it, in terms of power that's not a bad thing to have."

"Sure. You're one of the most powerful allies I could have. I know that."

"The most. The most powerful."

It was a striking declaration. With all his penchant for outrageous remarks, Adam was nonetheless consistently cagey (even with Terry, even when the two of them were alone) about his own place in office power-politics.

"Let's face it, kiddo. If push comes to shove around there, which isn't something I'm aching to see happen, actually, people would look at me skeptically for about fifteen seconds. They'd ask themselves, *Do we really want to put Hamill, Hillman in the hands of that greasy Polack? Can we really bear to have as our captain someone with a j-c-z consonant cluster in his last name?* And then they'd look at Sam Junior and say, *God he's gorgeous, went to Harvard Law, never farted in his life, he's our man* . . . But then they'd stop and think, and then they'd say, *But there's just one drawback with Sam—he's an empty suit.* No guts, no gumption, no real appetite for work. Christ, the guy actually goes around talking about how family weekends are sacrosanct. *Sacrosanct!* Not so sacrosanct for associates, though, who are billing the hours while he's collecting the bucks. Now am I misreading things?"

"I'll buy what you say . . ."

"Look, things are changing round here. Remember when we all had to pretend that old man Hamill day after day was being some sort of lovable curmudgeon, when in fact everybody knew he was a two-faced turd and a vicious unprincipled weasel to boot? Or remember when all the young associates had to sit enraptured at lunch while John Hillman recapitulated the *Times* and the *Post*, which admittedly he was eminently qualified to do, since he used to spend *all* morning reading newspapers in the lounge?"

"I like Hillman."

"So do I. He's entertainment in a firm that's not exactly a laugh a minute. It's a riot, listening to him loudly inform his secretary where he's going to be for the next twenty-two minutes, and the next twenty-seven after that . . . You'd think he was Henry Kissinger, when instead he's this affable klutz whose work consists of looking like he's working, but the point is that no one laughed very *openly* about him till a year or so ago. Power is shifting, there's no doubt about it. But the point is, I may have my share of the power, but I can't stop the talk. The whole thing would be a helluva lot easier if you'd just go out and break a leg. Give yourself an excuse for staying away. Can't you develop an ulcer?"

"I'm working on one."

"Are you with me so far? No more than two months? And vacation time if we can't pull off some sort of medical excuse? I think, actually, that may be the route to go—we'll fake some sort of medical excuse."

Terry was saved the need of a reply by a buzz from the phone. "Yeah?"

"It's your sister," Bertha said. "Kaye."

Count on Bertha, in all her false hyper-precision, to supply Kaye's name—as though to identify *which* of Terry's many sisters wished to speak with him. "Put her on," Terry said.

In his most dire lawyerly voice he began, "Terry Seward speaking . . ." No sense in making things easier for Kaye.

"I was just callin' to see how you're doin' . . ."

Indisputably, she was sinking fast. Even two weeks ago, would she have dropped two g's in a mere six words? Well, perhaps in the halls of Hamill, Hillman all sorts of talk was currently circulating about how Terry Seward was slipping, but in his personal life he had grown sharper than ever. He was beginning to see the people around him, all of them, with cleansed eyes.

"Well I'm doin' fine. And howya doin', Kaye?"

"Well we're fine, we're both fine. Glenn has really been such a boost. You know we've been lookin' for a hall, for the reception, and he's been *such* a boost. This is where his real estater's savvy is absolutely in*val*uable."

When a pause opened up, Terry promptly vowed not to break it. Whatever mischief or probing she was intent upon this morning, he wasn't going to assist her in it.

Kaye seemed to hesitate. "This week," she began, "last Tuesday it was, would you believe two different drills go out the same day? Two different makes, two different rooms, and both of them out within an hour of each other? And then to top it off one of the girls has gotten in *quite* a family way, doesn't even know for sure what *race* she's bringing into this world, and of course she doesn't want Dumph to know a thing. You know Dumph is *quite* moth-eaten and Catholic about such matters, but somehow I got cajoled into keeping it a secret from him. Lordy, what a disaster."

Which of course from Kaye's standpoint it was anything but. For this was Kaye maneuvering in her element, right smack in the middle of a hot little scandal with one of her "girls," scheming against the forces of the uptight, the straitlaced, the (heaven preserve us) old-fashioned.

"I mean *any*body would have noticed by now, the girl's half as big as a two-car garage. And another one of the girls, Estelle, suddenly she's decided to go punk on us."

"Go punk?"

"Comes in here all Halloweened out—"

"Halloweened out?"

"Green lipstick, *emerald* green, like she's auditioning for MTV. You got a minute? Is this a good time to call?"

"Well actually I was sort of in the middle of something." But what he'd been in the middle of—negotiations with Adam— had terminated with a brief wave of farewell: Adam had beat a retreat the moment he'd ascertained it was Kaye on the phone. "But I've got a minute."

"Well you know we've really gone *all* over town, Glenn and me, you honestly cannot imagine the hours of legwork we've logged in. And at last, at last, Terry, we've found just the most exquisite place, it's called the Excelsior Club, on Glidden Park, and it—the building, not the park—dates back to the eighteenth century. Or maybe the nineteenth but it's got the most wonderful kind of established *ambience* about it, Terry, we're talking the absolute epitome of non-tackiness."

"I don't doubt it."

"It's the sort of place where we could be really *proud,* you and me, to see Diana feted on her big day. Oh I wish you could *see* it, you ought to come over just for a look-see."

"I trust your judgment. Yours and Glenn's."

"It's the sort of place where those Kentucky Drills, with all their obscenely huge piles of bucks, wouldn't have anything *on* us, you see. What does Kentucky have on us? I'm sure there can't be a more beautiful place in all of Kentucky for two young people to get themselves hitched. But Terry, we're talking now over two g's just to rent the venue. And that's probably a conservative guesstimate. It may be closer to three really."

The conversation had veered unexpectedly. He'd thought the focus was to be his mental health, with an emphasis on its frailty. But Kaye had led him in another direction entirely. She had taken a branching wherein it was fully in her interest to assume that he was—mentally, and, even more, professionally—as entrenched and dependable as ever.

"You're looking for money," Terry said. "Well I'm sure I can be of some assistance."

As gambits went, this one proved pleasingly discombobulating.

"Well yes, well great, Terry, God you see it's . . . What the thing is is that that old way of doing things isn't going to cut the mustard, that the thing is is there's going to be a lot more of what you might call fancy folks, Peter's family and relatives and friends, coming over from Lexington, than we ever initially thought is what it is."

"Not just us white trash . . ."

"We're talking now about really a hundred coming from his side of the family. And an *hors d'oeuvres* bill, that's just the *hors d'oeuvres,* of about twenty-two bucks a pop."

"And that's just the *people*. Think about the cost of stabling their horses."

The little joke tickled Terry, as it would Adam. Terry had already mentally budgeted another twenty-five hundred dollars for Kaye, but at the thought of the joke, and how much more biting it would prove if the amount were greater, he upped the figure: "I'll tell you what I'd like to do, Kaye. I'll send you out a check today for four thousand dollars. You be as frugal as you can, I know you're doing your best, and whatever's left can go for Diana's wedding present."

"The point is you just can't shoestring it the way you used to. When Ralph and I got married, I can safely say we didn't soak Mom and Dad for more than a sum total of five hundred clams. You know, Terry, I did think about going to them for help, this time around."

"No, no, you did the right thing. You come to me."

"This is going to be the most picture-perfect day in the whole world, Terry."

"I don't doubt it."

"We could consider this one a loan, Terry."

What's the difference? "I'd prefer we call it a gift."

"I have my IRAs . . ."

"You keep your IRAs."

"I just wish there was something I could do for you, Terry. You know, with that famous self-sufficiency of yours, you make any sort of repayment a real tough nut to crack."

Actually, there was something Kaye could do for him: she could start referring to money as *money*. Wouldn't these occasional, awkward, anxiety-fraught moments when she came to him with her palm extended be enormously less excruciating if she weren't after *dough* or *bread* or *clams* or *green* or *scratch*? And another thing she could do (while going about the business of revising her speech) would be forever to forswear expressions like *pain in the tushy*. And—come to think of it—he would gladly give her another five hundred dollars, twenty-five crisp twenties, if she would stop referring to black men as *black dudes*.

"And how 'bout you?" Kaye went on. "You know, I was just saying to Glenn, last night it was, that we don't get to see enough of you. If the drive's a strain, there's always the train. Gee, a slogan. And we'd meet you at the station."

She didn't know, of course, that he'd been in Baltimore quite a lot lately. "Work keeps me pretty busy."

"And work's fine?"

"Work's fine."

He hadn't told her, either, about his plans to take a leave. Was it crazy to suppose she need never know? If Bertha were to remain on the job, why couldn't Kaye be told, each time she called, that he was simply away from his desk, or in court, or on the road? It was only two months he'd be away, after all. (Inwardly, he'd already bent to Adam's urgings on that score.) The fact was, he didn't think he could bear Kaye's concerned, sympathetic questions were she to learn of his plans. On the other hand, how in the world was he to justify to Bertha the need for a deception? And was Bertha, with all her odd veering candors, even capable of carrying out a simple ruse of this sort?

"Everything's fine, finefinefine," he chanted brightly. "Work's buzzing along, I'm taking one day at a time, billing what's billable, keeping the airwaves safe for democracy. Listen," he said, in a resumption of his normal voice. "I got to run. I'll put the check in the mail today."

"Now you keep in mind what I've been saying," Kaye offered by way of a conclusion, to which Terry replied, "Will do."

"We really don't get to see *enough* of you," she went on. "Come on out and hang your hammock for a night."

"I'd like that, I'll see what I can do, bye for now," Terry said and put down the phone. Then he announced aloud to himself, in a slow and solemn voice, as though he were speaking at an FCC hearing, "Statistically, most men have some sort of hobby. That's to be expected. That's normal. My friend Adam, for example, he follows baseball. My friend Kevin's got his fish . . . My own particular hobby is philanthropy." He rose from his chair and went over to study himself in the mirror.

His face encouraged him. A little pale, perhaps, but the beard was coming in with unexpected vigor. He hadn't been sure, really, that he *could* grow a beard.

"I'm generous to a fault," he said aloud, and the words recalled a little ghastly daydream-vision he hadn't entertained in years . . . It was a line of thought that had vexed him over and over again in college, or maybe it was high school. In any event, it had once obsessed him. The problem it posed was so simple, and yet so utterly unanswerable: one day, a spiritual agent (an angel, or Jesus maybe, or maybe the Good Lord Himself) comes down to ask you whether you will give up one joint of your baby finger in order to save a little girl in Jakarta who's dying of cholera—and of course you will. And the next day it's, Will you also give up two toes in order to stop a schoolbus in Appalachia from tumbling down a ravine?—and of course you will. And the next day it's, How about agreeing to have your right foot severed at the ankle in order to undo that deadly fire you read about in today's paper which razed a children's hospital in Peru?—and of course you will. And then it's, Your left arm off at the shoulder in order to keep a Danish ferryboat from capsizing into a merciless gray sea? (Of course!) And your other shoulder in order to reverse the most recent Armenian mud slide (who am I to say no?), and in the end what happens is that you wind up flat on your back in a high-ceilinged windowless room and you might as well be an upended turtle, for you haven't the means even of turning yourself over. Physically, you can do nothing, nothing but lie there limblessly, and now you have at your disposal all the time in the world to ask yourself: Where did I go wrong? Where should I have drawn the line?

He went over to the filing cabinet to look up the name Ralph Wogus. The file was thicker than he would have supposed. It was by way of Ralph, Kaye's deadbeat of an ex-husband, that Terry's career as a philanthropist had commenced. And here it was, the fateful letter:

Dear Ralph,

I learn from Kaye that problems have developed as to the future direction of Diana's education—to wit, that you have suffered in recent months unexpected and doubtless temporary financial reversals which result in your feeling reluctant or at least hesitant to commit yourself to undertaking the bulk of those admittedly enormous expenses that would be incurred were she to attend Dartmouth, as she seems to have her heart set on doing. (It occurs to me, by the bye, that the astronomical cost of higher education in America is one of the gravest problems facing our nation's citizenry, and I would be immensely grateful if you, in your political capacities [as a way of drumming up business connections, Ralph had served for a time on some local California Republican committee], *would investigate potential solutions.) I am immensely proud of Diana for having been admitted to Dartmouth College, and hence have endeavored to make clear to her that the mere fact of having gained admittance to so selective an institution is a significant honor in itself, which will remain with her even if she never sets one foot upon its campus. Not surprisingly, however, the girl has had some difficulty reconciling herself to this interpretation. She seems to feel that not admission per se but actual attendance is the main point here. It's an argument whose gravamen is, as I think you would have to concede, powerfully persuasive. I am prepared to underwrite, therefore, any of her uncovered expenses during four years at Dartmouth College, including tuition and lodging. I thought that you and Kaye might arrange between you the handling of the costs of transportation, books, and incidental expenses.*

I understand that you and your new housemate are about to be blessed with issue. I am afraid that I am unable, at the present time, to guarantee the expenses of his or her higher education.

I don't doubt for a moment that ours is a business climate in which a person of your adaptable attributes must thrive in the long run.

Sincerely yours,

It left him smiling, even now. He was a writer by profession—if the composing of legal documents qualified as writing—and this letter was in many ways the summit of his creations. Nothing else he'd ever written had brought to him joy quite so complicated and encompassing; certainly he'd put more effort into it, on a per word basis, than he'd given to any other composition. He'd subjected it to four painstaking drafts, struggling to arrive at just this winning compound of detachment, sympathy, fairness, generosity, and (subtly throughout and unignorably in the final sentences) an *up yours, Ralph* snottiness.

The process of revision had also offered—besides the tremendous satisfaction of shaping a good piece of writing into a sort of personal masterpiece—the reassurance that he was not behaving crazily. Wasn't the whole business proceeding with a measured, incremental, lawyerly sobriety? That's what he'd told himself—though he'd later felt a dizzy and giddy thrill (had felt, in fact, like someone engaged in a risky undergraduate prank) when addressing the envelope and affixing a stamp.

And he'd mailed off the letter before consulting Betsy . . . There'd been a sinking in his stomach when the envelope, with a last fluttering wave of brightness, had plummeted into the darkness of a mailbox on 19th Street—for suddenly he'd felt queasy at the thought of his wife. What if Betsy simply refused to permit it? She would put her foot down, she would squash the offer flat, and what would he do then? She'd always been a little jealous of Diana—who, when she was a little girl, used to vow (as little girls will) that she would marry her uncle someday, and who, even as an almost grown woman, had remained close to Terry in a way that no other female, with the natural exception of Mob, could be. And Betsy had been a jealous woman. It was important not to forget that. She'd been jealous of anyone—young or old, male or female—who was an intimate of his, and her jealousy wasn't so bad really, for he'd mostly enjoyed the sense of being needed which these demands of hers imposed. Nevertheless it did leave him occasionally suspecting that he carried too much of the burden in their relationship. She'd said herself, a couple of times, that part of the problem was that she didn't have enough friends of her own. *That* was why, weekend after weekend, she would be off—accompanied or alone, she didn't seem much to care—to her family in Charlottesville.

So what happened? Had Betsy blown her top? No, not at all . . . After making an off-the-point and oddly bitter remark about Kaye, she'd acquiesced quietly, as though this were a matter that didn't properly concern her. She'd been "doing better" lately; the dosages (which, all the doctors had assured him, were minuscule anyway) had gotten smaller and more precise; she'd seemed herself again, in virtually every way. Yet here she was agreeing to the forfeiture of thousands of dollars without a tremor of nervousness, without a solitary crackle of anger.

"The girl's worked hard," he'd told her. "She's entitled to a good school."

And Betsy—dispassionately, as though in the long run the money had no connection to her—had said, "That's very generous of you."

In actuality she probably *should* have been concerned about her husband's irresponsible ways with money. In small matters he was unimpeachable, the very antithesis of the impulse buyer: he was somebody who would hardly buy a clock radio or a toaster oven without consulting *Consumer Reports.* But when it came to larger sums, and the domain of grand gestures, he was of another stripe entirely. He'd surprised himself on the night of the Crash—October 19, 1987—when, according to a quick tallying, he'd found himself with a one-day loss of over forty thousand dollars. What he'd felt primarily wasn't despair (though there was some of that) and still less panic (though a touch of that as well) but a weird buoyant satisfaction, an inexplicable sensation that justice had been meted out on a global scale. It was as though one person in his head was calling to another *Take that!* or *So there . . .* It was a little like the feeling he'd sometimes had in his vaulting days, when, having botched a couple of jumps, he'd been left with but a single remaining shot at salvation: *You're up against the wall now* and *You've got to make this one good . . .*

Money—and wasn't it one of the few rules you could count on in life that *everybody* was inconsistent about money? In Vegas once, on business, he decided to while away a few minutes at the blackjack table, where he quickly lost something like forty dollars. The loss kept him up all night; it was dawn before he'd finally fallen into a crumpled sleep. Robbed was how he felt, as though the whole arrangement—the clockless walls and the women in tight cocktail dresses, the lights and the strong drinks and the multicolored chips—had been a deception tantamount to robbery. Lying on his stomach, in a room high above the thievery, he had thrashed about in a furious thirst for vengeance, preferably of a violent nature: he would find a way to strip the casino of hundreds, thousands, millions of dollars. For the fact was that however much money he might make at Hamill, Hillman, he would always be out *those particular forty dollars*—which the dealers and the bartenders and the glossy girls had stolen from him. They had robbed him of his money and then gone on to watch him walk away as a loser . . . And that was how it was: with a loss of forty dollars he'd obliterated all promise of sleep, with a loss of forty grand he'd slept like a baby.

Of course one could argue that, purely in business terms, the investment in Diana had paid off. Who'd been irrational? In the long term, Dartmouth would clearly return far more to her financially than he'd put into it. (In terms of the extended Seward family, he had invested brilliantly, hadn't he? And didn't it make sense for him to think in such terms? Though he'd always planned on having children, and still did, he'd reached a point in his life where he had to face the possibility of, as the law would say, dying without issue . . .) She was talking about law school, and her Dartmouth B.A. would surely ease her into a good school. (Sometimes, just for fun, he liked to think she might end up at Hamill, Hillman; he saw himself helping her along in that, too . . .) And if she'd not gone to Dartmouth, she would never have met this Peter of hers, who would bring her, apparently, money on a scale to dwarf Terry's original investment.

It was 12:10. He opened his office door. Bertha had begun her lunch break but hadn't yet started to eat. She was chewing gum and reading a magazine.

"Bertha, you want to go out to lunch with me?" He appended, as a courtesy, "Are you free?"

"I brought my lunch." This was, naturally, voiced as an accusation. It was clear to Terry that Bertha liked going out to lunch with him—something the two of them did once a month or so—but she was never one to have her lunch hour casually infringed upon.

"I should've extended the invitation before. Actually, there's something I want to talk to you about."

These words, evidently, lent the invitation an air of obligation; Bertha gave a shrug that seemed to speak of resignation or duty and said, "Okay."

"You ready to go now?"

"Not *now*. I've got to get ready."

"I'll wait for you here. I'll take a look at your magazine."

Terry sat in Bertha's chair, thumbing backward through the pages. He stopped when he came to a picture of a pretty woman—a beautiful woman, in fact, with a radiating grin—and though he'd never seen the TV show she starred in, he began to read about her with interest. She'd just broken up with a man who also was, evidently, a TV star. "Life goes on," she was quoted as saying. And, "I'm a natural risk-taker. That's what acting's all about. When I cut my bangs everybody said I'd absolutely lost my mind. But I just went ahead and had them cut anyway."

Bertha was a long time gone in the ladies' room and when she returned she looked in no way altered. To glance directly from the flawless woman in the magazine to Bertha was a bit of a shock. She hadn't even combed her hair. They rode down the elevator in silence broken only by the pumping of her chewing gum. On the street (it was cool, this mid-November Wednesday, with winter in the air) they hesitated.

"What would you like, Bertha? Anything you like . . ."

"*You* have to decide. Lunch was your suggestion."

"Yes . . ." By Terry's way of thinking the logic of this remark was hardly watertight, but he let it stand. "How about Japanese?"

"It gives me the stomachache. The one time I tried it."

"Thai?"

"That's the same problem."

"Mexican?"

"Honestly, whatever you want."

The sight of Bertha on the street, pink bubblegum dancing briskly in her mouth, reminded Terry that she was never "meant" to be seen anywhere other than in an office. Away from it she manifested—even in simple transactions like buying a cookie, or mailing a package—a wobbling unease; she was, simply, not at home in the world.

"We'll go to Zona Mexicana," Terry told her.

No doubt about it, she was a strange bird—as Squirrely Kopp in his own subterranean way was strange, and even Adam, in some ways, was strange. Why was it that he should spend his life surrounded by misfits and oddballs? Why (Terry had to wonder) were these the people he was closest to?

But it was a much more at ease Bertha who, in a booth at Zona Mexicana, went after the guacamole dip. For such a small woman she had quite an ardent appetite. This was something the two of them shared, actually: metabolic systems to which calorie-counting was an irrelevance.

He asked after the widowed aunts she lived with, Celia and Margaret. One had been a secretary and the other had worked for the phone company; one was moody and taciturn, the other cheery and garrulous. But for all the tales Bertha'd regaled him with over the years, he'd never quite straightened out which name went with which job and character.

He let her ramble on for a while (a story about how Celia was feeling inconvenienced by Margaret, or Margaret by Celia, because the former or the latter had moved into the room of the former or the latter while the former or the latter's bedroom was being painted), but when she arrived at an end, or at least a stopping place, he said, "So how's the rest of your life?"

"The rest?"

Her voice sharpened, as though defensively or, even, uncomprehendingly—as though, that is, for Bertha there was no "rest," no additional existence. Or as if she had no inkling what this "rest" might consist of.

"Well how are things at the office, for instance?"

"*I* don't know. You're at the office more than me."

"I mean from your side of things." He saw that her reply had given him a favorable opening, and he added, "Actually, I'm not going to be at the office. For a while. Just between you and me, I'm going to be taking a two-month vacation."

It was disconcerting—the way she greeted this revelation. As though she'd expected it. Or as if it were the most natural thing in the world. He'd expected her jaw to drop to the floor. *There's been talk,* Adam had said, and Bertha's matter-of-fact response might well be evidence of such talk.

"It's all my own idea," he hastened to reassure her. "And as for you, of course your job'll go on just as before. You could straighten out the files, or whatever. Only I've been thinking," he added (actually, this idea—meant to win her over, or at least to erase that knowing expression on her face—had only just this moment occurred to him), "that you might have Fridays off while I'm away. At the same pay, of course. I'll be doing some research at home. And I may go away now and then."

"When would this be?"

"Well I'd like to think beginning some time this month, but I've got lots of loose ends to tie up. Before Christmas, certainly. Or probably. Anyway, not much later than New Year's. You know, you might want to use that time to get away yourself. Take some of your vacation time. Don't you ever long to get away from Washington, Bertha?"

"I can't," she said. "Not right now."

"Your aunts?"

"No, oh no, all sorts of things." Bertha gave him what might be taken for a meaningful glance. She was making up, apparently, for that sad show of depletion a moment ago, when he'd asked after the rest of her life. "A lot of things," she repeated.

"Yes . . ."

Those crooked little fingers of hers had been busy; she'd

nearly finished off the guacamole. He said to her, "How about another order of this stuff? Before we settle on some lunch."

"Whatever you want."

He looked around for their waiter. They could use a couple more Cokes, too.

"But what will you do?" Bertha asked him.

"Hm?"

Terry turned back toward Bertha, whose eyes behind her glasses were locked upon him.

"But what will you *do?* What *kind* of research, Terry?"

It was unlike her to approach him like this, by name, so frontally and forcibly. She sounded strangely anguished . . .

"Well I've got some research, Bertha. It's cross-disciplinary, actually—physiological, psychological, historical. I've got all kinds of research, Bertha." He not only wasn't making much sense but—clearly—wasn't even fooling Bertha into thinking he was doing so. Scrambling, he took refuge in a kind of parody, a show of stuffy pomp which, even if she did not find it amusing, she might accept with the lenient patience usually accorded any show of his kidding. "I will pursue my interests, Bertha, temporarily throw off the shackles of the law in order to broaden my outlook and extend my horizons, explore the life of the mind."

With this culminating phrase Terry discovered that he had unwittingly hit upon an explanation at once resonant and candid. So satisfying was it, in its multiple echoings, that after pausing to indulge in another novel delight—the slow stroking of his beard—he once again avowed it, this time in an expanded formulation: "Bertha, I plan to devote myself to exploring the life of the mind."

Part Three

A SINGLE INVITATION

Horizontal Chitchat

"For the life of me, I can't tell if he's coming out of a muddle or going into one."

"Tell me . . ."

"Well you know he's actually not the dope you first take him for, and he does have this real gift for work, which is something he's always had. You set him on an idea, really *on* to it, and he's a bulldog. It's the high school valedictorian in him. Not the quickest guy in the class, no way, but the teacher's pet, the humble one always eager to do every little scrap of homework, doesn't matter how repetitive or inane it happens to be. He does have his pretensions, you gotta say, and if I hear him once more utter the phrase *from a historical standpoint,* I think I'll take poison. But hell, you gotta admire how he's gone after this. Just once in his life, this something strange happens to him, and instead of pushing it aside, like most people would, or coming in here with it, like I guess maybe I would, Amanda, he sets out like some screwy knight errant, carrying this banner called Truth. You have to laugh, but it shows something. It shows— can I call it a real depth of spirit?"

"Why not? Why does the phrase make you uneasy?"

"Who said it does? It's just it's not a phrase I'd usually think of applying to Terry Seward. But you know, it really is as if he's deepened."

"People change. Isn't that the premise we begin with, you and I?"

"People change? *He's* changed, anyway."

"And yet . . ."

"And yet?"

"You seem to be edging toward a qualification."

"Oh well hell he's nice—I mean in the conventional sense, the sense that makes people describe you as a *nice fella* and a *good guy*—and he's got mosta the blind spots you associate with niceness. He blocks out all sorts of things."

"You don't believe that . . ."

"What?"

"About niceness. About niceness and blind spots."

"It's a way of protecting myself? Of resisting change? If niceness equals blindness, then I've got some justification for remaining the crusty little shit I've always been? That what you mean?"

"Give me an example. Of one of his blind spots."

"Could give you a coupla dozen. Try this one. On the morning of the day when he sees his visitor, probably no more than twelve hours before, he meets a woman on an airplane. Quite attractive woman, who's leaving her husband and full of talk about leading a new life. A new life this, new life that . . . So I say to him, This sort of talk of hers has got obvious connections to the arrival of your visitor. And he nods knowingly—oh God, it's almost fucking *adorable,* this doe-eyed knowing nod of his. And I say, After all, what's another word for a new life but a resurrection? and this time his jaw drops. He's *never seen it . . .* And never seen, very clearly anyway, that the girl on the plane's a source of guilt. That the swamp vision, the vision in the cabin, she's a police woman. You wouldn't think in this day and age *any*body could be as repressed and uptight as he is. Shit, he doesn't even see that the visitation might be related to his fear of vanishing."

"Vanishing?"

"That's not his word, but it's what he means when he talks about being scared each time he moves from one neighborhood to another, one stage of life to another, that he's a little less alive than before. It's really quite an obsession of his, as he may finally be starting to realize. He tells me this sort of daydream-nightmare the other day in which God comes down and asks you to give up your baby finger to save some poor starving child in Ethiopia or whatever and so of course you say okay, and then He asks you to give up your toes to stop some orphanage in Calcutta from going up in flames, and you say okay, okay, and so on and so forth, until you've been lopped off to the point where you can't even roll yourself over—and you know what my first thought is? My first thought is this: what the hell *is* this, Terry? You been stealing my daydreams or what? Honestly, Amanda, now have you ever heard of a daydream more suitable for *my* subconscious than this one, where you got self-mutilation, altruism, and fear of the big knife all rolled into one?"

"I'm not sure I see the connection . . ."

"To?"

"To vanishing . . ."

"Well with both of them, the fear of moving and the fear of the Lord's requests, you wind up only half there. *That's* what I mean. And what better antidote is there to a fear of vanishing than to learn that even the dead can come back, huh?"

"So what does he think it is—the vision in the cabin?"

"I think he actually thinks it's his actual honest-to-God wife. Really. And sometimes I do too, actually, but we'll get into that one in a minute. The screwy thing is, it's easier for him to accept the notion that ghosts walk the earth than that he's carrying around in his brain a woman who's going to slap his face the moment he gets a hard-on. Sexually he's pretty much of a mess. Somewhere between adolescent and pre-adolescent."

"Why do you say that?"

"I'm projecting, am I, Amanda? Turning the world into a place where there isn't a sexually healthy man left in the world?"

"Why do you say that?"

"You know, you're developing a very annoying habit of not answering my questions."

"Cut it out, Kevin."

"No, I mean it. I've been through all that and I want no more of it, Amanda. Years, all those fucking years of shrinks playing the brick wall for me, bouncing my questions back at me like throwing a ball into a wall. I thought your whole approach, directionism and all that, was supposed to be different. I want a human being, and at eighty bucks a pop is that so much to ask?"

"*Would* you cut it out, Kevin. It's been a long, lousy day, if you want to know the truth, and I don't *need* this . . ."

"Tell me about your long, lousy day, Amanda. Tell me about the screwiest person you talked to today. That oughta cheer me up."

"Should we call it a day? There isn't much time left . . ."

"You wanna refund me the unused minutes?"

"Happily, Kevin. Only too happily."

"Well I ain't leaving," he declares, and laughs merrily. Whenever they reach an impasse of this sort, the silence is usually eased for him by the cries of children at play. No doubt it's a coincidence that her office overlooks a playground, but it's a blessing all the same—and probably a productive blessing at that. Those voices are a counterpart, an inspiration, an invocation. They are an alternative commentary. In all his years at this, all the couches he has in effect rented, hers is the place that gives him the greatest sense of fulfillment, of rightness, of something like home.

"Shall we go on, Kevin?"

"Sure."

"You might apologize first."

"Sorry."

"Do you want to give me your spiel now about how I'm playing the leather-clad dominatrix, whip in hand, because I dare to ask you for an apology?"

He chuckles again, gleefully, crosses his short legs on the couch, stares at his stocking feet. "Next time, Amanda. Next time."

"You were talking about your friend Terry."

"You know what he calls me? Squirrely. Fucking flattering, isn't it? My nickname from freshman year. *Just* the sort of nickname you'd want to be given, isn't it, if you were a shell-shocked little shitface from Texas who'd come up to Princeton feeling half gone toward a nervous breakdown . . . You shoulda seen his face. It was the night we smoked the pot, the night he got so sick. His face gets this big pissy grin, he asks me can he ask me a big *big* favor, and he's blushing, I swear, and then solemn as Moses he says, Can I call you Squirrely?"

"How did it make you feel? The request."

"I dunno."

"Did it make you uneasy?"

"*Are you scared of the closeness, Kevin?*—is that what you're saying? You know, Amanda, under the circumstances I'm not particularly unnerved at the thought of male-to-male intimacy. You're not holding out the threat of the psychologically unknown here."

"Or did it please you?"

"You know, I kind of wish I *would* feel some clear sign of attraction to him. Actually, I think it's his niece I got the hots for."

"His niece?"

"The legendary Diana. She's up at Dartmouth. I've never seen her, incidentally, only her photographs, which Terry's yanking out of his wallet every five minutes. But I had a dream about her. I think it was her. She was all in white."

"Totally in white?"

"She's getting married this summer. And I'm going to be there—Terry says he wants me to come. She's really the one bright star in his life. Figure it out. He's got this horrible smothering mother who he refers to, without the least sense of irony, as *Mob*. He's got this horrible grasping vulgar older sister. He's got this little browbeaten father. He's got the tragedy of his dead wife, and the knowledge—which he won't go near, incidentally—that the loss of this fat, depressed mule of a woman who was always deserting him for her parents' house does maybe have its compensations? He's got this ghastly, horrible, worse-than-horrible friend Adam, who leads him like a pet monkey on a chain, I mean the deference here is absolutely dis*gust*ing, he's this guy with this big braying donkey's laugh whose idea of a hot time is flirting with over-the-hill dog-faced cocktail waitresses. Why are you smiling? You know, just because I describe somebody's life as horrible doesn't necessarily mean it isn't actually horrible."

"You were telling me about your dream."

"My dream? Oh yeah. Anyway, in the dream Terry brought her to the shop. He brings this pretty young thing to the shop, and then he disappears, goes to watch the hamsters run in circles or something, and I lead her out back to show her the reptiles."

"And . . ."

"And will you think it's a cover-up if I don't remember? Does it necessarily mean I'm repressing something ghastly?"

"What does she look like?"

"Pretty. Pretty pretty. Enough to make the heart in a bald little ogre like me go pit-a-pat. Pit-a-pat."

"Does she look like him?"

"Listen to you—listen to your mind. He's this silly-looking guy who parts his hair down the middle . . . Actually, though, want to know something? Maybe the human interests me—interests me physically—less and less? And who's to say that isn't a good sign? The last time I mentioned what I call my Plague Fantasy—the notion of something more powerful than the bubonic plague or AIDS eventually wiping everybody off the planet—you gave me your watch-out-Kevin-the-screwball-in-you-is-*really*-coming-out-now look, but I honestly can't stop thinking the world would be a better place without us. You can see the fantasy as a show of enormous aggression and misanthropy, etcetera, etcetera, but you could also see it as a sort of fair-minded appraisal by somebody who owns a couple of pet stores and naturally spends a lot of time thinking about animal extinctions. There's a good case to be made that it's a shame the animals didn't push Noah and his family right off the ark. Of course there are days when I think maybe we do exaggerate our own destructive powers. When I think it's some sort of macho thing—that we're relishing the notion that we're such big-dicked bastards we can even give Mother Nature a screwing. Maybe we're not as big as we think? You got to ask yourself, Would the planet really smell much better today if no one in the history of the world had ever farted? But then there are days when I know in my heart that we're really much more vile even than we imagine. We're killing the only decent planet in the universe. Collectively, that's the one major thing we're doing. Killing the planet. Forget all the other news. Throw away all the newspapers. That's the biggest fact there is."

"Nothing else about the young woman, Kevin?"

"Hn?"

"The woman in the dream."

"No, but I had another dream—the night after the girl-in-white dream, actually—and in this second dream I was masturbating in the back of the shop. Where the reptiles are. Spilling my seed right there among the snakes and lizards. All those scaly, crawly, cold-blooded little bastards. Baring my snake to the snakes, huh? And you know what? It had a curious feeling of fullness about it. Self-sufficiency. Holy shit, I belonged."

"You sure this was a dream?"

He laughs, again boisterously, and recrosses his legs. "I'll leave that up to you."

"It's a way of bringing her back, isn't it?"

"Who?"

"Who do you think?"

"Pat? My great love—my reptologist? Why in the world would I possibly be interested in bringing back the one woman I ever had a decent, loving relationship with?"

"So how *did* it make you feel? When he asked to call you Squirrely?"

"You know the odd thing is, she was probably right—*she* here being my aunt."

"Your aunt?"

"My screwball aunt. Now I know you think I go around thinking everybody's screwy so I can project my problems on them, etcetera, etcetera, but in her case I'm on pretty solid ground, aren't I? I mean here's a woman who literally winds up in the loony bin. But if you want to know why she went seductive on me—something, I need hardly say, neither of us was *all* that keen on—it does make a kind of sense, doesn't it? You got a lunatic woman who's not only a lunatic but a religious lunatic, and whose lunatic of a husband may be trying, in the world's *most* bizarre and roundabout fashion, to turn her nephew into a heaven-help-us homo . . . what else is she going to do? And you could say it worked, couldn't you? I'm not a homo—but I'm not quite a real hetero either, am I? I figure you got three categories here, heteros, homos, and who knows."

"It's misleading to talk about seduction, isn't it?"

"Go ahead—be a stickler."

"It's not being a stickler—it's just a matter of simple facts.

In both cases, him and her, there's a big difference between the symbol and the act, between psychological and actual, physical—"

"*You're* a fine one to say that the psychological isn't real."

"It's not a question of re*ality*. It's a simple matter of who actually put, or in this case didn't put—"

"Argue it out with fucking Freud. I know what I know. I lived it. Every fucking day."

"Maybe this isn't a situation anyone needs to argue about . . ."

"Meanwhile I got this kid coming into the shop every day for a week. Mooning around for hours at a time. Half an hour in front of the fish. Half an hour pondering the hamsters, which I wouldn't have thought possible. Well, I'm pretty sure what he's screwing his nerve up to, but the fact is I got more help than I can use at the moment."

"And?"

"And of course I guessed it. Guessed it exactly. Only detail I hadn't anticipated, he's got this terrible stutter. He wants a juh-juh-juh-job."

"What did you say to him?"

"I said to him, Fuck you, if there's one thing I can't abide it's a goddamn stutterer. I hire you, I said to him, and the next thing you know you'll have the parrots asking for a cuh-cuh-cuh-cracker."

"What did you say to him?"

"Hired him after school two days a week. Four-sixty-five an hour, and it's goddamn charity is what it is. It's money thrown away and I figure you ought to reimburse me half, Amanda. You're the one always going on about my need to make fucking human contacts."

"I'm proud of you."

"Save your goddamn sympathy."

"You know you're really becoming foul-mouthed."

"Now that's interesting. This time you've truly hit on something *interesting*, Amanda. Because you want to know something? I almost never am normally, outside this room. You don't have to believe this—"

"I believe it. It's certainly nothing to boast about . . ."

"But it's true. The only place I ever seem to curse is right here. Right fucking here. Now why is that? What do you think that means?"

"I don't know."

"Why am I someone different here than out there? Huh?"

"Sometimes when I say I don't know, it's because I don't know. Let's say we're exploring it, you and I."

"But what do you think? You must have a theory."

"I told you before, there are all sorts of transitional stages that might be useful. Something between 'in here' and 'out there.' Various groups . . ."

"Shit, Amanda, can you see me going to some fucking group?"

"Tell me why you don't think it would do you any good. Some of them are quite reasonably priced, you know."

"Back to money, are we? And why *is* it that we're so goddamn sure that tightass Kevin won't be in the pink of health until he agrees to bankrupt himself?"

"What do you think you need, then?"

"Nothing. Or just what Terry's little cutie-pie on the airplane was looking for—a new life. Sign me *up!* Or maybe a woman who would come to me out of a cloud and say, Keep your dick in your pants when you go anywhere near those lizards and snakes." He laughs, uncrosses his legs, crosses them once more.

"Tell me about Terry."

"You tell me about Terry, Amanda. You've listened to me on the subject long enough."

"All right. For starters, he's good for you. This is the best thing in a while. I've said before—you need friends."

"I've got the kids at the store."

"Friends your own age. A peer milieu, if you will. In place of troubled teenagers. In place of parrots and hamsters and sea horses."

"I told you about what I chose to read to Terry? The night of the pot? When he got so sick and asked me to read to him?" He laughs.

"You need people of your own age to care about, to worry about."

"Well I do worry about him. Even if that was a mean trick. I mean what I read. Mermaids . . ."

"Tell me why you worry about him."

"We're just about out of time, aren't we. And what should I say before the gong rings? You know, speaking of things he will not go near, absolutely *will not go near,* he won't touch the notion that his wife's death might not have been an accident."

"Why do you think it wasn't?"

"I do, I mean I do think it was an accident. I'd bet real money on its being an accident. But in *any* accident of this sort there's always the possibility of suicide, isn't there? Or of a sort of languor that's very *close* to suicide? And if you won't face that— well, then you've got a fire in your bed sheets, don't you?"

"Fire and water . . ."

"Fire and water: good for you, Amanda. Good for you . . . You know, I said earlier that Diana's the one real something special in his life, but actually suddenly he's got two something specials. He's also got the knowledge that he's the sort of guy who's seen a ghost. And of course he's totally *unzipped* by this, even though he's been waiting all his life for what he used to call his *one extraordinary thing.* It's hilarious, really. I mean, he's the world's most unlikely mystic. That's the best part of this story. That's really the one enormous charm of the thing—it's sort of a Meet John Doe Meet the Bride of Frankenstein thing, huh?" Laughter. "Amanda, for Christ's sake he's a goddamn Republican. I've befriended a goddamn Republican. The world's going to hell, we're killing off all the animals, we're poisoning the planet, and I've befriended one of these we've-got-to-be-practical Republicans. I ask you, is there anything more impractical in the whole world, anything more short-sighted, than the Republican Party?"

"John Doe meets the Bride of Frankenstein. Maybe you should have been a moviemaker, Kevin."

"So what does he do? He goes after this ghost of his as if it were a legal problem. A matter of establishing precedents, interpreting rules. But it's a whole lot more intractable than that, isn't it? He's yanking up the—the underpinnings of his life, with my help, and I worry he's in for a big sense of letdown. Maybe even a bad shock."

On the playground, below, a boy calls *Got you* and another voice, so high and shrill in its strangled urgency that one cannot say whether it issues from the throat of boy or girl, replies, *But you never touched me.* The boy announces *You're it!* and the other voice—frantic, gone shriller still in its sense of rampant unfairness, of justice waylaid—replies, *But you never touched me. You never touched me at all.*

A Single Invitation

There is a world out there. The phrase arrived as he was padding barefoot into the kitchen, which he found awash with morning sun. He recited the words aloud. The light was brilliant and to step into the thick of it was to enter a keen awareness of natural bounty—a sense of things outdoors beginning to teem underneath the unseasonable February sun. The kitchen windowpanes, winter's dust ground into them, had turned glowingly opaque in all the dazzle, but the backyard swelter beyond them was no less real for its invisibility; it was, if anything, more lush and resolute for that. On the other side of those luminous rectangles lay outspread an earth too spirited to repose until the calendar said it ought to; unmistakably, spring was here.

He fixed himself a cup of mint tea. For the moment, anyway, he was off caffeine. This wasn't a regimen he intended to stick to. He had merely been curious, having cleansed alcohol from his life, what it would be like to follow a diet without obvious vices. It had been three weeks now since he'd eaten any meat and did he feel any alteration yet? He couldn't say . . . But the mint tea in the morning, the club soda undarkened by scotch at night, the vegetarianism all day long—these things had the supplementary benefit of erecting a sort of barrier around this unique and too brief interlude in his career; they distanced him from those suit-and-tie corridors that had enclosed his existence in the past and would do so in the future. Adam liked to call it "vacation time," but in his own heart of hearts Terry much preferred to think of himself as "on leave." The latter had a headier sound to it, and these were heady days.

He was wearing blue sweatpants and a gray sweatshirt he'd slept in. One of the unforeseen boons of America's ongoing fitness craze was that it allowed a grown-up to spend the day proudly and publicly in his pajamas. Actually, he had no exercise plans for the day, and hadn't really given himself a workout in weeks. Although daily exercise might be thought naturally to go along with temperance and vegetarianism, in his mind it was all too closely bound up with the pressures of the office—with, specifically, Adam on the road, swimming laps in an unlit motel pool long after midnight.

More than ever he felt the need to take some sort of trip—make some sort of pilgrimage. It would be fun just to disappear, perhaps, for a day or two. Get on a plane, on a train, get into the Audi and just head out—but where? The destination wasn't something he should fix himself. By rights, it ought to come on its own. Neither of the obvious choices attracted him. He could head back to the Dismal Swamp, observe it in a new light and season—only, he didn't want to go back there. Or he could drive down to Charlottesville, where Betsy lies buried, but there, too, was where he didn't want to be right now. The urge needed to clarify itself, as surely it would. In the meantime, he was a would-be pilgrim without a destination.

Terry sat at his kitchen table, savoring a sense of outspread amplitude. The green aroma of his mint tea bloomed in his head as he repeated the morning's phrase: "There is a world out there."

The question was: Where to go in it?

He had a great many tasks on today's docket, including one special one, in the living room, that he'd been saving as a treat for himself. But this would wait another ten minutes or so. He also needed at some point to do a grocery shop, and there were the kitchen windows to wash, there were many windows needing washing. Let it in—let the spring light in! In retrospect, it was funny how much he'd worried about this period away from the office, fearing the time might hang too heavily on his hands and he be compelled to confess to an internal bankruptcy. One of the many surprises of these past few weeks had been his constant sense of busy plenty. It was almost enough to make him wonder how in the world he'd ever managed a full-time job. Getting dressed, eating his meals, running errands, doing the reading he needed to do, seeing people occasionally—these things packed his day utterly.

He took a slurping tentative sip from his tea and found it still too hot to drink. He could wait. He would watch the steam rise from it—disappearing just at that wavery point where truly interesting shapes began to emerge.

He recalled an afternoon, a dark, damp, skin-penetrating winter afternoon of many years ago, when he'd come home numb from school and Mob made him a cup of hot chocolate. Sitting in the breakfast nook, alone, waiting for the chocolate to cool enough to drink, daydreaming about something or other (probably glory of some sort), he'd stared out into the darkness, over the back fence at old Mrs. Wheatley's place, and had seen a head dart past one of her upstairs windows, only this wasn't the widow's head—not her gray-haired bun but a quick jumpy gold flash that could only have belonged to one of her grandchildren, come for a rare visit. And that was it, was the sum and substance of his vision—one moment's tremor of gold—and yet, improbably enough, he'd retained it. He'd stored it up as one of those joys so uneventful they seem to persist by virtue of their littleness, having always succeeded in being overlooked when the mind cleared itself of clutter.

Lately, he'd been recalling all sorts of things out of childhood—frequently enough, and passionately enough, that he'd had to reappraise just what that period had consisted of. Over the years, whenever the subject of his upbringing came up, he would report that he'd had a "happy childhood." Certainly he'd escaped the catastrophes that had afflicted various of his acquaintances—for him, no proximate deaths, no divorce in the family, no grave illnesses. (The odd fact was that the first corpse he'd ever laid eyes on had been his own wife.) Back then, he'd lived a step by step ascent—with the promise of future vistas that, he'd known from the start, ranged beyond anything the flat-open landscapes of Iowa might contain. He'd been—for a time—consistently fortunate.

In recent weeks, though, he'd come on another feeling: a peculiar suspicion that to describe those days as *happy* was to simplify them, diminish them. When the memories came back lately, they returned in a field of enhanced, exaggerated pigments. Everything was dusted with a sort of dancing dust, the grit-glitter vibrancy of enchantment, and it was as if those days had taken place in a world of spellbound tints and lusters, and this was an inkling somehow obscurely connected to that evening at Kopp's when he'd made the mistake of trying pot again (but that evening had been so calamitous he could hardly bear to pursue connections there).

Whatever—whatever. And it was connected as well to his impression this morning of the luxuriance of his yard, unseen beyond the glowing windows. Could it truly be that in his take on the world something mystical had gradually dissipated—so gradually, so imperceptibly as to leave no trace of vacancy or loss behind? There was a wealth of evidence to suggest quite the contrary, wasn't there? Hadn't his life grown more rather than less interesting over the years? His view of the world richer with time? It had occurred to him lately that perhaps he should have gone to a shrink—not to deal with his loss, and still less to deal with his apparition or whatever, but merely to analyze questions of perception. The not always clear truth was that the loss of Betsy had been so monumental a loss—had so upended his world—that he sometimes felt he could no longer reconstruct the world she'd inhabited, or the world he'd inhabited before they'd met. Over certain memories, over certain objects, there floated this dancing dust. There was indeed a world out there . . .

He sipped from his tea, which had cooled to the point of perfection. He had work to do, of course—research that needed to be got at—but before he took it up he had a treat in store. It was waiting for him in the living room, and surely every day ought to begin with a treat. He lifted cup and saucer and brought them with him, through the hallway. He stopped at the threshold of the living room. There it was—empty, full of potential—in all its fifty-five gallon transparent glory: his new aquarium.

Kopp had volunteered to help with the setting up, but Terry had wanted to do it alone, and at this stage, anyway, he didn't need any assistance. When was the last time he'd bought anything that had so thrilled him, that quickened his hands in quite this tight, jumpy, jubilant way? He'd pondered each detail, read all sorts of pamphlets, even checked out other stores, though he'd known he would make all purchases at Just Off the Ark. Curly had suggested starting with a twenty-gallon tank, but he'd yearned for something larger. Their disagreement had turned comical: Kopp the salesman urging him to economize, while Terry the customer talked himself toward ever more ambitious designs.

He'd brought it all in from the car last night: the tank itself, the tank stand, the cover, the bags of gravel, the fake coral, the box that contained the pump, filter, thermometer. Before going to bed he'd sponged out the tank, but that was as far as he'd gone; he hadn't permitted himself even the first step toward assembly. The tank had held nothing but air all night. Today was the day—this sun-flooded morning—he was destined to launch the creation of his little living micro-eco-system.

He carried a twenty-pound bag of sand-colored gravel back into the kitchen and set it down on the table. He had bought more than he would need, probably—twenty pounds of black and forty of tan. Though he generally carried a tune so clumsily it was no fun to sing or hum, even in solitude, this morning a song was on his lips: "I *co*-ver the water-*front*, I *c*over the sea-ea . . ." He clicked the scissors in time to the music, creating an effect a little like castanets: "Will the *one* I love be *com*ing back to *me?*"

He hauled the bag of sand-colored gravel to the kitchen sink, where was waiting the largest kettle in the house. (A wedding gift from whom? So much day-to-day information had been lost with Betsy's going . . .) He hung the bag over the kettle's edge and opened its mouth slightly, creating a satisfying snake-like slither as the little stones oozed onto the kettle's white ceramic floor. When the bag's contents were all but depleted, he upended it with both hands and gave it a shake to free the last of the stones. A fine gravelly dust floated in the air.

He began filling the kettle with water. He had switched to another song:

> Oh, dear, what can the matter be?
> Oh, dear, what can the matter be?
> Oh, dear, what can the matter be?
> Johnny's so long at the fair . . .

By the time the water level had topped the stones, it was carrying a gray scrim of powder; this stuff was dirty. He plunged his hands in and combed his fingers through the stones, to dislodge any dust that might be trapped below. Meanwhile he let the water keep rising, rising, rising until it overflowed. Then, with a grunt, he tipped the kettle with one hand, cupping the other hand as a sieve beneath the flow. He didn't want to send any gravel down the sink.

After draining the kettle (which could not have been drained as well as he thought, for the load of gravel was *far* heavier on the way out of the kitchen than on the way in) he carried it into the living room and, turning his hand into a claw, emptied the contents onto the aquarium floor. The wet gravel clung to everything—to his hands and to the hair of his forearms and even to the front of his shirt. He had envisioned this as a much neater job than it was turning out to be.

Finally with his palms he smoothed the stones level. They filled the tank to a depth of an inch or so—just high enough to extend slightly above the black metal rim of the base; they would be visible.

He started on another twenty-pound bag. This one held black stones, for he had decided on a striated effect. Again he carried, dumped, rinsed, carried, dumped, smoothed. In his envisionings he'd neatly, crisply laid the bed of black on the bed of sandy stones, but it wasn't quite like that. The stones fell in clumps, and in the smoothing—careful as he was—they mingled, the tan and the black. He didn't have quite the sharp, layered lines he'd foreseen. At last he stepped back to survey his work.

Okay, this was going to be fine—this was going to be close to perfect. It wouldn't be long until the whole thing was humming with life, flashing with the glints and the dartings of undersea appetites. He was going to get some jumbo neon tetras; they'd grown on him over the last few months. They were less spectacular than painted glassfish, but comelier in the long run. He liked the way groups of them sometimes moved as one—throwing at the viewer first a blue side and then, with a telepathic simultaneity, a red side. And he would have plants, dried ones first (no plastic plants in his tank!) and later the real, the rooted article.

It was already clear to him, before a drop of water had been placed within it, that his new aquarium would be far more gratifying even than he'd figured. It would conform, that is, to the norm of these last few weeks—for he was coming to assume that life would periodically dole out to him profound and unforeseeable pleasures. These days he found himself savoring all sorts of things he scarcely noticed as a rule: how, for instance, the color of his raspberry jam on his morning slice of toast graded from a blood-red to an almost plasmic yellow as it thinned under the blade of the aluminum knife, or how, at day's end, the removal of a food particle in your evening's flossing eased a pressure you hadn't recognized—but one present all along, ever since morning, for the removed particle proved to be a raspberry seed. Fate was dealing him a compensation; this sensual enhancement arrived as if in recompense for the frustrations of his research. He had worked hard, and he deserved rewards of one sort or another.

Ironically, for all its associations with the wild and woolly, the literature of hallucinations had turned out to be tedious and unhelpful and predictable and *tame*. He had gamely slogged through page after page of both the medical literature and a number of first-person accounts. He had kept notebooks. He'd started with two, which he had grandly (and, he liked to think, wittily) entitled SCIENTIFIC DATA and OTHER DATA. They corresponded to what Kopp would call the Guest Hypothesis and the Round-the-Bend Hypothesis. But in time, as the subjects ramified, he'd found it useful to open other folders: there was a historical folder (devoted chiefly to the development of the science of psychical research) and a folder containing firsthand accounts and a folder of vocabulary terms. It turned out that he had had what was designated as a *positive hallucination* (the seeing or hearing of what wasn't there), as opposed to a negative hallucination (not seeing or not hearing what was there). But nothing, in the end, seemed to have any solid bearing on his own experience. The scientific materials, with their discussions of flash cards and sensory leakage and meta-analysis, or rods and cones, or statistical deviations and normalizations, captured none of the incident's force. And to look at some of the photographs—to see a human receptor prepared for the Gangfeld procedure, headphones strapped to his ears and halved Ping-Pong balls settled over his eye sockets—made Terry positively squirm. It was a

little like reading about prosthetic devices for male sexual dysfunction—surely there were some things that ought to be left
alone? Meanwhile, the firsthand accounts almost invariably
seemed, in their credulous fluency, the work of either lunatics or
charlatans. They were only a step removed from those people in
Bertha's tabloids who, pursuing the last step in miscegenation,
mated with extraterrestrials.

Even the mere business of obtaining the books had been dispiriting. No, more than that: it had been sullying. He'd never
properly understood before the atmosphere surrounding the
"Occult" section of a big bookstore—at least that of a bookstore
in a troubled, often fairly demented city like Washington. To
browse there was to stand among titles like *Within the Within* and
Squaring the Circle of the Bermuda Triangle and *The Psi-entific
Mind,* and to come upon self-help books guaranteed to teach
you how to talk to your houseplants in a mere six weeks' time.
It was to rub shoulders with people who literally smelled of
drugs, with others who handed you "$2 off Zodiacal Sale" cou-
pons for palm readings, with others who debated vociferously
with themselves while picking up titles like *The Multiple Mind*
and *The Myth of the Individual*. It was—as truly had happened to
Terry one afternoon, as he stood in a bookstore in Dupont
Circle—to have a very tall and very black-haired young woman
(the roots of her hair a sandy blond) point to you and declare,
"You are a victim of major karmic turbulence . . ."

*A victim of major karmic turbulence? Actually, lady, I'm a commu-
nications lawyer,* is what he should have replied. (The best lines
usually got away from him.) So far, the only satisfying side to
his work had been the purely historical. He had investigated
psychical research as a phenomenon of time and place, reading
a good account of the origins of the SPR, the Society for Psychical Research, founded in England in 1882. This "science" he
was investigating, such as it was, extended back over a hundred
years. And it was founded in what surely was a proper—i.e., a
sober-minded—spirit. Its first report promised that "our pages
are far more likely to provoke sleep in the course of perusal than
to banish it afterwards." He'd also read William James and Al-
dous Huxley and looked into the spiritualists in upstate New

York, and the famous forging of data at Duke. He had toyed, years ago, while still in college, with the idea of history graduate school, and while he had no complaint with the law as a profession, still it *was* a little unnerving to see how at home he felt with this sort of research.

And he'd gone on writing letters—crisp, concise, reasonable letters—to various researchers and authors. It turned out that there were three scholarly organizations in New York: the American Society for Psychical Research (founded in 1885!), the Paranormal Research Institute, and the Psi Center. Each of them published a journal. The materials were voluminous. He wrote his letters care of the publisher, care of the institute, care of the magazine—trusting that *something* in all this out-go must reach its rightful recipient. He wrote asking for clarification, for verification, for supplementation; he wrote asking, in effect, *What's new?* There were many, many accounts to investigate—there were whole books that purported to list verified psychical experiences, with names and addresses attached, and he wrote letters somewhat at random, as caprice moved him. He wrote to the Harvard-educated psychiatrist-author of a book called *Revisitations,* asking for more information about a patient, a woman, who had seen her deceased husband down in the basement; he'd been operating a jigsaw. (A neighbor discovered her—she'd fainted—and discovered as well, beside the jigsaw, a well-turned-out mortise joint.) He wrote a letter of inquiry to a Dr. Paul Noolan, an optometrist whose account of how his deceased twin brother had come to him during a blinding blizzard in the Cascade Mountains and led him to safety had seemed oddly moving. He even wrote to a psychical researcher in California who'd known a woman who one morning came downstairs to find a pineapple upside-down cake cooling on her sidebar; when she cut it open, she found the turquoise ring her Hispanic cook had always worn, before passing on four years before. And so forth. Terry wrote such letters all in one go, four or five at a time—lest he give himself time enough to ponder closely his own behavior.

He was asking, in effect, *What's new?,* but so far the replies had been silly, or unhelpful (referring him to things like what he'd already read), or nonexistent. More and more these weeks away seemed in practice what they were in name: a vacation. (It occurred to him how he might best answer, on his return to work, the inevitable *Where did you go on your vacation?*: "I went to Never-never land.") But if he had found nothing resembling an answer, or even a method toward an answer, he had nonetheless found something almost better perhaps: an unlooked-for talent in himself for tapping into the wordless, interconnected elations of his surroundings. There were mornings when he would swear that the knife in his hands was pleased to be spreading the raspberry jam, that the toast underneath the knife was thrilled to be receiving it . . . He was happier than he'd been in—how long? These days felt good. These days *he* felt good. And yet, if what he had found in himself was heartening it was also patently fragile, and the thought of going back to work, of being buried once more in the thick of things, was bleak beyond words. How would he protect himself?

He laid in another bag of sandy-colored stones. The effect, whether from up close or from across the room, was dramatic. He picked up the phone and rapidly tapped out a familiar number.

"'Lo."

"I've just put the stones down. Sandy, then black, then sandy."

"There's no point in it. They're going to get all jumbled up. First time you give 'em a suction cleaning, they're going to get all jumbled up."

"You're supposed to ask me how they look."

"How do they look?"

"Fine. Very nifty. *Promising.*"

"You washed out the tank first."

"I washed out the tank first."

"You putting the water in today?"

"I'm putting the water in today. And everything else. What's dinner?"

"I dunno, why don't you come on out here?"

"Why don't you come on down here?"

"I dunno. I like Baltimore food better."

"You're hopeless," Terry said. "Come on, I've been out your way three times this week. It's your turn. We'll eat Chinese—

two vegetarians. And then we'll go eat cheesecake at the Oven Door."

"Come on out here, we'll eat cheesecake at Carlo's."

"You're hopeless. You do know you're hopeless? Hold on— I've got a knock at the front door."

"Call me back. I got things to do."

"I'll call you back."

Terry hung up the phone. By the time he reached the living room, Adam had already stepped inside.

"You're all dressed up," Terry said.

"It *is* a work day, correct me if I'm wrong? According to the traditional, that is to say the old fart's, calendar? You're not losing track of what day it is, are you?"

"Hardly," Terry said, and laughed with a bright charged guiltiness—for this was a plainspoken lie. A couple of times, lately, he'd found himself off by a day. Time was moving faster than his own internal clock told him it ought to be moving. "So why aren't you at work?"

"Running some errands. Speaking of running, you look dressed for a run. Been out yet?"

"Thinking about it. You want some coffee?"

"Got some already made?"

"I was just thinking of making some." Terry wasn't about to confess to Adam, who was already formidably armed for debate, that he'd recently given up caffeine.

"Who do you know in Iceland?"

"Come again? I don't know anybody in Iceland."

"Germany?"

"What are you talking about?"

"Why are you suddenly getting letters from Iceland and Germany?" Adam had the morning mail in his hands.

"Iceland?"

"Tryggvi Hannibalsson? Surely the name's a fabrication? He's maybe some sort of arctic pornography dealer or something? Or could it be you're—"

"Tryggvi Hannibalsson. Oh good Lord—let me see it."

Adam handed over an airmail envelope and a manila envelope, retaining for himself the rest of the mail. The airmail envelope, almost unreadable for her sprawling handwriting, was from

Terry's sister-in-law, or ex-sister-in-law, Heidi. He decided he'd open that one first. It was a long letter, mercifully typed, and he scanned its contents quickly as he headed out into the kitchen. It appeared to be dutifully full of news—long paragraphs devoted to her Frankfurt apartment, a recent trip to Cologne, her children's schooling. On the bottom of the third page Terry found the one passage of true interest to him: "Yes, I too constantly think of Betsy, and I do feel constantly that she is still right here. Of course she will always be right here, just as long as I'm here, as long as you're here. And wouldn't she have liked Frankfurt! I think about this all the time, especially when I go to a little park nearby, where there are all sorts of . . ." and so it went, responsible and affectionate and utterly earthbound. Clearly, Heidi had had no visitations. And to whom, besides himself, was Betsy likely to appear if not to Heidi?

The manila envelope, the one from Tryggvi Hannibalsson, held a photocopied article, from the *Psi Center Journal,* with a short letter attached:

Dear Mr. Seward:

I have been slow to answer your interesting letter. It took some time to reach me here in Iceland, forwarded from North Carolina. It would not be possible to talk with you in North Carolina because I am no longer conducting research there. But I will be leaving soon for New York City, where I could be contacted at the Psi Center on East 72th Street. I will be working there for a few months at least, beginning in mid-February.

I am glad that you found my essay interesting. I enclose a more recent effort that may interest you.

> *Sincerely yours,*
> *Tryggvi Hannibalsson*

"What is it, let me see."

"It's from a guy I wrote to. Don't you love his name?" Terry handed over the letter but not the article to Adam, who had taken a seat at the kitchen table. Terry filled a kettle with tap water. A week ago he'd banished, as a temptation, his coffee machine to the basement.

"What's the article?"

"Some of his research. He's sort of a statistician—at least he takes a very statistical approach. It's all pretty rigorous."

"Let me see."

"In his own way, he's as rigorous as anybody at City and Country. That's my father's old insurance company."

"Let me see."

Regretfully, jittery with misgivings, Terry handed over the article and turned busily to the task of coffee-making. He rattled through the cupboards in search of a paper filter.

"You are kidding, aren't you, Babe? Putting me on? 'Putative Encounters with the Recently Deceased: A Further Study.' This is some sort of hoax?"

Terry turned and delivered a little oration. It was articulate enough, though his flustered emotions drove his inflections upward, converting declarations into questions:

"He's done some very interesting things, Adam. For instance, he went and talked to people in two completely different countries, Thailand and Holland, who had been, you know, clinically dead? To see what the similarities and differences were, trying to get at what's cultural and what's innate? I mean it's very interesting, even if you're a total skeptic. Such things are interesting sociologically, at the very least?"

His speech concluded, Terry immediately returned to the task of the coffee: setting out a sugar bowl, some half-and-half, a couple of cups.

"You do understand that this is somebody who writes articles about putative encounters with the recently deceased? Are we talking about the same thing here, Champ? Huh? *People who see spooks?*"

"Actually, of all the people I wrote to, he was the one I most wanted to hear from. There are some real loonies out there, Adam. I can tell you right now that they far outnumber any—"

"It is a hoax after all, isn't it? You know, for a while I thought you were going off the deep end, but now at last I'm wise to your game. This is something you and Squirrely cooked up, isn't it? You're testing the limits of *my* sanity?"

"Cut it out, Adam. This has nothing to do with Kevin, and you know it. And this man, Hannibalsson, he's a real scientist."

By way of reply, Adam merely repeated, in a deep, fruity voice, the essay's title: *Putative Contacts with the Recently Deceased: A Further Study*.

Terry poured Adam and himself cups of coffee, sat down, added a generous amount of half-and-half to his own cup, stirred into it two teaspoons of sugar and—all without recalling that he had forsworn caffeine—took a large swallow. It was only as the stuff eased burningly down his throat that he recollected himself. The coffee was distressingly satisfying—he'd missed it more than he'd realized.

"Oh God," Terry said, "I've got something great I want to show you."

"Mm?"

"Come on." He led Adam back into the living room and with a big sweep of his arm indicated the empty aquarium.

"It's—it's a trophy case? Something for your pole vault medals and ribbons?"

"Cut it out. It's an aquarium."

"You don't do things by halves, do you?"

"It's fifty-five gallons," Terry reported proudly.

"It's a big responsibility."

"Oh I know. I've been reading up all about it. Ammonia levels, nitrates, purification tablets, *algal invasions* . . ."

"I mean financially."

"Oh come on."

"No, I mean it. What have you sunk into it so far?"

"I got everything at cost. From Kopp. And it's not as though I've promised to put any of my fish through college." Terry turned to the tank and addressed a hovering cloud of imaginary fish, who were listening to him in fetchingly big-eyed, Disney-ish wonder: "Although I do want you all to know that if any of you kids are admitted to Dartmouth, you don't have to worry your pretty little heads about the bills."

"I came by to tell you that your girlfriend's going to be in town tonight."

"Diana?" It was the obvious assumption.

"Allie. Allie Collier. She doesn't seem to mind if *I* call her Allie."

"Here? What's she doing here?"

"This, that, and the other. And the Marquette licensing. And something to do with the FTC I think. Anyway, I told her I'd meet her for dinner. I told her *we'd* meet her for dinner."

"I kind of got other plans."

"What kind of kind of plans?"

"It's just that I told Kopp I'd meet him."

"And that won't keep? You can't put that one off a day, pal? What's tonight's seminar topic—putative contacts with the recently deceased?" Adam guffawed.

In his suit and tie Adam across the living room looked imposing—looked almost larger than life, as though he'd grown wider, taller in recent weeks. The light in here was dim (the room did not catch the morning sun as the kitchen did) and it was hard to judge how much true impatience, how much feigned despair was on his face.

In his uncertainty, Terry standing there in his sweatclothes felt shakily vulnerable. "All right. What time?"

"Eight. At Buccatino."

"I'll be there."

Terry turned and padded back into the kitchen, dropped into his seat at the table and sipped at his coffee. Tepid—and yet it still tasted marvelous.

Adam also took a seat, but immediately announced, "I better be going."

"So how are things at the office?"

"We're billing time, we're billing time. You know, you're keeping out of there much better than I ever thought you could."

"It's alarmingly easy . . ."

"Well I suppose if you're going to get out, it makes sense to really get out. So tell me—what's a typical day? Today, for instance? What's today's itinerary?"

Terry sipped his coffee. "Reading, research, maybe some correspondence. Of course today's sort of special cause of the aquarium."

"I wish I knew what you were after. I mean really *after*."

"It's hard to get that across to you when you're always telling me you don't want to hear about it . . ."

This was a fine refutation, which Adam-the-litigator must in fairness acknowledge as such; he lifted one eyebrow on his massive forehead and nodded.

"A while ago," Terry went on, "that time at Kopp's when I smoked the pot and got sick, I recollected something I guess I'd forgotten. This was years ago, when Betsy and I went to a party where for reasons I needn't go into now we got dragged into this party game where we had to describe ourselves with just one word."

"How godawful."

"I know, I know, very touchy-feely and all the rest, but let's not get sidetracked. Anyway, what does Betsy write? How does she sum herself up? Do you know she actually wrote ARTISTIC? And you know something else? The thought of her writing that has really been haunting me these past few weeks."

"Understandably. Me, I'm haunted at the thought . . ."

"No, I really *have* been, and not for the reasons you might suppose. Artistic? Ar*tis*tic? Here's this woman who can't draw even a proper stick figure, who plays no musical instrument, sings almost as badly as I do, has never acted or anything of the sort, doesn't write poetry—thank the Lord—doesn't sew quilts or weave baskets, doesn't even build solar doghouses or model railroad cars, *doesn't even garden,* and yet how at the end of the day does she decide to sum herself up? Artistic, that's how."

"Was she sort of shit-faced? Lots of things can be explained away once you assume somebody's totally shit-faced."

"The point is that I'm left sometimes wondering, Who the hell *was* this woman? The point is that sometimes things that I *know* happened, and that I saw with my very own eyes, like the time she wrote ARTISTIC at the party, seem far less real to me than something that maybe never did happen, like the incident in the cabin."

Rising from the table, Adam looked at Terry searchingly, and said, "I gotta go, we'll talk tonight."

"Okay, eight o'clock, at Piedmont, I'll be there. Don't worry."

"Piedmont? I said *Buccatino.* Boy, you really *are* losing the grip. By the way," Adam said. Again that eyebrow had risen. "What was your word?"

"My word?"

"What did you write for yourself that night?"

"Me? I wrote SOLID," Terry told him.

"Tiger, you're all right," Adam said and extended his hand—which seemed so oddly, awkwardly formal a gesture that Terry's glance dropped from Adam's, settling on the sun-dazzled table. Adam had scarcely touched his coffee. It was the other man, the one who'd renounced caffeine, who had drained his cup.

"You've grown a beard since I saw you last," was the first thing Allie Collier said when they stood across from each other once more; "And you haven't," was his answer, which was apparently the perfect reply. She laughed warmly, shook his hand with what seemed affection.

Hit the right first note and the rest's a snap—he was witty, he was intelligent, he was fully at his ease. And wasn't it funny that all day long he'd been dreading this meeting, just because in his mind she was somehow tied up with the night in the cabin? But what did she have to do with that—or with everything upsetting and bewildering that had followed as a consequence? She had no connection to what had happened, the link was purely an accident of timing, and there was nothing the least bit alarming about her. How had he possibly perceived her as so hard and alluring and mysterious? She was neither so pretty nor so tough as he'd envisioned. No, she was simply an attractive, lively woman who—no less or more than the majority of lawyers he met—was out to make a living. And that cross-eyed gaze of hers? The one that had seemed so elusive, conspiring, manipulative? A fluster of uncertainty—that's what he read there now.

On a day when he'd already succumbed to the vice of caffeine, there could be no compelling reasons for forgoing alcohol. It was even possible that the two contending vices—stimulant, depressant—might strike a metabolic harmony; he ordered a martini. And though he did not order a second when Adam did, he helped himself *quite* liberally to wine at dinner.

Talk flowed on all sides with an unpushed alacrity. Adam told with great success a story about an old law school classmate who'd been nicknamed Muffy because, seeking perfect silence, he'd worn acoustical earmuffs at exams. Anyway, Adam had recently read that Muffy had been indicted for securities fraud—which opened the prospect of Muffy's making license plates in a prison factory, earmuffs still clamped to his head. This led Allie to tell the story of how, when she was at college (Kenyon), the guy who, though she hadn't met him yet, would later be her husband (and, later still, her ex-husband) had been famous throughout the dorm for always sleeping behind 1) a locked door, 2) an eyeshade, and 3) earplugs. One night, the fire alarm went off (a false alarm, naturally) and a couple of overly zealous football players, eager to put their shoulders to work, immediately broke down his door. At this invasion, a blindfolded, deafened young man ("Larry was—is—wonderful, but he's pretty weird") bolted upright, like some zombie in a comical horror film.

This anecdote would have led Terry, a few months ago, to a couple of choice Kopp anecdotes—but he was no longer going to exhibit Kevin in this way. Happily, he didn't need to. For this was truly Terry's night to talk. Judiciously refilling his wine glass now and then, he touched on all the bases—Iowa; Mob and Dad; Dad's famous solar doghouse; his own new aquarium; and the time a drunk had come forward when he and Adam were leaving Memorial Stadium, thrown himself at Adam's feet, and cried out, "You go beyond all *recognition*." What a pleasure it was, as the wine replenished itself and the steaks arrived (vegetarianism, too, was on holiday) to indulge in this sort of talk—without any of Kopp's little probings and qualifications, his gnomic commentaries and squirming eruptions of sharp-edged laughter . . .

Conversation began to get sticky, though, once Allie said to him, "So you've been on a long vacation?"

"That's right. Vacation, leave. Something like that."

"Where you been vacationing?"

"Well I haven't really *been* anywhere, though I'm planning some sort of trip or other. I've been doing research."

"Research? What kind of research?"

"Oh, that's a long story . . ."

And Terry would have been content, probably, to leave the

issue there had Adam not added a wholly superfluous deterrent: "And a boring one . . ."

"I suppose you could call it psychical research," Terry interjected.

"Psychical research?"

"Well Terry's making it sound a whole lot more exotic than it is—" Adam began, but Terry cut him off:

"I've been looking into a mystical experience."

There was a pause, succeeded by a short exchange—of looks, of words—that was unmistakably to be the evening's summit: this the moment from which each subsequent moment must be a descent, a glancing-over-the-shoulder retreat. "Your own?" Allie said to him, and stared him in the eyes. Her own eyes danced with candle flame, with wine, with their own inborn optometrical waver, but behind that dancing was a gemlike steadiness. He glimpsed it there. He had enkindled her curiosity, no question about it, but in this opening up of hers (to which he tried to bring a similarly wide-open, soul-open gazing) he read a pledge of authenticity, of receptivity, of a willingness to follow this question wherever it led—as if she, intuitively, understood his quest. He felt a stirring at the base of his stomach, below his recidivistic carnivore's vitals. She was wearing a beige silk blouse that bared a narrow V below her throat, and though the light in here was too dim for making out such things, he knew from their previous meeting that she was light-handedly freckled there. Fire danced on the curved undersides of her earrings.

"My own . . ." Terry replied.

"Can I—do you mind if I ask what sort of experience this was? You see, the truth is I have a sort of special, personal—" She paused. And what was she on the verge of confessing to?

"I don't *mind*. Quite the contrary. Of course it's a difficult—"

Adam interrupted: "Oh God I can't bear to listen to this. Listen now, if it's *weirdness* you're after, you want to hear something weird? I had an uncle who was a bigamist. No—bigger than that. What's bigger than big? Trig—he was a trigamist."

Whether or not he was prepared actually to unravel the sole mystical experience of his life before Allie's cross-eyed gaze wasn't quite clear to Terry. Meanwhile, Adam's words were a distraction—simultaneously an annoyance, a relief, and a puzzle (what uncle was this?). And while Terry was working on sorting it all out, Allie dropped her gaze, sipped her wine, and volunteered a confession of her own: "You talk about vacations or leaves, I'm going to be leaving Freeley, Polk."

"You are?" Adam said. "For what? When?"

"Well my brother, he's in the antique business, in Chicago, and he's asked me to go in with him."

"The an*tique* business?"

"Oh he's a very big deal. You know anything about antiques? Ever hear of Charley Collier?"

"Antiques?" Adam repeated. "But what will you do if it doesn't work out?"

"Well, theoretically, I'll be on a one-year leave. But I don't plan to go back."

"But what will you do if it doesn't work out?" Adam persisted. "Two years from now, say—what will you do then?"

Allie sipped from her wine. Her thoughtful reply struck Terry as not merely wise but valiant and beautiful. Just *beautiful*—the way she swung her face toward Adam, licked her lips at both corners, and said, "Well then, I guess I'll find a new job. I'll deal with that reality when it comes to me."

"I think that's great," Terry said. "I think that's just marvelous."

"Nn," Adam grunted at Terry, meaning *You would* or *Naturally*.

Terry wanted very much to tell Allie how very much he admired her, or wanted perhaps to expand upon the topic of his research, and in this state of indecision he watched the conversation proceed under Adam's firm guidance. That was all right really, since a sort of affable muddle—could his body already have grown so unused to drink?—had settled upon him.

Adam had taken up control of the conversational flow, and when he gave it back to Terry, which he did before too long, everyone's words moved with the spin Adam had placed upon them. Terry talked about a number of things—Gawana, Mob and Dad, his new aquarium—but there was seemingly no way to reintroduce the topic of his research. The clearing of the dishes, the arrival of three cups of cappuccino, Adam's signing for the bill—each of these developments was, in its way, an obstruction or an evasion. For one moment Terry had held her gaze purely with the vigor of his own gazing, and everything since had clouded that lucent instant. His own conversation, which was meant to bring it back, or bring it closer, was itself a retreat, and what else was he left to ask himself, as he shook her hand at the end of the evening, while a cab waited for her, its door swung wide, except, *Have I made an utter fool of myself?*

"Have I made an utter fool of myself?" was indeed the first thing he said to Adam when, Allie having been given a wave of departure, the two of them got into their own cab.

"What do you mean?"

"It was all too"—Terry swung his hand in a circle in the dark in the back of the cab—"much." Enclosed within this circle was not only the drinks and the coffee and the steak (though Adam could hardly appreciate all of this, since he knew nothing about the new caffeine-free temperate vegetarianism), but Allie, too.

The cab dropped them at Adam's, where life immediately turned quite comfortable. Adam heated up some coffee and they watched a set and a half of a tennis match between two guys Terry had never heard of. One was a hulking dark Venezuelan and the other was a hulking blond Swede. The match was taking place in Tokyo. Adam—for obscure reasons—began rooting for the South American, who won the first set seven-five. When the Swede came back to win the second set (suddenly the Venezuelan couldn't put in a first serve to save his life) Adam clicked off the set. "Let's go for a run."

"All right. What time's it?"

"Late."

Adam was quick to change into some running clothes (he was always quick about that—as though, for all the time he spent in a suit, athletic gear was his natural dress) and they drove over to Terry's in Adam's Datsun. Adam had been pretty quiet for some time—at least since Allie's departure—but now, driving up Connecticut Avenue, he uncorked a large topic. "What was the title of that thing again?"

"What thing?"

"Mr. Hannibal's thing. His article."

"I don't remember exactly."

"Well, how about inexactly? 'Purported Encounters with the Recently Deceased'—is that it?"

"That's it—or pretty close."

"I don't get it."

"Get what?"

"What you're doing."

A car speeding rapidly the other way cast Adam in a blinking shudder of light, like that of a camera flash, supplying Terry with a still photograph of his friend—a big-headed, big-shouldered figure hunched broodingly over the steering wheel. "Neither do I. I don't know what I'm doing," Terry said. "I don't have a clue. No, no, not a clue"—oh, but this was fun! For this was the true beauty of his leave from the office: the opportunity, suddenly, to say, *I don't understand any of it* . . . "And you know what else I don't get?"

"What?"

"Hamill, Hillman. Now there is one phenomenon I truly do not get. If you stop and look at it from the outside, I mean. What is it we do? What is our job? Well, we work our butts off to see that *our* clients, who we don't really know but who are probably a gang of crooks, get an FM or TV license in Tuscaloosa or Battle Creek or Boise, instead of *their* clients, who we don't know but who no doubt are a gang of crooks. In either case the clients are likely to be mere stand-ins, aren't they, providing some pretense of local control for the big guys who are really going to buy them out or pull the strings. Local control, roots in the community and all the rest of it, which half the time means putting a suit and tie on some low-level Hispanic or black and dragging him out as a showpiece, which is so pitiful you want to *weep* on his behalf except that he stands to clear maybe half a million dollars for the performance he's putting on, yes it's a sham—okay, okay. I can accept that. I can even accept the notion that you may have fifteen parties battling over station rights, and in fact not one of them actually wants those very same goddamn rights. Do they want to broadcast? No, *they don't want to broadcast*. No, they're all in it for a payoff, aren't they? *Fifteen* parties—that's what we had for Cincinnati Channel 66 last year, each earnestly trying to prove why *they're* the most qualified licensees, and I'll be damned but not one of 'em—our clients included, by the way—not one actually wants the actual goddamn license. Okay, goes with the territory, etc., etc. But all that aside, what does this license entitle you to do? Well, it gives you a shit monopoly, doesn't it? You, and you alone, are entitled to fill your little niche of the airwaves with absolute rot and twaddle. Do you ever just stand back for a moment and take a look at the fifty channels, or whatever the hell it is, you get on your fancy hookup? Go through them one at a time, I mean? Historically speaking, has there ever been anything more pernicious, more pernicious to the collective American mind, than what we're offering? Mud wrestling, monster cars, 'Hogan's Heroes,' 'The Dating Game' and its Bachelorettes, 'Pimp for a day'—"

"It's a little late in the day to be getting sanctimonious, isn't it?"

"Sanctimonious? I'm just pointing out the obvious, Adam. No, not even the obvious—the unignorable. Right this minute, even as we drive along here in the dark, the air is abuzz with 'The Beverly Hillbillies,' 'Gilligan's Island,' pay-as-you-watch fake-fuck shows . . ."

"What are you calling for? Censorship?"

"We're talking in just a couple years of having four, five hundred channels available to most home viewers across the country. *Four or five hundred!* Freedom of choice, freedom of choice— God if I hear that phrase again I think I'll puke. Tell me this isn't *truly* what the American people have chosen. Do tell me they've been duped and this isn't *really* what we want, because if it is I'm heartbroken. Just heartbroken. But on the other hand, if they *have* been duped, where does that leave you and me? What are our roles in this? What does this say about our jobs? Aren't we complicit? *Freedom of choice*—I mean does that phrase honestly make you feel good about what you do?"

"It's a living."

"Isn't that what the dung beetle says? About the turd he's crawling around in?"

"Listen to you . . . I think *some*body around here was into the wine tonight . . ."

"Adam, seriously now, don't you ever wonder what you're doing? What the sum total effect of your life, if you could throw all the relevant data into some monster number-cruncher, would be?"

"Now you *are* getting sanctimonious."

"Okay, I'm sanctimonious. I'm a pompous little heated-up twit. But humor your little twit pal all the same and answer his question anyway."

There was a silence. Terry realized he was out of breath.

"Sure I wonder," Adam said. "I just don't see what good making an ass of myself would do."

Terry in recent months had entertained all sorts of jumbled feelings toward Adam—embarrassment, guilt, gratitude, frustration, fondness, penitence—but in this moment he felt something new: a sense of Adam's depletion, his intransigent narrowness, his final insufficiency. This was not only a novel feeling but an unwanted one, and he retreated from it hastily: "Yeah, you're right, I know, sorry." And then he added—as though Adam's comment applied only to this evening, which it unmistakably did not: "I've been making an ass of myself all night long."

"Is that yours, by the way? About the dung beetle? Did you come up with that?"

"No," Terry confessed. "It's Kopp's."

"I thought so . . ."

Terry giggled—a sound that rang oddly inside the car. "Not surprisingly, he's full of vivid zoological imagery."

Adam waited in the car, the engine running, while Terry went in to change. Terry's glance took in the new aquarium—the flash of the tetras—as he hurtled up the stairs. He slipped into sweatpants, sweatshirt, cotton socks and running shoes, leaving his dress shoes, shirt, tie, and suit scattered on the floor.

Any suspicions that he might yet be slightly drunk were stilled the moment they came to the tall, commanding fence surrounding the high school track. His glance with cutting clarity picked up every glint and twist of moonlight on its chain links. His eyes missed nothing.

He ascended effortlessly ten feet or so, fingers and toes in the little diamonds, and swung his leg weightlessly over the top. He used to clear higher heights than this at one go, lofting over

them with the aid of a fiberglass pole. He let himself drop and
came down not too badly, just a moment's jamming stiffness in
his right ankle, and he was back in stride once more.

The first lap, Terry moved in pure exhilaration. The air was
cool—perfect—and the moon, like a beach ball among break-
ers, bobbed unsinkably overhead. He could run like this for
miles, with Adam pounding along steadily at his side.

"The thing about vaulting," Terry said, "is there's a moment
when you're running just as fast as you can toward the pit, just
as fast as your legs'll carry you, and there's another moment,
near the top of your vault, when you're pushing just as hard as
you can with your arms, pushing yourself up those last few crucial inches, but in between, in between those moments there's
another moment, the real moment, when you're doing pretty
much nothing, when you're truly letting the pole carry you,
you're going along for the ride is all, which sounds easy but
you'd be surprised at how many people can't do that, they muck
it up, they strain when they shouldn't be straining. And that was
something I was good at—the going along for the ride. There
were all sorts of vaulters who were faster, and a hell of a lot
stronger in the forearms, but I'd beat them because I knew how
to go with the flow of things, I truly understood that vaulting
isn't something you can do better by doing it *harder*. I don't want
to overwork the symbol of the thing, but I just wanted you to
know, Adam," Terry said, "that I've always had that gift for
going with the flow of things."

"Meaning in this case what?"

Meaning in this case what? What *had* he meant? What *was* the
lesson he'd intended? "Meaning not to worry I guess. I know
what I'm doing."

In the second lap his ankle began to stiffen—it seemed he'd
come down harder than he'd understood—and his stomach began to churn. It wasn't that he was feeling the least bit winded.
But there was the food and the drink—they were beginning to
act up inside him.

At the start of the fourth lap, he dropped out. "It's all that
fancy dining," he called after Adam, who continued to pound
down the gravel straightaway. "I ate and drank too much . . ."

He walked a little ways into the track's inside oval and lay down in the grass. Immediately he felt better. The moon was high overhead. There were some clouds and these seemed to slide behind instead of in front of the moon, and as a kid one night, so many years ago, he'd not quite been able to believe it when Dad explained that the moon, despite all appearances, lay much further off than any cloud. How was he to believe any such thing, when his eyes irrefutably told him otherwise? And what was a child to do (what was a thirty-eight-year-old man to do?) when his eyes told him one thing and his solid wise father another?

What else did it remind him of, this breathing into the moon's face, lying here in the live grass in the dark in the dead of the night? And when was the last time he'd given the moon his all in this way? Stared at it with the replete and earnest longings of his heart? Months? Years? However faraway that moment might be, however distant the moon itself might be, was there any reason, with all of its clarity now flooding over him as he sprawled in the grass, for not conceding that he didn't understand that man whose crunch-crunch-crunch on the gravel approached and receded, approached and receded?

And did not understand Squirrely Kopp, though they had shared each other's food and talk and soiled laundry smells for a whole academic year, many years ago. And had not understood Betsy, who had said to him, as though in forgiveness for the very shortcomings of his understanding, *You, you're a holy terror.* Sweet Betsy, who'd lifted a card, with something in her gesture of the dragging coaxed shyness of a novice stripper, and something of a novice stripper's dawning pride as well, which held one word, ARTISTIC—although to be honest she was no more artistic than a leg of lamb. What in the world had she been thinking of? No, it was evident—lucidly evident, lunarly evident—that the only person on the planet who truly understood him, and whom in truth he understood, was Allison, was his Allie, was Ms. Collier, who had shared with him tonight that likewise blazing moment, and even if she did give up the law, thereby all but ensuring that their paths would fail to cross professionally, what was to stop him from walking bright as you please into her antique store one day, asking her advice, plunking down a hundred bucks deposit on a chair or something,

what was to stop two people from becoming lovers who so obviously were made for each other?

"You want to call it, Champ?" Adam was breathing hard.

"It was the food. And the drink." Terry scrambled to his feet.
The mistreated ankle groaned beneath his weight. "I'm a victim
of my own excesses."

"Oh, we've had quite a night, pal," Adam said and, jokingly
coachlike, threw a hand over Terry's shoulder.

And with Adam's heavy material touch, in this moment on the
high school track, Terry saw what was so obvious it seemed impossible he hadn't realized it before: Adam was Coach Kramm.
At our age everyone you meet is someone you've already met, Kopp had
told him a while ago, words which Terry had shrugged off but
which were probably true; by now, it was all a mere reshuffling
of the few basic figures in your psyche. And, psychologically
speaking, who Adam was was that man in the windbreaker, forever urging you on—it's all in the mind, it's all in the mind. *She
was unclean,* Kramm had said, of his vanished wife, while grip-
ping the steering wheel as if he meant to shatter it.

"You want to come in?" Terry said, when Adam had swung
the car into Terry's driveway.

"For just a minute . . ."

"Look," Terry said, throwing the front door open. "I added
an algae eater."

"Hey what happened to you? Your back, you're soaking wet."

"My back?"

"The ground must have been wet. Where were you lying?
You better watch out. You're going to catch cold."

"No. No, no," Terry reassured his coach. "It's funny, isn't it?
I've never felt better in all my life."

"Now this isn't so bad, is it?"

It was time to play the lawyer with Adam. "What this is
'this'?"

"This place, Mack. This fancy cup o' java."

The two of them were sitting over cappuccinos in The Bitter
Almond, a new little cafe on M Street, not far from the office.

"This stuff is great, Adam." Terry took another sip. "I like this place," he added—though the *this* Adam had been tacitly referring to was *this world* or *this way of life.* In the weeks since Terry had returned to work, Adam—bless him—had been behaving as though Terry were some sort of prize summer associate, who needed to be wooed not only by Hamill, Hillman, but by the larger lawyer's life it embodied. To see Adam proudly, proprietarily, pointing out the new office carpeting, or the wonders of the expanded office computing system, was great fun. And The Bitter Almond, too—here was one more credit to be tallied in some sort of grand psychological accounting: wasn't this a nice place? And wasn't this a fine *cup o' java?*

"You know, I'd better be off," Terry said.

"Another plane to catch . . ."

"Another plane to catch. Tulsa."

It had seemed the only sensible, the only workable way to go back to work—simply to throw yourself into it, with all the hearings and the meetings and the travel, all the hectic craziness of the old days. The truth was (even if this was something Kopp couldn't be told) that it had felt good to come back. Terry had been ready. For it had grown boring, his "research." No, more than boring—oppressive, dispiriting, and, with every day, more painfully irrelevant. Was it his fault if, in all his reading, he'd never once come across anything that threw any true light on what had happened to him? After a while it had been no better than reading novels, poems—once more the disconnected feeling that the book in his hands was failing to reach him where he lived. He had given it his best shot—hadn't he assembled something like a hundred pages of notes in all? Terry stood prepared, at any time, to turn over to the proper authorities all these self-exonerating materials, but who were the authorities? The fact was, no one seemed interested enough even to challenge him. He had notebooks devoted to the history of psychical research, to firsthand accounts of mystical experiences, to scientific materials about hallucinations, to terminology, to "miscellaneous things." But it was now time, literally and metaphorically, to close the books—although there still lay ahead of him the conversation he'd arranged with Tryggvi Hannibalsson. Actually, he was looking forward to that. It ought to be fun, weird, and—who could say?—maybe even illuminating.

"You'll be back tomorrow?"

"Back tomorrow. And then I'm off on Friday to New York."

"For what?"

"A deposition. And some other things."

"What sorts of things?"

"Non-legal."

"Non-legal?"

What was the point, at this point, of deception? "I'm off for a talk with Tryggvi Hannibalsson. You remember—'Putative Contacts with the Recently Deceased.'"

"How could I forget?"

But on Adam's face there wasn't any of the bitter vexation this announcement would have provoked a couple of months ago. He seemed amused—even pleased. Terry's return to the office, with its convincing display of being fully back in the saddle, had seemingly transformed altogether the long "vacation" he'd indulged in. What had once been seen by Adam as cause for worry and shame now was interpreted as a display of admirable willfulness and independence. Terry's show of cockeyed stubbornness was almost something to be proud of. "Well that oughta be quite interesting."

"I think so. I hope so. I'm gonna go up with Kopp."

"More interesting still . . ."

"Truth is, I'm feeling really guilty toward him. I think he's feeling ignored. You know I hardly ever see him these days—which isn't surprising, since I hardly see anybody. But you know I really do like Kevin."

"Sure. He's quite a character." With Terry's return to work, Adam had undergone a change of heart toward Kopp as well.

"He's more than that: he's a good guy, Adam. He's very generous—I mean in everything but money. And he's lonely you know. I don't think he's got many friends."

"Take it from a close friend: friends are vastly overrated." Adam laughed approvingly at his own joke. "It's work that keeps us together—right, Champ? Work, work, work."

"Speaking of which, I better run."

"I'll get this," Adam said, and snatched up the check.

This was another of the benefits of having in effect become a summer associate: Adam was picking up every tab in sight.

But if things seemed changed in all sorts of ways at the office, there was nothing the least bit altered about Bertha. Some things were not meant to change. She greeted him now with the news, "Your sister called. Kaye."

"I'll call her later."

"Also Mr. Seward. Your father."

"My father?"

"He said if you could call him in the next forty minutes he would appreciate it. That was twenty minutes ago. Twenty-two minutes ago."

"Thanks." Terry went into his office and closed the door. Calls from Dad were a rarity.

The phone had rung eight times—Terry was thinking about hanging up and redialing—when his father answered.

"It's me, Dad."

"Terry. How are you?"

"Well I'm fine. And how are you?"

"Well fine, fine. I'm fine." The silence that ensued seemed Dad's to break, which at last he did by saying, "Me personally."

"How's Mob? She there?"

"Oh she's out. She's over to the post office and the market. She'll be back soon."

The message Dad had left with Bertha meant, then, *Call me before the Mob returns.*

"And how is she?"

"In most ways, you could say she's fine as ever. She did have a big argument with Bea Dwyer, though. It's a week ago, and they're still not speaking."

"That's terrible," Terry said, hoping to sound concerned when, in fact, the news came as a relief. Was that all that lay behind this call? The thought unclenched him. "They've been the best of friends since I was a kid."

"Since long before that."

"So what happened?"

"Well I tell you, Terry—you know my own opinion is the Mob had had too much to drink."

"To drink?" And Terry clenched all over again—tighter than he'd been in weeks . . .

"Well it's now and then you know she does do that sometimes, Terry. And I don't really know what's to be done about it—if anything *is* to be done."

She stared straight out, Mob did, from the photograph on his desk, taken some ten or so years ago: a broad face (steady quick-witted eyes, strong jaw, broad ropey nose) that said, No non-sense. That was what, unmistakably, her face said: *No nonsense.*

Meanwhile, there was a cry for help—that's what this call was. The world's most adaptable, uncomplaining, resourceful man was asking his son for help.

"You say sometimes—well, what do you mean? How often do you mean?"

"Oh not all that often. And I don't keep a log of such things."

"But you must have some idea."

"Well I'm not suggesting every night, Terry. No, nothing like that. Maybe twice a week? Anyway, more often than before. I see it increasing. And it scares me."

It scared Terry, too, and it was as though the very geogra-phy of his existence now opened up before him. Here he was sitting on the twelfth floor of a modern security-guarded office building, but there, out there, lay the city—and beyond that, mile by mile, was a system of roads and highways, all of whose engineered banked veerings, turn-offs, cloverleaf inter-changes inevitably wound westward, toward that trim yellow house where a small-boned white-haired man, worried lest his wife return home any minute, was confessing to his son, *It scares me.*

"You see," Dad went on, somewhat puzzlingly, "I have expe-rience. I know what it can do."

"Experience?"

"Personal experience," Dad explained—which was no expla-nation at all. "Family experience. It scares me."

"Yeah, sure, these things are scary." Terry exhaled into the phone. "It's just it's not clear to me what I can do, Dad." Quite clear to Terry, though, was that the whole business was unques-tionably his own fault. None of this would have happened— would it?—had he been the sort of son who stood by his parents geographically, psychologically.

"Well, they have these clinics you read about. The ones you

always read about. I thought you might know something about these clinics you always read about."

"I don't know a thing really. But I think that's another sort of thing entirely. I mean with them we're talking *really serious*."

"I thought"—Dad's voice went apologetic, whispery—"you might have had some experience with Betsy."

"No, no. You see, Dad, Betsy's experiences were totally different. That was depression. That was chemical—that was a totally different thing."

"Well, they have clinics for that, too, don't they?"

Terry took a shot at a joke: "These days, they've got places you can send your dog to be psychoanalyzed."

"Terry?" An urgency had crept into Dad's voice: "Listen, I better go."

Better go? And who was it, Dad, right this minute, who was marching up the front walk?

A darkness was closing like a door swinging shut, into which Terry threw a sort of flare: "Listen, I'll try to find out some things for you. Call me soon, call me collect, call me anytime."

The moment he hung up the phone, he dialed Dunphy's office. Kaye was the one who answered, for which he was deeply grateful. "It's Terry," he said.

"Well aren't you prompt."

"Prompt?"

"My call—aren't you returning my call?"

He'd forgotten all about it. "Right," he said. "Listen, I just talked to Dad, and he said Mob had gotten into a fight with Bea Dwyer, and they weren't speaking."

"Bea Dwyer, that old witcheroo, it's about time." Kaye laughed gaily.

"And he said"—Terry felt oddly constrained about this disclosure, just as though Kaye were not family and he were airing some ugly indiscretion—"and he said that maybe one of the reasons why they fought is because Mob had had too much to drink."

"Well I've told you that, Terry. There's no question about it— she hits the bottle now and then."

But even if that were true—*was* there any need to use an idiom like *hits the bottle* in connection with your own mother? He could envision Kaye's face as she tossed off the phrase: that nervous blink and momentary flutter of her eyelids, that look of pride and uncertainty which came into her asymmetrical pop eyes whenever she got off what might be thought of as a saucy remark. He said, "Can you talk right now? I mean, do you have any privacy?"

"Sure, I can talk," she said—meaning, he supposed, who needs privacy when talking about your mother's *hitting the bottle*?

"You mention the drinking, but it's nothing *I've* much noticed her doing."

"Maybe you're the only one who hasn't . . ."

"Hasn't what?"

"Hasn't seen and heard."

"Kaye, he sounded really upset."

"Well that's only natural, given his experience."

And there was that word again.

"What on earth do you mean?" Terry said.

"I mean his whole life, Terry. Obviously you do know that Granma Seward was a lush."

He glimpsed that face of Kaye's again: the blink and flutter, the lids leaping back to reveal a look of girlish naughty daring in her big eyes, and the possibility came to him, as it had now and then since childhood, that if some stealthy gloved stranger were to set a pair of strong hands to her neck and begin to throttle her, might not those eyes, with a little springing noise, leap right out of her head? "A lush?" he said. "Granma Seward?"

The schoolteacher? The family archivist? The keeper of the family tree? The only one among them who knew all the Sewards from the Seawards? The woman who, when he'd been a small boy, had played such a memorable trick on him? (This had been enacted in her kitchen, and they were *making* something, the two of them, grandson and grandmother, some recipe so secret she could not disclose, even to him, her fellow worker, what it was. . . . It turned out to be his own birthday cake.) A lush?

"Sure."

"I never heard that."

"It's not as if it's *announced.* It's just implied. Like so many things in his life. Obviously, Terry, the old man comes from a totally dysfunctional family."

"Kaye, they hadn't even in*vent*ed dysfunctional families when Dad was a kid."

"That's one of the reasons why he's so nutso on the subject of drink. That's why he doesn't drink himself."

"He drinks. Of course he drinks." Whatever was she talking about?

"When was the last time you saw the old guy have more than one beer?"

And did she need to call Dad the *old guy*? "He does, sometimes he does. It's just that alcohol doesn't agree with his stomach."

"Now isn't *that* convenient . . ."

The triumphant laughter with which she concluded this remark seemingly left him no continuation. He shifted direction, started over: "He just seemed very wound up. He was even talking"—and here again Terry felt a host of compunctions, as though he were on the brink of an indiscretion—"about her maybe going to some sort of clinic."

"Well that's absurd!"

"It is? That was my immediate—"

"Why, it's totally laughably ri*dic*ulous . . ."

"You think so?" Despite that image of the gloved stranger a moment ago, he felt at once enormously heartened by Kaye. Bless her! God bless his own big sister!

"He's totally irrational on the subject—don't you see that?"

"I did think it sounded extreme."

"Did he say how often she ties one on?"

"He said, I don't know, maybe a couple of times a week."

"*Well* then—I mean, honestly! Can you imagine sending someone like that to a *clinic*? How often do you have a little snort, Terry?"

"To drink?"

"To drink . . ."

"That varies a lot, actually. I quit totally a while ago, but then other times I'll go out with Adam, and I—"

"Well, I have something to drink every night."

"You do? I didn't know that . . ."

"Would you call me a lush? Would you call me a soak?"

"Of course not. Obviously not."

There was a pause, and in her dragging reply perhaps a suggestion of being just a little crestfallen at the speed or certitude of his denial. "I like to have a good time," Kaye went on. "I always have liked a good time, that's my nature. A couple of pops at night—what's the harm in that?"

"None that I can see."

"You do understand, don't you, Terry, that the drinking itself, Mob's, isn't the problem. Oh no. It's just symptomatic."

He could agree with that, readily enough, and did so: "Right, sure. . ." But he felt compelled to add, "Symptomatic of what?"

"She's bored."

"Bored?"

"Course she's bored. The old guy can't understand that, how could he, him the one for whom there never will be enough hours in the day. He can always go wallpaper his doghouse or set up an electric window opener."

"You make it sound as though he wastes his time, as though he's—"

"Oh, Terry, why *are* you so defensive? Don't you see how that's what's so precious and *dear* about him? Who else on this *planet* would look out the kitchen window and say, 'What this place really needs is a—' "

"So why's she bored, Kaye?"

"Why in heaven wouldn't she be? She's never really worked. She's never had any hobbies, except for terrorizing the city council." Terry laughed approvingly, as Kaye went on: "Her friends are getting old, some of them are sick, and most have lost a lot of zip. But she hasn't lost a bit . . ."

"No, she hasn't lost her zip, not one iota of zip," Terry said, and these words—especially *zip*—filled him with a kind of giggly wellbeing.

"She's got all her old pizazz, but she doesn't know how to *focus* it any more."

"I see what you're saying. I see exactly what you're saying." That was the surprising thing about Kaye—she could be quite astute, she really could.

"Maybe I ought to talk to Dad."

"You should, Kaye. You should, soon, but some time when Mob's not around."

"I'll do that."

"I'd really appreciate it if you would."

"Now listen, Terry, I've got another subject, and I'm taking it to you purely as a lawyer. This is legal counsel I'm after."

"Shoot."

"What sorts of penalties are there if I turn in my IRAs?"

"Turn them in?"

"No lectures. Purely as a lawyer now . . ."

"Well that's not really my field, tax law, and you ought to take it up with an accountant—but why are you talking about turning in your IRAs?"

"Terry, what would you know? I mean what would you know?"

"Beg pardon?"

"You've got no children . . ."

"Okay, I'll go along with that . . ."

"What would you know about the costs of a decent wedding these days?"

"But surely—"

"Do you know what the cost is of a decent band?"

"A band?"

"I mean somebody you can actually *dance* to—not a bunch of heavy-metalizers with earrings in their noses."

"I think you have to call them nose-rings. Earrings are pretty much restricted to ears. Does this mean there's going to be a band?"

"And a cake? Can you tell me what the cost per head is of a cake you can actually eat? I mean something that not only looks presentable but won't make you want to toss your cookies? I'm just curious now. Just as a matter of interest, can you please estimate for me how much that would set you back? I'm talking per head."

"Kaye, how in the world would I have any idea . . ."

"No, no. You're lucky, you're privileged, you can just sit there in ignorance. That's all right—you just sit there in ignorance, Terry. Why on earth shouldn't you?"

"That isn't the way I'd *most* like to think of myself, actually."

"Terry, this is not a request for a handout. I will not say another word if that's what you think. I'm speaking to you purely as an attorney."

"Kaye, you need those IRAs. What are you going to do when you retire? That's why they call them retirement accounts."

"Well I don't suspect I *will* need them, Terry."

Meaning what? Meaning she genuinely judged it likely that Glenn, who had displayed, so far as Terry could see, not the slightest eagerness to tie any knot, was going to marry her? Glenn wasn't rich, surely—but there was little doubt that he was sitting quite pretty.

Or was she meaning to convey, as that mostly stoical but perhaps faintly wistful diminuendo in her voice implied, that she simply was not going to be around when retirement came? That some malignity or other was going to carry her off prematurely from the land of the living? Is that what she meant?

"And why not? What are you getting at?"

Softer still went her voice, more maddeningly elusive and airy: "I just don't think so . . ."

"I'm not saying we have to cut every corner. I'm just saying that my understanding was that we weren't having some sort of absolute blowout, some sort of gala affair. In fact, my understanding was that Diana didn't *want* a lot of ostentation. She's told me that expressly a number of times."

"Can you blame the girl, she's only twenty-two, if she feels a bit insecure about joining the Drill family? These people are *grand*, Terry, they were written up in magazines."

"What magazines?"

"I don't know—it was called *Lexington* or *Kentucky* or *Horse's Life* or something. Diana sent me the clippings. There was more than one . . . Now can you blame her if she wants to show them she can deal with them on their own level?"

"These people are made of *styrofoam*, Kaye. *That's* their level. You make it sound as though they were responsible for the first transcontinental railroad. As if they built the Panama Canal."

"Can you blame her if she doesn't want anyone thinking she's some sort of servant girl? Some Cinderella?"

"Talk about absurdities . . ."

"If she doesn't want them thinking she's some vulgar little gold digger?"

"Honestly," Terry protested, but the epithet tore at him all the same.

"She's only twenty-two."

Diana was less than twenty-two—she was a teenager, she was eighteen—in the high school graduation portrait on his desk. She looked him devotedly in the eye, with what might be called shy confidence. (As a little girl she'd lost her upper front teeth well before most of her friends, but new ones had taken forever to come in. Kaye eventually consulted a dentist, and X rays were taken, which showed that the teeth were there in the gums, all right; they were simply taking their own sweet time. After a while Diana had grown self-conscious of the gaping hole in her grin, and her smile even now held, though her teeth were lovely, a diffidence, a tight-lipped self-consciousness.) Oh, that eighteen-year-old understood what he was only coming around to realizing: he would deny her nothing.

"Kaye," Terry said, "now if, let's just say if, I were to send you a check for another five thousand dollars, do you think we could hold our heads up high around those styrofoam barons?"

"Oh Terry, oh Terry, you give me a bankroll like that to work with, I'm sure we'll have the world's classiest affair. I'm sure of it! But Terry," Kaye said, recalling herself, "you really don't have to do this. I certainly never called with any intention of hitting you up for a nickel."

"You didn't call me—I called you."

"That's right," Kaye echoed—wholeheartedly, for she'd been exonerated. "That's right, you did."

"And no one's making me make the offer. I want to do it."

"Oh Terry, I do mean the world's classiest. You can hold me to that."

"And you'll call Dad . . ."

"Call Dad?"

"About Mob. About this whole business. The drinking. You'll reassure him?"

"You leave it to me, Terry. You just leave every last detail to me."

"I gotta run, Kaye. I'm off to Tulsa on business."

"I don't know how to thank you. *Diana* doesn't know how to thank you. She's going to look simply smashing, Terry. You just won't believe it when you walk her down the aisle. You know, she's not even going to in*vite* Ralph."

"Well that's up to the two of you. That doesn't concern me." Somehow Kaye had got it into her head that it mattered to him whether or not the girl's father showed up. Specifically, Kaye seemed to offer Ralph's absence as some sort of repayment . . . "I got to run, Kaye. Bye-bye."

But Kaye was never one to let you have the last word: "The *classiest*," she said. "You can hold me to that."

The moment he hung up the phone nervousness knifed him in the belly. Five thousand dollars—and where was it going to stop? When was he going to put his foot down? Or was he merely going to watch as he and his money dissolved away together? An angel of the Lord comes down and asks, Will you give up your baby toe to save a family of Eskimos from plunging through the ice? He rose quickly from his desk and threw open his office door.

The sight of Bertha, soaking an envelope in a glass of water, was magnificently reassuring. "What are you doing?" he said—though he knew perfectly well what she was up to. *Bertha* was never going to need to hit him up for a loan.

"This one never got cancelled. It's amazing, how many stamps the post office never cancels."

"What kind of stamp is it?"

"I don't know. The environment or something? Birds."

"No. I mean what size, what price." There was a more technical word, and in his rattled state it was reassuring to locate it: "What denomination?"

"It's a twenty-fiver."

"You know you're welcome to whatever stamps you need." Bertha always maintained, no doubt truthfully, that she handled her entire postage bill by means of uncancelled Hamill, Hillman correspondence.

"I don't believe in taking office property for personal uses."

And what was the implication of this? That he himself, with his minor pilferings of things like postage and office supplies, was a thief? That the *other* secretaries were thieves? Or was the remark simply one more Berthaism—and hence, by definition, not fully to be fathomed? "That sounds reasonable," Terry said.

"And I get more stamps than I can use this way, especially lately. It's unbelievable, how sloppy they're getting."

"You could open your own mini-P.O. Bertha's Slightly Used Stamps."

She pondered for a moment. "I'll bet it would be illegal."

"You're probably right."

"Of course I don't need all that many stamps." She added proudly: "I don't send many letters."

"No . . . You'll remember about the fish?"

It had become Bertha's job, whenever Terry was to be away for a couple of days, to feed the fish. He'd proposed it to her the first time as a joke—and she had eagerly seized at the opportunity. On principle, he didn't like to give her any task that smacked of old-fashioned coffee-fetching, in part because he'd never felt quite right about commanding any sort of subordinate, and in part because of that singular remark she'd once made about his being the best attorney at Hamill, Hillman to work for. But the first time he'd fretted about his fish, she'd leapt at the coalescing offer. And had leapt, subsequently, with each of his departures. In fact, she now held on permanently to one of his house keys. He'd come to understand that having a house at her disposal—an occasional refuge from Celia and Margaret, the widowed aunts—was one of the great treats of her life.

It seemed she was especially delighted with his VCR. When he'd asked her why she didn't have one herself, and pointed out how cheap they'd become, she came back with a brutally depressing reply. She said, *You just try telling that to Celia, her with the 'Why pay good money to watch at home when television costs you nothing?'* and with these words he'd caught a rare glimpse of Bertha's boxed-in home life, the atmosphere of resentment and censure that permeated the place's no-doubt overfurnished and underventilated rooms. Bertha didn't feel free even to buy herself a VCR.

On perceiving this, he'd wanted to take her bony bent-fingered hands in his and cry, *Throw them both out* or *Lock them in the attic* or *Get your own place*—but who was he to tell anybody how to put your foot down with family members? He was the one who couldn't take a call from his sister without emptying his wallet . . .

Bertha said, "How are they?"

"Who?"

"The fish."

"Fine. Terrific. They're growing quite fond of me."

He looked at her, sitting at her desk, with an envelope turning to pulp in a glass beside her, and was suddenly aware, though generally unobservant about such things, that she'd altered her appearance somehow. Gotten a haircut? Begun to wear some makeup? In any event, these days she seemed to be looking a little less like someone who, in his tireless fabrications, was going to end up in a supermarket tabloid: WOMAN IMPRISONED BY ELDERLY AUNTS—*Eats, Sleeps on, Bathes in Sawdust* . . . Perhaps his time away from the office had benefitted *her*, anyway.

In an unusual meeting of minds, Bertha seemed to glimpse that he was pondering his time away. "Is it good to be back?" she asked him.

"At the office?" he said, and when she nodded he told her, "Sure, it's good to be back."

"But you're glad you took your leave?" She gave him a hard, scrutinizing look.

"Sure. No question. Only—" The pressure of her bespectacled glance seemed to squeeze the subsequent phrase right out of him. The words came so unexpectedly—for he'd not been thinking any such thing—and so rapidly, that he was left no proper time for amplification or amelioration: "—only, the thing is, it's left me feeling so blue . . ."

"You feel different . . ."

"Different?" It seemed a word to leap upon. Surely it was a good sign? "How so? More-relaxed different?"

But Angelina wasn't going to be led this way. "Just different."

"You can remember?" he asked her. "After all these months, you mean you can honestly remember how I used to feel?"

The question evidently struck her as a little absurd. "Of course I can remember."

"I just meant that that's a lot of—a lot of necks. A lot of necks and shoulders. To keep straight I mean."

The words faintly flustered him. In alluding in this way to the bodies she handled, one after another, week after week, he might almost be calling her a tramp. However the last few months had maybe altered him, he had not disburdened himself of a sense of something slightly illicit in this business of hers.

Angelina, on the other hand, seemed to feel nothing of the sort. She radiated a proud satisfaction in the efficacy of her work—pride being (his rational mind told him) just exactly what she ought to feel. But further down in his mind, where the rational mind's jurisdiction gave way to the illogical and instinctual, he could not fully divest himself of associations of shame.

"They're different," she said. "Each person is different. Each person's problems are different."

"Is that what you meant—when you said I feel different?"

She answered with gratifying rapidity: "No no. You've changed."

And this last word touched him anew with hope. What did it mean, what did it say about his life, that the phrase *You've changed* made him feel so buoyant? He felt prepared to sign an affidavit affirming that the language boasted no more beautiful phrase than *You've changed* . . . And wasn't it possible that she, with all her talk of energy channeling and psychic blockage and personal flowage, had developed some sort of quick, instinctive feeling for such things? Was it all that outlandish to suppose that someone like Angelina could tell that he'd undergone what he was surely entitled to call a massive shift in his personal flowage? With his forehead resting against the cushion-wrapped bulge at the end of the table, and his eyes staring down at her feet through the opening provided for his face, he felt a wild sort of attraction billow out to her. She still wore those pointy tennis shoes. The difference was that it used to be only one of the baby toes poking through the canvas. Now, both of them had worked themselves clear.

There'd been another change as well. She'd asked him this

time to remove his T-shirt. What did this mean? It was a good sign, surely? And given the pace of their growing intimacy, wasn't it inevitable that they would become lovers in, say, twenty or thirty years?

The question brought him back to the phone call he'd had this morning from Diana, which had concerned his wedding invitation.

As the one chosen to walk the girl down the aisle, he found the idea of receiving an invitation at all just faintly comical. Was she sending an invitation to the maid of honor? Was she sending an invitation to the groom? But Diana, impeccably hostess-like, was intent not merely on sending him an invitation but on getting its form precisely right. Should she—she'd wanted to know—send him a "single"? A what, Diana? *A single invitation . . .*

"What do you mean?" he'd asked her.

"I mean is there anyone special you want to be there? Invited just for you?"

But still he hadn't caught her drift . . . Well there were various people, he told her. Adam, Kopp, a couple of neighbors, a couple of others from the office. But he'd already given her their names.

"I mean somebody for *you.*" She hesitated. "A date?"

And why *had* he been so slow on the uptake? A date for the wedding? He hadn't really given the matter any thought before now. He told her, after a pause, "No, you can send me a single."

And yet, lying on his stomach, staring at Angelina's narrow feet, having bared his entire back to her exploratory touch, he was visited by a fantastic idea: wouldn't it be marvelous to bring Angelina? *She* would be his date! Oh, he'd fantasized before about going out with her—he had even allowed himself, a couple of times, an extended reverie in which she moved in with him; she would rub his neck while they watched videos late at night. In those earlier fantasies he'd savored the notion of how much *she* might savor the business of helping him to spend his money. He would buy her fancy clothes. He would buy her a new pair of gym shoes. He would buy her a string of pearls that would make her face go on like a light. But in *this* fantasy, the one in which he circulated arm in arm with Angelina among the wedding guests, she wore no fancy clothes, no pearls. She was dressed just exactly as she was right now. He would bring as his date to Diana's elaborate wedding a woman wearing a Redskins sweatshirt, a loose pair of unisex chinos, a pair of tennis shoes in which her baby toes had poked free. Oh, the delicious thrill of—just once—doing something outrageous, something heedless and headlong and absurd! He would exaggerate it, heighten it, perfect it: he would introduce Angelina proudly to the Drills, to Peter, to Mob and Dad, to Shawn, and when anyone asked who she was he would wink roguishly and say, "She's my masseuse . . ."

And yet if the prospect of escorting a sweatshirted Angelina to the wedding was ridiculous, *was* it all that outlandish to suppose that she might go out with him to a movie, say? Or out to dinner? On the one hand, her clear indifference to almost everything he had to say might well be interpreted as a bad sign. Clearly, she enjoyed his company, but equally clearly, she found him most interesting when she herself was doing the talking. She'd said he wasn't to talk because he needed to relax, but still there was no ignoring that he'd never once made a remark that had piqued her curiosity. They chatted sometimes for a couple of minutes *after* the massage was over, and then, too, she showed no real interest in what he thought, did, aspired to.

Nonetheless, wasn't there a valid way of analyzing their relationship in which their talk, or lack of talk, was hardly significant? As her hands went to work on his neck and shoulders, and a sort of wakeful drowse settled over his mind, he would understand afresh that the realm of existence in which the two of them exchanged conversation was narrow—superficial—and mattered far less than you would suppose. For with her hands upon his body it was apparent that she was, indeed, highly attuned to him. Time and again it would seem as though her hands had made a mistake; her thumbs would go left, say, just when he was thinking that what his muscles were craving was to have them go right. But she would be correct. Over and over he would discover, as some knot or kink in his neck deliciously simplified itself, that she'd done the necessary thing. Better than he did she knew what he wanted—and does the world offer any revelation more fulfilling than the knowledge that somebody knows you better than you know yourself? Where else in the universe is there any real promise of a release from your own ignorance? As he drifted along on the flow of her ministrations, following her into a zone between sleep and waking, it would become unchallengingly apparent that here at last he'd unearthed the one person who truly comprehended him, and whom he truly comprehended. There were obstacles that would have to be negotiated, to be sure, including her fundamental apathy about the major doings of his life. And there was as well that boyfriend of hers—that computer-jock who was a "man of the spirit."

On the other hand, there were obstacles he might face with other women that he wouldn't face with Angelina. There was that phrase which, though he rarely spoke it and rarely brought it fully to mind (except when, as now, a drowse came on), still it had to be said was central to his life—*sexual dysfunction*—and these were words with which, in the case of Angelina, he would no longer need concern himself. Oh, no!—for every nerve in his body confirmed that with her he'd be a jackrabbit, would be Terry the stallion, he would be a fever-blooded bull! And she knew it too. She understood most things about him . . .

Sometimes her thumbs seemed to lead him one way while her fingers guided him confidently in another, and through his drowsiness he might have been a child, with a parent holding each of your hands, and the two parents in some sort of game pulling you in contrary directions. In his drowsiness he missed the beginning of what she was saying.

She was saying: "—seemed totally reasonable at first, this subdued monotonous voice, you'd never know he's a wacko. But then he raises his voice, real *loud* you know, loud like some thundering TV preacher, and he says, 'Every single one of these loaves is *malignant.*'"

"Loaves?" Terry said.

"And people are naturally backing away, I mean the guy's practically like *shouting,* but me I need some bread. So I go right up to him."

"Mm?"

"And I take down a loaf—there must have been a hundred of them stacked up there, and I say, '*This* one isn't, this one isn't malignant. I'm going to buy this one.' And I say, 'Would you like me to help you?' and I take another loaf down from the shelf and you know what I do? I pretend to like inspect it, and then I say, '*This* one isn't either,' and I hand it to him, and you know what he does? He takes it, he smiles at me, a real *radiant* smile, and walks away just as normal as you please."

"That was very clever."

"It's just a matter of dealing with each person on their own level."

"What about me?" Terry said and added, a little boldly, "Tell me about my level."

"I'm dealing with it now," Angelina said, and worked her fingertips more deeply into his shoulders.

Afterwards, as he was buttoning up his shirt, he said to her, "Sorry I've been away so long. It's been quite a busy and confusing time. All *sorts* of things have been going on."

"Uh-huh," she said.

"One of the things that happened was, I had this odd experience. It was really quite amazing. I had what I guess you'd have to call a mystical experience." *And your boyfriend, that man of the spirit, could he say this? Had he ever had a truly mystical experience?*

She looked at him closely. "Mm?" she said.

"I'd like to tell you about it."

"I'd like to hear about it," Angelina said.

Given all the hours he'd passed in her company, he'd rarely looked into her face. Her chin was weak, her adorable brown eyes were close-set, her tangled auburn hair was pulled back in a ponytail. The light in here was dim, but he thought he could make out freckles on the bridge of her nose. "You tell me all about it next time?" she said.

"What's that on your neck?"

"That?" she said. She had a red splotch on her collarbone. "That's just tension."

She offered this without the least show of self-consciousness. Evidently she saw no irony in the fact that she, who made a living by reducing stress in others, would carry such a mark.

She might dismiss it, and yet for Terry this mottled sign of fleshly vulnerability, of an incomplete mastery of personal energy flowage, was emboldening. He said to her, "How's the boyfriend?"

"Howard?" she said, with some surprise. You would think she hadn't mentioned him at every one of Terry's appointments. "He's fine."

"Do you two ever date?" Terry went on. "I mean people other than each other?"

She made no effort to disguise her look of frank appraisal. There was a waver in it, a momentary flutter, as if in the balancing of one thing against another, and in that instant he saw unmistakably that—however she might eventually answer him—such things were workable in principle. By means of her eyes alone, he knew with absolute fixity that there existed no insurmountable obstacle to her going with him to the movies or out to dinner. Such things were doable. If the spirit only proved willing, every moon-mad scheme in the world was doable—even that one in which she breezed into the wedding in ripped tennis shoes and he rakishly introduced her to the Drills as his masseuse.

But what at last she said, having sized him up thoroughly, was, "It's Howard, you see. He just won't permit it." She lifted those lovely hands of hers—those long, strong, miraculous healing hands—in order to enact a quick, ugly, mortal wrenching. "He'd wring my neck," she said.

He woke in the dark to the sound of breathing—Kopp's.

And lying atop the plane of his breathing, like a silver needle afloat on the surface of a pond, was a phrase, *This is not home either.*

New York—he was in New York, where he never slept well. Terry located the upper of the two little silver buttons on the left side of his digital watch and pressed down upon it to ignite the miniature light within: it was 4:27. Too early to get up, but late enough to offer the likelihood of no more sleep. Downstairs—down a swooning ladder of staircases—a metropolis was already coming awake with a creaking stiffness of horns and brakes. No, he was not at home here.

But there was that *either*—the phrase had been *This is not home either* (although already the words were fading and he could no longer be sure he held them in his head verbatim), and the phrase seemed to tell him that Washington, too, wasn't home. And where was it that he'd glimpsed or felt before (in a dream perhaps?) the place where he was meant to live? (Where else but in the free land of a dream had he beheld those white and gold and sea-blue streets, with their snow-knit, sunlit mountain crests behind them?)

Someone, down below, leaned hard into his horn and held it—a long rancorous blare of protest—and Terry could feel the uncontainable rage behind it, but who in the world could be feeling so angry while driving through the dark and mostly empty streets of Manhattan at 4:27 in the morning? What was the driver raging at? What was the crime, that so much rage was called for?

Of course Kopp slept through it all, just as he used to sleep when the customers would come, shy and sly and triumphant, saying, *You the guy with the jumping beans?* They had seen the ads of course: *if you haven't felt their warm rapturous throbbing in the palm of your hand, you have not really lived.*

The two of them were asleep again in the same room, though it wasn't as if other arrangements hadn't been available. Terry had made this plain a number of times, as they'd driven north in his Audi. (Driving had been Kopp's idea—a little money-saving gesture, evidently.) He'd offered Kopp a room to himself, courtesy of Hamill, Hillman. It would have been easy enough to book another room at the firm's expense. Or—since he liked to keep his expense accounts reasonably free of irregularities—Terry might have picked up the tab himself, which he would have been perfectly willing to do. But our ever-frugal Kevin had balked at taking two rooms.

And yet, while it was true that frugality was one of the Kopper's overriding passions, more than money had been involved, as Terry had belatedly realized just before turning in for the night. He'd been brushing his teeth, and hurrying the job a little so Kopp could have his shot at the bathroom, when it occurred to him that, some twenty years having gone by, they were together just as before—before, that is, Terry had informed Kevin that they would, come the following year, no longer be roommates. That announcement hardly sounded, today, like any sort of momentous decision. But momentous it had been at the time. Both of them realizing that—whatever Terry's bromides about the need to broaden experiences—Kopp was hopeless when it came to meeting new people. Terry was leaving him in the lurch, stranding him. And yet, two decades later they were roommates again—Kopp had finally gotten his way.

If Kopp wanted to share a room, let him have his way—in this as in all sorts of minor matters. Terry was feeling guilty. He had done it again—dumped Kevin. But this time around it was different, for this was purely a matter of scheduling. There simply were not enough hours in the day for Terry to go on indulging himself—as he had during his nine-week leave—in the endless, incurving chatter that Curly found so engrossing. No time, no time.

More than that, of course there was more to it than that: for the whole business had begun to seem futile—and if futile, then silly. And if silly, then sad. Unfortunately, Kopp's sort of chatter led precisely nowhere. Far more productive to accept the notion that, now and then, strange things simply happened. Sometimes, on the head of some poor soul or other, out of the blue, an inexplicability would descend . . . and when it did, talk was almost certainly unfitted for the task of its analysis.

Yet it was cheering, all the same, to have an appointment today with Tryggvi Hannibalsson . . . Terry had been looking forward to this. Let Adam, if he wanted to, go on ragging about Putative Contacts with the Recently Deceased, or let him change the name Hannibalsson into Son of the Elephant Man. But from where Terry now stood there could be no doubting that to hypothesize that nothing lay behind his visitation in the cabin was far more disquieting than to hypothesize that something or other did. Tryggvi Hannibalsson . . . The very name Hannibalsson . . . Oh, the syllables went winging through Terry's head while he felt himself tiptoe along a narrow causeway, a granular path, a sandy winding shallow-rooted easement between sleep and waking, but it wasn't as though nothing had changed since the days when they'd shared a room with a restless brood of Mexican jumping beans, because, for one thing,

Curly had become a noisy sleeper. He snuffled and sighed, rolled over, rolled over.

Curly was feeling hurt, neglected, and that was a shame, for Terry liked him—far better now than he'd ever been able to like him back then. What had changed in the meantime was nearly everything. A world had intervened. And there could be no reason now, as there had seemed reasons then, for feeling unnerved by the Kopper. Kopp was weird (or, as he himself was more likely to call it, screwy) but nothing more than that, and that was all right. Oh, he could still lash out with a malice that left you momentarily stunned—he'd done it tonight. But that was all right, too.

Kopp was hurting partly because he sensed that, in Terry's eyes, his whole take on things (or at least his take on the incident that had inspired Terry's initial call last fall) had begun to look ridiculous. These days it made Terry positively wince to hear Kopp refer to Hypothesis One and Hypothesis Two—albeit terms far preferable to the Guest Hypothesis and the Round-the-Bend Hypothesis. It was this awareness of Terry's discomfort that had led Kopp tonight, forking up a final bite of raspberry cheesecake, to lash out.

He had lashed out for a variety of reasons. For one thing, he'd been disappointed at the nonchalance with which Terry had greeted his observation about the psychological links between the accident and the purchase of an aquarium. But had Kopp honestly been thinking Terry himself was blind to the connection? Just how dumb, how obstinately stupid, did Kopp actually think he was? A man whose wife had drowned some two years before goes to considerable trouble and expense to set up an aquarium—and aren't the analogies here, the obvious symbolic yearnings for mastery and redemption, almost too obvious to point out? But, his eyes agleam with the overweening light of a man unfolding a revelation, Kopp *had* pointed them out—and he'd felt hurt, clearly, when Terry had brushed him aside.

So Kopp, a few minutes later, had lashed out—and what was Terry to reply? The words he'd wanted to confess to Curly, in a spirit of resignation tinged with gratitude and fondness, had something to do with the futility of thinking and of words—

but he'd lacked even the thoughts and the language for that. And what to say or do about these other feelings, the inner intimations that even now there might be something peculiar and outsize and all but imperceptible happening to him? Something still going on, even yet . . . This was like termites eating a house or microbes boring the marrow from a bone or the tide hollowing a cliff—but it was like none of these things. Something was moving, or had moved. And that was about as good as he could do.

Kopp rolled over once more, toward Terry, and in the hesitant, mistake-prone wash of dawn, or false dawn, the familiar face took shape. His lips were twitching: he was toiling toward speech. Like a baby he was, but a balding baby—a very homely baby. In the middle of a dream he was, and what benefit were all the months they'd lived side-by-side, sharing the same food and the same air and the same wall clock? None at all, if you couldn't begin (and Terry couldn't) to speculate on what might be going on underneath that threadbare scalp.

Even now, this trip, the Kopp full of surprises. Terry saw before him again the folder on Kopp's desk, puzzlingly labeled "Heaven-bound" (Kopp was in the bathroom, taking a last pee before they started the drive to New York), and once more Terry opened it instinctively, without pausing to question the ethics involved. Within, he'd found records of charitable contributions—to the World Wildlife Fund and a save-the-whales organization and Greenpeace and even a group called Preserve the Parrots. Individual checks had not been all that substantial—$50, $100—but there had been a great many of them, and Terry's rapid impression (he'd had to close the folder hurriedly, on hearing the bathroom door swing open) was that Kopp must give away at least a couple of thousand dollars a year. And who in the world would ever have predicted that Kevin Kopp, Princeton's tightest tightwad, would become a philanthropist? And—still more puzzling—why would the Kopper, with all of his bristling impulses toward self-justification, keep this sort of nobility a secret?

And had Kopp left the notebook out on the desk in the express hope that Terry would chance not only to spot it but to open it? (Not a bad bet, since the two of them had a long-standing tradition of covert prying into each other's lives . . .) Was it really happenstance, or some sort of devious design? In the end, there was no telling what Kevin was thinking.

No telling, perhaps, what anybody was thinking—and this was the fear that Curly, with all his sure, malign instincts, had been playing on tonight. What did Terry know with any certainty about—well, about, let's say, the woman he'd made his wife? Here was somebody you knew so well you could have identified her merely by the cadence of her footsteps on a flight of stairs, or by the little popping sigh her elbow sometimes released (her right elbow—the one she'd injured in a junior high gym class), or by the little, dimpling, much-kissed scar on her right thigh, or by the dozy, deodorized smell of her under-arms—but what in fact did you know?

Which meant that when Kopp, having licked from it the last smeary traces of cheesecake, brandished an empty fork like some miniature pitchfork in a children's satanic cartoon, and fixed you with a glare of hell-bent cunning, and said, "But according to Hypothesis Two, the Round-the-Bend Hypothesis, you had strong motivations for seeking reassurance and forgiveness," what was there to offer in reply? Kopp had probed in this direction before, but now, nudged by all the neglect and scorn you'd begun to show him, he'd lashed out openly at last: "You wanted to be told it wasn't a suicide, didn't you?"

Of course there was that, oh of course there was that. There were fronds turned to metal, overheated palm trees outside, each brandishing a phalanx of blades, and it was of course impossible to rule out, under just such killing circumstances, the narrow possibility of the accident's being no accident. Of course. Of course. And what good to point out that the vacation had been going well, Betsy bubbling with talk about future plans? What good to point out how the currents were tricky, the flippers and mask were rented and hadn't fit properly, the wind had shifted? Still that faint possibility; still the stain; still that network of sun-sharpened blades. Of course.

Before Kopp came along, no one had ever explicitly articulated the possibility, though others must have thought it, at least for a few gnawing moments. Kopp hadn't been the first, surely, besides Terry to think it . . . But did you need to speak it aloud? And if (playing the devil's advocate, with your little mini-pitchfork in hand) you went on to point out that she'd suffered bouts of depression, wasn't that to argue against rather than for the possibility? For she'd put those behind her, and she wasn't the only one to say so; everybody had said so. And if a person had self-destruction in her, was ever to be inclined in that way, wouldn't it have come to the surface during the depression and not well afterwards? She had weathered that. She had proved her own strength.

One accepts the other possibility, one has to, now and for all time (and especially at night, in bed, at four in the morning, waking to a world that will not lie flat) one accepts the possibility. Agreed. Or one had to accept it unless—unless one took as the simple and literal truth (and why not? why not accept what earlier generations would have accepted unquestionably?) the message she'd brought him. In that moment before the glass shattered and the blood issued so frenziedly from his foot, she'd said, *No one's fault,* and for all the blood that trailed in pursuit of her, all the hubbub and craziness, it had been a message of clarification, of assuagement.

. . . Or should have been. So it should have been, had he known what to do with her words, how to think about them—instead of letting them fester into greater doubts, a deeper-incising nervousness. He'd failed her, hadn't he—failed to *fit* her words into his life? Oh, he was in more need now than ever of a visit, a word, a look of placation. He was in need of another bitter miracle.

And what was to stop her from appearing to him now? What was to stop her, as Kopp snuffled and sighed, snuffled and sighed, from appearing in this midtown hotel room—why could he feel so heart-certain that this wasn't about to happen? What was to stop her, anyway, from appearing in a dream? (And wasn't it peculiar—dear Jesus, surely it was peculiar!—that as far as he knew she hadn't once, since that night in the cabin, appeared to him in any dream?) Something, even now, happening within him, shifting . . . *Artistic* is the word she'd held up, but she wasn't artistic. And *solid* he had held up, but he wasn't solid. And sometimes it was as though the two of them were tumbling down a chute, in so tumultuous and blurring a fashion that only at the extremities—a foot, a hand—was either of them distinctly visible. Tryggvi Hannibalsson—one took all such questions to the son of the Elephant Man. In this, as in so much in the modern world, one sought out the specialist. Get yourself a professional opinion . . .

He was returned from the shore of sleep by Curly Kopp, who was toiling toward speech. Outside, down all those flights of stairs, it was the city of Manhattan; and here, in this rented room, it was the city of a dream, and who in the world could confidently premise the alleyways and thoroughfares, towers and amphitheaters, balconies and sewers and shadowed parks of Kopp's dream city? Scrutinizing his old roommate in the tentative light, Terry read upon those homely, impacted features a show of effort—the pressure of trying to emerge, for once, into a speech free of obliquity, irony, cross-reference, understatement, overstatement: words at last that everybody could follow. And Terry Seward the communications lawyer, who specialized in radio and television licensing, now proceeded to broadcast a message toward that zone, wherever its location, in which telepathic impulses are fielded. *Go ahead* is what he advised the Kopper. *Speak up,* he told him. He said, *I'm here,* and *I am listening, friend.*

"So you are, literally, the son of a man named Hannibal?"

"Ah!—you understand about the system of Icelandic naming. Our unusual patronymics."

"Not really. I think it's just something I once picked up in a flight magazine."

"Ah!—so you have visited my country?"

"Not really. I stopped there once for a few hours, on my way to Europe."

"Ah! You were already *in* Europe, when you landed in my country," this man, Tryggvi Hannibalsson, pointed out. Whether characteristically Icelandic, or a personal eccentricity, this *ah!* of his was an unusual affirmation, produced on a sharp intake of breath. It was followed by a low bumpy giggle. Behind his thick glasses, his eyes came as close as eyes ever can to twinkling.

"Yes, sure, I suppose. This was years ago—back in the days when Icelandair was the cheapest way to Europe."

"So you have few impressions of my country . . ."

Actually, to speak of it as a country at all seemed, in the light of Terry's memory, comically grandiose. Arrival had meant winging down through a gray wet sky over a gray sea to reach a gray wet land. There'd been a scurrying into a little lounge that had felt more like an old ski lodge or small town bus station than an airport terminal, while rain ripped and broke against the panes. Terry had walked around sipping a bitter cup of coffee and looking at photographs of cliffs and waterfalls and pinched little hovels with grass sprouting out of their roofs. "*Very* few I'm afraid," Terry said.

"Now *that* is unfortunate. You see it is so beautiful."

"I can imagine."

Again Mr. Hannibalsson emitted a merry snort of hilarity—although, so far as Terry could see, nothing humorous had been ventured on either side.

He was a large man, maybe six feet two, and broad across the face and shoulders. His cheeks and hands were freckled. His neatly parted hair was gray—dark gray—on top, and snowy white along the sides. He was wearing a suit and tie. In moments of reflection he could look very much like a lawyer, and this meeting in a little office in a book-lined study in the Psi Center had for Terry a familiar feel; the two of them might be closing up preliminary greetings on their way to a discussion of "hard look" processing of FM radio applications.

—Or Tryggvi Hannibalsson might have seemed a lawyer had it not been for the loopy way in which mirth kept bubbling up in his large frame. Even the most mundane pronouncement tended to dislodge a giggle at its conclusion.

"You are a lawyer," Tryggvi Hannibalsson said.

"That's right."

"And what kind of law is your speciality?" The last word

came out in British fashion, with an extra syllable. His Scandinavian accent carried an overlay of the King's English.

"Communications. Especially licensing of radio and television stations."

"They would have taken *that* for a miracle, wouldn't they? A hundred fifty, two hundred years ago."

"Beg your pardon?"

"Everybody. Even the skeptics. They would have been forced to call it a miracle, would they not?"

"You mean—"

"Consider a moment this sending of voices and pictures unerringly through the air. What else could they have called it but a miracle?"

"I hadn't really thought of it that way."

"You are working to make people hear things and see things that aren't there . . . Is that not so?"

"That's right. That's true."

"You, my friend, are a miracle worker." Mr. Hannibalsson giggled and looked down at his freckled hands—massive hands, the fingers laced on the desktop. "Did you know that in the eighteenth century the best scientists did not believe in meteorites?"

"Really."

"What could be more absurd? I ask you, Could anything be more absurd than the notion of rocks falling out of the sky?"

"I've never looked at it that way . . . Is Hannibal an unusual name in Iceland?"

"Quite so. But not altogether unheard of. I am hoping to see it become more popular. And I thought of naming my son Hannibal."

"Or you could call him Hasdrubal. That was Hannibal's brother." It pleased Terry Seward, the former history major, to insert this picturesque detail.

"Yes, his brother-in-law."

"So what *did* you decide to call him?"

"John."

"John?"

"J-o-n, actually. That's the Icelander's John."

"So his name is Jon Tryggvisson," Terry said.

"Ah! Quite right." Mr. Hannibalsson looked very pleased.

"And what is your son doing? Is he in Iceland?"

"Well he's here in America, actually. He is a neurologist. He is studying at M.I.T."

And *this* news pleased Terry. For it was reassuring to think that this man with the bouncing merry eyes, and the queer and faintly macabre laugh, who committed his signature to articles with titles like "Putative Encounters with the Recently Deceased" and "A Comparative Study of Visions in the Clinically Dead," had produced a son sufficiently earthbound to have gained admittance to M.I.T. The son's work legitimated the father's.

"I suppose it is very complicated—the licensing of television and radio stations?"

"More complicated than it needs to be."

"Yes. The human race—we are great complicators, aren't we?" And he giggled again. Then, his face retaining its look of jubilation, he said, "And you yourself have had some sort of personal complication in the form of a mystical experience?"

Terry paused for just a moment. "That's right. As I wrote to you, I—"

"Please." Mr. Hannibalsson lifted his hands from the desk and—a strikingly vulnerable gesture in so large a man—spread them before his face, creating a sort of fence or screen, through which he said, "I was hoping, before we talked of such things, that you might fill out my questionnaire."

"Yes, of course. I said I'd be only too glad—"

"Our talk might influence your answers, you see."

"Yes, I can understand that."

"You must go into it fresh."

"I suppose I'm as fresh as I'll ever be."

But in fact Terry did not feel ready to undertake the questionnaire. This place itself had unnerved him from the first moment, as though there were something duplicitous—sinister—in the businesslike nameplate on the door (The Psi Center for Research into the Paranormal) and the pointedly ordinary coatracks in the foyer. What had he expected? Terry wasn't sure—but definitely not this antiseptic entryway, the pinging of a computer, the grinding of a printer, the sense of subdued industry among the technocrats. Had he been disappointed not to discover some dilapidated nineteenth-century mansion with curving staircases and a frescoed ballroom converted into a musty library? The actual library might just as well have held FCC broadsides or IRS advisory reports instead of the accounts of spooks and fetches it presumably contained. Doubtless his expectations had been unrealistic, but it had disappointed him faintly when the un-wild-eyed receptionist had requested his name for the guest list. Shouldn't anyone connected with a psychical research institute know that his name was not spelled S-T-U-A-R-T?

All of these things required some assimilation time. And before starting the questionnaire he wanted, as well, some solider picture of this big strange man with the very strange name who sat before him. "Tell me about Iceland," he said. "Are you from Reykjavik? I mean if it's okay, in terms of the questionnaire, if we talk a little first."

"I grew up on a farm near Mount Kringlan—perhaps you've heard of it?"

"I don't know. Maybe. I don't think so."

"It is famous for its eruptions." Another low giggle. "It last erupted in 1915. And before that in 1847. And before that in 1775. And before that in 1702. And so forth. Roughly every seventy years, you see."

"Yes."

"It is overdue." Giggle.

"Yes."

"Later I moved to Reykjavik to work for my uncle, who owned a printing house. He was quite well-to-do, by Icelandic standards. Of course that's nothing like here, is it?" His massive hands fluttered to weave a net, catching in the mesh of his metaphor all the gleaming upright glass-and-steel opulence of Manhattan. "But I had other interests . . ." Giggle.

"Are many people in Iceland interested in the things you're interested in?"

"You are referring to my studies? The articles I sent you?"

"Yes."

"Generally? As a people? As a people, I believe they are, rather. We're perceived as a superstitious people, you know, and statistically that may be an accurate perception. We have a very rich folklore. Perhaps you've read some?"

"I don't think so . . ."

"Ogres, sea cows, mermaids, ghosts, trolls, elves, *huldufolk*—which is the Hidden Folk. They're something between elves and people, I suppose. When I meet others in my field, they are impressed simply that I come from Iceland." He looked still more pleased—colossally pleased. "I am exotic to them.

"All my life," Mr. Hannibalsson went on, "I have been an exotic." He stared out the window—or, since the curtains were all but closed, stared at the vertical crack of light that represented the window. Not so far off, at the end of Seventy-second Street, the East River was flowing out to sea.

"You're the first Icelander I've ever really spoken with," Terry said.

"But you see," Mr. Hannibalsson replied, "I am not completely an Icelander. My maternal grandfather was German, and that made me, at least among the farms around Kringlan, an exotic creature. Of course, in America there's nothing exotic about being a German, is there? These days, I'm an exotic because of my Icelandic blood. But I may be more exotic yet." Giggle. "There was talk, you see, I don't know how much to be trusted, that my grandfather's father was a Jew, a Jewish trader. The story may be utterly without foundation, but the idea appeals to me."

Terry suppressed the ludicrous impulse to say, *Funny, you don't look Jewish.* Instead he asked, "How did you first become interested in this particular field of study?"

"Ah, but perhaps it would be better if you first filled out my questionnaire. I would be very grateful . . ."

"I'd be happy to."

"You could remain right here. I will return in let us say half an hour?" He removed from his folder a stapled little sheaf of papers, which he placed face down before Terry. "You could work right here at this desk. I think the whole thing should require no explanation."

"Fine."

Mr. Hannibalsson rose, smiled, and rubbed his huge hands together gloatingly, in a seemingly unwitting but wholly inspired parody of a B-movie's archetypal mad scientist. "I will return in half an hour."

"Fine."

"Half an hour." The door closed without a sound behind him . . .

The first portion of the questionnaire was reassuringly sober. Terry might almost be filling out an application for life insurance. Name, age. Marital status. Education. Profession. General medical history. Terry worked in pencil, slowly.

The shift in tone, too, was introduced soberly. Terry read: "You are filling out this questionnaire, presumably, because you have experienced what might be called a mystical experience. Please describe this experience as precisely and *factually* as possible. Feel free to use the back of this sheet if additional space is required."

Terry propped his elbows on the desk, placed his hands together, and rested his chin on his backward-extended thumbs. He read some of the titles in the bookshelf on the opposite wall: *Withinways, Mandala, Intimations, The Interior Flame.* Vowing to be both terse and impeccably factual, he wrote, "I flew from Washington, DC, where I live, to Norfolk, Virginia, where I was to spend the weekend in a cabin with my sister and her fiancé."

He halted, surprised to discover that he had, in referring to Glenn in these terms, already deviated from the realm of unchallengeable truths. Cross it out? Change *fiancé* to *boyfriend*? He decided to leave it and go on—but to proceed with a still more scrupulous exactitude.

He wrote: "I arrived at the cabin before they did. I poured myself a glass of water and then, having finished that, I poured a glass of whiskey. I had drunk only a little of the latter when I heard a voice behind me (I was standing at the kitchen sink). The voice said, 'Terry, Terry, no one's fault.' I thought I recognized this voice as that of my deceased wife Betsy, who had died in a swimming accident the year before. Naturally I turned around immediately. I saw, or thought I saw, her standing before me. She was standing in a sort of white glow. She was wearing a

T-shirt on her—" He halted. On her what? He continued: "her upper torso. She often slept in a T-shirt at night. Around her waist she was wearing a white towel, wrapped around her like a sort of skirt. Not surprisingly, in my great astonishment I dropped the glass I was holding. It shattered on the floor. When I stepped forward, to approach her, I cut my foot rather severely on the broken glass. I fell down. By the time I had re-covered—" He crossed out *had recovered* and continued, "had risen to my feet once more, she was gone."

He surveyed what he'd written and found it gratifying. He liked its matter-of-factness, its balance of reasonableness and skepticism. He liked the *or thought I saw;* he liked still better the *Not surprisingly.*

He read it through once again and this time perceived that, as a sort of legal document, a witness's affidavit, it was incomplete in all manner of ways. Neither the time of day nor the time of year was included. Nor anything about the drive to the cabin, nor about the cabin's location. Nor the headaches all day and the drinks at lunch. Not to mention, as well, any of those details that Kopp was always harping on—meeting Allison the night before, in Marquette; meeting Kelly that morning, and inviting her out to Washington; Bertha and the *National Enquirer;* the call from Angelina; the storm and the impression, all day, of fleeing a storm . . . The list went on and on.

Still, it turned out not to matter so much that his account was abbreviated since the questionnaire, with reassuring exhaustive-ness, took up most of the missing details. What time of day was it when this experience occurred? When was the last time you had slept and how many hours' sleep had you had? Were you under any medication? Were you under the influence of alcohol or rec-reational drugs? Was the place where the experience occurred familiar to you or new to you? Were you alone at the time?

Terry worked carefully—more than carefully: with joyful ab-sorption. Despite Mr. Hannibalsson's chuckling mirth, and the odd bouncy brightness of his gaze, he evidently knew how to pursue his study rigorously. Terry was gratified to discover two pages of visual diagrams of that peculiar sort in which the hu-man eye can just as easily discern one object as another. In the first of these, which was like something borrowed from an

Escher print, there was a patterned flock of white birds migrating to the right, or an army of pincered black insects scrambling to the left. In the next there was a white urn against a black background, or—by a process that was like flipping your vision over—there were two stylized black faces separated by a white gap that was no longer an urn but simple air. Terry was to indicate what each diagram first evoked for him—and whether or not the diagram "changed" as he continued to stare at it. Clever, surely Mr. Hannibalsson was extremely clever!—for wouldn't it be useful to know whether those people who had had "experiences" might also, in some quantifiable way, see things differently from those who hadn't? Gleefully, exulting in his mastery over his own visual powers, Terry made one diagram after another "flip"; he would unlock them all.

After the visual diagrams, Terry met a harder question, a multiple choice: "What would you say was the *intention* of your experience: A. to frighten you; B. to reassure you; C. to enlighten you; D. other (please specify); E. Not applicable." After grave deliberation he circled B, but added, in the space reserved for those who'd circled D, "Not necessarily the actual effect on me, however."

But the ever-anticipatory Mr. Hannibalsson had foreseen this possibility, for the very next question was: "What would you say was the ultimate *effect* of your experience on you: A. frightened; B. reassured; C. enlightened; D. other (please specify)." Terry circled D, and wrote, "Somewhat frightened, slightly reassured, not at all enlightened, greatly confused." This was a beautiful answer and left him feeling heartened.

It wasn't long after this, however, that the comforting commonsensicality of the questionnaire began to dissolve away. "How would you best describe your attitude toward money?" it asked: "A. very tight (skinflint); B. tight; C. average; D. loose; E. very loose (spendthrift)." And what possible relevance could this have? Terry wished Kopp were here to consult with; *he'd* be able to see in a moment just how aboveboard such inquiries were. And there were other, still more peculiar questions . . . "What is your favorite color?" And of what use could such information be? Terry wrote "Blue—sky blue" and proceeded to the next question. "If your experience involved seeing a person

or persons who was/were 'not there,' do you know what his/
her/their favorite color(s) was/were?" Terry was tempted to give
the wiseguy response—to write "Yes" simply and move
along—but the question brought him up short. What *was*
Betsy's favorite color?

He knew the answer, of *course* he did know it, but for one
hard-pressed moment, sitting in this cluttered office with the
curtains drawn, faced with question after question whose pur-
port he could not follow, he was unable to call to mind Betsy's
favorite color, and all at once he felt panicky. He laced his fingers
together on the desktop and squeezed hard, which turned his
knuckles white and his fingertips a bright purply-red.

He waited. On a pure beam of light the answer came to him.
Yellow, of course: the lapping of the sun, the food of the skin.
Betsy's depression first came on in January, and one of the medical speculations about her condition was that the shortage of
natural light had gotten to her—hence their first trip to the
Caribbean. Why *did* Hannibalsson have the curtains drawn? It
was a fine day, a day like so many in Terry's Iowa childhood, and
he felt, as he had so often during his recent leave from work, a
pulling upon his spirits, a drive which sought to lead him both
outward and backward—outdoors and back in time, to the
fields and playgrounds of his youth.

Was any particular color associated with your experience? Terry
wrote, "White. She—the vision—stood in a sort of glow."

When Terry came to *Are you afraid of dogs?* he laughed aloud.
For this was it, surely this was it: the juncture where the rational
and the mad firmly embraced each other. Those two parallel
lines of his life in recent months—the down-to-earth and the
out-to-lunch, the mundane and the lunatic—intersected here: in
this office, with this questionnaire.

There was a timid knock and Mr. Hannibalsson's large bespectacled head floated sideways around the door's edge. Terry
thought he detected mischief in the man's tilted grin. "How are
you doing with my little questionnaire?"

"Maybe another ten minutes?"

"Yes. Please take your time. Yes. Don't let me hurry you."
And the head slipped out of sight.

Do you have a lucky number? How often do you bathe? Do you consider yourself: A. overweight; B. average weight; C. underweight? And in the middle of this nonsensical jumble: Do you believe in God? Terry after a pause wrote "Yes," which seemed more accurate than "No" and perhaps just as accurate as any lengthier explanation he might tender. Has your experience altered your religious views? After another pause, Terry wrote "No," which seemed marginally more correct than "Yes," crossed out his reply and did write "Yes," and crossed this out as well. The result—two black smudges—seemed as true-spirited as any reply he was likely to elaborate.

Had you had sexual relations with anyone on the day of the experience? "No." If yes, was this the initial encounter with that person? Not applicable. Do you recall feeling any strong sexual attraction on the day of the experience? Terry, after a moment's deliberation, answered "Yes." Why in the world was he filling this out? If yes, was this attraction different in kind from your typical sexual attractions? Another one to mull over . . . Terry was on the verge of another affirmation when he read the next few questions: If yes, please explain in what way it was atypical and Did you indulge in a sexual act (interpersonal or masturbatory or other) as a result? And, If so, please describe. Defiantly, relishing his own illogicality, Terry scribbled "Not applicable" after all three. (Interpersonal or masturbatory or other?) It occurred to him, with a sharp inkling of betrayal, that Mr. Hannibalsson might be pursuing a purely psychoanalytical line—investigating, in Kopp's terms, only the Round-the-Bend Hypothesis. This hardly seemed fair. Indeed, it seemed unconscionable. For Terry had not come to the Psi Center for Research into the Paranormal with this understanding—and he'd come something like two hundred miles, at no small expense of time and money, to place himself here. Surely, if there existed any erudite, commonsensical, open-minded person on the planet who in a serious fashion ought to be willing to entertain the notion of paranormal visitations, that person ought to be a big, giggly Icelander named Tryggvi Hannibalsson who conducted elaborate surveys about putative encounters with the recently deceased.

Terry considered abandoning the questionnaire altogether

(what the hell business was it of anybody's what sort of *atypical* sexual desires he'd been experiencing?) but saw that this wouldn't constitute much of a gesture: he was nearly through. Besides, it might make him look like a prude. And the remaining questions were—Terry saw, glancing at the final page—a reversion to harmless nonsense. *If you had to decide, would you rather lose a hand or a leg?* And *What is your favorite season?* and *Which of these art forms do you prefer: A. Music; B. Painting or sculpture; C. Literature; D. Other (please specify).* And (a cruel irony, this!) *Do you consider yourself artistic?* Was he never, never going to be free of that startling night at Brad Boggs's when he and Betsy had been asked to encapsulate their souls in a single word? He jumped ahead in the questionnaire in order to answer this question now. NOT ARTISTIC he wrote in big block letters.

When Mr. Hannibalsson, a few minutes later, poked his head in once more, Terry was prepared for him. He had casually rolled up his sleeves and removed a newspaper from his briefcase. The questionnaire lay face down on the desk.

"You've been very kind." Mr. Hannibalsson took the other seat—the one that had been Terry's originally. Terry remained behind the big desk.

"I hope you'll find my answers satisfactory," Terry said, seeking with a faint coolness of voice to impart that his actual doubts lay not with his answers but with the questionnaire itself.

"Satisfactory?"

"Helpful."

"I'm sure they will be very helpful."

"Well Mr. Hannibalsson," Terry began, aggression rasping his voice slightly. "I was hoping *you* might be helpful to *me.*"

"You must call me Tryggvi, I beseech you. You see, Icelandic surnames are employed exclusively for identification and not as a means of address." He giggled.

This Mr. Hannibalsson—Tryggvi—truly *ought* to have been a lawyer. For someone working in a second language, he was a surpassingly articulate man.

"Yes, okay, Tryggvi," Terry began once more, the tentative note of aggression abruptly having fled his voice. "I was hoping you might shed some light on what your questionnaire would call my *experience.*"

"Tell me about it in detail."

"In detail? Well then, I suppose I would start with the morning—though the 'experience' didn't happen until that night."

"Yes. In the morning. And as much detail as you can recall."

Not since the days when he'd first hooked up again with Kopp—months and months ago now—had Terry gone into this with anyone. *That* occasion had been difficult; this one was singularly easy. Tryggvi's questions—and they were many—did not seem at all intrusive. The two of them might have been partners. They were probing this event together.

Piece by piece, shuttling back and forth in time, Terry assembled it all: rising at dawn in Marquette; meeting Kelly on the plane; having lunch with Adam; talking to Bertha . . . The brewing storm, the second flight, the drive in the darkness, the stops for gas and directions, the names posted on the tree, Absen, Butscher, Coldwell (which, Terry now belatedly came to see, were alphabetical) . . . The lock springing open so easily, and the jittery searching from room to room, the framed prints of the Indian and the buffalo and Botticelli's Venus, the wondering where Kaye and Glenn might possibly be; and the drinking of a glass of water, the pouring of a glass of whiskey.

Like that of someone taking notes, Tryggvi's gaze bobbed up and down, from Terry's face to his own lap. But his big hands, resting palm up on his thighs, were empty.

Terry felt as calm as calm could be. Tryggvi was especially interested in the vision itself. *What had she been wearing on her feet?* He didn't know—or maybe hadn't noticed . . . *Was it possible that the vision had no feet?* Under the circumstances, he had to say that pretty much anything was possible . . . *Was she merely bright—or did she actually seem to give off light?* That was hard to say, but he supposed it correct to say she gave off light. *Was it a sharp or a blurry vision?* Blurry—and getting blurrier all the time. Nowadays it sometimes seemed a sort of dream . . . *Was her hair up or down?* That wasn't easy either . . . But he would say down—yes, down upon her shoulders. *Had she looked in any way altered from life?* Well she was bright, of course, she was so full of light, but other than that, nothing he could recollect right now. Slimmer, perhaps. *Slimmer?* Slimmer than she'd been at some periods in the marriage; she'd gained a fair amount of weight at times. *Fat? Would you say she'd been a fat woman?* Fat? On no, not that.

And what happened next?

"Well, as I told you, I cut my foot pretty severely on the broken glass and I fell down, and when I got up she wasn't there. And after that, things got really blurry, though to some extent you could retrace my steps by the blood I left behind. I went outside, in pursuit of her, and then I came back in and tracked through all the rooms, and managed to cut my foot again, my other foot, only this wasn't so severe, and then when Kaye arrived, I'm not sure how much later but not so very long I think, I was standing in a little creek or river down behind the cabin."

Did you put all of this into your questionnaire?

"No. I kept pretty much to the facts."

But these are facts, aren't they? Didn't these things happen? You were standing in a stream?

"Oh, yeah, I was standing in the stream all right."

And then what happened?

"Well, nothing happened. You could say that nothing has happened ever since. That's really the point, you might say. I've gone back to work, I've left work, I've gone back to work again, I looked up an old college roommate, I read some books, I bought an aquarium—nothing has happened."

What happened after they found you in the stream?

"Well that's still pretty hazy. I'd lost a lot of blood, I guess— you'd be surprised at how much blood was in the cabin. They thought they'd have to take me to the hospital, but Kaye got the bleeding to stop and they threw a lot of whiskey down me. And I fell asleep."

Do you recall any dream?

"Nothing. But then I don't generally remember my dreams. And when I do, they can be astoundingly dull. I remember one dream in which I was painting a wall. That's a fact—painting a wall, one slow stroke after another for hours on end. I'm afraid I have a very mundane subconscious."

At this remark Tryggvi, who'd laughed or grinned at pretty much everything Terry had said up to now, showed none of the amusement he was supposed to. He said, somberly, "What color were you painting it?"

"What color? I don't recall. Something bright I guess. Something bright on a dark surface. There were a lot of colors in your questionnaire. Tell me about your questionnaire."

"Tell me first about the next day. What did you do?"

"I got up early and I knew I had to take a drive somewhere. I went out and discovered that the battery was dead on my rental car. So I gave myself a jump start and I started to drive. I thought I was going out only for an hour or so. But I drove for hours and hours."

"Where did you go?"

"At first I thought I'd go over to Jamestown. That's the first permanent settlement in North America. But then I decided to turn around and drive to Cape Hatteras. You know where I mean? On the coast of North Carolina? I'd always meant to go there. It's also a historical spot. That's where the Wright Brothers first flew a plane."

"What did you do when you got there?"

"Well that's funny. All day long I'd seen myself strolling up and down the beach . . . But my foot was in such bad shape I could hardly hobble. And I was very tired suddenly—almost unbelievably tired. I realized that my sister had no idea where I was, and I suddenly felt very guilty about that, and I called my parents, in Iowa—to let them know, and after getting things straightened out I found a motel room and went to bed. And as I said a minute ago—nothing has happened to me since."

Tryggvi Hannibalsson—the son of the Elephant Man—sat with his head bowed. He had been chronicling all of this in that imaginary volume in his lap: The Book of Unearthly Visions. Terry had been planning to ask about the questionnaire, but when at last his interlocutor's glance lifted to disclose a gaze that had undergone a sort of drainage—all merriment having receded, to reveal a dark gray melancholy beneath—Terry addressed an issue of far greater urgency: "I suppose my question, Tryggvi, is simple: having experienced what I experienced, what do I now do about it?"

"What do you do?"

"In what way is it supposed to change my life?"

"Perhaps the better question to ask initially is, Does your life need changing?"

"I wouldn't have thought so, frankly. Not until this happened. But this won't fit in my life."

"Well, my friend, have you any idea how many people in this country have had some sort of analogous experience? Some sort of mystical encounter?"

"I wouldn't have a clue . . ."

"Millions. Twenty million, if you want to be conservative with the data. Two, three times that figure if you read it differently."

"Twenty million?"

Terry was, in fact, accustomed to dealing with population figures of this magnitude (a grasp of television licensing required nothing less) but in this bizarre context the number sounded dizzyingly, insanely unreckonable.

"You are not a religious man?"

"Well I don't know—I suppose not," Terry said. "I didn't know quite how to respond when your questionnaire asked me just that. But I suppose you could say there are no great convictions . . ."

"Now that complicates matters, doesn't it, Terry? Let's be conservative and adopt that figure of twenty million. Well, most of these people who have some sort of mystical experience— something in the neighborhood of eighty percent of them—are religious, or quickly become so. For them, the experience is apt to 'fit,' as you say, rather easily into a larger spiritual world. They have been 'born again,' you see."

"I don't feel born again exactly. I've been changed, maybe, but I don't feel born again."

"Then we have what I call the Bertrand Russell Phenomenon. You know his work?"

"Not really, I mean obviously I know who he is."

"The great simplifier, yes, who once wrote a book called *Our Knowledge of the External World*? Now what does such a person do when he has a mystical experience?"

"He had one? Bertrand Russell?"

"And A. J. Ayer. Do you know A. J. Ayer?"

"He's maybe a philosopher?"

"Author of *The Origins of Pragmatism*?" The last word seemed to delight Tryggvi no end. His eyes twinkled. He said, "Now you see, that may be the category you belong in. You may be one of those who have difficulty categorizing your experience."

"I think you could safely say I've had trouble categorizing my experience."

Gravely Tryggvi nodded, evidently overlooking the note of grievous irony in Terry's remark. Trouble? *Trouble?* But why, on the other hand, should the irony matter, since the remark was true on its face?

"But you must see that you are still one among many, many people, Terry. You are part of a hidden army, don't you see? A sort of *huldufolk*—the Hidden Folk? Now if we take that conservative figure, of twenty million? And we reduce it by the eighty percent who can fit their experience easily into a larger spiritual world? That still leaves four million people, doesn't it, who had an experience that cannot be reconciled."

"So what do these four million people *do?*" Terry pressed him. "I mean other than wait for another 'experience.' "

"Ah, but you see the waiting is probably futile. Statistically, in most cases. Most of these experiences are what in my notation I call SVs. Single Visits."

"Single Visits?"

"As opposed to MVs—Multiple Visits."

"Multiple Visits?"

"The vast majority of people who have an experience never have another. That's true in about ninety percent of the cases. MVs are rare. Of course I'm excluding schizophrenia, drug trips—things of that nature."

So: okay, that was it, hey, all right, fine, gotcha, great, no problem . . . Terry had had an SV: *that's* what had happened to him. And after all of his painful, painstaking ransacking after the truth, how was *this* for a final explanation: *You been wondering for months and months, pal, what it was that happened to you? Well, hell, you had an SV—it's as simple as that.* Oh it was hurtful. It was all too stupid and plausible and stupid and hurtful for words!

And yet—and yet beneath the lightheaded absurdity, the

laughable ridiculousness in seeing the queerest occurrence in the
world trimmed to a pair of initials, there was a sense, too, of
distress, of anguished loss, of a dwindling hope of any genuine
clarification. "Four *million?*"

"You see, when you live in a country of two hundred and fifty
million souls, even very *odd* things, very *irregular* things, will be
measured in the millions . . ."

And who could argue with that? The big man was impreg-
nable, surely—for there was no strangeness, no quirk or aberration, that Terry might bring before him which couldn't be
slotted into his charts and grids. He was (and what a twist this
was!) he was, just as Dad was, a *numbers man:* he had all the
statistics on his side. And what was Terry left to do except to
say, as he did, "Well I haven't had another visit but I may have
had little hints, I guess you could call them follow-ups."

"Follow-ups?"

Terry reached down and patted his pants pocket. It was
there—the little cassette tape from his answering machine was
there. Terry had kept it all this time, in the top drawer of his
chest of drawers, safely stored on its bed of foreign coins. Physical evidence.

"A couple of times," Terry said. "Things like you know on
my telephone answering machine? Well, there's been a message
but the person or whatever doesn't say anything. There's only
breathing."

"*Breathing?*"

The utterly dismissive way in which Tryggvi met the news—
the robust skepticism in his voice, the shooing-away motion of
his big hands—seemed, under the circumstances, flagrantly unfair. How in the world could *he,* a man who, for heaven's sake,
put his name to articles about SVs, possibly treat such things as
inconsequential? And yet, in addition to feeling indignant, Terry
was now left feeling just a little fatuous. A breather on the
phone? Had he really brought it with him, the cassette tape,
carried it up from Washington just in case Mr. Hannibalsson
wanted to give a listen to a *breather?* But he wasn't about to mention now the tape in his pocket. Oh no. He changed the subject.
"So what do these four million people do? Let's assume you're
right, that it's likely there will be no other experience . . ."

"I can assure you of that, for on this I am certain. The statistics leave little doubt."

"No, I mean in my particular case. Let's assume *I* have no second experience—that I'm an SV or I've had an SV or whatever the hell it is . . . So what do I do? What do these four million people do?"

"Do?" Tryggvi repeated once more. "I suppose they do four million different things. They go on with their lives.

"When I was a young man," Tryggvi continued, "it may amuse you to hear that I resolved to become a famous writer, like the great Saga writers of old. So I wrote a story—and do you know it remains the only story I've ever written? I'm afraid it's neither a very artful story nor a very satisfying one . . . And yet if I may say so I think it has its charming aspects. Perhaps you would like to hear my story?"

Terry paused only a moment. "All right. Sure."

"Once upon a time . . ." this man actually began, and in that very moment Terry knew positively that he didn't want to hear the Icelander's story. No, what he wanted instead was to bellow in frustration, to bang his fist on the desktop, to hold a massive gleaming antique pistol against this lunatic's temple and compel him to explain his goddamned questionnaire.

". . . over the streets of Reykjavik, the clouds did a most peculiar thing: for approximately one hour they came all together, into one mass, and then they assembled themselves to form a date—complete with month, day, and year. Now the date itself is insignificant—call it May sixteenth, or July twenty-second, or any other day. The important thing is that this day was about a year off into the future.

"Now you must understand, Terry, that nobody could dispute what the clouds had done. After all, thousands upon thousands of people had witnessed it. Thousands of people had photographed it. Icelandic television crews had captured it unmistakably. It was a miracle—there could be no doubt about that.

"But, my friend, I'm very sorry to say that some people across the globe chose to disbelieve anyway. There will always be disbelievers, you see. They said it was a hoax or a military stunt pulled off by the U.S. Air Force.

"And some people saw it as proof of the existence of UFOs and some people decided it was a signal of the coming end of the world and they sold their belongings and went up on the mountaintops in preparation for the Day of Judgment.

"But most people just decided to wait and see.

"Well, the weeks and months finally passed and the day finally came, and do you know what happened?"

"No, what happened?"

"Do you want to guess?"

"I'd prefer to have you tell me, actually."

"*Not a thing happened, Terry.* Given the circumstances, nothing very unusual at all occurred. The day came and went. No volcanoes erupted, no tidal waves came crashing in. As far as was possible under the circumstances, it was a normal day.

"And then the scholars got to work in earnest, investigating the day from a million different vantage points, searching for the mystery they knew it must contain. Meanwhile, most of the religious people changed their outlook. They'd expected the end to everything, the Lord's Day of Judgment, but now they reasoned that the day must signal a beginning, the birth of a Messiah, and they turned to investigating all the children born on that day, to determine which one was the true child of God.

"But as the years went by, five, ten, twenty, thirty, it began to seem clearer and clearer to the historians that nothing very eventful had happened on that day, and clearer and clearer to the religious people that none of these children was the new Jesus or the new Buddha or the new Mohammed. And so people went on with their lives."

Tryggvi paused as if for breath, or to collect his thoughts. He removed his glasses, blew on the lenses, and replaced them on his face. Only then did it dawn upon Terry that the story had reached its termination. He said, mildly, "I'm not sure I get it. I'm not sure I understand your fable."

"Well it isn't a very artful or satisfying story, as I told you before I began it. But I suppose the meaning of the fable, my friend, is that for most people miracles don't matter very much. What is one more miracle? Does it mean more to a smoker than a pack of cigarettes? Does it mean more to a hungry man than a pickled herring? Life itself is a miracle—is it not?—and what additional miracle can possibly stand up to that? Life itself is a miracle, but so what? *So what?* The people find a way of ignoring miracles, don't they? They find a way of going on with their lives all the same. As you will do, my friend."

"But that leaves everything seeming so—" Terry began, and halted. What was the word, the one big-bordered word, that would enclose the peculiarity and heartbreak and insufficiency of Mr. Hannibalsson's advice? It seemed there *was* such a word inside him, but Terry, unsuccessful at dislodging it, was reduced to stringing adjectives together. "So pointless, so absurd, so defeatist . . ."

"So inconclusive?" Tryggvi suggested, which was closer, but still wasn't right.

"I just have trouble believing that everything I went through, on that night and since, doesn't *lead* somewhere."

"It's frustrating, isn't it?"

"To put it gently. It's more than that . . ."

"Maddening?"

"That, too. And more than that."

"Upsetting?"

The man was a goddamned thesaurus. "That goes without saying. Don't you see what it's doing to me? It's making a mockery of my life."

"Would you prefer, then, that the experience had never happened to you, Terry? That you had never gone to the cabin? That you had never had a visit, my friend?"

Oddly enough, this last question wasn't something that Terry had ever put to himself exactly. And now, and at once, Terry was struck by an impression of the question's crucial significance—as though, somehow, matters of great import poised in the balance of his reply. He was at this moment compelled to ask himself, as if for the first time, *What do you really wish, Terry Seward? Where would you seek to have your life come out?* What, at bottom, did he truly feel? And he was weirdly elated to discover himself able—weighing things all in all, one sort of life against another—in utter candor to respond, "No, I'm glad it happened."

He said them again, these words that had upon them the glow of high sunlight: "No, the fact is I'm very *glad* it happened to me . . ." They glowed because, in having chosen to cast his vote this way, in choosing to ally himself with embarrassment, puzzlement, chaos, expense, fear, and anguish, he had come down indisputably on the side of the angels.

And in this moment Terry knew it was time to go and he rose firmly from his chair and he stuck out his hand. He would carry his own words with him out of this place that was, surely, the strangest spot within this unfathomably strange city. He would wander out onto the streets of Manhattan, among the SVs and the MVs and the unflappable NVs—No Visits—and the out-and-out lunatics, not knowing for sure how to distinguish one from the other.

"You've given me a great deal of your time," Terry said, "and I want to thank you."

"And I want to thank you." The two men shook hands.

"If I have any more questions, may I write?"

"Please. You have my address."

A concluding question struck Terry. "Mr. Hannibalsson," he said, reverting to the banished surname, "have you ever had an experience of this sort?"

The big man released a final chuckle. "Four times," he confessed. "Four times, my friend. I am fifty-two years old. The first time, I was eleven. This was on the Kringlan farm. The second time I was twenty, and I was in Reykjavik. The third time I was thirty and I was in Kenya, at an altitude of nearly fourteen thousand feet, incidentally. The fourth time, I was here, in New York City, on Third Avenue just north of Seventy-ninth Street, and I was thirty-nine. Periodic, you see. Roughly every nine years, you see. Which means that I am due. Or overdue. Like Kringlan, the volcano." He was grinning from ear to ear, this man who was the joyfullest person on the planet. "I am waiting for another eruption."

(He woke to that smell he kept forgetting to remember. So faint was it, so perishable in its tendrilous extremities, that he could not seem to convey it with him all the long distances from sleep to waking. Somewhere he had read, years ago, that in the mile-high city of Tenochtitlán the Aztec imperial court used to dine on ocean fish, transported up to the palace by teams of breathless relay runners, this being the only way to ensure freshness in that torrid country—but in his own case some link in the relay chain had snapped and he couldn't bring the message of the smell intact to himself. This smell was feminine, and yet not something he altogether liked—if it was a perfume, it was unwisely chosen. Betsy had never worn any scent like it, he was all but sure of that; but why on earth was he smelling the smell of another woman in his bed?

(Possibly this was some sort of sign or clue from elsewhere, or some first signal of some sign or clue from elsewhere—but if so, it didn't seem anything to welcome. The mind had to do its work—analyze the analyzable—and possibly the way to categorize this newest bit of data was as another sensory aberration: you start by seeing things, my friend, you wind up smelling things. But if so, it wasn't something he wanted to recognize. No—something inside said, *Let it go;* said, *Ignore it;* said, *This is a sort of dream . . .*))

He woke to the sound of a doorbell ringing, repeatedly. He moved rapidly, jumping out of bed and throwing a robe over his shoulders, but hadn't even reached the top of the stairs before he recalled the events of the night before—including their ghastly, humiliating conclusion. Hence it was a great relief to discover that the person on the front porch was Adam—to whom the whole story could be recounted without holding back a single squirm-inducing detail.

"Did I wake you, Champ?"

"Mm. I flew in this morning early, and went right back to bed."

"Sorry. You know I already ran five miles today? Got to run early, given this heat."

"Or not run at all. Come on in."

"How was the graduation?"

"Weird. Upsetting."

"Weird and upsetting?" Adam looked pleased rather than sympathetic; he sensed a good story in the offing.

But Terry wasn't going to satisfy him—at least not yet. He

turned to his fish tank and said to the spotted clownfish, "Hey guy, you sleep all right?" The tigers were circling lazily, as if they, too, were slowed by the heat, although the water temperature was 78—just where it ought to be.

"Weird?" Adam repeated. "What way weird?"

"You want some coffee?"

"Only if you turn on the AC. I ran five miles already today."

Terry was generally sparing with the air conditioner. Adam teased him about being cheap, but it wasn't that. He didn't like its sense of hushed enclosure—the way it cut you off from the rest of the world.

"All right."

They trooped out into the kitchen. Terry turned on the air conditioner and threw two scoops of coffee into the coffee machine. "Good God," Adam said, "here are some more of them."

"Them?" Terry asked, although he knew—despite having his back to Adam—what Adam was looking at.

"More fish. You got another tank."

"Two new tanks," Terry confessed. "One for the bedroom. It's going to be sea horses in the bedroom."

"You do understand they're taking you over, don't you? How long before you flood the whole basement for them?"

"You don't know the half of it. I've started growing scales under my arms."

"Weird—you said something about last night's being weird."

"Scales under my arms aren't weird enough?"

"And upsetting—you said it was upsetting. You got a story for me or not, Babe?"

Terry turned and faced his friend, who was sitting at the table in gym shorts and a polo shirt, a look of happy, hungry expectation on his ruddy face. "You know what I honestly think?" Terry said. "I honestly think sometimes that I'm losing my mind. I am not speaking hyperbolically."

"You and everybody else in this town. It's the heat."

"I begin to say to myself, In what way am I going to make a fool of myself next?"

"Guy I read about in the paper this morning, he goes out into a crowded parking lot to take a leak, wanders around, finally happens to piss on the chief of police's car. Now the beauty of it is, the guy's a statistician. Later figures the odds at one-in-a-hundred-fifty. When it comes to making a fool of yourself, you've got *stiff* competition."

This was one way in which things had changed in recent weeks, or months. Last fall and winter, and even into the spring, Terry had repeatedly found himself insisting that he was in fine mental health—claims which Adam had met with a forceful skepticism. These days, it was the other way round. Let Terry so much as hint at some internal oddity and Adam would come hurtling forward to detect within it some further corroborating evidence of health and normalcy. And Adam seemed more than merely sincere in his interpretations: he seemed proud. His tacit message was that he had successfully piloted Terry through another crisis.

"So how was the ceremony?"

"Just like any other graduation—too long, too self-congratulatory. It was fine."

"And the bride-to-be?"

This was Adam's newest, and unfortunately almost inevitable, epithet for Diana. One of the advantages of having the wedding day imminent was that Adam would soon have to come up with something else. "She was fine."

"And Kaye?"

"She was all right, though you'd've thought she'd done it all herself. As if *she* was the one graduating magna cum laude. And Glenn, oh he was a riot. You'da thought *he* was the one who'd put her through school."

"I thought you liked him."

"Oh I do I guess. He's all right."

"And the groom-to-be?"

"Peter? Oh I don't know. Very Southern with the accent. To hear him, you'd think Kentucky was south of Mississippi."

"Good-looking?"

"Yeah, I don't know—sure. Maybe quite good-looking really, in this fine-boned long-nosed blond sort of way. At one point he kind of annoyed me, you want to know the truth. Over drinks afterwards."

"It isn't fair, is it? Nobody young ought to be good-looking. I'm talking guys. Girls are another matter. So what about his parents?"

"Very full of *charm*."

"Totally insufferable?"

"Oh I don't know, I'm just being a party pooper. Actually it wouldn't have been so bad if Kaye hadn't seen fit to pretty much kiss their hands as royalty—King and Queen Styrofoam."

"So come on. Have you got a story or haven't you?" Bare elbows on bare knees, his chin in his cupped hands, Adam leaned forward. Though the air conditioner was set on high, he was sweating profusely.

"Yeah. I got a story," Terry admitted. "Well a sort of story."

"Is it about getting annoyed at Peter?"

"No—though I suppose that could be sort of connected. I'm sure Kopp would see some sort of connection."

"So let's hear it."

"I can see already that it loses something in the telling." Terry sipped from his coffee. "Anyway, graduation itself was fine. Lots of photographs and clowning around. And then afterwards we went out for dinner—Peter and his family, Diana, me, Kaye, Glenn."

"Who sprang for the tab?"

"Peter's parents. Though I was willing to. They got to it first."

"Let them . . ."

"Anyway, dinner was all right. And then we went out for some drinks—except for Peter's parents, who'd found everything so charming they needed to go to bed, I guess. And Shawn, Diana's roommate, she joined us."

"She's pretty."

"How would you know?"

"That photograph of yours. Her and Diana and that beach ball."

"Well you know she *is* pretty pretty. Prettier than the picture would suggest."

"I like the way this is going . . ."

Terry chose to ignore the remark. "Anyway, there were six of us now. Kaye and Glenn, Shawn and Peter, me and Diana. And we each had a drink. I don't think anybody had more than that. I didn't anyway. But the truth is I'd been feeling sort of funny. Dizzy would be putting it too strongly, but there was this sort of floating jerky feeling. You know what this was like? It was like actually being in one of those old movies that don't have enough frames per second, so wherever you go there's a kind of continuity lost."

"We Polacks," Adam said, and laughed boisterously, "you know what we call that? We call that stone-dead drunk."

"But I'd only had one drink, and the feeling came over me even before I'd had that." The argument seemed important to Terry, and he was prepared to pursue it at some length. "Now how could I possibly be feeling drunk," he began, "when I was feeling that way even before—"

"Just a joke," Adam said. "Anyway . . ."

"I wasn't the least bit drunk."

"Okay, you weren't the *least* bit drunk."

"Then they bring out a couple bottles of champagne. This is supposed to be some great surprise and honor. We will now drink a toast to Uncle Terry, benefactor and etcetera, without whom etcetera, the world's most etcetera. Only, I know I'm feeling kind of weird, I've got this little alarm bell ringing in my head, so I only have one glass. It gets refilled, but I hardly touch it. And so we all sit there, talking about how exciting the future is, and how exciting the wedding is, and what a great guy I am, and needless to say I'm not saying much—just smiling and nodding modestly and being great old Uncle Terry.

"Then Peter starts going on, maybe more than he ought to, about being a classicist, you'd think to listen to him he'd just rendered all of Homer into rhyming couplets, and maybe I'm feeling a little annoyed because you know I've never studied Latin *or* Greek. And I point out, which is pretty interesting actually, that even though I never studied either one, still the book that maybe had the greatest effect on me in childhood was this illustrated collection of Greek tales. That thing really haunted me. Those gods in the clouds, they really did *scare* me, you know?"

The look on Adam's face made it plain: Terry was losing his audience. Just as he had lost them at last night's dinner. It seemed no one wanted to hear about the childhood book that had haunted him.

"It wasn't the gods' malice that unnerved me," he went on, nonetheless. "No, it was their languor. All these illustrations in which you'd see the people down on earth below, fighting battles, risking their lives in a million different ways, and there would be these figures in the clouds, lying down in the clouds and looking on idly, you know what I mean?"

"Sure. So then what? You were all drinking champagne . . ."

It wasn't a point he was ever going to convey adequately to anyone, evidently: the fear and the twitching claustrophobe's anger it had engendered in his boyish breast. Oh, but it pained him even now—to think of yourself down there upon the earth, battling men and demons, supernatural as well as human foes, while all the while, unbeknownst to you, among those distant reclining figures, who have limply thrown their heads upon each other's flanks, your strugglings are a matter of idle talk, of cozy horizontal chitchat . . .

"So finally," Terry said, "we all decided to call it a night and Kaye and Glenn go driving off in their car, to where they were staying, and that leaves me and Diana and Peter and Shawn in my car."

"I like where this is going . . ."

"I don't. And you have a sewer of a mind, by the way. Anyway, Peter and Diana have got to go pick up something or do something in Peter's room—"

"I wonder what they had to do in Peter's room . . ."

"Do shut up. And I drop them off and that leaves me and Shawn and I drive her back to her dorm and we sit there talking in the car—and *don't* tell me you like where this is headed. And then she sort of launches into this set speech. I mean she's suddenly some junior high school kid on Recitation Day. And her speech is all about what a wonderful great guy I am, how much Diana looks up to me, how wonderful and great it is that I would help Diana out when she really needed it—in short, just exactly what I've been listening to all night. Only, the difference is that all night long this sort of thing has merely left me feeling like a chump: there's the guy who got suckered out of all his dough, etcetera. But *this* time, I'm suddenly very touched.

Good lord, what a marvel, what a great guy I am! Gee whiz, who'da guessed it?—I'm some sort of fabulous wonderful human being! I mean, I was sort of choked up."

Given the look of ribald amusement on Adam's face, Terry was not about to confess that, in truth, Shawn's little rote delivery had so sweepingly moved him that for a second his eyes had brimmed and one scorching tear had tumbled down his cheek.

"So what did I decide was the appropriate response to this young woman who had just called me one of the world's most admirable men?"

"I can imagine . . ."

Looking at his friend seated bare-armed and bare-legged in his kitchen, hair damp with sweat, a cocksure leer on his face, Terry responded with words that he knew were a little cruel: "But that's just it. You can't, Adam. You just can't imagine."

Terry took another sip from his coffee, swirled it around in his mouth, swallowed, wiped his lips with the back of his hand. "You see, if I tell you I was attracted to her, that won't really begin to do justice to how I felt. Maybe if I went to the drawer there, got out a paring knife, cut a little wedge out of my index finger, signed in blood a document that said, I, Terry Seward, have never been so attracted to anybody—maybe that might do it. Because otherwise you can't imagine. You just can't. And it all came on so suddenly! In the darkness of this car I'm looking at this girl who's just delivered this speech about my elevated moral principles and I'm suddenly sitting there with what feels like the world's biggest hard-on, and I say to myself, I've never honestly wanted *anything* so much. Nothing in the world has ever seemed so desirable to me. Nothing. Never."

"What's so tough to imagine? I felt that way just this morning. They've got a really nice-looking new redhead, actually sort of strawberry blonde, up at the 7 Eleven."

"Do cut it out—it just so happens I'm *serious.* For anything *remotely* comparable I'd have to go back to eighth grade, Mr. Shober's Spanish class, when I looked over at Wendy Wentz and saw that a button had come undone on her blouse, and *I* became so undone that when the bell rang I couldn't—"

"You know, I had something just like that happen in eighth grade, only this one's name was Maria Hopkins, we called her

Maria Hotpants, and there was actually something quite fitting about—"

"No, I *mean* it. I felt like I was in eighth *grade*. I was planning this entire elaborate pathetic seduction, where we'd go up to her *room* and I'd sort of simultaneously advise her about her future plans and drop my trousers. I thought to myself, Terry, you are losing your mind. I thought to myself, You've got to get out of here."

"And? . . ."

"And I kissed her goodbye."

"And? . . ."

Adam's face was positively aglow with carnality. No one, no one else Terry knew savored so much as Adam did a story of this sort—titillating sexual encounters, tales of mixed arousal and embarrassment. As a rule, Terry avoided any investigation into what lay behind Adam's notably inactive social life, with its singular blend of bold flirtatiousness and quiet withdrawal. That was one of the things they did for each other as friends: neither probed the other much for explanations. Still, there were moments—and this, with Adam's face all lit up, was one— in which Terry unignorably felt there might be something a little peculiarly vicarious in his friend's sexual psyche: that Adam wanted less to be in the car with the pretty young woman than to hear about being in the car with the pretty young woman.

"Well," Terry said, "I'm not sure there's much more of an 'and' to this story."

"You mean that's it?"

". . . Well there's a little more." The urge to continue was in part a desire to fulfill Adam's hunger for a good story, in part an urge to lighten his own soul of its cargo of mortification. "You know, I thought this was a sort of nice-talking-to-you kiss, a have-a-wonderful-life kiss, but it turned into something much more. The problem was I sort of missed her cheek and hit her mouth. It was dark. None of this would have occurred if I hadn't missed her cheek."

"None of this? What do you mean by this?"

"Well her mouth was sort of open."

"Pray continue."

"And I sort of put my arms around her and she definitely put her arms around me. I wish I could tell you I was drunk. You were anybody else, I'd tell you I was drunk. But the fact is one of my hands was sort of half-on half-off her breast. More on, I guess. Quite a bit on, frankly. She was wearing this white blouse and I could feel her brassiere under it, and a big healthy bulge under the side of my hand . . ."

"And then?"

Terry looked his friend straight in the eye. "And then I let her go. And we were both sort of breathless, and we exchange this panting goodbye, and I watched her walk up to the front of her dorm, and I drove away."

"Oh God how *could* you? You *had* it . . ."

"Had it?"

"She wanted you, Champ. I mean you *had* it right there." There was real lamentation, there was heartfelt grief in Adam's voice.

"Adam, you don't understand how close I came. I mean I came *this* close"—Terry held out his left hand (the malefactor's hand, the one that had groped the innocent girl) and brought index finger and thumb together, until less than half an inch of air divided them—"*this* close, to feeling up my niece's roommate, and a lot more besides."

"You had it, Terry. *She wanted you.*"

"Can you imagine? Let's just imagine"—and the thought inserted a quiver into his voice—"Diana and Peter come back and *I'm in bed with Diana's roommate?* Can you imagine? And you want to know what happened next? I mean after Shawn and I say goodnight? I drive away and I break into a sweat. I don't mean damp under the arms, either. I mean suddenly drenched— you'd think I'd run four miles in all my clothes."

"Hey, that's healthy. That's just healthy self-expression."

"Well it didn't feel healthy. I tell you, Adam, I'm losing the grip."

"So you are, but not for the reasons you think. You're losing the grip because you *had* that girl and you let her go . . ."

"*This* close," Terry said.

"It's going to *haunt* you."

"Maybe."

"You let them go like that, ones you really want that much, and you know what happens? It haunts you forever . . . You know what I mean?"

"Sure."

"It *haunts* you—it haunts you forever."

What was Adam really saying? What was he confessing to? "I'll live," Terry replied.

"In any case, it sounds like you're definitely ready."

"Ready."

"For the big event."

"What event?"

"Your girlfriend's coming to town."

"Beg pardon?"

"Your girlfriend's coming to town." The long face had vanished: Adam all of a sudden looked extremely jolly.

"Adam, what in hell are you on about now?"

"I'm talking to Bertha yesterday, and by the way *she's* really blooming, isn't she? I'd like to know who or what's got into—"

"Just leave her alone, Adam. You leave Bertha alone."

"You think I'm kidding but I'm not. Anyway, I'm standing by Bertha's desk when the phone rings, it's someone looking for you, and wouldn't you know it, but it's your old friend Kelly."

"Kelly? I don't know any Kelly . . ."

"How soon we forget. How soon we forget . . . Use 'em and lose 'em, huh? Video store Kelly? Woman on the airplane Kelly?"

"Oh *Kelly!* Good Lord, why's she calling me?" The odd thing was, he'd meant it. When he said he didn't know any Kelly, he'd meant it. Blocked her right out.

"Forgetting our promises, are we? Didn't you tell her if she ever comes to D.C. you'll take her out for a night on the town? Well, she calls to say she and her friend Marty are coming to town on Wednesday. Poor girl, poor *poor* girl . . . So young and naive I think she actually took you at your word—"

"Wednesday! *This* Wednesday?"

"This Wednesday."

"Well that's so *soon.*"

"Soon?"

"I mean to make arrangements."

"Arrangements? This ain't no Superpower Summit we're talking here . . ."

"Wednesday. I can't do that. I've got to be in Detroit on Tuesday night."

"And what's that got to do with Wednesday? You come back Wednesday morning. Or you come back Wednesday afternoon."

"You'll come along with Kelly and her friend? I mean I'm counting on you to come along . . ."

"Me? I wouldn't miss it for the world."

"It's your niece. Diana."

"Diana." It was a bad time to take her call—he had all sorts of pressing papers on his desk—but he was going to have to talk to her sometime. Sometime soon. They hadn't spoken, not since graduation, though hardly a waking hour had passed without some thought of her—without his wondering, specifically, what it was, if anything, Shawn had told her about graduation night. The whole business had sunk its way so deep into his psyche that he'd even had a nightmare, a couple of nights ago, in which Diana had stood forth in a white, pointing fury and accused him: Shawn was pregnant. "Sure, sure. Put her on."

He waded in on a tide of words. "It's the young girl graduate come up against the cold hard adult world at last. So how's everything with you? Getting excited about the wedding I'll bet. You move from one celebration to another, don't you?"

"Terry, guess where I'm calling from."

"I don't know. Madagascar?"

"From New York. From Manhattan. I'm calling from the apartment."

"The apartment?"

"You know, where Peter and I are going to live."

"Well how is it? Tell me all . . ."

"I don't know where to start, it's full of all this incredibly *old* furniture. Very *dark* wood and these really ancient rugs. It belongs to one of Peter's aunts, who has just moved into some sort of *home*. But there's a good view of the park."

"The park?"

"The, you know—Central Park."

"You've got a view of Central Park?"

"That's the street we're on—Central Park West."

"Diana, what's your cross street?"

"The cross street? I keep forgetting. Hold on. Shaw-nee," she cried, "what's the cross street here?" A muffled cry came back. Shaw-nee? "Shawn says it's Ninety-first or Ninety-second."

"She's there with you?"

"These days we're in*sep*arable." Diana giggled. "She says I'm going to desert her once I'm an ol' married lady." More giggling, and a half-audible exchange of protestations ("I didn't . . ." "You did . . .") and then Diana said, and these words of hers might have been lifted right out of his nightmare of a few nights ago:

"You know why I'm calling, don't you? It concerns your misbehavior. You've been *very* bad . . ."

"Bad . . ." was all he managed to reply—his voice ruptured on the word.

"The car?"

"The car?" This was not happening. Pray God, this was not happening.

This was not happening, and Diana *surely* was not now about to confront him with what he'd done to Shawn in the car. No— surely not.

"The little card?" Diana said.

It seemed he hadn't heard her right. "What card?"

"The measurements. You told me you'd go and get measured. You promised."

"Oh. Right. Well I have. Well I haven't yet, actually, but I do plan to. But in fact I don't need to, because actually I already know my measurements."

"But the guy, the guy at the tux place, was absolutely in*sist*ent about this. He said you mustn't let anybody measure themselves, or use old measurements, or anything like that. They've got to be recent measurements *by a professional tailor!* He was so insistent he sort of scared me." She giggled.

"I'll do it today. Cross my heart."

"Would you—you can call Mom with them if you want."

"I'll do that. Diana, how big is it? The apartment."

"Oh it's going to be fine. There's a living room and a dining room and a what will be our bedroom, and a guest room where you must stay every time you come to New York, *you'll* be my guest"—giggle—"and a funny little thing that I guess will be okay for Peter's study. Although he says it smells like a *cat* died there."

Terry stared at the photo of her on his desk: did this girl have any idea of what sort of set-up she'd landed in? Or was she truly so young and unworldly as not to comprehend the extraordinary, the unbelievable good fortune in having been given, for your very first married lodgings, what sounded like a palatial apartment on Central Park West? Did she truly not understand that if he himself had headed to New York rather than Washington after law school, he would probably not be able even now, approaching fifteen years of practicing law, to land such a place? There were times when he could believe Diana truly was just as young and ingenuous as that, but there were other moments when he nervously caught inklings of a core of cunning, from which emerged the manipulations of a girl so freshly pretty that she didn't need to articulate her wishes (even to herself) in order to see them accomplished.

Was it possible, then, that *Diana* of all people had taken advantage of him? Either way, and whether she understood what she was doing or not, the notion that he was, in a sense, passing her on to Peter, so that she might ascend from a position of privilege to one of far greater privilege, momentarily disheartened him. He felt a sudden need to get off the phone, although the thought of leaving her to Shawn—inseparable Shawnee—was itself unsettling.

"Listen," he said, "I got some work to do. I gotta go."

"You won't forget? The little card?"

"The little card," Terry said. "I won't forget. Bye now."

The work on his desk called to him but he couldn't face it—not quite yet. He went out to talk to Bertha instead.

He found her hunched over something on her desk. It was a shoe—a little gray Adidas running shoe. "It broke," she explained. "After only three months."

"Your shoe?"

"The lace." Her hands—those old woman's bony, bent fingers of hers—were threading a pristine white lace through the gray shoe's eyelets.

"Three months," Terry said. "Wouldn't you think they could do better than that?"

"They *weren't* cheap," Bertha said, vehemently, as though fending off an accusation.

"I'm sure they weren't."

"I didn't lace them too tight."

"I'm sure you didn't. That was Diana," Terry added, which of course Bertha already knew; but the words provided a conversational bridge. "If I hear one more word about weddings, I'm going to scream."

Bertha's hands halted with a jerk and she glanced up sharply from the shoe on her desk. "You don't approve?"

"It isn't that. It isn't that. It's just all the *fuss* that's made. And all the expense, most of which I seem to be covering." The oddly steady intensity of Bertha's gaze compelled him to qualify: "It's not that I'm begrudging anybody anything."

"They don't have to cost a fortune," Bertha said.

"Tell that to Kaye."

"It's odd, it's really quite odd you should mention that," Bertha said.

"Mention what?"

"Weddings."

"Odd?" Terry said.

"I mean quite a coincidence."

"I'm not sure I follow . . ."

"From my point of view."

"Come again?"

Bertha dropped her gaze back to the shoe and, tugging hard, secured the laces in a tight bow. "Because, well, because you see it's today I'd been planning all along to tell you. That's all. *That's* what I mean. That I'd planned to tell you today and then here you go mentioning the subject first and that's what I mean by *odd*, I'm gonna get married."

In the face of this—the world's most flabbergasting revelation—Terry did somehow manage to squelch the incredulous

Congratulations that leapt to his throat, which might have been embarrassing; and managed to silence the swooping guffaw of laughter that longed to succeed it, which would have been more embarrassing still. "You're going to get married?" he said quietly.

Bertha looked up at him. All the blood in her bony little body had gone to her face. Never in all these years had he seen her look so flustered. "That's right . . ."

"Well—well that's wonderful, Bertha. Who's the lucky guy? Anybody I know?"

"His name is George." She offered the name with an almost defiant pride—as if merely to be named George were in itself a sizable accomplishment.

"Well that's a fine name, I've always liked that name. George. George. And what does George do?"

"He's a musician."

"A musician?"

"Well not professionally. But that's his first love. He teaches math."

"Math?"

"To eighth graders."

And with this piece of news there came to Terry's mind, full-blown, a vivid figure: a skinny little acne-scarred guy in glasses—a sort of female Bertha—who kept a freshly sharpened pencil parked behind his ear.

"God this is marvelous! And how old is George?"

"He's forty-nine."

"Forty-nine?" A good deal older than Terry had pictured. "Let's see, he's forty-nine, and you're—"

"It's a twenty-two year difference."

"Well. And when's the lucky day?"

"We don't know. You see, she doesn't want him to."

"She?" Of course: a steely little gray-haired woman—George's mother—who wasn't about to see her baby of a son carried off by this calculating, worldly younger woman . . .

"His wife," Bertha explained.

"Ah . . . George is married."

"He's getting divorced."

"He's been separated?"

"As of last week."

There was an inconsistency here—something that Bertha needed to have pointed out to her. "But if—well, if he was living at home, how did you—I mean isn't this all kind of sudden perhaps? I mean you can hardly *know* who he—"

Over the years Bertha had volunteered all sorts of peculiar pronouncements. In fact, no one, not even Kopp, had so regularly tested him with unfathomables. But nothing she'd ever delivered, or was ever going to deliver, could match for strangeness this moment, when she said deliberatively, as though clarifying a point for somebody who was thick in the head, "But we've been having an affair for nearly a year."

Terry felt himself blink hard. "An affair," he parroted, and wondered for just a moment whether for Bertha the word might carry very different connotations than were usually assigned to it. Did she know what she was saying? Understand that for most people the word had very definite physical connotations? Realizing that he was standing there with mouth agape, he added, "I see."

"She mistreats him," Bertha said. "She's intentionally cruel."

"Are there children?"

"Four."

"Four? Four children?"

"But they're all grown."

"Right. He's forty-nine."

Terry could not hold the woman's gaze. His eyes dropped to her hands, those ugly bent bony hands of hers which had—astoundingly, and, yes, perhaps admirably—reached out fiercely to seize at love. *Bertha* had grabbed at love. He turned, as though to re-enter his office, then turned toward her once more. "Where on earth did you meet him?"

"At astronomy class. We happened to sit together at the planetarium."

"Right," Terry said, turning again toward his office, where all of this would have to be pondered. "That makes sense."

And in the light of Bertha's wedding announcement, it did make sense—since it now appeared that whatever in the world was farfetched, mismatched, implausible, incongruous, unlikely or insupportable was destined to eventuate. Bertha and some middle-aged father-of-four falling in love under the stars, the artificial stars . . .

Everything made sense! Later that same afternoon, for instance, wasn't it only to be expected that the trip to St. Ferri's, too, would contain an upending revelation? "Waist, thirty-three and a half," Carlo the tailor said. They'd known each other for some years now; this was where Terry bought most of his clothes.

"No, no. The waist's thirty-two."

Much amused, Carlo smiled, exposing a new gold tooth. "I'll check it again." He drew the tape measure once more around Terry's middle. "Thirty-three and a quarter, thirty-three and a half . . ."

"But that can't be. I've always been thirty-two. Thirty-two is my waist size."

"I tell all my customers, in this business there is no always," Carlo said. "Thanks the Lord. Otherwise I'm out a job."

"But I've been thirty-two since high school!"

"Look at your suit. Look at yourself in the mirror there. See how you're pulling it down there, wearing it low? And see how the pockets are stretching here? And here? And it's pinching—see how there isn't any room left here?"

Terry stared into the mirror, wherein—right before his very eyes—a transformation took place: his body thickened, his belly distended. Surely he hadn't looked like this yesterday, or this morning . . . Surely there was some mistake! But it was a fact (one he could literally feel in his gut) that his suit no longer fit properly. Nothing fit. Nothing—anywhere—*fit*. It was pinching him, and with this realization he heard at last the little signal of abdominal distress that had been going out for weeks now: *You're squeezing me, you're squeezing me . . .*

"You put on five, ten pounds," Carlo estimated. "Not so much. Not so bad," Carlo reassured him. "You're a successful man. A successful man ought to eat well," Carlo advised him.

"Five or ten pounds . . ." How Adam was going to laugh! How long Adam had waited for this day—when the Great Metabolic Shift would occur and Terry would begin to pay for all the heavy wedges of cheesecake, the slick greased bags of take-out fries, the milk shakes, the tollhouse cookies, the hot pretzels . . .

"I can't believe it." But he had only to look into the mirror to see unmistakably that the body which had once—on a sun-shellacked day in Iowa, some twenty years ago—floated over a bar that stood twelve feet nine inches above the vaulting pit had gone lax and paunchy.

"You need some new suits," Carlo suggested.

"Or I need a diet."

"One or the other—you need one or the other. Get the suits now and the diet can wait." Carlo laughed.

"Something anyway. It's clear I need *some*thing," Terry said.

"Adam, hi. I'm so glad I reached you . . ."

"Where are you? Where you calling from?"

"Detroit." The shimmering band of light outside the window? That was the Detroit River. And across the river? That was a foreign country. That was Canada.

"*Detroit?* I expected you at lunch. I held off eating until one o'clock—at great physical cost, I might add. Hey, good Lord, you're going to be late."

"Listen, Adam, I'm not going to make it in tonight."

"Not make it in? You've *got* to."

"Can't. I got things I got to do."

"Things to do? What things? Hop on a plane right this minute. You mean you're not calling from the airport?"

"I can't. I got things to do—you know, businessy things. I've got another deposition, for one thing. I'll do that tomorrow."

"So hop on a plane now. Zip, zip. Pronto, pronto. You can hop on a plane back to Detroit first thing tomorrow morning."

"Adam, I can't."

"But you got to. Tonight's the big night. What about the girls? They're expecting you—they're expecting us."

"Well, that's why I'm calling. You've got to take them out yourself."

"My*self*? I don't even know them."

"I don't know them either. I mean I've never met this Marty.

And Kelly, I talked to her for all of one hour on a plane last year."

"But they're coming out to see *you*. That's the whole point. *You* invited them out."

"I know I invited them, but they're hardly coming to see me. *That's* the whole point. They're just coming to have a good time. To look around. To see the nation's capital. Just tell 'em I had business. Tell 'em we'll make it some other time. I mean you can still take them to Fanciulla's—they'll like that. And then to a bar or something—it's no big deal."

"What the hell is this, Terry?"

"What I was thinking was, this whole thing being my idea, its having been intended to be my treat and all, well, it *still* will be my treat. You take 'em out, do whatever extravagant thing you want to do, and stick me with the bill. Adam, I'm giving you a great opportunity to bankrupt me—hell, I'm giving you carte blanche."

A new tenor seemed to enter Adam's voice: a brusqueness born of slighted pride. It was as though his gallantry had been rebuffed. "I think I can afford to take the two women out to-night . . ."

"What I was thinking was, get somebody else to make it a foursome. Townsend, say. Or Solefield."

"What are you doing, Champ? Just tell me what you're doing."

"I mean it can't be *that* hard to find somebody who'd like to go out for free drinks with a couple of nice-looking young women."

"But you do see, don't you, that they are expecting you? That much you understand? That much is penetrating? And that I don't even know them? You understand that, too?"

"But they're not. Expecting me. They're just expecting a couple of lawyer-types in decent suits to take them out for a fairly fancy meal. It isn't *me* they're expecting. It isn't *me*," Terry repeated, and felt again the logical forcefulness of his argument—which was, really, the absolving factor in this matter.

"Well it's certainly not *me*. It isn't 'Dam Mikolajczak they're expecting."

"Listen," Terry said, "you'll be fine, it'll be no problem . . ."

And again he'd rankled Adam: "I'm not saying I can't manage. All along you've been acting like we've got some superpower summit here. I'm just hoping, to begin with, for some sort of explanation."

"I'll explain it all tomorrow," Terry said—words that, in their suggestion of something withheld, seemed tantamount to a confession of wrongdoing. He went on: "There's really not a thing to explain, Adam," which echoed in his ears as cool and unappreciative; and so he added, "I'll make it up to you when I get back"—which was his most dismal stroke yet. "Listen, I got to go, you know how to reach them, I'll see you tomorrow," Terry said, and hung up the phone. He needed a shower.

Before undressing, he checked once more to see that the room was locked, then went into the bathroom and—having heard such horror stories about crime in Detroit—locked this door as well. He stood for an endless, timeless stretch under a hot shower, finishing off with a blast of cold water—just the way they all used to do at the end of track practice.

He brushed and flossed his teeth with minute attention, sprayed his underarms with deodorant, gargled some purple hotel mouthwash and combed his hair. He shaved for the second time that day—though he hardly needed to—and decided to put on a clean shirt and a fresh tie for dinner. When he discovered that these made his suit look crumpled by comparison, he removed his second suit from its hook in the closet. But this one (a lightweight tan summer suit) perhaps clashed with the tie (a blue and yellow diagonal stripe) and he took another tie, a brown and yellow and green cotton paisley, from his suitcase. He set the old tie on the television, beside a stand-up cardboard advertisement for the hotel's private television system. Four of the eight available films were, he'd already noticed, "adult entertainment." This was another little wrinkle in the ever-altering field of communications law—the conversion of hotel rooms into mini-porn-theaters. He adjusted the new tie in front of the bathroom door's full-length mirror, ran a comb through his hair once more, and—a New York *Times* under his arm—went down to eat a solitary dinner.

The hotel restaurant, which had a French name, was all but

"It's the lobster, the lobster was bad," he said, as his insides gave way utterly, collapsing like a needle-pricked balloon, and what seemed to be a plurality of his internal organs spattered into the overworked bowl. There was nothing left inside him. Truly there was nothing inside him. Zilcho.

He'd come clean.

He walked on the outsides of his feet, trying to keep off the places where the glass had bit, over to the dripping telephone. They weren't going to get through, those sperm cells. Their call would never be placed. Outside, the sky had gone dark, the river had become a shifting net of glints, though still the current flowed on—ultimately eastward, seaward, to the very coast where was also found his home. He wiped the phone off with his left hand and smeared the hand across his forehead, as if mopping his brow. As he picked up the receiver, it came to him—the answer to the question Tryggvi had asked, and Kopp had asked, and even Adam had once asked, and on the night in question Kaye and Glenn no doubt had asked: *But what did it feel like?* They'd all wanted to know. It was the one thing everybody wanted to know: what did it feel like, exactly, to stand squarely before one of the risen dead? Everybody had wanted to know but heretofore he'd never been able to muster an answer, not until the prodding of this glass-honed moment, when at last he informed them all: "You want to know what it felt like? Do you really? Okay. It just so happens I know. Uncle Terry knows. For one instant it felt as though all the shit inside you had tumbled from your body. *That's* what it felt like."

When he got someone at reception, a woman, he said to her: "I need a car. What's the fastest way to get a rental car at this hour? I need a company that allows one-way drops. I'm going a long way." He was heading eastward, with the river. "Would they deliver, or at this hour would I have to take a taxi to the airport or somewhere? If so, I'll need a taxi there."

If he started driving now, he could be back in Washington before dawn, probably. Of course he'd have to clean up in here first, and pack up . . . He had so many things to do! He had to hurry. Hurry now, hurry. There were so many things to do.

Delays, delays, and he felt he was losing it—the crisp energy, the mighty transcontinental impulse—even though he moved as fast as he could: cleaned up, straightened up, threw his clothes into his suitcase. There was blood on the bathroom floor—a fair amount of it, wisps and smears and intact droplets of blood—but none in the bedroom, so far as he could tell. Fortunately, it was a dark carpet.

Delays, delays—the paying of the bill, the ride out in the taxi, the forms to fill out before the car was his. But then came a moment when, despite everything, it arrived: the moment when the whole of everything was his—the keys, the car, the journey itself. The journey itself—the long interstate journey—was his.

Terry turned the radio up loud—some sort of disco music—and when he reached the expressway he set his foot on the accelerator until it climbed to eighty, and he kept it there. Surely he wasn't going to get a speeding ticket tonight. You had to trust your luck. At some point, you had to trust your own dumb luck.

"This was a good idea," he said aloud, as he pulled into a service area for a cup of coffee. He was on the Ohio Turnpike. He'd been driving for two hours. "I needed this. Time and space. All God's children need time and space."

And, "So this is my pilgrimage," he said, again aloud, a few hours later, when he stopped once more for coffee. He'd crossed into Pennsylvania. "You talking to me?" a waitress asked him.

And an hour or so later, somewhere in the Allegheny Mountains, he began to feel drowsy, paralyzingly drowsy—his body was going down heavily—and he thought he might have to call it a night. It was something like three in the morning. The road was pretty much deserted, except for trucks. He pulled into a rest stop and headed for the bathroom, limping, for his feet were hurting him. The bathroom was empty. "You don't think I'm going to make it, do you?" he said. "But you're wrong. I'm going to prove you wrong."

He slapped himself on the face, once on the left side and once, stingingly, on the right, and said, "How's that for turning the other cheek?" He felt better, and knew that he'd not been spouting empty vows: he was going to make it all right.

Day was dawning—a woozy accumulation of fresh, glazed

tints and cooling silences—when he pulled into his driveway. "Who would have thought," he said, turning the key in the front door, "that in the end my pilgrimage would be to my own home?" He looked in on the big fish tank. Nothing was floating, belly up, on the surface. Bertha had done her job. On anguished feet he went upstairs, ignored the blinking light of his answering machine, threw himself down on the bed, and full in the bones of his face felt that runaway scent again, that unplaceable female odor, and at once he realized it was no illusion. This one, anyway, was no illusion.

Sometimes your senses tell it to you straight. Sometimes all you have to do is attend to them—carefully. This was no trick. No hallucination. It *was* perfume. Bertha's perfume. And one of the reasons—doubtless, *the* reason—that she'd always been so eager to play the caretaker, to feed the fish and water the plants, was that the job provided her with a safe, free, discreet, and comfortable trysting place. Bertha and forty-nine-year-old George. Filth. That was what they'd been up to. Right here.

The telephone was a prying tool, like the claw of a hammer, and isn't it funny how human a sound a simple iron nail can release from its narrow little body when it's uprooted from an old piece of wood?

That was one of his sounds, Daddy's, and all over the house you'd hear it, the pulselike pounding and the calling cries of nails going in, coming out, and you'd know once again in his hands simple dull dead lumber was taking shape according to designs he'd blueprinted right there inside the bones of his head. It was one of the keenest joys your life knew, that huge hunger rising in your own head which said, *Hey, what is it?*, said, *What will it be this time?*, said, *What in the world is he making now?*

The phone rang enough times, anyway, for Terry to recognize it and refuse to recognize it, come up, like a swimmer for breath, submerge himself once more, and come up. Yes. Gasping. Oh God it was the phone.

"Hello," Terry said. But where was he?

"Ohhhh." The voice came down a sort of slide. "Terry."

Kaye. It was Kaye and he was back in his own bed and the whole thing—oh the sheer monumental lunacy of it!—was behind him. He had made it, had overcome danger and lunacy and degradation, had driven all the way from Detroit, it was Kaye and she was hammering him for money. Again. He was home.

"Mm," Terry said.

"Terry you won't believe this, oh it's so awful, but everybody says it's going to be all right, it's going to be all right. It's going to be all right."

"Hn?" Not a dime—she would not claw another dime out of him. Not today, anyway.

"It's *Glenn,* Terry. Oh, Terry, yesterday when he's coming home early, I just knew he wasn't right, but he says fine, he's fine, so I go out last night to play bridge with some of the girls, even though I *knew* he wasn't right, and so I go out and oh Terry, *Terry,* he had a sort of heart attack or stroke."

The last word dealt Terry a muffled but a potent blow. He wasn't yet quite following her—he'd been waiting for the mad scramble of words to solidify into a plea for money. But this was no such thing, and Kaye—poor Kaye—was teetering on the edge of hysteria.

He sent a cry out to his sister: "Kaye . . ."

"Thank God, thank God, he was able to call the ambulance himself. Sitting there all alone."

"Oh Kaye, I'm so sorry."

"And I'm told that, as these things go, his wasn't so bad. The doctors say he's going to have a hundred percent recovery. Those are the words they used—one hundred percent."

"Well then," Terry said. "Well then, one hundred percent," Terry said. "It's going to be all right."

He sat up in bed and looked at the bedside clock. 7:57. He looked at the window: it was morning, not evening. He'd been asleep an hour or two.

"You know, Terry, most of my friends, the ones my age, they've had to *deal* with something like this. They've at least had a parent die or something. But last night I realized this is absolutely *new* to me. Of course Glenn's going to be fine, I'm not questioning that, but suddenly I had to face the possibility of how you lose somebody—somebody you love. I walked into that hospital and my knees almost went scooting right out from under me and I thought, Me, they're gonna hafta put *me* in here."

"You're calling from the hospital?"

"I'm home now. Glenn's asleep. But I'm going right back."

"That's probably what *you* need to do. Sleep."

"Oh I know it, I know it, but I can't do it. I *can't*. I'm going to lie down a while but I know I *can't*. Then I'm going to get right back up and go back over there. And where is Tyler in the midst of all this? You're no doubt asking, Where is Tyler at an important time like this?"

"Who's Tyler?"

"He's in Europe—that's where *he* is. He's somewhere, *some-*where on the coast of Spain and isn't that extremely *help*ful? Isn't it all too perfect? What am I supposed to do—call Spain and say, Give me Tyler, please, you'll no doubt find him sunbathing on some beach or other."

"Who's Tyler, Kaye?"

"Glenn's *son,* Terry. And isn't that just where you'd expect him to be, *on the coast of Spain,* when his father's lying in the hospital at what could well be death's door?"

"But it isn't as though anyone knew, Kaye. To be fair, you'd obviously have to admit there was no predicting—"

"Of course you never hear Glenn complaining, but if God forbid any son of mine—"

"What hospital's he in?"

"Glenn? Stafford. It's over on—"

"Yeah, I know where it is. I'll meet you over there. It's prob-ably an hour's drive—I'll be there in say an hour and a half?"

And since he was feeling, for once, no complicated blend of feelings toward Kaye—just an instinctual, loving access of sym-pathy—it seemed a spoiling shame that she would say what she said next:

"I bet this means he won't be able to go."

"Hm?"

"And of course it's too late to reschedule."

"Reschedule what?"

"Wouldn't you just *know* this would happen, Terry? After all the planning I've been doing for pretty much a solid year? There's simply no *way* it can be rescheduled. And what does that mean? That means I'll wind up alone on the day of the big do, doesn't it?"

"Well not really. And there do seem to be more important considerations at the moment. After all, Kaye, doesn't this seem to be a case of count your blessings?"

"Well there's nothing to be done, is there? And as I always say, What's the use of complaining?"

"Exactly. Exactly right. Listen, I'll be there in an hour and a half. Bye now."

When he rose from the bed, his feet sent crisp little shoots of pain to his head. He'd done it again, hadn't he? Hobbled himself . . .

Under inspection beneath the bedside light, it appeared he'd cut himself three times: in the left arch, in the right baby toe, and in the ball of flesh beneath the right big toe. He recalled a childhood story, a bit of Mob's wisdom—how someone some-where sometime somehow heedlessly left a minuscule sliver of glass in a wound, and it sped like a mortal arrow through his bloodstream to his heart. Not the sort of image to be entertain-ing today, as Glenn lies in a hospital bed . . .

He limped into the bathroom, found some tweezers in the medicine cabinet, and made his way to the landing, where good strong sun streamed in through the window. He sat down on the top step and turned his right foot to the light. Gently, with the pad of his index finger, he tapped the cut on the baby toe. It was sensitive, and it seemed there might still be some glass in-side it. He tried the one under the big toe, and this one, too, hurt him; this one, too, left him in doubt. Then he switched feet and tapped on the little wound in the arch, wincing sharply, and knew instantly that no glass remained in the other two wounds. The glass was *here*. If it was in there, you knew it. You felt it.

After much hurtful prodding with the tweezers into the tight little bruised mouth of the wound, after a good deal of twisting and wincing and swearing, he brought it up to the light, shorter and slenderer than an eyelash: the little transparent filament that had intended to murder him.

He hobbled over to the shower and stood up a good long time beneath its downward pushing. His thoughts were like the legs of an inexperienced skater—they kept suddenly dropping away beneath him. It was hard to concentrate on anything.

He cut himself while shaving, which was something he almost never did—nicked himself not once but twice. "I'm turning myself into a piece of hamburger," he announced. "I believe in the possibility of real transformation and so I've decided to turn myself into a hamburger."

He was slow this morning—slow in dressing, in making his coffee, in eating a bowl of granola. He would find himself pausing, only to be awakened by the thudding of his heart in the bridge of his nose.

He left his granola unfinished and opened a carton of cherry yogurt. The granola had been too effortful—demanding too much in the way of serious chewing—but the yogurt was splendidly right. The fruit was blended or whipped right into it, so there was none of the messiness—or, if not messiness, complication—that comes of being required, with each bite, to settle upon a suitable balance of fruit to yogurt. It was all done for you, which he appreciated. It was a sort of compliment, after all, an assumption that you had better things to do with your time than to fiddle with your food.

On the Beltway, his bright red Audi afloat on a bobbing stream of trucks and cars, Terry recalled the time when Kaye's first boyfriend had dumped her. Big sister—at that time she'd been a high school kid, sixteen or so, which meant he himself was about eleven. He'd understood only dimly what was going on—caught a sense of smothered turbulence and desperation, her serial consultations with Mob and Dad behind closed doors, the sound of tears, both parents urging him to go out and play, to ride his bike, go visit a friend, all of it culminating in Kaye's flinging her bedroom door wide open and rawly moaning, "Nobody loves me *enough*." The words had hit Terry with real force, and was it improbable, almost thirty years later, to read into that cry of hers the beginning of his dealings with Kaye as an adult? For he'd sensed immediately its keen perceptiveness, had known in that instant that not even God Himself loved Kaye as much as he loved the rest of the Seward family. And if, over the years, his sense of God's presence had grown hazy, nonetheless his suspicion had remained steadfast that something as large as Life itself did not love Kaye *enough*. Every year, every setback only went to confirm it. She deserved better—oh, she deserved love. And if she drove everyone a little crazy with her plucky but at bottom self-pitying complaints, was she not entitled to issue some form of protest? What is a person to do, after all, when it is Life itself that doesn't wholly love you?

An hour and a half, he'd promised Kaye, but it was closer to two-and-a-half hours—closer still to three—before he'd completed the drive, parked the car, and reached the reception desk. Only then did it occur to him that Glenn might not be allowed visitors. *I'm his brother,* Terry was prepared to say. He was guided to another reception desk, where he was told he could visit Glenn for five minutes. He realized, as he approached the room, that he probably should have brought something—flowers, booze, chocolates, a book. His own heart went *thud,* heavily, delicately, as he stepped across the threshold of the cardiac patient's room.

But there he was: no vision of death, no man on the subsiding slope of another world. Just Glenn—Kaye's boyfriend, the real estate man—in a pair of aquamarine pajamas, his face upturned toward a television whose screen was invisible from where Terry stood.

There he was, a man united with machinery. Terry saw at a glance—a darting and recoiling glance—that Glenn was hooked up to all sorts of equipment. Dials, wires, monitors. This was the probable future of all of them, Terry knew—the fate of Dad, Mob, Kaye, himself. In the end most of us wind up here, married to all sorts of intricate, hopeless paraphernalia. And the future ought to be faced—he knew this, too. But the truth was, he fared no better than Kaye in hospitals. Worse, probably. Did she, too, take shallow breaths in here, as though leery of drawing deeply into the lungs the unshakable scent of death? And where was Kaye?

"Hiya," Terry called softly and, getting no answer, in a louder voice he said, "My goodness, don't you look comfortable."

"Well, well, look what the cat brought in."

"Hiya—you don't look sick to me."

"But *you* sure do." Glenn set his face to launch into that exaggeratedly sociable salesman's laugh of his, but immediately recollected himself. His mouth snapped shut, he drew a protective hand to his chest, he turned up his lips in a guilty smile.

"I was up all night," Terry said. "It's a long story."

"Have a seat."

Terry sat in the chair by the window. There were some flowers, some roses, on the sill. In his pajamas Glenn looked at once younger than usual—almost little-boyish—and older, which in fact he was today, for he'd felt it again, last night, on the back of his neck: the coldest breath there was, death's very own.

"I understand you called the ambulance yourself."

"That's right."

"That's great—that's great you could do that." Terry kept his eyes on Glenn's face. He wasn't yet ready to take in the surroundings. Some piece of equipment nearby seemed to be making quiet zapping noises of crisp extermination, like the sound of a mosquito zapper. Another was making little digestive gurgles; it might well have been drinking Glenn's blood. Meanwhile, in the back of Terry's head, something was turning round and round like a children's merry-go-round.

"Nothing to it. Just making a call."

"I mean that you were able to."

"Able to? Oh, I was able to *drive*. I could have driven here if I'd had to. It was nothing really. Nothing more than a touch of angina."

"Kaye said something about—about a stroke."

A look of fear, pale as lightning, crossed over Glenn's features. "Stroke?" he echoed.

Had Terry revealed something he shouldn't? Had the truth been kept from Glenn? Or was it possible (it certainly was possible) that Kaye had the details wrong?

"I suppose they're looking into that," Glenn went on. "I'm not sure they really know. Of course why tell me, huh? Keep the customer happy, huh?"

"It looks like they're treating you all right," Terry said.

"Oh this was all minor-minor. All strictly little-league stuff.

You know I'm an old hand at the ticker business. And did you know that sometimes people have a stroke and it's so minor they don't even notice? Whatever this was, it wasn't much of anything."

"I see," Terry said, with a weary sense of being confronted with much too much to interpret. It would seem that Glenn in his narrowing dismissals wasn't going to be any more informative than Kaye in her expansive lamentations. A nurse or a doctor—what he needed to do was to talk with a nurse or a doctor. Once he got out of here.

Truly, though, Glenn didn't look too bad. His voice was softer today, and slower—less in it of the veteran salesman's patter—but he was still the old Glenn. "Well I'm glad to hear that," Terry said. "Mighty glad to hear that."

"I've got just a little numbness, in my chest and arm, but that'll pass, that'll pass."

The buttons on the chest of Glenn's pajamas were undone, and there, pale on his pale chest, was the lingering evidence of that perilous trial Terry had so often heard about: the long scar left by the six-hour bypass operation.

"I'm sure it will," Terry said. "Where's Kaye?"

"Haven't seen her. Not for a while anyway."

She'd gone to sleep—that's what she must have done. She'd managed to fall asleep.

"Well I'm sure she'll be here soon," Terry said. "She'll be pleased to see you're looking so well. She sounded so worried when she called."

"Ka-a-aye," Glenn said, in a wistful or meditative tone, and halted, as if he'd said enough—which perhaps he had. "She's a worrier," he continued, and again there was that outreaching laugh, and an abrupt halt, and a dumb-show flutter of his hand to his chest.

The silence that opened for the two of them admitted murmurs from the television. "We're talking bigger than gold . . ." "What's bigger than gold?" "Think bigger. Think really big . . ." Terry now was struck, as he had been numerous times over the past year, by how little he had to say to Glenn. The two of them were forever being placed, thanks to Kaye, in a kind of circling intimacy that neither of them knew quite how to negotiate. Fate set them side by side but supplied no bridging words of conversation. Fate had, in fact, done more than that: had arranged it so that after the strangest night of Terry's life, eight months ago, and now again, after what was probably the second strangest, the first man he would happen to speak with would be Glenn.

Terry's gaze wandered uneasily over to the roses. A little card was pinned to one of the stems, and on it a message that, in the cruel mazelike windings of his fatigue, he found absolutely inscrutable. In a big, looping, childish hand it read—"One flower for each pound. I love you both."

"She's a worrier," Glenn said again.

"Well, you did give her a scare . . ."

"You know, a gal like that, she'd be better off without a fella like me. I told her that flat out. Don't think I didn't. I told her, I'm a bad investment. But what are you gonna do? The gal's got herself hooked up with a bad investment."

Glenn's face above his aqua pajamas took on, unmistakably, a faint flush of exultation, which brought tardily home to Terry the vital knowledge that—as far as this man in the hospital bed was concerned, anyway—Kaye was never going to be granted her dearest wish. Never, she would never drag *him* to the altar. No. Never. What Glenn derived from their relationship might not sound like very much, but it was nonetheless too precious ever to be forsaken. Here he lay in blue pajamas, someone already abandoned by two wives in succession and a very bad investment besides, and yet someone who nonetheless possessed a woman who was foolishly throwing away prudence, reputation, practicality, all in the name of love for *him*—this was ongoing sustenance. Glenn coveted this knowledge with every fiber of his damaged but still functioning heart: a woman was *sacrificing* herself for him.

Terry stared once more at the roses. He had found the handwritten message such an enigma because he'd assumed that these were Glenn's flowers—which, even if they'd borne no message, clearly they were not. Leftovers, many days old, they were instead the offering of a husband to a wife who'd given birth to a nine-pound baby. *One for every pound. I love you both.*

It was as though Terry had never been so tired while still upright, and to rest his gaze upon the flowers seemed a tangible refreshment, as comfortingly tactile as any pillow plumped beneath your head. Steadily his gaze went into the flowers, in time penetrating into, as it were, the very soul of the rose—wherein Terry discovered a revelation . . .

How peculiar it was, how very peculiar indeed, that any flower's heart could look so inorganic! So coldly mechanical! The little bedraggled knot of pistils and stamens might as well be a knot of soldered circuitry—a network of those trim little plastic-coated wires Dad was always inserting into one project or another. The mysterious rose? The enchanted rose? The legendary rose? All a fabrication, an illusion . . . *This* was the core and conclusion to the protracted, enraptured, petal-by-petal disclosings of every lover's rose: a ripped and pitiful straggle of wires. Nothing more.

Part Four

MULTIPLE VISITORS

Horizontal Chitchat

"This isn't so bad—in fact, it kind of grows on you."

"It's bitter."

"Bitter is what it's supposed to be. That's what gives it character. Or depth. Or whatever it's supposed to have."

"I say, Who needs character, Di? I say, Screw character. It's bitter bitter bitter."

"That's what makes it champagne."

"I'm going to put some orange juice in." She rises from the pillows on the floor. "You want some o.j., Di?"

"Mine's fine the way it is." Diana, pillows beneath her hips and stomach, remains on the floor. She is watching the bubbles leap in the wide-mouthed glass. She calls to her friend, who has stepped into the kitchen, "You can really spend a *mint* on this stuff. Guess what our bill's going to be just for champagne alone."

"I don't know—seven zillion dollars?"

"Close—well over a thousand. Or maybe that's well over two thousand. I forget. And we're not even drinking the real French stuff. Not that the stuff we ordered isn't good. It's from California and Peter says it's fine. He says French wine is generally overrated. But if you're talking over two hundred guests, you're soon talking a couple grand in champagne bills alone."

"It's not a matter I need ever worry myself about, my dear." Shawn returns to the room carrying a can of Sunblossom Diet Orange Pineapple Drink and her fizzing champagne glass, into which some of the Drink has already been added. In a hushed, high, declamatory voice she announces, "As for me, I shall never marry. I shall devote my life to my studies, to caring for my aged parents, and—and to being an in*cred*ibly easy lay . . ." and shrieks with laughter.

"Shawnee," Diana says, as though reprovingly, but she is laughing along with her. "You know you are incorrigible."

"Di-hard, I just learned something useful. You want to know something? Never, *never* laugh too hard when you're carrying a full champagne glass. I spilled half of it." She dangles her dripping hand before Diana's face. "You wanna lick?"

"In*corr*igible."

Shawn settles herself and refills her glass. Like Diana she lies on her stomach, propped upon her elbows. They are facing each other, with only two or so feet between their faces. "Help yourself to some more," Shawn says.

Diana picks up the bottle. Moet & Chandon is what the label says. "This is really from France." She lifts it high enough to stare at the bottom, where she finds a price tag. "Shawn, do you know what this bottle cost?"

"Seven zillion dollars?"

"Twenty-eight ninety-five. Your father's going to mur-r-r-der you."

"No he isn't. He's never even going to notice. There are seven zillion bottles down there. And if he *does* notice, I'll tell him we drank ourselves a wedding toast. I can't believe you're getting married the day after *tomorrow*."

"*You* can't believe it . . ." Carefully Diana fills her glass to the brim. "You can tell this is very good champagne," she says.

"It tastes bitter to me," Shawn says, and adds, in a falsetto imitation of Diana, "but that's the way it's supposed to be."

"Forty-eight hours from now I'll be a married woman."

"Forty-eight hours from now, I know what *you'll* be up to."

"Shawnee, honestly—don't you think about anything else?"

Shawn laughs appreciatively. She loves this role, or pair of roles, which the two of them have codified and refined over their years as roommates: Diana is an innocent, a fresh-faced kid, an ingenue, and she herself is a sophisticate, a woman of the world. And also something of a slut. Much of the fun lies in the intimate understanding that an outsider would scarcely suspect this little game—or, if informed of its existence, would probably be unable to guess which girl played which role. For to the outside world they dress in pretty much the same style and talk in pretty much the same fashion. "Drink up," she says. "That's the advantage of adding the o.j. It goes down easy as Coke."

"I am drinking up—it's just I'm savoring it."

"You're going to be a married lady, in Man-hat-tan Ci-ty."

"And you're going to be a working girl right here in Phil-a-del-phi-a. It's not as though we're going to be so far away . . ."

"That's the advantage of working for Daddy. I mean he can't fire me, can he?"

"I don't see how."

"I don't know. Frankly, I don't know if this is a good idea at all. I mean I'm only doing it to make him feel better."

"How do you mean?" Diana senses that things quickly might sour; it's nearly impossible for Shawn to talk about her father without growing morose.

"I suppose if he gives me a job, and an apartment, well then he won't have to feel so guilty."

"So guilty about what?"

"You know—on account of his always having been a total shithead."

"Mm," Diana says, sympathetically. "What does your mom think?"

"Think? What does *she* think? She doesn't *think* anything about anything, obviously. She can't even see what he really feels about her."

"Mm," Diana says. She sips from her champagne. "You know I think I will try a little of it with the o.j. in it . . ."

"Help yourself, kiddo."

Diana pours an inch or so of the Drink into her glass, takes a small sip and then a much larger sip. "That does go down easy. I guess that's because it's such excellent champagne."

"I guess. How about your dad?"

"What about him?"

"You feel bad? His not coming?"

"Sort of. Not really, though. It's really like I hardly know him, you know? And Mom wouldn't have heard of it. She's been waiting almost my whole entire life so she could not invite him to my wedding. It sounds sort of gooey and sentimental, but it really does mean a lot to her—not inviting him. It's kind of like the wedding's really for her. And besides, I've got Terry."

"God you're so lucky. To have him, Di."

"Don't I know it? That was the other thing about my dad—you know he's got this big huge fat stomach now. I'da had to walk down the aisle arm in arm with this guy with this big huge fat stomach."

"I mean not just the way he looks. Terry, that is. I mean somebody who's so terrific and all that."

"Don't I know it? God can you imagine? You've seen Peter's father. Mr. Tennis, Mr. Gorgeous, even at his age, and there I'd be parading down the aisle with this guy with this big huge fat stomach?"

"Somebody who's so sensitive. And I like his beard."

"I don't—I don't at all like his beard. And Mom's been after him to shave it off. I've been after him too, and I asked her to sort of ask him to, but it's up to him of course. I just hope he'll be all right."

"It looks nice. It looks very—"

"Very much like the Newt? You and your bearded newts . . ."

"Oh God, Di, talk about ancient *history,* that isn't even a show I *watch* any more. No. Terry's beard is totally different. Very poetic maybe? What do you mean you hope he'll be *all right?*"

"Well you know his wife died. My Aunt Betsy."

"Of course I know that but that was *ages.* I was only a *sophomore . . .*"

"Well, what do I know, but Mom keeps insisting how it's made him kind of like *funny*? And how he's like he's gotten funnier this year? I mean there've been these sorts of incidents—don't ask me what."

"Like what?"

"Well the beard for one, and leaving his job for a while, and the night I told you about, when Mom found him bleeding in that cabin place. All sorts of things. Is there any more of this stuff?"

"It's better this way, isn't it? With the o.j. in?"

"Are you hungry?"

"I thought maybe popcorn . . ."

"Twist my arm, darling."

"First we'll kill the bottle."

"Bang, bang," Diana says, and knocks the bottle over on the floor. Nothing spills from its mouth as it rolls away from them. "Man, you are a *goner.*"

Nudging each other, as a sort of joke, elbows into ribs and hipbones into hipbones, the two of them wander into the kitchen and Shawn sets a foil-wrapped tray of popcorn into the microwave. She disappears for a while and when she returns her face glows pink with triumph. She holds up a dark green bottle. "Di," she calls. "I looked and looked until I found one that's absolutely *right.* Guess what this one costs."

"I don't know . . ."

"*Fifty-four ninety-five!*" she cries and simultaneously the two of them shriek with laughter.

"Lots of butter?" Shawn asks, when things have calmed down a bit.

"Oh, what the hell, sure—lots of butter."

"Lots of salt?"

"Definitely lots of salt."

Shawn sets a stick of butter into the microwave. "Are you enjoying your stag party?"

"Stag-ette. Remember—we agreed to be stag-ettes."

"Are you enjoying your stag-ette party?"

"It's perfect."

"Not too big? Not too splashy?"

"It's heaven, darling."

"You bring the bottle, I'll take care of the popcorn."

When the two of them are settled once more on the floor, propped on pillows and facing each other, the big bowl between them and their glasses newly refilled with champagne-orange-pineapple-juice cocktails, Shawn says, "I suppose it's time to prepare you for your wedding night . . ."

Diana giggles. "Prepare me?"

"Okay, kiddo, do you know about the birds and the bees?"

More giggles. "Sort of. A *little.* Oh, please *do* tell . . ."

"Okay, now what's it you do when the groom first takes down his pants?"

"Ooh, I don't know, Shawnee. Initiate me."

Shawn sits up. "You stare like this"—she opens her eyes so wide that the irises show as clear circles—"you point like this"—she raises her hand slowly, slowly, like someone in a cinematic trance—"and you say, *That? All of that?* But it will never never *never* fit in little old me!"

Diana hiccups loudly, as she sometimes will when she's been laughing a great deal. "Then what?"

"And do you know what you say when he finally inserts his throbbing member into your Mound of Venus?"

"What?" she replies, but the word is broken in half—creating an absurd gasping sound—by another hiccup of laughter.

Shawn rolls onto the floor, on her back, and wiggles her long legs in the air. In a mincing, quivering voice she replies, "I'm a complete *woman,* a complete *woman,* a complete *woman* at last."

She sits up abruptly and, a look of proud sobriety settled on her face, upends the can of Drink over her glass. It's empty. "Shit," she says. "Wait here.

"God," she says, a minute or so later. "Isn't that just like the old shithead—setting a real good example for everybody? What a role model, huh? Seven zillion bottles of wine in the house and is there *one* can of juice, I ask you? What's he trying to do—turn us all into winos? If that's what I become, we'll know who to blame, won't we? Anyway, I thought we could mix it with Diet 7-Up. Or there's Cherry Coke, but maybe that's sort of gross and disgusting? I brought it along anyhow."

"I'll try the Coke. You know, I still can't believe it. That in two days I'm going to be a married woman."

Shawn hands her a refilled glass and says, "*You* can't believe it."

"Shawn, d'you think Peter will lose his Southern accent in New York City?"

"Why should he? He didn't in college."

"It's just I'd be so sad if he lost it . . ."

"What difference would it make? It's not like the two of you actually ever converse or anything. It's not as though the two of you ever hold an honest-to-goodness conversation."

"Oh come on, cut it out."

"I mean, like what's your typical conversation?" In a chirpy, wonder-struck falsetto Shawn calls, *Again?* And in a husky Southern drawl she answers, *Ba-beh, don' you fret yourself, we got time for anothuh.*

"Shawn!"

"*I* don't know what goes on behind the closed door? And I want to tell you I am shocked, shocked and deeply revolted, at the two of you . . ."

Diana feels her face flush with embarrassment. Shawn's little enactment has heated up all sorts of emotions inside her—including pride and happiness and amusement—but what she feels made broadly visible on her face is simple embarrassment. It *is* true—it really is—that she and Peter spend an inordinate amount of time in bed. She has already vowed to herself that, when they get to New York and he has settled down to the serious business of his graduate studies, they will both display greater self-containment. She thinks of Peter, and wonders what he, with all his dear, sweet, decent Southern attitudes, would think if he could only hear the two of them now. But there is something else. She remembers now that there is something else.

"Shawn, can I tell you a secret? A it's-probably-nothing-but-maybe-it's-a-super-huge-deal secret?"

"I'm all ears." Shawn takes her ears in her fingertips and stretches them out as far as they will comfortably extend from her head.

"Cross your heart and hope to die?"

"Dead as a doornail. Dead as a dead dog on the side of the highway. Dead as a dead person. Dead as a dead whale stranded on some—"

"That'll do. Okay. Okay, you see the thing is, I'm late. Five days late. Of course that hardly sounds like anything, but you know how *regular* I always am."

"But—but you don't really think so, do you?"

"No—yes—I don't know. Shawnee, I don't know what to think."

"You don't really think so."

"I don't know."

"You know, if you are, you probably shouldn't be drinking," Shawn says, and promptly realizes that she has cast a cold shadow on the long-awaited stag-ette party. She shifts direction: "But hell, what do the scientists really know? Killjoys, party-poopers, every last one of them, bunch of nerds and twerps is what they are, and not one who—"

"No—but you're right, isn't that right? I shouldn't drink, should I? Isn't it funny? I never thought," Diana says. Her voice is almost a whisper: "Good Lord, I never once even thought . . ."

"But haven't you been careful? About prevention? I'll bet you've been careful."

"*Super* careful," she replies. "Every time, *super* careful."

"Listen, I've known you to be late before. And remember those times I was late? It's nothing. Being late is normal. If you're *not* late, that's probably when you need to worry."

"I don't feel any different."

"*Well* then—that proves it, doesn't it? You'd know. Of course you'd know. You'd *feel* it. Drink up," she says, and drinks deeply. But Diana does not lift her glass. "You're going to love New York," Shawn says.

"I don't know."

"You'll love it."

"What if I hate my job? What if I can't *get* a job?"

"You know how long it's going to take you to get a job? With *your* charm? About two-and-a-half minutes. The first guy interviews you, he's going to sign you up."

This was another longstanding and mutually rewarding little joke of Shawn's—that there was no man on earth who could stand up to Diana's *charm*. But now the little joke fails to please. Quite the reverse, in fact. For in her mind Diana beholds a sort of image of herself, and she is sitting across a table from a man who is interviewing her, and though his face is darkly obscure she still can feel the way he's eyeing her and knows he is checking her out, up and down, while all the time pretending that what's at stake here are other things—business things—or that his interest is kindly and avuncular, and she resents his dapper dishonesty, his sham decency, but resents still more the unreasonableness of his desires: for who in the world is *he,* who has no face, to covet the parts of her he's coveting?

"But what if I don't like it?" Diana asks. "What if I don't like being a paralegal?"

"Maybe that means you shouldn't go to law school? You're doing just the right thing. Looking before leaping. I wish I was doing what you're doing. Rather than working right here for the Shithead."

"Well there's nothing says you can't. Maybe we could even work at the same firm, Shawnee, and you could come stay in our guest room until you find a place . . ."

"Move in with the newlyweds?"

Another ponderous silence descends upon the two of them. Shawn refills her glass and, after a pause, Diana refills hers.

"You know they're actually going to play 'Here Comes the Bride' when I walk down the aisle. You don't think that's going to make people throw *up* do you? It was Peter insisted."

"I can't believe you're trying to get him to shave it off."

"Who? What?"

"Terry. His beard. Just so you can walk down the aisle with this clean-shaven lawyer type. Honestly, sometimes you're all too prissy and disgusting for words."

"Oh I don't *care.* It's not as if I *care.* At least he's not this big old fat huge stomach type of guy, and it's not like I'm *pressuring* him either."

"No but you did say you were having your mom pressure him. Once again letting her do the dirty work. I just think you might want to leave him alone for once."

"Leave him *alone?* Why of all the absurd, I mean the absolutely ridiculous . . . You act like I go around harassing my own—"

"You know he kissed me . . ."

"What? Who?"

"Terry."

"Kissed *you?* What are you talking about?"

"Graduation night. In his car. In the dorm parking lot."

"*Kissed* you? Terry? Kissed *you?* Well, that was a graduation kiss."

"On the mouth."

"He did not . . ."

"Right on the mouth."

"He did not. He doesn't kiss *me* right on the mouth, and I'm his niece!"

"Right on the mouth, he most certainly *did* right on the mouth. It was a *long* one."

"Oh God Shawnee, you're incorrigible *really*. You don't know when to stop. You know at times this bimbo routine of yours doesn't exactly—"

"But he did. It's no kidding. What do you mean—bimbo routine?"

"He did not . . ."

"Did so—he even opened his mouth a little so he could work his tongue right in. You know it was the first time I've ever kissed a guy with a beard—I mean a real kiss. Lots and lots of moustaches, but this was my first beard."

Silence—another moment's silence. "Now let's get this straight," Diana begins. "If I understand you correctly, you're saying that my Uncle Terry, my own mother's only brother, he pulled you over in some *parking* lot and gave you a French kiss?"

"He even sort of grabbed my boob . . ."

"*Shawn!*"

"But I'm telling you he *did* . . . Listen, it was perfectly sweet and everything. I'm not saying he was at all *boorish* for heaven's sake."

"You're saying that my Uncle Terry tried to feel you up—is that what you're saying? Let's get this straight, okay? He grabbed at your tits—is that what you're saying? Huh? *Huh?*"

Shawn hesitates, her certainty dissolving beneath this unforeseen, aggressive show of vehemence. She realizes that she is recalling the incident through two veils of alcohol, and it's hard, suddenly, to keep the matter absolutely focused. She feels Diana's *force,* so close upon her. She'd expected none of this. She'd expected giggling, warmth, that roommate's sense of nuzzling closeness, the comfort of longstanding intimacy. Instead, she faces anger, self-righteousness, and a startling show of rectitude. "Okay, all right," Shawn says, "I'm not a hundred percent sure of the boobs bit. I mean we'd all had lots to drink . . ."

"Well I am. One hundred percent sure. That he didn't try to feel you *up* for Christ's sake."

"Okay, all right, but he did kiss me on the mouth. *And* got his tongue in. That one's a hundred percenter, Diana. Do whatever you want to me, but that one's a hundred percenter."

"Well if he did, *if* he did, which I don't believe for a minute—"

"Do whatever you want to me, I can't run away from the truth."

"But *if* he did, you *got* him to do it. Let's get that straight. It was all your doing. Because I don't doubt that for a *minute.*"

"What are you saying, Diana? Huh? So, Little Miss Magna Cum Laude, who I might point out wasn't above pulling some pretty cute maneuvers on her male professors, *Ooh, Professor Winston, if you wouldn't mind sort of writing all my footnotes for me that would be just lovely,* now is calling me a bimbo, huh?"

"I'm just saying you just think everything in pants is just dying to get into your *pants.* That's what I'm saying."

For a moment Shawn feels an encouraging, steeling sense of indignation flare within her chest, something that might match Diana's self-righteous raging. But it dies within her, leaving her with very little to say except, her voice trembling a little, "Okay, so now at last I know how you really do actually feel about me."

"And you think Peter's trying to get into your pants."

"*I never said that.* Jesus, Di, I never once said any such thing."

"You *implied* it. Plenty of times. *Plenty* of times. Hell, you even think my Uncle *Terry's* trying to get into your pants."

"I never said that. I just said he kissed me. You're the one who's jumping to conclusions. I suppose there's no difference between kissing and—and all the rest of it! Is that what you think? That there's no difference? Huh? *You're* the one with the big huge dirty mind suddenly."

"*Me?* But kissing isn't the only thing you said. I won't repeat it—what you said about the man who has been better than a father to me." This last remark fills Diana with so strapping a burden of emotion that she isn't sure she can utter it once more, but she manages to, just: "I won't repeat what you said about the one man who's been better than a father to me."

She sees Terry as she says these words—his round face, his brown hair parted in the middle—and knows he must be safeguarded. She needs to protect him and preserve him, for the world is more full of girls like Shawn than he could ever imagine. In all of his sweet innocence he can't begin to grasp what they're really like—just how very *bad* most women can be. Yes, he does need a woman in his life (she has been saying this for months and months now), he does need somebody to replace Betsy, but where is he going to find somebody who isn't out to trap him, to mislead him, to soak him of his money, to keep him down? Where is he going to find somebody who's good enough for him? Who is going to protect him from all the Shawns of this world?

"Now I know at last what you really think of me," Shawn says. "It took me a long long time, but I'm glad at last to know the truth about what you really do think of me. And I'm just very glad to find it out before you went off and got married. I'm just glad to find it out *before it's too late.*"

"You don't care who it is. That's the one thing about you: you don't care who it is. You go on thinking things like that without any regard to *who* it is."

"Now I know at last what in your so-called heart you truly think about me," Shawn wails and feels this declaration, toward the end, collapse in her throat. She gasps over the final *me* and her eyes flood with tears.

And yet, just as she is completely giving way, blindly letting loose the sequence of brutal wails that is waiting within her chest, she hears the one sound that is more welcome to her than any other in the world. It's Diana, gasping. Yes: Diana, too, has begun to cry. Yes, they are crying together.

Shawn crawls across the floor and throws her arm around her best, her dearest, her true heart's only true friend.

"I can't believe it," Diana cries, and her warm firm shoulders are shaking. "In two days I'm going to be a married woman."

"*You* can't believe it. Stop and think how *I* feel."

Multiple Visitors

"Sir? . . . Oh I'm sorry, did I wake you?"

"No, not at all," he corrects her, with a forcefulness born of an urge to clarify that his is not any polite and perfunctory denial; he has truth on his side. "I was just closing my eyes."

"It's breakfast—I only wanted to know if you wanted breakfast."

"I don't think so but some coffee." He runs a smoothing hand over his hair and down his beard. "Could you get me some coffee?"

"That'll come round just a minute."

"Where are we now?"

"I don't know . . . Maybe another hour and a half?"

"Where does that put us?"

"Put us? Maybe across the Mississippi?"

It seems the land below might as well not exist for her, the flight consisting purely of the duties needing doing before the final disembarking. She is blonde and pretty in a somewhat tired, smudged-looking way.

"And we're going to arrive on time?"

"That's what they tell me."

He will be present at the church, just as he is supposed to be. Everything will come off without a hitch. This decision to head out to L.A. yesterday, which meant returning home on the morning of the wedding, had not been completely logical, he is now willing to concede. What if the flight's cancelled? everybody had objected. *They're not going to cancel every flight from L.A. to Washington,* he'd told them. You'll miss the rehearsal . . . *They can fill me in an hour before the ceremony begins . . .* And what about the rehearsal dinner? *I'll see everybody at the reception.* Defensible replies, all of them, and isn't he about to prove how groundless their many objections had been? For he will be there, just as he has pledged. And yet in his heart he knows that the trip—a couple of meetings about a cable franchise in the San Fernando Valley—could easily have been delayed. No, the truth of it is that he'd relished this image of himself as somebody who, at the last moment, would descend from the skies to assume his role in the great ceremony. And it is for this sensation, the opportunity to embody this particular glittering image, that he missed last night's rehearsal and rehearsal dinner, and also risked, to some small but not wholly negligible degree, missing the wedding itself. But he will do no such thing; he is going to make it just fine. You have to trust to that unseen control panel inside you that can pilot you—just as surely as this plane is being piloted—over thousands of miles.

And when, an hour and twenty minutes later, they touch down at National, there isn't even a shudder or a bump. The wheels meet the runway in a partnered embrace. The flight is fifteen minutes early.

And no wait for a cab, either. Everything, everything without a hitch. He gives the cabbie his destination and adds, "Some day, huh?" It's a beautiful morning, a beautiful Saturday in July— a perfect sort of day, there could hardly be a more spectacular perfection for the solemnizing of marriage vows.

"Sposed to rain."

"Rain? Rain?—sure doesn't look it."

"Eighty percent chance of showers," the cabbie replies. He's a big man with a gruff voice who wears a baseball cap pulled low over his forehead. "That's what they said on the weather last night."

"Makes you wonder how in hell they come up with their numbers, doesn't it? Sometimes I think they pluck 'em out of a hat. It better not rain. I'm going to a wedding this afternoon."

"Eighty yes, twenty no. Take your pick, take your pick. You could bet it either way—all depending what kind of a spread they give you."

"It's my niece. I'm giving her away."

"I was married once." His seems a voice of studied brusqueness. He's a broad-shouldered man who is quite a bit over-weight—this much Terry can discern from the way his neck bulges over the collar of his yellow polo shirt. And the photo-graph over the taxi medallion reveals that on top he's bald as a baseball underneath his baseball cap.

"Not any more?"

"Left me. Thirteen years ago it was. Went out to visit her sick aunt in California and never comes back. Sick aunt? Sick joke's what I call it. I call it a very sick joke."

"That's just where I'm coming from. California."

"If you saw her, you didn't need to say hello from me."

"She still out there?"

"Now that is exactly what I don't know. I don't know *where* she is and you know something else? You go and put a five-dollar bill on one side of the table and you put an envelope with her address in it on the other side of the table and you ask me to pick one—me, I take the five bucks. Every time."

"Still, you got to admit it's a perfect day for a wedding."

"If it don't rain . . ."

They ride the rest of the way in silence. But when the driver pulls up at last in front of his house, Terry can hardly resist: after paying the fare, he holds out five dollars and says, "Let's just say here's that five-dollar bill you mentioned? Now tell me the truth—you sure you wouldn't rather have your wife's address?"

The cabbie handles the test with impeccable macho aplomb. He licks his thumb and index finger, clamps the bill between them, tucks it into his shirt pocket, spits toward Terry's ease-ment, says, "The fiver'll do me fine"—and roars off down the street. Terry, overnight bag in hand, heads up his front walk. The screen door is closed but the front door is open.

He steps inside and calls, "Anybody home?"

Anybody home? Into the living room from the direction of the kitchen, advancing with an elderly woman's stiff-limbed shuffle, she comes. In that initial instant, before he has even called out a greeting, her enfeebled motions press hard upon his lungs; it hurts to breathe suddenly.

"The Mob," he says softly.

"Well, well," she says. "Well, well."

She raises her chin, holding out her face to be kissed. She is just his height, or a fraction of an inch taller. Older people are supposed to get smaller, to dwindle under the weight of their advancing years, but she doesn't. There are times when he would swear that, if anything, she has shot up over time. He sets his lips on her cheek and makes a little snapping noise. "You're looking fine," he says. "You tired? Did you sleep okay?"

"*You* look tired."

"I ought to be, I hardly slept at all, but I don't *feel* tired, I feel—well I don't know. But it's very exciting, isn't it, Mob? Your granddaughter's getting married today. Isn't that something? It's a perfect day for a wedding."

"The weatherman said it's a sixty percent chance of rain."

"Eighty's what the cabbie told me. Better, we're getting better all the time, aren't we?" Terry laughs buoyantly. "Come on out in the kitchen. You had your coffee? You eaten? How was the dinner last night?"

"Well it was very grand, Terry—it was a very grand affair."

"Not exactly your cup of tea, huh, Mob?" Terry says, and laughs once more. He claps a hand upon her hefty shoulder, guiding her toward the kitchen. She is a sworn foe of grandness—always has been—and, as such, has been a perennial scourge of all those in Gawana who might be guilty of "looking down their noses." This is something she simply will not countenance, and among the town's elite—its few doctors and lawyers, Mr. Wilbur who owns the car dealership, Lucinda Stitt at the Century Hotel, Reverend Klinken, Father McClatchy—she can claim, in her time, to have taken most of them "down a peg or two."

But now—discomfiting Terry a second time—she says, "Oh no, no, it was, it was impressive. It was lovely. Those are quite some people, those Kentucky Drills," she says and, distressing Terry yet again, releases a hearty grunt of relief as she eases into one of the kitchen chairs.

"You seem to be limping a little," he says.

"Had a little fall."

"A fall? Here?"

"No, no. Home. Not much of a fall, really—just gave my ankle a twist."

Terry takes a seat across from his mother. "And how was Diana?"

"Well, since you ask, Terry, I can honestly report that I've never seen her look so lovely. She had a glow—that girl truly had a *glow*. I don't know where in the world she comes by her looks, it's the most extraordinary thing. Not from poor Kaye."

"Kaye doesn't look so bad. None of us do. You make us all sound so *homely*." He follows this with a laugh.

"Nothing of the sort—nothing of the sort. Kaye is a perfectly fine-looking woman. But she never had a *glow* like that. The girl looked celestial. She looked otherworldly. Never—not even as a teenager would you have called Kaye celestial. Not even on her wedding day, which I remember vividly."

"Ralph's not coming."

"Who?"

"Kaye's husband? Your son-in-law? Or ex-son-in-law?"

"Oh I haven't forgotten *him*. Though many's the time I wish I had. I warned her against him. All the time I did."

"I know you did. You did everything you could."

"The day before she married him, I warned her against him."

"I remember . . ."

Mob says, "Kaye's not to be blamed for leaving *him* out today."

"Well it was Diana's choice."

"Diana's?"

Mob seems tired, and slow, and—more disquieting still— vague. She doesn't seem altogether here. "Where's Dad?" Terry says.

"Running a few errands. He took your car," Mob informs him, and a quickening eagerness in her eyes and in her voice seems to solicit Terry's disapproval or censure. She might in this moment almost be a schoolgirl, for this is an ageless look: the gleeful expectation of the habitual tattletale.

"Hey, that's *fine,* I told you that was *fine*—yesterday, on the phone, and also in the note I left you . . . Use the car, I said. Use everything, I said. Just as if it were your own. What sort of errands?"

"He's up to the hardware."

"The hardware store . . ."

In another of Bradford Boggs's little idiotic party games, many years ago now, all the guests were asked to write down on a piece of paper a place that depressed them and Terry wrote *Hardware Stores.* The other responses had been disappointingly predictable (hospitals, morgues, churches, singles bars) and Terry's answer had been taken up eagerly, as a flash of wit, but he hadn't intended to be witty—had merely, as instructed, listed the first thing that came to mind. For they always did send his spirits plummeting: those rows and rows of tools and gadgets he didn't understand and yet (as the son of a crackerjack handyman) ought to understand. They spoke—those gleaming, banked rows of merchandise—of a connectedness with one's home, a nurtured pride of ownership, a love of husbandry that he'd never been able to feel, quite. "You want some coffee, Mob?"

"You had your breakfast? You look like you need your breakfast."

"I'm not really hungry. But maybe I should be? I feel so—so I don't *know* that I just don't want to eat a thing."

Terry pours himself nonetheless a big bowl of Kellogg's cornflakes, adds milk, sprinkles on a teaspoonful of sugar, and is going after a second spoonful when Mob cuts him off: "One, Terry. Just the one. I always tell you that—ever since you were a little boy I've told you that, for all the good it's done. With cereal, the one ought to be plenty."

"Right you are, right you are." The words come out as a sort of chant; with everything he says this morning, he's just on the verge of song. "Actually, I'm dieting. Or sort of dieting. I eat hardly anything one day and then I'm an absolute *glutton* the next. I'm just beginning to get the hang of this business. Me, dieting—can you believe it, Mob? Did you know I've gained nearly ten pounds this year? Seven, anyway."

"Saw it the minute you walked in."

"Surely it's not *that* obvious."

"Terry, I'm your mother."

"No doubt about that, Mob," Terry says, winks at her, and successfully hoists a large, precariously stacked spoonful of cornflakes to his mouth. Under his teeth the flakes crunch a little less satisfyingly than he'd hoped. Gone a little stale. He tries a second spoonful, which seems soggier still, and sets the bowl down on the counter—he really isn't very hungry this morning. "So tell me more about last night . . ."

"He's really a very nice-looking young man, isn't he?"

"Peter?"

"Now who else would I mean?"

"Well I suppose he's nice-looking. I have a little trouble with that accent. Come off it, huh? For instance, did you know that Lexington, Kentucky, is no further south than Washington, DC? I mean they're pretty much *exactly* the same, the very same degree of latitude, I checked it on a map. I thought somebody ought to actually check it on a map."

"They really are very well-to-do people, aren't they? The Drills. Everything that Kaye has been telling me was God's truth, wasn't it?"

"Aw, Mob, not you, too." Terry shakes his head at his mother. "Not you, too. Don't you see? Don't you see it's all styrofoam? That's all their money is." Terry pours himself a cup of coffee and joins her at the table. "There's no weight to it, if you see what I mean, and how you going to take that sort of money seriously?"

"She has a tendency to exaggerate . . ."

"Kaye?"

Mob nods thoughtfully. "But she wasn't exaggerating, was she? They're really very grand people, aren't they?"

"I don't know, let's just say Diana won't have to worry about how to put her kids through college. They won't have to call on Uncle Terry." A thought strikes him: "Those kids of hers, they would make you a great-grandmother, wouldn't they? Imagine that. You'll be a great-grandmob."

He expects laughter but instead she flutters her hands, as if to brush his words away. "Oh no," she says. "I'm not so sure I'll see that."

And what is *she* suggesting? Here, too, such ponderous words—she and Kaye both lately, with these vague threats about not being long for this world . . .

"Sure you will," Terry replies, and laughs gaily, to rally her.

This morning she is uncharacteristically tired or morose or dejected about something, and as such she poses for him a sort of obstacle: what is he to do with this big, driving woman, whose force for the moment seems depleted, whose edge is blunted? She represents to Terry—who dropped down out of a luminous sky this morning, his blood humming with a conviction that everything today must come off without a hitch—an obstruction, a challenge.

"You haven't eaten your cereal," she says.

"I'm not really hungry. Anyhow, it's stale."

"I'm going to make you an egg."

"There's really no need . . ."

"I'm going to make my boy some breakfast. Now you stay there."

Mob rises from her chair and limps over to the stove. She sets a frying pan on the left front burner.

"That one's out," he tells her. "Broken."

"Out? Not any more it isn't."

"What do you mean?" Terry asks but knows the answer even before the words are fully spoken. "Dad," he says, and grins at her.

"And some new light bulbs in, and your lamp upstairs fixed, the one in the guest room, and he sharpened your knives, and he did I don't know what all in addition. Do you know he thought to pack a knife sharpener, because last time he was here he noticed all your knives were dull? I wish someone would tell me how that man does it. How he goes on and on and on the way he does without ever slowing down." These words might be taken as praise, as admiration—surely the way Mob herself would characterize them—but at bottom they seem instead a forlorn declaration. Underneath them it would appear there's a cry of resentment, perhaps not so much with her husband as with fate itself. She shuffles over to the refrigerator, from which she removes a carton of eggs and the butter dish.

"You do all right yourself," Terry says. "We should all do so well as you at the age of seventy-one."

She shakes her head at him. She is not going to allow herself—or him—this comfort. "I get heavy in my bones, Terry.

You know old people are supposed to become so light, winding up all light as some itsy bird, the way my own grandmother Pfeiffer did, who you never knew, but me, me I feel myself day by day getting heavier in my *bones*." With a steak knife she whacks off a huge wedge of butter—nearly half the stick—lances it with the tip of the knife, and shakes it above the pan. It lands with a terminal *thump*. "It's as if that man simply doesn't stop to ponder. As if only once he stopped to ponder, the heaviness would get to him, too." She waits a moment for the heat to work, then lifts the pan, turning it this way and that, as the rectangle of butter skates round and round its metal rink.

Her words call on Terry to defend his father, but the only thing he can think of to say is, "We should all be doing so well at seventy-three."

"Remember what you used to say about my eggs?" Her voice has turned wistful. "How nobody could cook an egg like me?" She cracks one egg, two eggs into the pan, which welcomes them with a friendly hiss. She tosses salt over them liberally and adds a couple of gentler shakes of pepper.

It's true he used to say that. He'd always liked his eggs over easy, which week after week she would manage for him with hardly a yolk broken. For so big a woman, she'd always shown in many regards a darting sureness of touch.

"Course I remember. How are things in Gawana?"

"They say all the young people are on drugs. They talk about a 'gone' generation. Do you suppose they're all on drugs?" She turns from the stove to peer sharply at her son.

"How in the world would I know?" Terry says, and sees, from her expression, which clouds instantly, that he has let her down. He is, even now, her boy and the closest link she has to those young people (their faces, with each passing year, more and more unfamiliar) who have claimed as their birthright the streets of Gawana. "Actually, my personal suspicion is that that's all greatly exaggerated," he says. "They're good kids there," Terry says. "Gawana kids."

"Used to be."

"Still are, still are," Terry insists. "Kids in a place don't change that fast."

Mob takes down the spatula from the rack over the stove and with clipped motions she goes at the eggs. "Damn," she says. The profanity surprises him—disappoints him. "S'all right," he tells her.

"I can make you another. I'll eat the broke one."

"It's all right. I'm sure it'll be fine."

Limping, she comes forward and sets before him a plate with two eggs upon it, the whites spotted brown with butter. One of the yolks is broken. With another grunt, she lowers herself back into her chair.

"Great," he says, even as he realizes that he wants no eggs this morning. No, he's wanting out—that's what he's wanting. Looking down at his plate, he feels his mother's eyes upon him, fixed upon her son and his steaming breakfast, and her close supervisory devotion is another obstruction. Airborne was how he'd begun the day, high above the clouds at dawn, and that's how he wishes to stay. He wants to fly. A giddiness, a hopefulness, an intimation of proximate mastery—all of these things are imperiled by her watchful presence this morning.

It is a relief, then, to hear—or to feel in his sinews—the approach of a familiar car. "I think that's Dad," he cries, and rises from the table.

He crosses quickly through the living room and reaches the front door as his father, a cap on his head and a brown paper bag under one arm, is coming up the walk.

Years ago, Betsy once said something that had made him laugh at the time, but that on many later occasions he'd regretted her saying. The two of them were lying on the floor together, watching a black-and-white movie whose name Terry has forgotten, in which something momentous had unfolded—a murder, perhaps, or a kidnapping, or the outbreak of a war—and the camera, panning the street, had caught sight of a grizzled little man in a cap who was holding up a newspaper and calling *Extry, extry, read all about it,* and Betsy cried, her voice riding a cascade of laughter, "It's your father, Terry, that guy looks just like your father!" Which he did—the man in the cap had looked a lot like Dad.

But the resemblance she'd hit upon ran deeper than either

Betsy or Terry had realized. For with this remark Terry began to discover his father in all sorts of movies—old movies, invariably, the black-and-white sort, in which Dad was always cast in the role of the "little man": he was one of the jittery small town investors who came clamoring into Jimmy Stewart's savings and loan association desperate to withdraw his little stake in *It's a Wonderful Life;* he was one of the downtrodden longshoremen who shuffled fretfully from side to side as Marlon Brando exhorted them to toss out corrupt Lee J. Cobb in *On the Waterfront;* he was standing in Grand Central Station when a mortified William Powell, playing a seamy politician, found himself wandering in his pajamas through a subway station in *The Senator Was Indiscreet;* he drove cabs, waited in soup lines, and huddled over illegal campfires, extolling the quality of a can of baked beans. That's where Dad was to be found. "Hello, hello, hello," Terry calls.

They shake hands on the front porch, in the bright sun.

"I took your car," Dad confesses sheepishly.

"Good," Terry says. "That's excellent, I *told* you to. It's a good car, isn't it? A truly excellent car? Best car I ever owned, I love it. Whatcha got in the bag?"

"Caulk. You're out of it, aren't you? I looked high and low."

"I just may be fresh out of caulk, Dad. Fresh out of caulk, that's me." Terry laughs. "Now why in the world are you buying caulk?"

"It's those bathroom tiles—the upstairs bathroom."

Instantly, unexpectedly, Terry has to turn his head away—for with his father's words, and the sharp sunlight, he feels come to his face the stinging threat of tears. What we have on display here, Terry realizes, is a man who apologizes for borrowing your car when he's gone off to buy caulk for your bathroom tiles. That's the sort of man we have here. And you could call it wonderful, this unmatched kindness and solicitude, which it is, indeed it is wonderful—but how could you totally ignore the fact that, at some level of the psyche, the little man was, even now, nervously trying to earn his keep?

The brief burning moment passes. "Come in, come in," Terry urges and leads his father into the living room.

"I meant to tell you," Dad says, "that that's a mighty impressive aquarium. Did you do it all yourself?"

"Yes I did it all myself and don't you pretend for one moment to be impressed, because if you'd got started on an aquarium, good heavens, you'd have built them a—a retirement home." This little conceit comes out sounding peculiar, and Terry adds, "You'da built them a bowling alley, Dad. Or a shopping mall! Or a fire station! Don't *you* pretend to be impressed, I can't bear it. I can't bear it," Terry repeats. Then, "Mob!" he calls, "Mob, guess who I've got here?" And Terry prances into the kitchen and, with a flourish of his hands, as though presenting to her somebody she hasn't laid eyes on in years, indicates Dad—who, cap still on his head, humbled by the fanfare, switches the paper bag from one hand to the other and back again.

"Wudja buy?" she says to him.

"Just a little caulk. For the bathroom tiles."

"Terry, your eggs are getting cold."

"I'll get to them in a minute," Terry replies, although he does not want them and knows he will never want them. He feels a need to stay on his feet, to move, to gesture broadly. This is quite an exciting thing: to have his parents here in his own house on this sunshine-flinging day of days.

There's a moment's silence, which Dad breaks. "Your car's idling a little high. I could look at it if you want."

"I know it is. I've been saying that to myself—it's idling high."

"I don't like to tinker with another man's car without permission. A car's a personal thing. Some folks prefer a high idle."

"No, that's just what I've been saying—that it's idling high. But it's a good car, isn't it? You know," Terry says, "I've been thinking about getting rid of it. They kind of expect us to, at the firm. In fact there's an arrangement where I can get a new car, a lease car, for almost nothing," Terry says, and observes himself, having moved so expeditiously from the realm of partial to absolute fiction, growing ingeniously persuasive; this is improvising that carries on its fast-moving surface the burnish of true inspiration. "Which means it makes sense to get a new one, in fact it's actually uneconomical not to, if you stop and think about it, so I was thinking, well, you might want this one. You might want to try an Audi, just once. I could give it to you for practically nothing."

One glance meets another's, Dad's and Mob's, and in the exchange some understanding clearly passes. Parent to parent. Then Dad says, "Now that's a very generous offer, son. But you know our Olds is doing fine. I think we've got another hundred thousand miles in her."

Dad has never understood the ongoing American attraction to the foreign car—the early Volkswagen bugs, and later the Toyotas and Hondas, the Yugos and Hyundais. Why would anyone buy foreign when Detroit assembles such a topnotch machine? And for him, of course, Detroit always did . . . His Oldsmobiles would run a hundred thousand miles without a knock or shimmy, and with a little touching up they'd run a hundred thousand more. For him, those Motown vehicles would shoulder down the road all day with the patience of packhorses and, come evening, would purr like a kitten in its master's lap. Terry marvels anew at an ancient difficulty, one that came up with pointed force on festive occasions, at Christmas and birthdays: what do you give a man of such dexterous, consummate self-sufficiency?

"What you got in the bag?" Mob asks Dad, just as though she hadn't asked him a moment ago.

"Tile stuff. For the upstairs bathroom."

She nods once, heavily, and gets to her feet. It isn't apparent what she's doing or where she's headed as she shuffles from the room, but a moment later Terry hears the bathroom door click shut.

"You want these eggs?" he says softly. "Me, I ate on the plane."

"I'm afraid I'm up to the brim, Terry."

And now it is their turn—the two men, father and son—to communicate gaze to gaze. Terry winks at his dad, for this occasion obviously calls for a time-tested maneuver: one of many techniques the two of them have evolved for Pacifying an Angry Mob. With his fork Terry rips away more than half of the mat of egg on his plate and slides it onto a paper napkin, folds the

napkin over the egg, and deposits the tidy bundle in the waste-
basket under the sink. When Mob returns to the room, she finds
him seated at the table, a square of egg poised on his fork.

He lifts the fork to her in greeting, says, "Great, Mob," and
pops the bite into his mouth. The eggs have gone thoroughly
cold, but he does manage to swallow.

Mob does not return to her seat at the table. She stands in the
doorway and says, "We all better get ready."

"Lots of time," Terry says. "Lots of time."

"*You* ought to go lie down," Mob says. "That's what you
need."

But Terry does not want to lie down. Far from it: he wants to
fly. "I'm all right. I'm *fine*."

Dad clears his throat. "Speaking of getting ready, I was wondering, Terry, maybe I could borrow some shoelaces? I snapped
a lace last night, at that dinner of theirs. Of course I should have
brought another pair. Or bought some when I was out just now.
I can't believe I forgot to do that," Dad says, and seems—judging from the stricken, incredulous look on his face—to find this
lapse genuinely inexplicable.

"Shoelaces?" Terry echoes eagerly. A string—a broken
string—promises to tug him loose from this overburdened
kitchen. "We'll go out and get some now. We'll both go." Terry
rises from the table and says to Mob, with a nod at what's left of
the eggs on his plate, "Sorry, gotta go, gotta run."

And yet Terry, for all his talk of hurry, decides, the minute he
has Dad in the car beside him, not to head to the corner CVS.
He wants a chance to talk—more, he wants a simple chance to
drive, to accelerate. He swings onto Wisconsin Avenue, which
is surprisingly free of traffic this morning, and heads out—toward the suburbs, toward open land.

After a while Dad says, seemingly less in reproach than in
dispassionate curiosity, "They're not so strict around here about
speed limits?"

"Golly." Terry'd been doing over 60 in a 45 zone. He brakes a
bit and says, "So how was the party last night?"

"Well, I snapped that shoelace."

The answer tickles Terry, who throws his father a grin and

says, "But even above and beyond that. Above and beyond the shoelace. What do you make of what I suppose you would have to call your granddaughter's in-laws-to-be? To say nothing of the groom . . ."

"Good people. All good people, Terry. Don't you think so? Which is just what you'd expect of Diana, now isn't it? Maybe they're a little—" He breaks off. "I don't know."

"You were about to voice a reservation?"

"Not one I can put a finger on, Terry. I just felt a little bit at sea."

"And that's not anything a good Iowa man likes to feel, is it? Who did you talk to?"

"Mostly to Mob, I'm afraid. Maybe I wasn't such a good socializer? But I did talk to the woman, the groom's mother, Mrs. Drill. To her, too."

Mrs. Drill—and she, what, twenty years younger than he was?

"What did you talk about?"

"What did we talk about? I guess about life insurance. How it works." Dad adds, uneasily, "Hope I didn't bore her silly."

"Everybody's interested in life insurance. Or ought to be."

"Well *I* always have been. But then I'm a numbers man."

And speaking of numbers, how many times has Terry heard Dad proclaim *I'm a numbers man?* When Terry was a boy, the words had been fortifying; they were a testament of hidden ability, of strength in reserve. Later, during a long stretch of adolescence, the same words had distressed him, for they had come to resemble an unwitting confession of narrowness, of spiritual destitution. These days they are, with all the reverberations they carry, not just commendable but reassuring. They speak of a godsend: for numbers are what have provided this man not merely with a career and a lifelong passion, but with a vision of the world.

"Not your fancy numbers," Dad goes on, as he usually will when the subject arises. "None of your transcendental numbers, your irrational numbers, your so-called imaginary numbers. But the numbers of a person's life. The numbers of your average American citizen, white or black," Dad says, "male or female," he says, and there resides in this declaration of inclusiveness a call to a fundamental, heart-stirring democracy. "The chances of life and death, illness and injuries, birth and marriage—the timeless things. The timeless things."

Over the years, Dad had watched the ascent of the women's movement with more amusement and wonder than anything else—certainly showing it far less hostility than had Mob (who, with all her social frustrations, her perpetual strugglings against the town's power brokers, theoretically might have embraced it). But in one of the movement's ancillary repercussions he had found cause for anger, vexation, indignation: oh, he had bitterly opposed the adoption of genderless insurance rates. "Don't they see they're en*ti*tled to pay less for car insurance than men?" he used to point out in a hopeless, cap-wringing fervor. "And don't they see that if you live longer, as they do, in fairness you should ex*pect* a higher premium? Otherwise they're getting a free ride." *A free ride* . . . In his outrage over this state of affairs, he could not seem to grasp that for women, no less than for him, it was not finally a matter of dollars but of principles. In his eyes, genderless insurance ran against everything he'd supported and husbanded throughout his long professional life. Always he had yearned, in his perfectionist's accuracy-chasing way, to see life insurance companies take into account not a smaller number but an ever greater number of categories. No one, no one must get *a free ride;* no one be forced *to pay anyone else's way* . . . In theory, in its pristine disembodied state, his profession would factor in virtually *every*thing about your life (what you did for a living and how long your maternal grandfather had lived, your preference for skimmed over whole milk, your penchant for an after-dinner cigarette, your weekly trips to the local swimming pool, your habit of absentmindedly leaving the stove on), all in order to ascertain that equitable figure—not a dollar more, not a dollar less—which represented your fair contribution to that fiendishly intricate apportionment of risk and responsibility known, for convenience's sake, as life insurance.

"I leave the light-years to the astronomers," Dad goes on. "I leave the nanoseconds to the atomic scientists. But there's a space in between, and it's a pretty big space, let me tell you, Terry—and that's where life insurance enters in."

No doubt Mrs. Drill had been treated to a speech along these very lines last evening, and Terry (though he has little cause to do so, having met her only once, at Diana's graduation) envisions her responding to it with a sort of backhanded, wealthy-woman's condescension. With ennui. And at the thought of her doing so, of her daring to treat his father like that, Terry pushes so hard against the steering wheel that his palms ache.

He's cheered up, though, by the pharmacy—and who could resist a place like this? It's done up in glossy primary colors, as a sort of kindergarten, with two simple sets of signs hung over the aisles. The first are printed in lowercase letters ("candy," "snacks," "school," "greeting cards"). The others—seemingly designed for the illiterate—are illustrations: an upturned pair of lips, which are smiling over the Chap Stik, the mouthwash, the smoker's denture cleansers, the gum stimulators, the Blistex; an ear that eavesdrops over conversations arising beside the wax removal kits, the Q-tips, the Stopples; a foot that marches above the bunion cushions, the toe sleeves, the corn removers, the mole foam, the Cloud Pillo. (The condom section, Terry notes, carries no visual diagram—he laughs aloud.)

The two of them swing past a pyramid, built entirely of spray deodorant, taller than either of them.

"What size laces do you need?" Terry says.

"The ones I had seemed about right. Those were fourteen inches."

"You measured them?"

"I held one up. From my elbow to this little mole here"—Dad points to a black dot on the outer edge of his palm—"that's twelve inches. Comes in very handy. Sometimes you don't have a measuring tape."

"Sometimes you don't," Terry says, and laughs brightly, for in truth it elates him, this little demonstration of how the "numbers man" has put into his employ the mole on the side of his palm.

Dad locates his shoelaces; meanwhile Terry decides to buy a pack of cherry gum—when was the last time he'd bought a pack of gum? He has two pieces already unwrapped and in his mouth by the time they return to the parking lot, where he notices that the sky has clouded just a little. These are cumulus clouds, white and playfully fluffy, but they bear a hint of gray within. Will it rain? Surely it won't rain. Still, the gray-in-the-white hurries him along, back up Wisconsin; he's risking a ticket deliberately this time.

Suddenly it's gotten late: it's after one o'clock when he and Dad pull into the driveway. Terry races up the walk, through the front door, and up the stairs, actually savoring the clock's mounting pressure, the need now to move quickly and efficiently. He turns on the shower before undressing, lest time be wasted waiting for the water to warm.

He shampoos his hair and, while letting the lather sit, soaps himself downward, from head to toe. One of his earliest memories concerned bathing. He'd noticed—he'd probably been no more than four years old at the time—that his father when he washed him always started at the crown of the head and worked down, whereas Mob had no set system. And one time he'd asked his father why he proceeded so unvaryingly. And Dad explained that if you start low and work your way up the dirt's going to drip down into what's already been cleaned, and so it was always better to work from the top down, and these words served Terry as perhaps his earliest memory of a true intellectual illumination: he'd marveled and marveled at them! Indeed, they had left him, in a child's rapt way, dumbstruck—though it wasn't so much the logical penetration of Dad's analysis, great and incisive though this was, as the revelation that hard-headed logic was applicable even here, in a simple matter like bathing . . .

As he rinses his hair, the water drumming on the crown of his head echoes with music and he begins to sing. What pops into his head is a wistful lament, but he gives it a cheery uptempo rendering:

> *When I want rain, I get sunny weather,*
> *I'm just as blue as the sky.*
> *Since love is gone, can't pull myself together,*
> *Guess I'll hang my tears out to dry.*
>
> *Somebody said, Just forget about her*
> *So I gave that treatment a try,*

And strangely enough I got along without her,
Then one day she passed me right by . . .
Oh well, I guess I'll hang my tears out to dry.

He wraps a towel around his middle, turns on the overhead
fan, opens the bathroom door a little to speed up the clearing of
the steam, and, having just this moment arrived at a decision,
takes down a pair of scissors from the medicine cabinet. He will
confound them all. He cannot see himself yet—that shapeless
wedge of a face in the mirror might belong to anybody—but he
will emerge soon enough. Working by touch, he begins to trim
away his whiskers, which fall into the sink in sticky little
bunches that are surely too insubstantial ever to have masked
anyone's face, and by the time the mirror clears the beard is
gone. There's still some cleaning up to do with the razor, but it's
his old face back again.

Is and isn't—for it's not quite his old face . . . It seems altered.
He stares hard at himself. Under cover of the beard, it's as
though his bones and cartilage have played around a bit. He
grins, scowls, stares at himself by turns pensively, entreatingly,
quizzically, opens his mouth as if to blow out some candles, lifts
his eyebrows, lowers his eyebrows—hoping to surprise in himself one expression indubitably his own.

Full reassurance in this matter does not come until, stepping
into the hallway wearing nothing but the pants to his morning
suit and a T-shirt, he encounters the Mob. "Terry, what have
you done?" she cries so forcefully that she unnerves him.

But she answers her own question: "You shaved your face,"
she says and comes forward to plant her big, heavy palms upon
his shoulders. "Oh my, there you *are,*" she says. "Hiding there
all along." And this woman who throughout the morning has
been limping and moping now bubbles over with gay laughter
like a girl's. "There you *are,*" she crows again.

"Did you think I'd gone somewhere?" he answers. "Did you
think I'd gone away?"

Mob has been uplifted, and it is as though her discovery of an
unlooked-for joy removes some final impediment to the afternoon's preparations. Things everywhere move smoothly and

within minutes all three stand ready in the living room: Terry in his morning coat, Dad in an ancient but still quite presentable gray suit, and Mob herself in a lavender dress of a shiny and rustling material. "Okay, then," Terry announces to his parents. "It's time to go marry the girl."

Mob sits in the front, beside her smooth-faced son, Dad in the back. The Audi hums along. Shortly after they swing onto the Beltway, Dad says, "That's how it is with a fine car like this, you don't get any shaking at expressway speeds"—which may be a way of signaling surreptitiously (without alerting Mob) that Terry's speeding again. In any event—good Christ!—the speedometer has climbed over eighty. Terry slows to seventy and sets the cruise control. A glaze has settled in—the sky is definitely clouding over—but it will not rain. Terry is sure of it.

It's nearly three o'clock by the time Terry pulls up before the church. He'd promised to arrive by two-thirty at the latest. "I can let the two of you out here," he tells Mob. "While I go find a parking place."

But Mob says, "We'll come along with you."

Her voice has gone soft—uncharacteristically timid—and could it be that the Mob's a little unnerved at the prospect of this "grand affair"? Terry finds a parking spot only a block past the church and though it's a bit tight he slides neatly into it, marveling at how well the Audi handles and marveling still more—with less unease then simple disbelief—that he'd only a few hours ago tried to give away this car. His thirty-thousand-dollar Audi! What *could* have been in his mind? The three of them—Terry and Mob side by side, Dad a couple of steps behind—walk briskly under a bright if cloudcast sky. They haven't yet reached the front of the church when a woman in a green dress and sunglasses comes hurtling down its steps and clatters toward them. It's Kaye.

"Terry, Terry, Terry, you're late, you're late," she cries. "I was *sure* something happened. I was *sure* something happened to you."

He laughs at her and takes her hands. "What coulda happened? Now what coulda happened, Kaye?"

"I was *sure* something happened to you. Come in—you've got to get in. You've got to talk to Reverend Foreman."

She takes his arm firmly in hers, rattling on about one thing and another, and how often has she done this to him, or with him? It was one of the defining features of his childhood: this being marched off by a tugging, chattering Kaye, on some matter or other of squeezing urgency. He laughs once more, expressly sending this latest laugh skyward, to the massed but docile clouds and the looming steeple of the church. She's so preoccupied, she's failed even to notice about the beard . . .

The tall but very stoop-shouldered, grizzle-haired, bespectacled man who will be performing the ceremony—the famous Reverend Foreman—is everything that Kaye at the moment is not: collected, unhurried, and, perhaps, ironically amused. Terry has heard Kaye, for months now, rattle on about the Reverend's voice, and truly the deep, distended syllables that issue from the man's throat are extraordinary: mellifluous, plangent, dignified. Here is a gentleman born for the pulpit.

"Do I understand," the Reverend says, or intones, once introductions and the briefest of small talk have been exchanged, "that you are the fellow who will be es-corting our very lovely bride down the long aisle?"

"That's right," Terry says.

"And have you done this before? Served in this capacity?"

"No, sir. It's a first for me. I mean I've been to weddings, I was even married myself. But that's a long story." Terry feels himself getting pulled away in all sorts of directions. He laughs. "New, it's all new to me."

When, a couple of days ago, Terry divulged to Kaye that he would be missing the rehearsal, she'd protested frantically. To hear her talk, you'd think that his was a role of treacherous complexity. Instead it turns out to be, just as Terry had expected, what Adam would call unbungleable: merely a matter of standing in the lobby (which Reverend Foreman, voice prepossessingly vibratory, refers to as the narthex), waiting for Diana to appear, and then walking her up the aisle to the strains of the wedding march. That's it, really. "Now you will be standing right here, watching what you might call a sort of parade, a sort of pageant," the Reverend explains. Terry has a dim sense that at some point in his life he has heard a voice as theatrical as this, but if so it must have been on the radio or in the movies; clearly, no one he has ever encountered face-to-face has dared to risk tones so sweepingly melodious, so parody-tempting.

The Reverend, stooping toward Terry, says, "My boy, you will be watching as one beau-tiful bridesmaid after another goes by." Each word emerges from his throat with a sort of flicker or glow upon it; each comes encircled by a halo of light.

"All right," Terry says.

Where has Kaye gone off to? And where is everybody else? The Reverend has effectively backed Terry into a corner of this lobby, or narthex. The intense air of performance surrounding this man—the woodwind voice, the grizzled upright shock of hair, the curious piercing fixity of the gaze behind his thick glasses—is a little oppressive. Terry has never been absolutely comfortable with men of God. Women of God, yes (he has an instinctive soft spot in his heart for nuns), but the men, the priests and ministers and rabbis, have always creeped him a little.

"And you will let each of them pass—won't you, my boy?— and then there will be a lit-tle pause, and finally the most beau-tiful of all, the bride herself, will come your way."

"Right," Terry says. The Reverend's breath seems to smell of lunch meat.

"And she will take your arm and you will walk up the aisle slow-ly, slow-ly, slow-ly."

"All I have to do is stand right here."

"And choose the right one. There's that, too, my boy. You must choose the right one. It's all a matter of waiting for the right little girl, don't you see?" And the Reverend, releasing a humming, evenly spaced chuckle, squeezes Terry's arm.

And with this squeeze the famous Reverend, for all his years, for all his practice and calculation, at last oversteps. Oh, what this grizzle-haired, impeccably robed holy man has to say in praise of the bridesmaids' beauty might well pass itself off as something charming—a show of old-fashioned gallantry—did Terry not, for just a moment, detect something else, something radically unfitting, in the scheming old man's gaze. Dear Lord, sweet Jesus yes, there's something else to be found in that gaze— there's a brisk, naked avidity there, without any question *it is there*, and when he speaks of beauty, of this little "parade" of feminine lovelies, well, he's smacking his lips over all of them, he's indulging in riotous speculations. *That's what you're up to, isn't it, you scheming old lecher?* Terry in barefaced shock gazes up into the elderly features, but that little flaring of carnal mischief, having hotly declared itself, retreats behind the shelter of drooping eyelids and a veil of distended syllables. He's a crafty one, the Reverend Foreman—a very crafty man.

"Why don't we run through a little practice?" the Reverend hums, and calls to Kaye, who stands nearby, "My dear lady, would you mind stepping forward?"

Terry is guided to the spot where he will wait for the bride and the Reverend positions himself beside him and slightly behind him. The old man's face can no longer be observed, but his meaty breath is right at Terry's ear. "All right now, all right now, here they will come, here they come," chants this polished old charlatan got up as a man of God, "all the beautiful *girls,* one after another in their matchless finery"—but Terry sees nothing of the sort. The Reverend is seeking to arouse visions in his head, a pageant of temptresses rustling forward, passing before his eyes, but Terry will not be so aroused; he merely waits where he is supposed to wait. "And here she comes, at last, the one you've been waiting for," the Reverend declares, and Terry's bride does indeed step forward, garbed in green. It's Kaye. She takes his arm—the very arm the Reverend has just now released—and brother and sister begin to march up the long aisle, past empty pew after empty pew. "Slow *down,*" Kaye says, "slow *down.* What's with you today, you're going a mile a minute. I simply cannot believe it, can*not,*" she says, "that after all this planning I'd wind up alone today. Wouldn't you know it? Wouldn't you just know it? I'd be here alone while Glenn's lying there watching the boob tube in a hospital bed? And where is Miss Quiggles? Where on earth has Miss Quiggles gone off to?"

Mrs. Who? He is scarcely listening to her. Kaye requires no listening to. He understands she is trying to weigh him down, as she has been attempting to do ever since his birth. She is holding on to him lest he rise, but the church is ambitiously tall, its arched ceiling climbs and climbs over their heads, and didn't he once, despite her, vault twelve feet nine inches into the air, and hasn't he, his whole life, figured out ever so many ways of out-leaping her? And will do so again?

Still, it depresses him—or depresses that sector of his mind which listens and attends to her, nods and grunts assent. It's grim, this marching to the altar, as if for the rest of his life, as if for eternity everlasting, bound arm in arm to this jittery, pop-eyed, indefatigable source of minor disgruntlements. "So what happens today, Terry? They tell me today, this *morning,* that the drummer's sick, he's got hepatitis, which isn't something you'd think they'd want to broadcast, but there it is, and I'm not to worry because they think they can come up with somebody else."

"The drummer? They're going to bring a drummer in here?"

"The drummer in the *band.* For the reception."

"Oh . . . By the way, I was sorry to hear about Glenn."

"Glenn?"

"This little relapse or whatever it is. But I gather that he'll be fine."

"He'll be *fine,* oh *he'll* be fine, it's *nothing,* all the doctors say so, but what I want to know is where is Miss Quiggles? That's the one question I'd like answered. But isn't he a peach, Rever-end Foreman, isn't he *dear?* God, isn't it a shame he never went to Hollywood? I mean, instead of spending his whole life—or maybe I shouldn't say that here? Sorry, God. Forgive O Lord Kaye's little no-no. But he doesn't do much any more. Reverend Foreman."

Terry thinks about warning her—someone definitely ought to be warned about dear Reverend Foreman. But he reins him-self in, recognizing that Kaye has never been any good in situa-tions of this sort; she panics and loses her head. The whole situation requires clearheaded analysis. It requires just the right sort of ally.

"He doesn't do much what any more?" Terry says.

"He's retiring. You know, he must be nearly seventy-five."

"Seventy-five!" Not comforting news, no—quite the reverse: all the more reason that the man's covert leers and nudges are something unspeakable. "I would have thought ten years younger."

"Over seventy if he's a day. It's all that clean living that keeps him young," Kaye says, and gives what is probably intended to be a racy laugh—the implication naturally being that, unlike the irreproachable man of the cloth, she herself frequents cock-fights, opium dens, waterfront bars, swinging singles orgies. Poor kid, she has no concept, doesn't understand a thing . . .

They have reached the steps of the altar. "Now what do we do?" Terry asks.

"Now you go away. You'll go sit down right there, there'll be an empty seat right there in the front pew. Oh I *do* wish Miss Quiggles was here!"

"And what will you do? Where will you sit?"

"Sit?" Kaye says. "I'm not going to sit! I'm going to be married! I'm the bride, remember? You know," she says, "maybe we better run through this again. With some more people. We need more people."

"More people?"

Terry turns around and, materializing as if in response to this request, a young woman sashays up the aisle toward them. She's pretty, whoever she is, in a long sky-blue dress and flowers in her hair, and he is reminded somehow of Angelina, whose hair is always up, in a ponytail, as her hands go to work on the torso outstretched beneath her, but this woman in the sky-blue dress keeps coming forward, toward him, to him; she takes him by the arm and cries, "Terry!"

He looks and of course it's Shawn; he hadn't recognized her with her hair up. "You shaved it!" she says. "I almost didn't recognize you."

"I didn't—well, I almost decided not to—" he begins, but Kaye cuts him off with a little shriek.

"You shaved your beard!" she cries. "Do you believe it, I didn't even notice. Not until this moment did I even once notice! Do you see what a state I'm in?" she asks triumphantly. "Now do you all see what a state I'm in?"

"Diana said she'd been after you to shave it."

"Oh it was hardly Diana's doing. It was just something I decided this—"

"Terry," Kaye says, "when did you shave it off?"

"I mustn't kiss you," Shawn says and laughs and he doesn't

know what exactly to make of this—what is she saying? "I have to keep my make-up pic-ture per-fect," she says, and giggles, and of course it is all right; it's fine; it's just a bit of fun.

"That's the state I'm in. *Now* maybe you all see how it is with me."

"I told her you shouldn't shave it, because I liked the beard, but you look good without it, too. Younger, maybe?"

"It was just an impulse," Terry explains. "At the very last minute."

"And weren't you naughty not to come last night . . ." She still has hold of his arm. Everyone wants his arm.

And yet it's hard to believe that this woman with her hair up and the flowers in her hair is Shawn—though surely it is Shawn. He needs to step back, to peer at her hard from a distance, but she has hold of his arm.

"Business," he tells her. "I was in California. I fly a lot."

"Terry, when did you shave it off?" Kaye asks.

"You know I'm about to become a businessman?" Shawn says. "Or is it better to say businesswoman? Person of business? In Philadelphia. Starting next month. First I'm going to Majorca, though."

"That's a good way to start," Terry tells her.

"Terry, when did you shave it off?"

"Have you ever been to Majorca?"

And the way she asks him this, unblinkingly, with an urgent pressing down upon his forearm, the words might almost be framing an overtakingly wild and thrilling proposition. "Never," he tells her. "Not yet . . ."

"We better run through it again. We'll need somebody else. Where in the world is Miss Quiggles?"

"Who the hell," Terry says, "is Miss Quiggles?"

"She's the wedding consultant, Terry."

"*Wed*ding consultant? Wedding con*sul*tant?" Which is to say, one more person whom he has, without knowing it, placed upon his payroll.

"I've only told you about her a hundred times."

"I thought consultants were people who arranged leveraged buy-outs, industrial privatizations, that sort of thing."

"She tells us all what to do and where to wait," Shawn explains. "We're all frightened to *death* of her."

"Well here's *some*one who could stand in," Kaye says. "If it isn't Adam Mikolajczak."

Adam: striding up the aisle in a wrinkled gray suit; extending his hand to Terry; announcing, "He's back—he's back in town." Adam is sweating.

Terry says, "Who's back?"

"The smooth-faced Terry Seward." Adam laughs ringingly, that overloud lunge of a laugh—as though he has pulled off some great witticism.

"Since this morning," Terry says, wishing suddenly that everyone would quit making such a fuss over nothing.

Adam looks around, says, "Hello, sweetie," to Kaye, kisses the air beside her ear, and glances at Shawn.

"Hi. I'm Shawn. I'm Diana's roommate."

"I'm Adam, Terry's office-mate, so to speak"—and again that extravagant, ringing laughter. Adam seems nervous—it's as though merely to be present at a wedding, even somebody else's, makes him nervous.

"Now Adam, you're just the person we need," Kaye says. "You're about to get married."

"Is that right? Today's my lucky day . . ."

"We're acting this out for Terry's benefit. So he can practice giving the bride away. You're going to be the groom."

"And are you," Adam says to Shawn, indulging in a little courtly nod that is almost a bow, "the blushing bride?"

"*I* am," Kaye replies with such jolting forcefulness that she herself has to laugh. Then she says, "That is, with your permission, Adam."

Adam recovers gracefully, as he often will in matters of gallantry: "As I said a moment ago, today's my lucky day."

So Kaye establishes the little tableau: Shawn must stand on one side at the head of the altar, as the maid of honor, and Adam on the other, as the groom. Both are positioned to look down the aisle. "Come on," Kaye says and once more takes Terry's arm. "We'll do the march again."

"All the way? Do we need to?"

"We need to."

"Okay, all right, whatever you say."

And this time, too, walking up the aisle, Kaye chants, "Slow *down* slow *down*. You're going a mile a minute today."

"*I'm* going a mile a minute?"

"That's right—you're going a mile a minute."

At the end of the long aisle Shawn and Adam stand waiting, and isn't it peculiar? Isn't life all too *odd*? This little pantomime presents Terry with a chance to deliver up his sister to Adam in marriage—just as (briefly, once) he'd envisioned doing in real life. "It's kind of dark in here," he says. "I like it."

"That's because of the weather."

"The weather?"

"Terry, haven't you noticed it's looking like rain? An hour ago, when the sun was out, this was a completely different place."

"The stained glass?" Terry says.

"The stained glass. Now," Kaye says, "at this point, Terry, you'll give a little nod to Adam, who's really Peter, the groom, and you'll walk slowly *slowly* over to that seat right there. Meanwhile, I'll keep walking forward, toward the minister, and the groom will turn, everyone will turn with me, and I'll stop and the minister will begin to speak. Is that clear?"

"Totally clear," Terry tells her. "It's clarity itself."

"And you can handle that?"

"Handle? What's to handle? Handle? I walk up the aisle and I take a seat. That's all there is to it. Where's Mob and Dad?"

"They're in the lounge. Come on, I'll show you."

Kaye leads the three of them down the aisle. Adam has struck up a conversation with Shawn. Terry falls behind the pair of them, taking the opportunity to inspect—for the first time, really—this church, with its dark wooden walls, its successive panels of stained glass, its balcony in the back, behind which dimly glimmers a mini-metropolis of silver organ pipes. If it's all a little forbidding—well, these are the solemn trappings that ought to mark any true marriage. It's a perfect spot for a wedding.

In the narthex, where in not many minutes Terry's responsibilities will begin, Kaye meets a neat little middle-aged woman, into whose arms she practically drops. "*There* you are."

"I was just having a word with a member of the janitorial crew. They had a section of the parking lot blocked off, goodness knows why. I suppose it was all some silly mistake. Whatever it was, it is no more. Everything's shipshape now, my dear."

The indispensable Miss Quiggles is who this must be, and Shawn in reporting that everyone was frightened to death of her obviously had been joking. She's a trim, mild, rapid-speaking tranquil little woman who wears her gray hair in a bun. "That's the essential rule about a wedding," she says. "No point, not a single point, is an unimportant point."

And yet there *is* something sharply authoritarian, something of the unchallengeable air of the veteran schoolmarm, in the way she tells Shawn now, "*You* ought to be with the other bridesmaids. In a wedding, there's a place for everything, my dear, and you're not in your place."

Shawn melts away, and Miss Quiggles begins a nodding, pacifying conversation with Kaye, leaving Terry a chance, the first such chance in a couple of days, to speak with Adam.

"Hey, where do I sign up?" Adam says. "Me too—I too want to neck with her in a parking lot."

"What are you *talking* about?"

"Who do you think? Shawn—she's a real looker. A boost for iron-poor blood is what I call her."

"*Do* cut it out. Right now."

"How was California?"

"Fine—it was okay."

"No adventures?"

"No adventures," Terry says firmly.

"You meet any women work in video stores?"

"Okay. I owe you one."

"*I* owe *you* one," says Adam, who, in reference to a night that Terry in his embarrassment can hardly bear to mention, has thrown out various hints that Kelly's friend Marty had found him *quite* to her liking.

"I met no one."

"Hey, I just met Marrying Sam, at least I assume he's Marrying Sam. Where in the world they dig him up? What an ex-cep-tion-al speaker. We ought to get him in front of a jury, huh?"

"I see him in the role of defendant, actually," Terry says and lifts his eyebrows meaningfully. "You know actually—actually, Adam, he's a dangerous man?"

That look on Adam's face of being wakened, his curiosity whetted, is so satisfying that Terry cannot regret the interruption that cuts him off. "Terry," Kaye says, "I want you to meet Miss Quiggles, the wedding consultant."

By way of parting with Adam, Terry places a hand upon his friend's arm, says, "Don't worry, I'll explain it all later," and nods a couple of times.

Terry has just entered into a conversation with Miss Quiggles (who sends Adam packing with the same neat aphoristic forcibleness with which she'd dispatched Shawn) when a little man comes shuffling forward, whom Terry, catching him in a sidelong glance, for a moment fails to identify.

Once before, some months ago now, Terry had failed to recognize Kevin . . . That was the night in the Benchmark, when Terry, Adam, and Kevin were first brought together. Back then, what had momentarily misled Terry was Kevin's glasses; now, it's the suit. Has Terry *ever* had a glimpse of Kevin in a suit and tie before? It seems not. And Kevin is not only in a suit: he's aswim in a bright royal-blue-and-red double-breasted suit with wide lapels and pleated trousers. More than ever, he looks like a circus comic.

"Kevin!" Terry cries loudly, jubilantly, and thrusts out his hand.

Kevin flinches—recoils—a little, but not so thoroughly or so far as to fail to be caught up by Terry's outstretched palm. The two of them shake hands.

"So glad you could make it," Terry calls, in a show of expansive hospitality; there's a sense here of a dramatic tableau, a broad-gestured encounter upon a stage, though in fact nobody is watching or listening.

"Yeah," Kopp says. "Gooda be here."

"Quite a day for a wedding, isn't it?"

"You bet. Listen, I wanted to ask you what to do about the present. I brought 'em a present."

"Bring it to the reception."

"That's the thing," Kevin says. He is speaking quietly, at a volume many notches below Terry's own. "Something came up, that's the thing. At the store. That's why I can't make it to the reception."

There is guilt in Kevin's eyes—an old, hard-pressed, dolorous guilt—and Terry on the instant knows what this expression signifies: one more case of Squirrely Kopp's retreating fretfully from a grand social occasion. It is an admission of weakness. It is a cry of inadequacy or insufficiency, in answer to which Terry feels rising within himself a wash of cleansing affection for this little buffoonish man in the too-big, too-loud suit, and feels compelled to say—though this really has nothing to do with anything—"Hey, guess what? Bertha's getting married."

"Bertha?"

"Yeah. Bertha. She's—she's blossoming. Blossoming! Who would have guessed that out of all of us *Bertha* would be the one to blossom?"

"Married?"

"Not today. Not today, thank God," Terry says, waving his arms somewhat absurdly, and adds, in a consoling voice that is more absurd still: "You two would never have hit it off, incidentally."

Kopp says nothing. Instead, he does what, over the years of their acquaintance, he has always done best: merely studies Terry, with glittering eyes that are nervous, penetrating, merry, scornful.

Under the intensity of that gaze Terry's voice plunges in volume. He says, "So what's the gift, Kevvie? Whatcha get 'em?"

"I got 'em two things really. Two presents. A subscription to *Natural History* magazine—"

"They'll like that—"

"And a photograph. It's a nature photograph. It's an original signed photograph by Scott Mead—you know who he is?"

Terry hesitates. Should he know who this is? "I don't think

so. Not that that means anything. I know zilch about photography."

"He's one of the most famous nature photographers in the world. He's in *Natural History* all the time."

"Sounds great. I'll bet they'll like that."

"I thought you might come out to my car now. I got it in the trunk. Just round the corner from here."

"Sure. Okay. What's it of? The photograph."

"Coupla lizards."

"Lizards?"

"Some Komodo dragons, actually. It's a fantastic picture. A really incredible picture."

"I'm sure."

"I looked through this whole portfolio of amazing stuff, Mead's stuff, but this was the most amazing of the bunch . . . Come on. You can pick it up now. You can give it to them for me."

"It'll take just a minute?"

"Just a minute."

Terry is heading out the big church door when a voice summons him—summons the two of them—back inside. *"Kevin Kopp. And you haven't changed a bit."*

Why does Kaye say things of this sort? Is she blind? Would she have Kopp believing she's going blind? Since she last saw him, Kopp has lost half the hair on his skull and has put on fifteen pounds. At least fifteen.

Kevin does not tell her that she hasn't changed—she whose hair has also thinned a bit since the two of them last met and who has also put on fifteen pounds. At least. He says, "Hi."

Kaye launches a flood of words and high-flung laughter—the visit to Princeton twenty or so years ago, with Ralph and infant Diana, who was just a *baby* then, and isn't it amazing that that little baby is getting married today, where *has* the time gone? But her real concern is not reminiscence, not Kevin at all—as the telling change in her voice makes clear when she says, with steely quietness, "Terry, where did you think you were going?"

"Just out to Kevin's car, Kaye. He's got a gift for Diana in his trunk. I was going to move it to my trunk."

"Terry, you are *not* leaving this place," she sternly declares, and offers a high-pitched laugh to cover the sternness. "Not after the way you've nearly driven me nutso these last couple days. And we've got scads to do yet," she says. "Scads to do. So you better come with me. I'm not letting you out of my *sight*," she says. "Kevin, it was so fabulous to see you and I look forward to a good long chat at the reception. And a dance—do you dance? Terry, you can collect the gift then."

Kopp has backed a step or two away from her and his skittery gaze jumps to Terry's face. What Terry reads in his friend's eyes—an ambiguous expression—might be an appeal for help. Kopp just might be asking that Terry eventually, at the reception, make the apologies for his absence which he himself now feels unable to make. *Don't blow my secret,* Kopp may be saying. Or the look might signify something else entirely. That may be exasperation in his eyes—as if Kopp is mutely asking why it is that Kaye, like her brother, is so *determinedly vapid.*

The old roommates, Terry and Kevin, lock gazes for an ambiguous moment—a parting moment—and then Kopp is gone and Terry is following Kaye down a dark corridor, toward the lounge, and Kaye whispers, "At the reception I want you to keep an eye on Mob." "Keep an eye on her?" Terry says at normal volume. "To see she doesn't have one too many," Kaye whispers again, and Terry, again pointedly at normal volume, begins, "Keep an eye on her? Why of all the absurd—" but he has to halt. They have reached the lounge.

Dad is talking to Mrs. Drill, and Mob, who is looking tired, is talking to an old couple who must be some Drill grandparents. Terry moves toward his father and overhears Mrs. Drill—who has her back to him—say, "Oh, but you positively owe it to yourself. You positively do. From the minute you step off the plane you'll be saying to yourself, 'There truly is a heaven right here on earth.'"

"Hiya, hiya," Terry says, and Mrs. Drill swings abruptly around. For just a moment on her face there may be a shadow of indignation toward whoever it is who has shown the effrontery to interrupt her. But if so, this is instantly replaced by a wide smile. The fact is, she's a good-looking woman. "Mr.

Seward," she says, in an accent that renders Mister as Mistuh.
"Or perhaps I ought to say *young* Mr. Seward, but then again
your father seems to have ample enough youth himself to qualify for that distinction."

"Better call me Terry, then."

"Correct me if I'm mistaken, but weren't you bearded the last
time I saw you?"

"Shaved it off."

"I regret to say that since our last meeting I myself have made
no such notable alteration—may I say improvement?—in my
appearance."

"You still look fine," Terry replies and, hearing these words
echo as somewhat unimaginative, even bluntly ungallant, he
adds, "Stick with a winner, isn't that what they say in Kentucky
Derby country?"

"You remember Diana's Uncle Terry, dear," she says, catching
at the sleeve of her husband's pinstripe suit jacket.

"Of course."

He's tall, Diana's future father-in-law, six feet two or three,
half a foot taller than Terry, with an impressive head of wavy
hair. He has gone prematurely white—silver, really—a color
dramatically set off by the ruddied rich tan, or tans, of his face.
In the middle of his copper-bronze features, far off, float a little
pair of wan blue eyes.

"How are things in Kentucky?" Terry says. "How's the styrofoam business?"

"Getting by, getting by. And how are things in the nation's
capital? And the television licensing business?"

"We're keeping the airwaves safe for democracy." It's a line of
Adam's—and one which Adam himself can deliver with real
panache, as though uncorking a keen witticism, but one which
in this context sounds smartalecky. One of the things Terry has
always liked least about himself is the way that in conversation
he, as a "little guy," sometimes feels almost physically over-
borne by a "big guy." This is especially the case with new acquaintances. What he says next is something that is utterly out
of place and that he'd had no intention of saying: "I took a
couple of months off from work not long ago to do private
research. I was studying the phenomenon of hallucinations."

That pale blue gaze undergoes a shift, a sort of withdrawal or subsiding. Mr. Drill is in a sense backing off—but clearly there lies, behind his retreat, a mind actively at work, interpreting and categorizing. When the two of them first met, at Diana's graduation, it had not taken Terry long to conclude that, whatever complaints you might have about Peter's dad, the guy was no dope. His mildness, refined to the verge of blandness, is nothing but a front.

"That must have been quite an interesting interlude."

"It took me all over the place, even to a psychic research center in New York. Are you interested in hallucinations?"

"Well it's a very thought-provoking thing, isn't it? The human mind? The most complicated piece of construction in the universe, or so I'm told."

"It all started last year, actually, when I went out to a cabin in Virginia."

The goal, Terry senses, is to drive this man out of the realm of conventional responses. There's a real possibility of getting him on the run. "This was out near the Dismal Swamp, by the way—"

Her voice—Mrs. Drill's—cuts across his own: "*There* he is," she says. "If it isn't the Man of the Hour. Son, you remember Terry Seward, Diana's uncle?"

"Sure."

It's the groom himself—who, it must be said, cuts quite a figure in his black tuxedo and yellow bow-tie. Actually, the tie is not so much yellow as gold—as Peter himself is gold. In person he's blonder, more the golden boy, than in Terry's memory.

"How are you, Terry?" The two of them shake hands. The young man has a firm, a forthright grip. Though not so large as his father, he's probably six feet tall, and Terry at last appreciates that what everyone has been saying about this young man, over and over, with seemingly ridiculous insistence, is only fair and accurate: truly, he is surpassingly good-looking.

"Sorry you missed the party," Peter says.

"Party? I missed a party?"

"Last night."

"Oh. Yes, right sure, sorry I missed it too. But what can you do? Business, business, business, right? I flew in from California this morning." The moment he utters these words Terry experiences, illogically, a visceral slither of uneasiness. It is just as though he'd uttered a lie and may be caught out in it; for so distant does the flight now seem, so remote from where he stands, that it could hardly have taken place this morning.

"Well," Terry says, "you're looking very, I don't know, splendid."

"Thank you kindly."

Terry confides a little boast. "You know, I'm not feeling the least bit nervous"—and then, realizing that this may sound a trifle odd vis-à-vis the groom, he adds, "And what about you?"

"Myself, I haven't a doubt in the world, Terry. She's—she's splendid, isn't she? She's first off the line, isn't she?"

Terry stares hard into the young man's eyes, which are larger and deeper than the father's, and isn't there also something a little indecorous in this sort of appraisal? And isn't there also something a little too blithe, too unthinkingly assured, in the way that Peter addresses him by his first name? Not that "Mr. Seward" would be appropriate or desirable, but there are ways and there are ways of being called Terry.

He continues to stare at Peter, whose blond locks fall in a neat sculpted wave upon his forehead. And looking at that forehead, looking up at that forehead, Terry sees (with something of the lure of the forbidden in the glancing, so that he might almost be peeking up a woman's skirt) sees (and immediately experiences a little spurting squeeze of jubilation in his chest) sees that beneath the sculpted wave the young man's scalp climbs farther than it ought to: Peter Drill, everybody's golden boy, has begun to lose his hair.

"It's hard to believe we'll be off to Italy tomorrow," Peter says.

"Italy?"

"Our honeymoon."

"Right," Terry says. "And then Greece."

"And then on to Turkey. I suppose the whole thing might look a little extravagant, if it wasn't directly related to what I do . . ."

Although Terry knows perfectly well what the young man's implying by this, he says blankly, "What you do?" For, of course, Peter doesn't *do* anything, and it's arrogant young pomposity to suggest otherwise. He's a college kid, and what he *does* consists of eating pizzas with his buddies, playing cards, going to parties, drinking beer, sleeping in . . .

"I'm going to be studying Classics. At Columbia. This fall."

"That's right," Terry says. "That's wonderful—that you've got the leisure to do something like that." Oh, but the thought festers in the hot pit of the stomach—even while Terry fully understands that the resentment he's feeling isn't altogether rational. But for the moment it's as if he himself had suffered a childhood of scurrying destitution—as if his youth had been given over to peddling papers and gathering empty soda bottles in vacant lots rather than to playing softball and cruising on his ten-speed around and around the benightedly benign streets of Gawana, Iowa. He resents their money, these styrofoam millionaires, and the way that it leaves them believing themselves entitled to carry off their brides to Italy, Greece, Turkey . . .

At Terry's talk of "leisure" Peter's face undergoes a slow clouding. His untroubled features admit a darkening suspicion perhaps. Or maybe it's merely (for, let the truth be told, this kid is not the swiftest) simple befuddlement. In any case, Terry in the periphery of his vision sees a woman bobbing by, a blonde with flowers woven into her hair, and this is Shawn and so he says to Peter, very decorously, "If you could possibly excuse me just a moment . . ." And to Shawn he says, as he takes her arm, "You'd be saving my life, darling, if you showed me where the johns are located."

The whole of her face enters into her smile and in this moment, having just now recognized that she understands him perfectly, he thrills to his own good fortune in having at long last discovered a woman who understands him perfectly. She leads him out of the room and down a corridor in which her heels click-clack, click-clack. His head is full of perfume. She is giving it off, he is taking it in; they are made for each other. She says, "Would you like to go see Diana?"

"Isn't that supposed to be bad luck?" he asks her, and she jostles his arm, and laughs appreciatively, as though he has pulled off a fine little joke, and says, "That's only true of the groom . . ."

"Right," he says, and laughs with her, but he doesn't want to see Diana quite yet. "I think I'll wait," he tells her. "Just the john for now."

"Well that's right here." And indeed they are standing in front of a door that reads MEN. "Do you dance?" she asks him.

"Dance? You mean dance?"

Again she laughs appreciatively. "Terry, will you dance once with me? At *least* once?"

"When?"

"At the reception."

"Okay. Sure."

"You will?"

Hasn't he just told her that he will? "Sure I will. That is, if you don't mind if I step all over your feet."

"I think I'd like that," she says, and looks down at her shoes, which are sky-blue like her dress. The flowers in her hair—those, too, are blue, sky-blue. His favorite color. "I'm looking forward to that."

He smiles gratefully at her—thankful for this little jest of hers that grants him a departure—and nods, and retreats into the bathroom. There's no one here. Though he badly needs to urinate, nothing comes. It's the oddest thing: he has to pee and yet he can't pee and what does this remind him of? He stands a good long while with the pants to his rented morning suit down, but nothing comes.

Seeking some sort of conclusory gesture, he washes his hands thoroughly and dries them still more thoroughly on a fibrous paper towel. He pauses at the door. Surely the girl is gone by now? He needn't wait any longer?

Boldly he pushes the door open and finds himself in an empty corridor. He decides to explore the church a little and wanders off in the opposite direction of the lounge. He passes a ladies' restroom and some empty classrooms and halts before the door of the church library. He tries the knob and finds it locked. He studies the titles in the window (*The Second Self; The Living Message; Birth & Rebirth; The Christian Guide to Sex and Marriage; Life: What's Next?; A Personal God?; Love, Romance, and the Lord; Miracles in a Scientific Age*) and is made uneasy by them. He has put such titles behind him and how long ago it now seems, those days when he would venture, with the queerest mixture of antsiness and exultation, into those odd little nooks of bookstores where the weirdos and nut-cases naturally congregated—sections marked OCCULT and NEW WAVE and SPIRIT and RELIGION AND MYTHOLOGY. That was another life ago.

He is bothered, too (though not out of any feelings of prudishness), by all these references to sex, right here at the doctrinal heart of the church. No doubt the intention is admirable—but doesn't it represent a sort of caving in? And isn't it necessary that something, somewhere, doesn't cave in? There are forms of enlightenment that are really only apologies for weakness, aren't there, and don't these books represent a confession of weakness? Or do they reflect (a deeply unsettling possibility) the sly intervention of that repulsive old goat of a minister who so tenaciously refuses to retire?

His head jerks—he has been daydreaming—and he realizes he ought to be heading back, but it is as though the entire lounge has been air-lifted elsewhere, for it simply is not sited where it's supposed to be. That's clear. A thought—a highly irrational thought—hits him, chills him: *could the wedding already be over?* Has he missed it? Of course not . . . and after a minute's wandering he goes down some steps (though he doesn't recall going up any steps with Shawn) and here is the lounge, only a queer thing has happened: everyone's gone except for Kaye, in her green dress, who is pacing inside it.

"Sis," he calls, meaning to be funny, "where's everybody?" and of course she yells "Terry!" as though she hasn't seen him in months and rushes forward and seizes his arm.

"Where have you been?" she cries. "It's any minute now."

"Just to the john. Where's everybody?"

"They've all been seated. I'm next. I'm the last to be seated. And then Miss Quiggles will take you up there, where you're going to stand, and then the whole thing will start in earnest."

"Hey, hey now, it's all right, it's all right," he tells her. She is practically shouting.

"Come sit," she says. "Terry, come sit with me."

And so it comes down to something as basic as this: brother and sister together seated, arm in arm, waiting for everything to commence. And where else could they have expected to end up? Wasn't this arranged from the outset? She's older than she was, of course, and the new permanent cannot fully conceal the way her hair has thinned on top just a little in recent years, so that sometimes you're suddenly conscious of the scalp underneath (an awareness that each time stabs him with guilt, and why exactly has he come to feel she has lost some hair so he might keep his own intact?). He notices also that there's a gray smudge—like a bit of ash or dust—on the front of his sister's dress, and is about to mention it when he catches himself. It would only upset her.

"Do you remember when Diana was born?" she asks him.

"Do I remember?" What an absurd question. "I was at home, Gawana, when the call came through. And I remember the first time I ever saw her. She'd just woken up and she was wearing this little white and pink sweater and this little white frilly cap. I remember everything about her. Remember when she broke her arm? It scared me, Jesus, the way it hung there, it hardly looked *human*."

"Isn't it funny, the way it all turns out? You're alone and I'm alone."

"I don't feel so alone, Kaye. It's all in your state of mind." *All in the mind,* a voice echoes.

"If this were some sort of storybook story, Diana's father would be the one walking her down the aisle. I'd still be with Ralph and you'd still be with Betsy. But I'm not even with Glenn today—isn't it funny?"

"I guess. It's just the way things have worked out, Kaye."

"You know what was the very first thing Ralph said when Diana was born? Maybe not the *very* first but damn close to it. He picked her up in his arms and said, 'Someday, little girl, I'm going to walk you down the aisle.'"

"Maybe you should have invited him today . . ."

"It seems to me he *forfeited* that right. Long ago. And in any case, it was none of my decision. It was Diana's." Kaye sounds bitter. But after a moment she exhales, seemingly releasing the bitterness within, and admits, "I don't know, maybe I should've. Not sent him a letter or anything—just a plain invitation maybe."

In the face of this admission of error—or what is, anyway, as close to such an admission as Kaye is ever likely to make—he feels he must offer some partnering disclosure. She is seeking to make this, as it should be, a special moment, and he feels pass from him a wild, buoyant sort of love—something as light on its feet as a flat stone sent skipping across a smooth body of water—out toward this middle-aged woman in a smudged, unbecoming green dress (and one winces even to think about how much time and money went into its purchase), who cannot keep from swearing even while seated in a church. No one loves me *enough,* she'd cried once, nearly thirty years ago, but hasn't he, her little brother, done his best? Where to begin to tell her all he needs to tell her?

What comes to mind hardly seems adequate, though it's a start: "Speaking of funny, you know what's funny? You'd think that being here today would remind me in all sorts of ways of my own wedding, but it doesn't." He pauses and gives her the point of his confession: "It's as though I've never been here before."

"I remember your wedding very *well,*" Kaye says. "I remember everything about it. You looked too young to get married, my little baby-faced baby brother."

He decides on another confession and this one is something else entirely: "This may sound odd but you know what's the oddest thing about having been a pole vaulter? Maybe I shouldn't bring this up, I know there's nothing more tiresome than reflections of a former jock about his former glories but, as you'll see, the *principle* of what I'm saying has nothing to do with sports. The important thing, you see, is that I might never have done it at all. It's the merest chance that I happened to give vaulting a try. A total *accident.*

"Now if you look at it objectively," he goes on, "it's almost certainly the thing I've done best in my life. Not that I was fantastic or anything, but given where I was living, and the kinds of equipment and instruction we had, I was pretty darn good. I was certainly better at that than I was at being a history student at Princeton, or a law student, or a communications lawyer, or a husband, maybe—though I've been perfectly okay at all those things. But the experience of vaulting—which, after all, was pretty tangential to my life even when I was doing it, I mean I've never been any sort of serious jock by temperament—can't help but leave you feeling that you may never discover what you're really good at. *That's* my point, and it's haunting, isn't it? You may never stumble on the *one thing* you're honestly meant for in life, just the way I could so easily have never stumbled on vaulting—you know what I mean? You ever feel that way?"

"I suppose," Kaye replies and these abstracted words of hers tell him he has again failed to offer something suitable. But that's all right. He feels ready to try again. And again. He is brimful with talk today, and if only given enough time, he will link it all up—for everything he says is connected to everything else. The network is there, for those who would strive hard enough to see it.

He says, "You want to hear what strikes me as the very *essence* of adolescence? The one thing that epitomizes all its awkwardness and discomfort and embarrassment? Let me tell you something I've never told anybody except Kopp." This is better. *This* is the sort of thing he ought to be confessing to his sister.

"Okay, I was at this retreat," Terry says. "You remember there was that period when I went a couple of times on those Methodist weekend retreats. Now this is sort of embarrassing—in fact, given my age and sensitivity at the time, it was probably the most embarrassing moment of my life." It embarrasses him to think of it now, and yet Kaye ought to know this story, surely. For it is something the two of them share, with each other, and with nobody else in the world: the physical unlikelihood of their parentage, the fact that in a cabin full of pubescent boys who were discussing grown-up sexual habits under the cover of darkness, the mere phrase, "*My* Mom and Dad," the mere thought of little Everett Seward climbing into bed with the Mob, had been sufficient to raise from every bunk peals of raucous, hideous, unstoppable hilarity. "We were all lying in our beds, this was after lights out, and we got on the subject of, you know, of how often our parents—"

"I believe it's time, my dear." It's Miss Quiggles. "But what's this?" she says, and steps forward. A magician's cloth has materialized in one of her hands and with a few rapid strokes the smudge on Kaye's dress is gone. "It's time to seat the mother of the bride."

"Yes. *Good,*" Kaye says, with that vigor of hers that comes so close to grimness. She mounts to her feet.

"I'll be back for *you* in a minute," Miss Quiggles tells Terry. "Now don't you wander off."

"Would you rather come with us now?" Kaye says.

"I want to sit for a moment."

"Now don't you wander off," Miss Quiggles says.

"I'll be right here."

"Terry," Kaye says, "if you wander off I'll simply *kill* you."

"Nothing could make me desert my post."

Miss Quiggles conducts his sister from the room, though Kaye's voice—the last words he has from her—carries back to him: *I really will kill you.*

He, too, rises to his feet. "Won't *that* make a headline?" he asks aloud. He envisions it as a tabloid feature—something along the lines of MOTHER OF BRIDE SLAYS BROTHER IN CHURCH. There's a mirror on the wall opposite and he says to the shaven, smooth-faced version of himself that occupies a place there, "I don't hold anything against anybody about any of this." He paces the room, turns abruptly, and says, "I'll listen to evidence of *any* sort." He says, "We all stand ready in the eyes of the Law."

He does need to urinate and now that he knows the way it will only take a moment. He can be out and back in no time and nobody will even know the difference. "Be back in a sec," he says, and heads out of the lounge and down the corridor.

"I was never the kind of boy who would pound nails into the school floor," he says aloud, and adds, "I've just stepped off a plane."

The church library: he needs, also, to gaze once more into that library window. To study the titles, to remember how it was, so long ago, when he'd taken his leave . . . He has nearly rounded the bend in the corridor when that incontestable voice—tough as steel; he, too, is scared to death of her—commands him: "This way," she says. "This way now."

Terry swings around. "Right . . ."

"Are you feeling ready?" Miss Quiggles asks.

"Ready? I'm perfectly ready."

As they walk up the stairs she says, "It's a perfectly lovely day for a wedding, isn't it?"

"They said it was going to rain but I knew it wasn't. It's not raining, is it?"

"Raining? Heavens no," Miss Quiggles tells him. "The sun has come back out." And she adds, just as though she were talking to a kindergarten boy, he might just as well be heading off with a fresh crewcut to his first day of school, "Mister Sun is shining, shining, shining brightly."

Indeed, the lobby—the narthex—is awash with sun. The big front doors of the church have been thrown open. The doors from the narthex into the nave are open as well. Organ music floats in the air, inside and outside, as free as the wind.

"You're to remain here, out of sight," she explains to him. "Just the way you've been told. The girls will be along in just a minute now."

"What are those guys doing?" he whispers back at her.

"You might call them the gatekeepers. They're keeping the latecomers out of the way. Now don't you pay them any mind. The only thing *you* need to remember is *slowly, slowly, slowly . . .*"

He has to pee and he shuffles a little under the burden of his unspoken need. To distract himself he stares out the front door, at the white concrete of the steps and the sidewalk, which are so flooded with sun they have become almost golden. White is supposed to be the spectrum's culmination, the union of all the world's colors, but there exists, he perceives now, a gold lying on the far edge of white . . . He has a sense of the woman at his side, consulting her watch, signaling with her hands—making sure everything gets done that ought to get done. Such concerns are no concern of his. He stares out the door, at the blinding light, and a peacefulness is breathed into him. He, too, might be a creature without borders, as free as the wind.

"Here they come," a voice at his side, or in his head, announces, and one by one the beautiful women stride toward him, with flames, with flowers in their hair. Each one of these women, each of these torsos gift-wrapped in his favorite shade of blue, is an ingenious lure, and that revolting old lech of a reverend had it precisely right: it is all a matter of waiting for the right girl. It is all a matter of being true. One of these flowered blue bodies belongs to Shawn, whose breasts he has pawed, once, in a dark rented car, and he recognizes her, she gestures him hither with her eyes, and she is coming toward him, but he holds to his post and she must turn away. And for a moment the women are gone. The parade is over.

—When she comes, the one for whom he has waited, letting the others pass him by, she comes in immaculate white. The genuine article, the bride, and right here is where she certainly is. She has stepped forth from the photographs on his desk, risen from the white sweater that was wrapped around her torso the first time he saw her, more than twenty years ago. She comes forth steadily, on unseen feet, just as had been planned, and links an arm in his arm, and this is the touch, the arm, the linkage for which the day's every other claiming arm was a precursor. He feels her there right beside him. The pathway before them is long but perfectly straight. On either side is a sea of heads.

But this time it's all different. It's a different church—more light is spilling through it than it can possibly contain. And it isn't graying Adam at the end of the aisle but a tall golden-haired figure whose neck is ringed in gold. The light is buzzing round his head and this time it's also the tall old hunchback who is waiting, honey in his voice, squalor in his mind, and someone should have been warned about him but no one has been warned. Too late, it is too late now to warn her, there is nothing to be done except to trust to fate and to the girl's good common sense. This time it is all different, no place on earth could encompass such solar profusions, and wasn't it only to be expected that the church's every colored window should shatter simultaneously in an implosion of glass? He has begun to cry. "Slowly, slowly, slowly," a voice beside him, or inside him, whispers and with a gigantic awareness of triumph he takes up the stately pace of their glory walk. The sea of faces has parted, to the left and to the right. Music washes in and out of his ears and it is not Adam before him and none of these people, these visitors—

Diana least of all—are quite who they would claim to be. He is weeping, copiously, but that is all right. All the windows have broken, flinging sharp glass everywhere, but it is merely a matter of coming down lightly, of proceeding with a measured cautiousness, and he knows exactly what is to be done.

Through a sea of faces he conducts her, toward that shore where the others stand waiting, and he is weeping all down his face and onto the floor and there will be hell to pay over this. There will be talk. There will be teasing and kidding to live down, speculations and inquiries to answer to, nods and whispers, nods and whispers—but he can persevere through all of that. There will be hell to pay, but everybody will simply have to learn that they are dealing with no ordinary man, for he is somebody who entertains visions, and this is his fate and these are something he alone can negotiate. Slowly, surely. Surely, he guides the full figure in white, who is now his responsibility alone, leads her with slow sureness through the long sea of humanity. Let them look. And let them say what they will— whatever talk they want to talk. But let it never be said of him that he failed to bring the girl safely to shore.

A NOTE ON THE TYPE

This text of this book was set in a film version of a typeface named Bembo. The roman is a copy of a letter cut for the celebrated Venetian printer Aldus Manutius by Francesco Griffo. It was first used in Cardinal Bembo's *De Aetna* of 1495—hence the name of the revival. Griffo's type is now generally recognized, thanks to the research of Stanley Morison, to be the first of the old-face group of types. The companion italic is an adaptation of the chancery script type designed by the Roman calligrapher and printer Lodovico degli Arrighi, called Vincentino, and used by him during the 1520s.

Composed by Graphic Composition, Inc.,
Athens, Georgia

Printed and bound by R. R. Donnelley & Sons,
Harrisonburg, Virginia

Typography and binding design by
Dorothy Schmiderer Baker